Laura Lippman has been awarded every major prize in crime fiction. Since the publication of *What the Dead Know*, each of her hardcovers has hit the *New York Times* bestseller list. A recent recipient of the first-ever Mayor's Prize, she lives in Baltimore, Maryland, and New Orleans with her husband, David Simon, their daughter, and her stepson.

To find out more about Laura visit www.lauralippman.com.

Praise for Laura Lippman:

"I love her books." Harlen Coben

"Laura Lippman's stories aren't just mysteries . . . they are deeply moving explorations of the human heart. She is quite simply one of the best crime novelists writing today." Tess Gerritsen

"Exquisite as fine jewellery." Lee Child

"What a knock-out she is. A really superb multifaceted storyteller whose Baltimore-based crime and suspense novels are so much more than mere whodunits." *Daily Mail*

"One of the most distinctive voices in contemporary fiction . . . Lippman has once more challenged, realigned and ultimately transcended the boundaries of genre." *New York Observer*

LAURA LIPPMAN

And When She Was Good

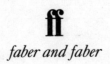

faber and faber

First published in the United States in 2012
by HarperCollins Publishers
10 East 53rd Street, New York, NY 10022

First published in the United Kingdom in 2013
by Faber and Faber Limited
Bloomsbury House, 74–77
Great Russell Street, London WC1B 3DA

Typeset by Faber and Faber Ltd
Printed and bound by CPI Group (UK) Ltd, Croydon, CR0 4YY

A CIP record for this book
is available from the British Library

ISBN 978-0-571-29965-2

FSC
www.fsc.org
MIX
Paper from
responsible sources
FSC® C101712

2 4 6 8 10 9 7 5 3 1

For every woman I know,
but in particular the three L's—
Lauren Milne Henderson
Linda Perlstein
Lizzie Skurnick
—who manage, despite vast distances, to keep me well
fed, well shod, and reasonably sane.

Monday, October 3

SUBURBAN MADAM DEAD IN APPARENT SUICIDE

The headline catches Heloise's eye as she waits in the always-long line at the Starbucks closest to her son's middle school. Of course, a headline is supposed to call attention to itself. That's its job. Yet these letters are unusually huge, hectoring even, in a typeface suitable for a declaration of war or an invasion by aliens. It's tacky, tarted up, as much of a strumpet as the woman whose death it's trumpeting.

SUBURBAN MADAM DEAD IN APPARENT SUICIDE

Heloise finds it interesting that suicide must be fudged but the label of madam requires no similar restraint, only qualification. She supposes that every madam needs her modifier. Suburban Madam, D.C. Madam, Hollywood Madam, Mayflower Madam. "Madam" on its own would make no impression in a headline, and this is the headline of the day, repeated ad nauseam on every news break on WTOP and WBAL, even the local cut-ins on NPR. *Suburban Madam dead in apparent suicide.* People are speaking of it here in line at this very moment, if only because the suburb in question is the bordering county's version of *this* suburb. Albeit a lesser one, the residents of Turner's Grove agree. Schools not quite as good, green space less lush, too much lower-cost housing bringing in riffraff. You know, the people who can afford only three hundred thousand dollars for a town house. Such as the Suburban Madam, although from what Heloise has gleaned, she lived in the most middle of the middle houses, not so grand as to draw attention to herself but not on the fringes either.

And yes, Heloise knows that because she has followed almost every news story about the Suburban Madam since her initial arrest eight months ago. She knows her name, Michelle Smith, and what she looks like in her mug shot, the only photo of her that seems to exist. Very dark hair—so dark it must be dyed—very pale eyes, otherwise so ordinary as to be any woman anywhere, the kind of stranger who looks familiar because she looks like so many people you know. Maybe Heloise is a little bit of a hypocrite, decrying the news coverage even as she eats it up, but then she's not a disinterested party, unlike the people in this line, most of whom probably use "disinterested" incorrectly in conversation yet consider themselves quite bright.

When the Suburban Madam first showed up in the news, she was defiant and cocky, bragging of a little black book that would strike fear in the hearts of powerful men throughout the state. She gave interviews. She dropped tantalizing hints about shocking revelations to come. She allowed herself to be photographed in her determinedly Pottery Barned family room. She made a point of saying how tough she was, indomitable, someone who never ran from a fight. Now, a month out from trial, she is dead, discovered in her own garage, in her Honda Pilot, which was chugging away. If the news reporters are to be believed—always a big if, in Heloise's mind—it appears there was no black book, no list of powerful men, no big revelations in her computer despite diligent searching and scrubbing by the authorities. Lies? Bluffs? Delusions? Perhaps she was just an ordinary sex worker who thought she had a better chance at a book deal or a stint on reality television if she claimed to run something more grandiose.

A woman's voice breaks into Heloise's thoughts.

"How pathetic," she says. "Women like that—all one can do is pity them."

The woman's pronouncement is not that different from what Heloise has been thinking, yet she finds herself automatically switching sides.

"What I really hate," the woman continues, presumably to a companion, although she speaks in the kind of creamy, pleased-with-itself tone that projects to every corner of the large coffee shop, "is how these women try to co-opt feminism. Prostitution is *not* what feminists were striving for."

But it is a choice, of a type. It was her choice. Free to be you and me, right? Heloise remembers a record with a pink cover. She remembers it being broken to pieces, too, cracked over her father's knee.

A deeper voice rumbles back, the words indistinct.

"She comes out of the gate proclaiming how tough she is, and when things get down to it, she can't even face prosecution. Kills herself, and she's not even looking at a particularly onerous sentence if found guilty. That's not exactly a sign of vibrant mental health."

Again Heloise had been close to thinking the same thing, but now she's committed to seeing the other side. *She may be mentally ill, yes, but that doesn't prove she chose prostitution because she was mentally ill. Your logic is fallacious. She happened to get caught. What about the ones who don't get caught? Do you think they catch everybody?*

The deep voice returns, but Heloise is on the couple's wavelength now; she can make out his words. "She said she had a black book."

"Don't they always? I don't believe that truly powerful men have to pay for it."

At this point Heloise can't contain herself. Although she always tries to be low-key and polite, especially in her own neighborhood, where she is known primarily as Scott Lewis's mom, she turns around and says, "So you don't think governor of New York is a powerful position?"

"Excuse me?" The woman is taken aback. So is Heloise. She had assumed the self-possessed voice would belong to another mom, fresh from the school drop-off, but this is a middle-aged woman in business attire, talking to a man in a suit. They must be going to the office park down the street or on their way to a day of brokers' open houses or short sales. There has been an outbreak of auctions in the community, much to everyone's distress and worry.

"I couldn't help overhearing. You said powerful men don't pay for sex, yet the former governor of New York did. So are you saying that's not a powerful job?"

4

"I guess that's the exception that proves the rule."

"Actually, the saying should be the exception that *tests* the rule. It's been corrupted over the years." Heloise has spent much of her adult life acquiring such trivia, putting away little stores of factoids that are contrary to what most people think they know, including the origin of "factoid," which was originally used for things that seem true but have no basis in fact. There's the accurate definition of the Immaculate Conception, for example, or the historical detail that slaves in Maryland remained in bondage after the Emancipation Proclamation because only Confederate slaves were freed by the act. The purist's insistence that "disinterested" is not the same as "uninterested."

"But okay, let's say an exception does prove the rule," she continues. "Let me run through a few more *exceptions* for you—Senator David Vitter, Charlie Sheen, Hugh Grant. Tiger Woods, probably, although I'm less clear on whether he visited professional sex workers or women in more of a gray area. I mean, you may not think of politicians, actors, and sports stars as inherently powerful, but our culture does, no?"

People are looking at her. Heloise does not like people to look at her unless she wants them to look at her. But she is invested in the argument and wants to win.

"Okay, so there are some powerful men who pay for sex. But they wouldn't risk such a thing unless they were very self-destructive."

"What's the risk? It seems to me that sexual partners whose services are bought and paid for are more reliable than mistresses or girlfriends."

5

"Well—"

"Besides, they didn't get her on sex, did you notice that? She was arrested on charges of mail fraud, racketeering, tax evasion. They couldn't actually prove that she had sex for money. They almost never can. Heidi Fleiss didn't go to jail for selling sex—she served time for not reporting her income. You know who gets busted for having sex for money? Street-level prostitutes. The ones who give hand jobs for thirty bucks. Think it through. Why is the one commodity that women can capitalize on illegal in this country? Who would be harmed if prostitution were legal?"

The woman gives Heloise a patronizing smile, as if she has the upper hand. Perhaps it's because Heloise is in her version of full mom garb—yoga pants, a polo-neck pullover, hair in a ponytail. It is not vanity to think that she looks younger than her real age. Heloise spends a lot of money on upkeep, and even in her most casual clothes she is impeccably groomed. The woman's companion smiles at her, too, and his grin is not at all patronizing. The woman notices. It doesn't make her happy, although there's nothing to suggest they are more than colleagues. But few women enjoy seeing another woman being admired.

"You seem to know a lot about the case," the woman says. "Was she a friend of yours?"

Heloise understands that the point of the question is to make her disavow the dead Suburban Madam with a shocked "No!" and thereby prove that prostitution is disreputable. She will not fall into that trap.

"I didn't know her," she says. "But I could have. She

6

could have been my neighbor. She was *someone's* neighbor. Someone's daughter, someone's sister, someone's mother."

"She had kids?" This is the man, his interest piqued, in Heloise if not in the topic, although Heloise has never met a man who isn't fascinated by the subject of prostitution.

"No—that was just a figure of speech. But she could have been, that's all I'm saying. She was a person. You can't sum up her entire life in two words. You didn't know her. You shouldn't be gossiping about her."

She feels a little flush of triumph. It's fun to claim the higher moral ground, a territory seldom available to her. And Heloise really does despise gossip, so she's not a hypocrite on that score.

But her sense of victory is short-lived. The problem, Heloise realizes as she waits for her half-caf/half-decaf, one-Splenda latte, is that people *can* be reduced that way. How would Heloise be described by those who know her? Or in a headline, given that so few people really know her. Scott's mom. The quiet neighbor who keeps to herself. Nobody's daughter, not as far as she's concerned. Nobody's wife, never anyone's wife, although local gossip figures her for a young widow because divorcées never move into Turner's Grove. They move *out*, unable to afford their spouses' equity in the house, even in these post-bubble days.

What no one realizes is that Heloise is also just another suburban madam, fortifying herself before a typical work-day, which includes a slate full of appointments for her and the six young women who work at what is known, on paper, as the Women's Full Employment Network, a

7

boutique lobbying firm whose mission statement identifies it as a nonprofit focused on income parity for all women. And when people hear that, they never want to know a single thing more about Heloise's business, which is exactly as she planned it.

1989

"You have a nothing face."

Helen hadn't realized that her father was even in the house. She had come home from school, fixed a snack for herself, and was heading upstairs when she heard his voice from the living-room sofa. He was lying there in the dark, the television on but muted. The remote control was broken, which meant one had to get up to change the channels or adjust the volume. So her father stayed in the dark, stuck on one channel. Helen thought of a saying used by her AP English teacher, the one about lighting a candle rather than cursing the darkness. Her father preferred to curse the darkness.

"I mean, it's just there, you know?"

She stopped, caught off guard. She should have kept going. Why did she stop? Now she was stuck, forced to listen to him until he granted her permission to leave.

"Not ugly, but not really pretty either. Unmemorable," he continued.

From where she stood, she could see her face in the cuckoo-clock mirror that hung at the foot of the stairs, a curious item to her, because it combined two things that shouldn't be combined. If you glanced at a clock, you were usually running out somewhere, worried about being late.

Yet the mirror invited you to stay, linger, attend to your reflection.

"Just another face in the crowd. There must be a million girls that look like you."

Helen had brown hair and blue eyes. Her features were even, proportionate. She was of medium height, relatively slender. But her father was right. She had noticed that unless she took great pains with her looks—put on makeup, wore something showy—she seemed to fade into the background. It bugged her. And Hector Lewis was very good at knowing what bugged people about themselves. If only he could make a living from it.

"If I looked like you, I'd rob banks. No one would be able to describe you. I can't describe you, and I'm your father." A beat. "Allegedly."

Helen knew he was challenging her to contradict him, to defend her mother's honor. But she didn't want to prolong the encounter. This was fairly new, his verbal abuse of her, and she wasn't sure how to handle it despite watching him dish it out to her mother for much of her life. It had never occurred to Helen that he would start to treat her this way. She had thought she was immune, Daddy's little girl.

"What are you gawping at?"

That was her signal that he was done with her. She climbed the stairs to her room and started her algebra homework, which required the most focus. Math did not come as easily to her as her other subjects. She charted her points, drew lines, broke down the equations, imagining the numbers as a wall that she was building around herself, a barricade that her father could not breach. She put an album on her record player, one of her mother's old ones, Carole King. Most of her albums had been her mother's, which wasn't as strange as it might sound. Her mother hadn't even been twenty when Helen was born. The music was yet another boundary, the moat outside the wall of algebra.

But Helen knew that if her father decided to get up off the couch and follow her into her room, continue the conversation, nothing could stop him. Luckily, he seldom wanted to get up off the couch these days.

Helen had been baffled when her father started in on her the week before last. If he saw her eating dessert, he warned her about getting fat. "You're not the kind of girl who can get away with an extra pound. You take after your mother that way." If she was reading, he pronounced her a bookworm, a bore. If she tried to watch a television show, he told her she'd better bring home a good report card, yet she had been close to a straight-A student for most of her life.

She asked her mother why her father was irritable, but she shrugged, long used to her own up-and-down dynamic with him.

Then Helen finally got it. Her father was putting her on notice because she had seen him at McDonald's with Barbara Lewis, even though Helen hadn't given it a second thought at the time. In a town of fewer than twenty-five thousand people, everyone ends up at the McDonald's at some point. They had been in the drive-through lane. *Why not?* she told herself as she locked up her bike, skirting his eye line as she walked inside. She went to McDonald's with all sorts of people, didn't mean anything. Money went a long way at McDonald's. You could get a large shake and fries for what some places charged for a shake alone. Her father wouldn't want to go someplace expensive with Barbara, because she was always trying to shake him down for money. He wasn't treating Barbara, he was showing her how little he cared for her.

In Barbara's defense, she did have four kids with Hector Lewis. So even though she had a decent job and he had none, he probably should be helping her out, at least a little.

Hector had left Barbara fifteen years ago, after impregnating nineteen-year-old Beth Harbison. Helen was born seven months later. Meghan, Barbara and Hector's youngest, was born four months after Helen, and Helen had no trouble doing that math. "That was the last time he was ever with her," Helen's mother often said, as if it were something of which to be proud, that he went back to have sex with Barbara only once. "And she still won't give him a divorce. So why should he pay her any support? A woman can't have it both ways."

But someone was having it both ways, Helen realized that day outside McDonald's. There might not have been another baby after Meghan, but there had been sex. They had probably had sex that very afternoon. Perhaps it was Hector who kept persuading Barbara not to divorce him. That way he never had to marry Beth, whom he blamed for keeping him in his own hometown, an indistinct place just north of the Mason-Dixon Line, not quite a town yet too distant from anywhere else to be a suburb. "Like a wart on somebody's asshole," her father said.

Helen had not told her mother about seeing her father at McDonald's with Barbara. She wondered if he knew that. If Helen had a secret and another person found out about it, she would be extremely nice to that person. But Hector Lewis didn't behave like most people did. "He just loves us so much," her mother was always telling Helen. He loved them so much that he left his other family when Beth became pregnant. He loved them so much that he refused to work more than a few hours a week, and then only jobs where he was paid cash money, which he spent on himself. He loved Beth so much that he made fun of her and, on the occasional Saturday night, beat the crap out of her. "He gets frustrated he can't do better by us, but if he got a good job, on the books, Barbara would take everything. He just loves us so much."

Please, Helen prayed, *make him love us a little less.*

Shoot. She had left her history book in the kitchen. She couldn't do her homework without it, but she couldn't get it without walking through the living room again. She imagined she was invisible, hoping that would make it so. Sometimes if you acted as if something were true, it became true.

"But you better not do anything bad," her father called out as she walked by. She was confused for a moment. She was in the middle of her homework. What could she be doing that was bad? Then she realized he was still having the one-sided conversation he had started an hour ago, about

13

her nothing face. Having suggested that she had the perfect look for a criminal, he was now outraged that she might become one, which she had no intention of doing. Helen wanted to be a nurse. Actually, she wanted to be a history professor, but she understood that wouldn't be allowed, that it would take too much time in school with no guarantee of a job. A nurse could always find work. Her mother was an RN, and her pay supported the household.

"I won't," Helen promised, hoping it was the right thing to say.

"You better not," he said, his voice rising as if she had disagreed with him. She wondered if she should try to get out of the house until her mother came home. It was five o'clock on a winter Thursday, too dark and cold to pretend a sudden errand on her bike.

"I said I wouldn't." Despite her best efforts, a note of exasperation crept into her voice.

"Are you getting smart with me?"

"No, sir." Her voice was very tiny now, a mouse squeak.

"I said, *Are you getting smart with me?*"

She tried to speak so he could hear her. "No, sir."

"ARE YOU GETTING SMART WITH ME?"

"N-n-n-"—she could not get the words out. This was new, at least with her. But this is how the fights with her mother began. Her father kept hearing disagreement where there was only appeasement. "N-n-n-n-"

He threw his beer can at her head. His aim was impressive; the can struck her temple. Empty, or close to, it didn't hurt, but she flinched, then continued to the kitchen, trying to remember why she had started to go there in the first place.

The house was small, but it was still shocking how fast he came up from the sofa and into the kitchen behind her, grabbing her shirt at the collar and whirling her around to face him.

"I—will—have—respect—in—my—house." Each word was accompanied by a slap. The slaps were surprisingly dainty and precise, as if he were beating out a staccato rhythm on some improvised piece of percussion. Helen had had a drum set when she was a baby. She knew because she had seen the photos of herself playing with it, but she didn't remember it. She looked so happy in those photos. Did all babies—

Now he was banging her head on the kitchen table. Again he seemed to have absolute control. It was so slow, so measured. He was still speaking, but it was hard to focus on the words. Something was bleeding. Her nose, she thought. She heard another voice, from very far away. "Oh, Hector, oh, Hector." Her mother was standing in the doorway that led from the carport, a bag of groceries in her arms.

Her father acted as if he were coming out of a trance, as if he had no idea how he came to be holding his daughter by the scruff of her neck.

"She was very disrespectful," he said.

"Oh, Hector." Her mother put the groceries on the kitchen drainboard, dampened a paper towel, and applied it to Helen's gushing nose.

"I think I might have a concussion," Helen whispered.

"Shhh," her mother said. "Don't upset him."

And that was the day that her father went upstairs and broke every single album she had, cracking them across his knee as if they were very bad children who needed to be spanked. That was okay. Albums weren't cool. Not that she could afford CDs or a player, but she could live without the albums. She liked to listen to WFEN, a station that broadcast from Chicago, available on her little portable radio late at night. It wasn't a particularly good station—it played soupy ballads, things that were old-fashioned even by her mother's standards—but she liked the idea that her radio could pick up something from Illinois, even if it meant a night listening to Mel Tormé and Peggy Lee.

"That's old people's music," her father said, standing in the door.

She started, but he was already gone. Maybe he had never been there at all.

That weekend her father went out and bought her a Sony Walkman and ten tapes from Lonnie's Record & Tape Traders. Indigo Girls and Goo Goo Dolls and De La Soul, Dream Theater, and Depeche Mode. She couldn't begin to figure his selection criteria. He also bought her a heart-shaped locket from Zales. Her mother exclaimed at how pretty it was. She wasn't envious that it was Helen who had gotten all these gifts. She seemed happy for her. Helen understood. Every beating she got was one her mother didn't get. Hector's beatings were a finite commodity. A man had only so much time in the day.

A few weeks later, when her mother fastened the locket around Helen's neck as she prepared to go to a school dance—with a group of girls, because she was not allowed to date until she was sixteen—Helen said, "I saw Daddy at McDonald's. A week or so before."

Before was understood. Her mother didn't say anything, just smoothed Helen's thick dark hair, which she was wearing in a ponytail very high on her head, so it cascaded like a plume. With eye makeup and a new dress, she wasn't a nothing-face tonight.

"He was with Barbara," Helen said. "Barbara Lewis." She picked up the purse that her mother had lent her for the evening, a beaded bag, one of the few nice things her mother still owned, and sailed out the door.

Tuesday, October 4

Heloise stops at one of her favorite sushi places on her way out of Annapolis. Tsunami, an unfortunate name in 2011. What can the owners do? Heloise is sympathetic to the challenges inherent in rebranding. When she had to change her name, she felt the need to stay connected to her original name, and not just for business reasons.

Why? Chopsticks poised over her sashimi, she can no longer remember why it was important to her to keep the first syllable of what some might call her Christian name while holding on to the surname of the man she despised more than any other.

Is her father the one she despises the most? The competition, after all, is notable. She considers the top candidates. Billy. Val. No, her father's still the champion asshole of the world, because he was supposed to love her and he didn't. The other men didn't owe her anything, except perhaps the money and time stolen from her. Besides, if her father had been a different person, perhaps she wouldn't have ended up with a Billy, much less a Val.

Usually Heloise has no use for the blanket blame applied to parents. This was true even before she became one. Earlier this year she was entranced, almost in spite of herself, in a murder trial featuring a seeming monster of a mother who eventually was acquitted of killing her daughter. The woman's behavior did seem inexplicable—if she didn't kill the child, she did *something*. Yet the hate for the woman is so virulent that Heloise can't help trying to find a way to empathize with her.

Heloise and Paul Marriotti, one of her oldest and favorite clients, had ended up talking about the case in the lazy half hour they allowed themselves after business was done. Heloise didn't linger with many men—most didn't want their paid companions to linger—but Paul enjoyed her company and often bounced ideas off her, paying for the extra time if he went on too long.

"This Florida murder case," he'd said to her. "It's the kind of thing that makes people want to write legislation just to showboat. I'm dreading the kind of stuff that's going to come through committee next year. As if we need to make it illegal for women to kill their children."

"Only women?" Heloise's challenge was smiling, good-natured.

"Oh, the bills will be gender-neutral, but this is the case that will be in the back of everyone's minds. The bills will be framed as better oversight of abusive, neglectful parents, but everyone will know the subtext—the next bitch must not get off."

"You mean the next white bitch. With pretty little big-eyed white kids whose photographs make them suitable poster children. I don't recall the same national outcry when they discovered that child in Baltimore who had been starved and so deprived of basic care that his development was essentially stunted for life."

"Heloise, if you want clients with bleeding-heart-liberal politics like yours, you're never going to make a dime. Social workers and public defenders can't afford you."

"I'm a socially progressive libertarian," she said.

He gave her an affectionate smack on her now-clothed hip. Yes, they had an easy, playful rhythm much like— what? Not a marriage because there were never recriminations or resentments. Not a friendship, although they were friendly. They were collegial colleagues, two people who had worked together for a very long time, with positive benefits for both. She could disappear tomorrow and Paul wouldn't miss her that much.

Yet it surprised her when Paul said, "Next week—do you have anyone new?"

"New?"

"New to me. I need a little novelty."

"Of course," she said, conscious not to allow any emotion to show on her face. Would the cashier at the diner care if the man who always bought a York Peppermint Pattie at the end of his meal decided that he wanted a roll of LifeSavers instead? Not if she owned the diner and made a profit either way. Besides, it wasn't the first time that Paul had branched out. One couldn't call it straying, right?

"I'll send you January."

"January? Get out."

"We have a new theme right now. January, April, May, June, July. You wouldn't like November, though. She's very frosty."

The joke, groaner that it was, allowed her to establish

equilibrium. Paul wanted to try someone new. That was fine. It wasn't a comment on her. She would bet anything that he would switch back to her after a time or two or three with January. Which was no knock on January, whom Paul really would enjoy. He liked a little ice, a coolness, a reserve. Heloise would never send him June, busty and ripe, a volcanic Italian girl in the mold of the 1950s knockouts Loren and Lollobrigida. Besides, whichever girl she sent, he would return to her. He always did. As much as Paul needs novelty now and then, he likes talking about his work even more. And as smart as Heloise's girls are, they can't sustain long conversations about the inner workings of a statehouse committee, which is really Paul's principal turn-on. He loves to talk about his work, and she, the perpetual student, likes to listen. How does a bill become a law? What does it take to get it out of committee? What will happen if there's a House version of the bill? It's like *Schoolhouse Rock*. With sex. Heloise wouldn't say that the sex is secondary to Paul, not at all. He always gets right down to it, makes sure he gets his money's worth. In that way he reminds her of someone paying for one of the big fancy brunches at a downtown hotel, the kind of guy who loads up on shrimp and lobster, whatever the most expensive items are. But once sated, Paul starts to talk, and she doesn't always bill him for that part, although she would not tolerate that kind of laxness from one of her girls. She especially likes the secrets he entrusts her with, the feeling she has when something she's known for weeks finally shows up in the news.

No, she'd told herself back in the hotel room. It would all

21

be okay. This was why most madams didn't compete with their own girls, just sat back and took the fee off the top. She had to concede that ego, and even a little greed, had kept her in the game long past the point where she could have retired to a straight management gig. She relaxed, listened to what Paul was saying about a brewing scandal.

Then, all at once, she could barely listen at all. She felt light-headed, heard nothing except her own blood—not so much a pounding in her ears but the sense that all her blood was draining away. She was like an animal in fight-or-flight mode, only she couldn't choose. She jumped up from the bed, saying she had to go, sat back down, glanced about frantically for her purse.

"Hey, don't look so stricken," Paul had said. "I told you, I just need variety. It's no big deal."

It had been easier, Heloise thinks now, stabbing at her sashimi, to let him assume that she was unnerved by his request for a new girl. Because she had no idea how to tell Paul that her unmasked moment of panic had nothing to do with him. It was the confidence Paul had shared about an investigation into the faked credentials of a ballistics expert, someone who had testified in dozens of homicide cases over the past ten years. It has turned out that everything on the man's résumé related to his professional credentials is pretty much bogus. So far the gossip has been kept in check, but it's going to get out, and then every case in which he testified will be up for grabs. Possible retrials, petitions for pardons.

Paul had nattered on as if it were just another bit of gossip, an interesting inside story. To him it was.

He had no way of knowing that one of the men sentenced to life in prison, based on the expert's testimony, was Scott's father. But then Paul doesn't even know that Heloise has a son. Scott's father doesn't know either.

She looks around the sushi bar, almost empty at this hour of the day, and fantasizes about jumping a busboy and taking him into the bathroom and telling him her life story. Forget the zipless fuck. What Heloise wants is a *conversation* with no consequences.

Maybe she could start gabbing to the sushi chef, who doesn't seem to have a great grasp of English. Who could be a better confidant, smiling and nodding without comprehension as she tells her life story between sips of green tea. *I never really wanted that much. Maybe that was the problem. My dreams were so small—to be a nurse or a history teacher, to marry a nice boy, to love and feel loved. I might as well have aspired to win a Nobel Prize or fly to the moon. And I never meant to hurt anyone, yet people around me have gotten hurt, over and over again. It's not my fault. It can't be my fault.*

Instead she asks for the check. She tips well. She always does. But her hand shakes as she fills in the amount, puts her copy of the receipt in her billfold. If Scott's father was to be released— No, no, no. It's not fair. *Possible,* she corrects herself. It's not possible. Heloise long ago reconciled herself to the idea that all is fair in love and war, which is just another way of saying that nothing in life is ever fair, because life is love and war.

1990

Helen could never understand how her father had landed any woman, much less two. But as her studies in world history advanced—she was admitted to the AP class as a junior, a real achievement—she gained insights into how the scarcity of a commodity made people irrational. She read about the tulip boom and bust of the seventeenth century and figured there would have to be a Hector Lewis bust eventually. Not that men were scarce in her town, not in general. If anything, Helen wished there were fewer of them, that she could get through the day with less catcalling and trash-talking as she rode her bike to and from school. She may have had a nothing face, but her rear end, propped up on a bike seat, was apparently quite memorable.

Yet the pool of men available to women such as her mother and the first Mrs. Lewis—as Helen thought of Barbara—was tiny. And Hector was good-looking, she supposed, although it's hard to see one's parent in that light. A few girls at school had said as much. His looks were secondary, however. By refusing to belong to either woman wholeheartedly, Hector kept both in a state of dynamic tension. When Helen's mother dared to complain about anything, he disappeared for a few days, probably to visit Barbara, although he always denied it. And every time he spent the night at Barbara's, he reset the clock on their separation, making it more difficult for either one of them to obtain a divorce. It wasn't often, no more than once a year, but that was all it took. Each woman wanted what the other had. Barbara wanted Hector to live under her roof and resume being a father to their four children. Beth wanted the surname of Lewis, the official status of Mrs.—and the obvious sexual chemistry he enjoyed with Barbara.

This, too, was new information for Helen. She thought men left women for fresher, more exciting sex. But her parents seemed to have a most lackluster life in that department, even though Beth Not-Really-Lewis was prettier in every way than Barbara Lewis—thinner, younger, better kept. Eventually Helen worked out that her father preferred sex with Barbara because it was forbidden, dirty. Sex with her mother had been that way only in the beginning, when he was cheating on his wife with the naïve nineteen-year-old country girl who worked as a carhop, of all things, across the street from where he sold cars. Once he got Beth pregnant and decided to move in with her, it wasn't furtive anymore, and therefore it wasn't fun. When he returned from his weekends at his first wife's home, there was a brief interlude where he had loud—and, presumably, satisfying, at least to him—sex with Helen's mother. But that honeymoon phase wore off quickly, and then the only way they could have sex was if he hit Beth first.

When he started hitting Helen, she knew enough to worry that it might become sexualized. She wasn't that

25

much younger than Beth had been when she met then-thirty-six-year-old Hector. But her father never transgressed that boundary and seemed to think well of himself for it. He talked a lot about filthy perverts who had sex with their own daughters, how disgusting they were, what he would do to any man who dared to commit such a crime. Helen was not comforted by these diatribes. She worried that her father was protesting too much, that he was locked in a battle with himself he might lose. She kept herself as plain and unprovocative as possible, wearing her hair in two braids in an era when other girls had big, teased hair, and sticking with a preppy style that was considered out of fashion unless one was an actual preppy or a mean girl in a John Hughes movie. She became grateful for her nothing face, which she did little to enhance and then only at school, where she daubed eyeliner beneath her lashes. She was learning that her father was right in a way: There was a virtue in not attracting attention.

Still, throughout high school she could feel the tension building in the house. *Something's gotta give,* Ella Fitzgerald sang on her father's record player. He loved old jazz standards, which was the hardest thing for Helen to reconcile with her sense of him. He was an oaf, a boor, a lout in so many ways. Yet he loved beautiful music.

And Hitler wanted to be an artist, she learned in world history.

The breaking point, oddly, came over her report card. Oddly because it was a very good report card, all As except for a B in home economics. Yet her father focused on that

B. She couldn't remember her father ever looking at her report card before. She had long given up on trying to impress him. But he found this one on the table, awaiting her mother's signature—and, Helen could admit, maybe a little praise, wan and tired as her mother's praise tended to be—and he began to harangue her for not making straight As. Yet she knew it wasn't the lone B that bothered him but the As themselves. He did not want her to think she was better than him.

Too late.

"World history," he said with a sneer. "Trigonometry." He stumbled on that one. "English III. Aren't you good enough for English I?"

"English III is what they call junior English."

"French. Freeeeeeeeeeennnnnnch. The only thing on here that's going to help you in this world is home ec, and that's the one you got a B on. There's nothing worse than being book-smart and world-stupid."

Her mother sat quietly at the table all the while, working the jumble. She worked the jumble, then the crossword puzzle; she read the advice from Dear Abby; she absorbed the hints from Heloise. She read every single word in the slender local newspaper.

Helen knew better than to defend herself, yet—"It's not my fault that we don't have a sewing machine at home. That's what pulled my grade down. I couldn't work at home, like the other girls, and—"

He hit her, the report card crumpled in his fist. He was smart about how he hit people. Usually to the side of the head, with his fist, maybe in the stomach. Sometimes a kick. But he almost never left a mark.

"Oh, Hector," her mother said, picking Helen up, whispering in her ear not to antagonize him, not quite able to conceal her relief that it was Helen's turn to be hit. "I'm sure she'll bring the grade up next semester."

"Why should there be another semester for her? She's sixteen now—she can drop out and go to work. Why should she have it better than you or me?"

Neither Helen nor her mother dared to point out that Beth had finished high school and gone on to get a nursing degree while Helen was a baby. Facts only infuriated Hector Lewis. He considered them a personal affront, unfair and sneaky. Give Hector Lewis a fact and he'd answer with a fist.

"If she wants to go to school, then she has to get a job, kick in her share of the rent and the food she eats. She eats a goddamn lot of food."

"Hector—" Her mother cared enough about education to want to see Helen finish school. Or maybe it just galled her that Barbara Lewis's kids would all have high-school diplomas, maybe even college degrees, and Beth was very competitive with Barbara. The three older ones were all at the local satellite campus of the state university, getting by on grants and student aid; the youngest, Meghan, was almost as good a student as Helen.

"It's only fair," he said again. And Helen understood, even though she didn't want to. She understood her father in a way that no sixteen-year-old girl should have to understand a parent. Where most people wanted their children

28

to have more than they did, Hector wanted Helen to have less. Perhaps it was his guilt over the other four children, essentially abandoned. Perhaps the only way he could keep getting up in the morning was not to be left behind by anyone close to him. At any rate, he meant it. She would have to get a job, pay her way. It would be harder to keep her grades up, which would make it harder to get a scholarship. He was setting her up to fail.

He succeeded beyond his wildest dreams.

Wednesday, October 5

Scott plays soccer. His grandfather probably would have been appalled if he had lived long enough to see this. Not that Heloise would have allowed him to see Scott, much less have a relationship with him. Watching Scott now from the sidelines, she wonders how many grandchildren Hector Lewis has in the world. She knows that her half sister, Meghan, has four children, but Meghan has moved to Florida, and Heloise never kept in touch with the other, older children from her father's first marriage. Why would she? When she was a kid back in Pennsylvania, they didn't even acknowledge her on the street, although the oldest boy sometimes screamed after her, "Your mother's a fucking slut!"

It was interesting how hot and red one's ears could get on the coldest day in a Pennsylvania winter.

No screams here on the sidelines of Scott's soccer game. No one would dare. There is a long list of protocols for how parents are to behave. They must be models of good sportsmanship. They must not make suggestions to the coaches. No excessive celebration. Even cheers must be muted. Not that Heloise is a person given to excessive celebration, but *still*. She hates rules derived from the bad behavior of a few.

She always stands apart on the soccer field, her

conversations with the other mothers polite yet fleeting. She's not sure whose fault that is. She has stopped trying to figure out if she's standoffish because the other mothers snub her or if she's snubbed because the other mothers sense she's standoffish. For the most part, she tells herself that she's happy for their neglect. It makes life that much easier, and Heloise is not the kind of person who disdains anything that makes life easier. Cake mix for the class cupcakes? Bring it on. Hiring a tailor to make the "simple" priest costume that Scott wore as Father Andrew in the school play on the founding of Maryland? Yes, please. Heloise doesn't necessarily throw money at problems, but she does apply it in bold, confident strokes.

True, she encourages incuriosity in most people. Yet it's still hurtful to see how easily people fall into line with one's desire to be ignored. What if she needed their attention? What if she had a crisis? There are only two people she could call: her au pair, Audrey, and the man who is standing here next to her, Tom. Come to think of it, the mothers are paying attention to *him,* and he's not even that attractive. Broad-shouldered and barrel-chested, which has never been Heloise's type. Pleasant-looking but not handsome. He is undeniably masculine, however, a man who somehow projects his ability to take care of those he considers his responsibility.

Heloise is lucky enough to fall into that small group of people.

"You don't have anything to worry about," he is saying now, in the most conversational tone possible. Tom and

Heloise long ago mastered the knack of having serious talks in casual tones. "They're not going to release a lifer like Val because of one bad expert. There was an eyewitness, remember? At worst they might agree to a retrial. But the evidence will be reexamined by a certified expert, and it will hold up, because ballistics are pretty cut and dried. Val's staying put."

"You're always so certain. You told me I'd be safe forever once he was locked up."

"And so far I'm right." Tom shields his eyes against the late-afternoon sun. He actually tries to follow the game, and Scott within it. Heloise has never allowed him to meet Scott, at least not since babyhood, but Tom enjoys watching him from a distance. Tom would have liked to be Scott's stepdad, but it just wasn't to be.

"Forever is a long time," Heloise says.

"True. So let's say I don't see this being a threat in your lifetime, based on those insurance charts about life expectancy."

It is October, usually the most beautiful month in Maryland's most glorious season, although lately it has become hot and undependable. Still, Heloise feels that fall is a new beginning, as many people do.

"It's interesting," Tom says, "that you called me today. Because I was going to call you."

"About the ballistics expert?"

"No. Damn, you have a one-track mind at times. Fact is, I'm coming up on my twenty, Hel. I think I'm going to retire, move over into private security."

"I can't afford you on the payroll full-time."

He smiles, acknowledging her joke. He's never taken a dime from her. "No, no, you can't. And you won't have anyone else like me, going forward. This is something you actually should worry about. The guy coming up behind me, he wants to make a name for himself. He wants to make big busts, get attention."

"I'm a small fish. They almost never go after anyone at my level."

"Your client list has some folks that would be of interest to any prosecutor trying to make his bones."

"I don't live in the city limits."

"But you conduct a lot of business in the city. I'm pretty sure I know which hotels are friendly to you." Tom and Heloise have always been very careful not to share too many details, although Heloise has never been shy about providing Tom with information on other vendors, those she perceives as threats or competition.

"Okay, so I just won't cross city lines for a while. There are plenty of hotels near the airport. Besides, half my business is in private homes."

"Be careful, Hel. That's all I'm trying to say. I'm not going to be there to tell you what's going on, where they're looking. It's true your operation should be fine. But if you get sloppy or hire someone untrustworthy—"

"Won't you stay plugged in, at least for a little while?"

"The new guy's going to want to make the office his. You can't blame him for that. I've got to give him space—or risk having people wonder why I'm still so interested."

"Maybe I really *could* hire you full-time." If she got rid of the two drivers who work for the car service—after all, their primary job is providing security for the girls—or found another way to economize, she could probably come up with a competitive salary.

"No thank you, Heloise." Very formal of him. He seldom uses her "new" name, although at this point Tom has known her as Heloise much longer than he knew her as Helen.

"Oh, don't be so gallant. Revenues aren't what they were, but I bet I could match your current salary, for a lot less work, and you'd be drawing your pension, right?"

"I can't work for you." Eyes on the game, hands in his pockets.

"Why not?"

"Because what you do is illegal."

Oh, so he wasn't being gallant at all.

"That's never stopped you from being my friend." *Or wanting to be more,* she yearns to add.

"I owe you. You gave my department a big case, put yourself at risk. I want you and Scott to be okay, so I've done what I can to look after you. But I can't take your money."

"It's not blood money, Tom. Jesus."

"Look, just because I turn a blind eye to what you do, that doesn't mean I approve. I'm a captain in vice, Heloise. I'm supposed to arrest people like you."

"So why don't you?"

She holds her hands out to him, fingers dangling toward the ground, wrists bent. The other mothers probably think it's a tender gesture, a woman asking her husband or boyfriend to warm her hands in the deepening chill of a fall evening. But Heloise is miming the act of being handcuffed. Something, by the way, she has never been, not even once.

"Stop," he says. "Just stop." Then: "Scott's team is lining up for the penalty kick. Another soccer match ends in anticlimax. I swear, I do not understand the fascination this game has for so many people. It's boring as crap."

He's trying to extend an olive branch. She takes it, dropping her hands and the subject. "What do you think about that . . . situation?"

"Situation?"

"The next county over. The one in the garage."

"Oh." Tom's face is a study. "About that—be careful, Hel."

"I always am."

"Be extra careful."

"What are you telling me?"

"As much as I can for now."

Scott's team wins. He's more interested in the snacks offered after the game than he is in the victory. The light has disappeared very quickly, as it does this time of year, leaving a pink stripe on the horizon. Tom vanishes before Scott finds her on the sidelines. Tom has always respected the fact that no one—well, almost no one—can have access to both sides of her life. He's unusual in that he even knows that Scott exists, a fact she has kept from her clients and employees.

Yet he has been judging her, as it turns out, all these

years. The moral relativism of the situation sends her reeling. She *knows* men. She knows that Tom desires her, would have given anything to marry her, raise Scott as his son. Is this payback for her not wanting him in return?

Or did Tom imagine that he could rescue her from herself, bring her back to the legitimate world? The way Heloise sees it, the legitimate world kicked her out when she wasn't that much older than Scott. Turned away from her, shut the door in her face.

Besides, if she's being honest—she always knew she could do better by herself than being a cop's wife. Than being anyone's wife. Because being someone's wife would mean being dependent on someone else for money, which was where the trouble always began. It wouldn't matter if the guy was a cop or a Wall Street bond trader—to go to a man, palm out, asking for money, to seek approval for every purchase—Heloise doesn't want to do that again, ever. When her father made her get a job, he unwittingly taught her the power of money.

She is so busy brooding about Tom's insult that she forgets at first to consider the real problem he has handed her. *Tom is retiring.* She will have no one on the inside. Careful as Heloise is, he has been invaluable to her a time or two. But mainly there was the *idea* of Tom, which gave her confidence, an indefinable asset in business.

Snack time is over, and Scott runs across the field. He's no longer one of the best soccer players, but he's beautiful when he runs. Her son is eleven now, almost twelve, but in seventh grade because of his December birthday. There is a lankiness that wasn't there last year. It might not have been there yesterday. His red hair is darkening, his freckles are less numerous, his brown eyes more foxlike since his face shed its baby fat. She wishes she couldn't see his father's face in his, but it's there, always. She can live with that, though—as long as she never sees anything else of his father in him.

"Mom, could we have a date?"

"Audrey put hamburger meat out to defrost."

"It will be okay for another day," he says, quite earnest. "We studied food safety in science last year. The important thing is to defrost food in the refrigerator, not on the counter."

"Oh, Audrey always does that."

"Then can we go to Chili's?"

She hesitates. Part of her wants to teach him about thrift and value, remind him that one can't always have what one wants. But that was the kind of lesson Hector Lewis claimed he was teaching her. Besides, Scott called it "a date." And it's Chili's he wants, not the Prime Rib. A plate of nachos, free refills on soda, the televisions on in the bar, whereas Heloise never allows any screens at dinnertime.

"Of course," she says, yearning to smooth down his hair, ruffled in the wind. But she knows better. "Of course."

At the restaurant, over fajitas for Scott and a taco salad for her, she listens to Scott's cheerful report about school, her eyes catching the scroll of headlines on the television behind his head. There's the Suburban Madam again. Why did Tom tell her to be careful? She's always careful.

Fastidious with her records, within the law on taxes, scrupulous about screening clients.

She decides that Tom's just a grump. Perhaps it wasn't his idea to retire at all and he is being forced out, and that's why he was unkind to her. Another reason not to marry. If a man wants to be grumpy with her, he has to pay for the privilege.

Il Cielo was supposed to be the best Italian restaurant in town. Given the town, this was not saying much. It wasn't even true. There were small roadside taverns that did much better by the hearty, pasta-heavy dishes that people thought of as traditional Italian fare. Il Cielo was the most *pretentious* Italian restaurant in town, with gilt-frame chairs and white tablecloths and tiramisu, considered avant-garde at the time, in that place. The ceilings were painted to resemble a pale blue sky with wisps of clouds. The effect might have been pretty if the slipshod brushwork hadn't been so noticeable. Plus, the sky had been filled with chubby angels that floated across the ceiling, most with harps, one with a bow and arrow.

The owner's wife, noticing Helen's eyes drifting upward, mistook her gaze for admiration.

"Don't you love my cherubs?" she said.

Helen, who had written a paper on cherubim in her class on comparative religions, yearned to show off her knowledge, to explain to Angela Papadakis that she had made the common mistake of thinking that cherubs were little angels, when they really occupied a much more interesting and specific role within Judaism and Christianity. The figures on Il Cielo's ceiling were, more correctly, putti.

39

But she wanted a job, so all she said was "Yes."

Although Angela's second husband, Gus, owned the restaurant, it was Angela's project, the kind of gift that a smitten widower bestows on a second wife. Gus was in his sixties, a dour-faced Greek man who ran two successful diners. But plump, pretty Angela, twenty years his junior, wanted something with *class,* and he had given her Il Cielo instead of a lavish wedding. She paid far more attention to the decor than to the menu. The result was that the food was mediocre but inoffensive, whereas the dining room was painful to contemplate.

Part of the problem was that Il Cielo was very dark for a place meant to evoke the sky. The pale blue paint, the light colors throughout, could not combat the inherent gloom in the squat, windowless building, a random piece of real estate that Gus owned. (He may have been enraptured with his new bride, but there were limits even to rapture.) Often Helen ended her weekend lunch shifts thinking she was going out into a dim, dark world, only to wind up blinking at the sun, which had been shining all along.

The weekend lunch shifts weren't the best, but she was the new girl and she needed to schedule work around school. She waited on Saturday shoppers, women who, true to stereotype, took forever to split the bill and almost always undertipped. She waited on men who tried to cup her behind. She found that if she started at their touch yet said nothing, they left larger tips. She even waited on a few rich kids from her school, the kind with cars and endless allowances, but they pretended not to recognize her. She

40

was like a bad smell, a fart, and the only polite thing was to ignore her. She preferred the men who reached for her behind.

She was surprised that anyone wanted to touch the waitresses, given the drabness of their uniforms. They were brown velour, short sleeved and V-neck, perfectly straight, with fabric belts. The thinnest girls appeared shapeless in them, while the girls with shapes looked like bulging sacks of potatoes tied at the middle. Helen could not understand why Angela wanted the girls to be so drab and clunky, clashing with the dining room. It was rumored that Angela had landed her then-married husband-to-be while waitressing at his diner, where the girls wore short skirts and tight blouses. But could Angela really think that the young women here wanted gloomy Gus just because she had?

Then Helen met Angela's son, Billy.

"Watch out, new girl," said Rhonda.

"I'm not interested," Helen said. She wasn't. Oh, Billy was very good-looking. He had dark hair and eyes, a charming manner. But she didn't have time for a boyfriend. A job and school were all she could handle, and she was barely handling school. Her grades had dipped here and there, just as her father had hoped.

"Doesn't matter if you're interested, only if he's interested."

"That's illegal."

Rhonda laughed. "Yeah, well, enjoy taking it to the Supreme Court while you're out of a job. Look, the best way to handle it is to give him what he wants right away, and he'll leave you alone. If he gets *too* interested, his mom gets mad and you'll be history."

"I'm not interested," Helen repeated.

"Well, then you're really fucked."

Rhonda's dire warnings seemed off base. Billy was kind to Helen, nothing more. He was being trained to manage the restaurant, at least according to Billy and his mother. His stepfather seemed less convinced of this plan. He had a point: Billy came and went as he pleased. For a day or two, he would appear in a nice suit. Then several days would go by when he wasn't seen at all. Or he would show up late in a shift "to go over the receipts." This involved shoving a few twenties into the pocket of his very tight, acid-washed jeans. They were fashionable—at that time, in that town—and Helen wouldn't have minded having her own pair, but she couldn't afford them. She could pay for them, but she couldn't afford having her father notice them. She had realized early on that the advantage of being a waitress was that her father couldn't know how much she made in tips. She'd been squirreling money away ever since. But he would get suspicious if she showed up with anything new and expensive. So while she hid money in books and soap boxes and in the toes of her shoes—never all the money in one place, because then she couldn't be wiped out—she could never figure out what to spend it on that wouldn't catch her father's eye.

At any rate, she thought Rhonda was wrong. Billy had no use for her. There were other, prettier girls at the restaurant, closer to Billy's age and therefore with more freedom to date. He helped her at times, but that was in keeping with his need to learn the ropes. For example, the restaurant had a "signature" dessert, which was nothing more than Marshmallow Fluff with syrupy canned strawberries worked through it and then spooned on top of ice cream. The Marshmallow Fluff, purchased in bulk, often arrived frozen, and Helen found it impossible to stir the strawberries through it in order to achieve the even color and distribution that Angela required. Angela was always more interested in how things looked than in how things tasted.

"Let me show you," Billy said when he found her struggling with the mix one day. He led her to the sink, instructed her to wash her hands up to the elbows, almost to the hems of the cap sleeves on her ugly uniform.

Billy then rolled up his sleeves. He had nicely muscled arms for a slender man. Olive skin, which was odd, given how fair his mother was. Big brown eyes. Helen still didn't have aspirations toward him. He was twenty-three, he drove a nice car, he wasn't looking for some silly high-school girl who was still forbidden to date despite being almost seventeen. Besides, Angela wouldn't like it, and Angela, not Billy, made the schedule. Helen wanted to get weekend evening shifts, which meant the best tips—and, better still, being out of the house on the long weekend evenings, when Hector was often at his surliest.

"Do what I do," Billy said, then plunged his arms into the fluff, almost up to the elbows. "It's the only way," he said, seeing how startled she looked. "That's why you wash up so thoroughly. You have to squeeze it through. It's a little like milking a cow. I bet you did that, right? On the field trip to Wentworth Dairy? Every kid in this town has milked a cow at Wentworth."

This was true, and the acknowledgment of this insubstantial bit of shared history made her like him. It was unusual for people to include Helen in things, to point out what they shared. People always seemed more interested in cutting her out.

Timidly, she followed. It was cold; she suppressed a squeal. Billy, after all, hadn't squealed. But it didn't feel awful, and after a bit the sensation was oddly pleasant. "You can squeeze too hard," Billy said, "and then you'll break up the berries. You have to massage it."

Deep in the fluff, she felt his fingers brush hers. A mistake, she thought, but he twined his fingers in hers before moving on, looking deeply in her eyes. At that moment Rhonda came into the prep area, and her expression of disgust shamed Helen. Was this what Billy did with all the girls?

He swore it wasn't. He began driving her home. Of course, given her family situation, she didn't dare let him linger in front of the house. When she explained, leaving out the uglier details, why she couldn't sit in a car with him in front of her house, he began stopping a block away, two blocks away, and then, one afternoon, many miles away, at his mother and stepfather's house, which was grand and new by local standards.

"I just need to check on the dogs," he said. "The folks are out of town."

She had just turned seventeen, but she knew what was going to happen. She wanted it to happen, had already told the lies—she was working a double shift, she'd just stay at the restaurant between the lunch and dinner hours—to make it possible. She wanted Billy as she would never want another man as long as she lived, although she didn't know this at the time. But Billy turned out to be the only man she ever selected for herself, for her own pleasure. And she didn't really choose him, unless taking a job at Il Cielo was a way of choosing.

He undressed her in front of the fire in the living room, carried her into the bedroom that surely must be shared by Angela and Mr. Gus. If she were watching a movie, Helen would have found the scene cheesy. But she was living it, and she loved every minute.

For the rest of her life, Helen would hold on to this memory. The fact that it ended badly didn't corrupt how it began. Whatever his intentions—and, in his own way, Billy did care for her—*her* intentions were pure, she was honest, she was in love. Later, when she was older, she would even dare to ask herself if her mother might have felt the same way with her father, that first time, but she couldn't bear to believe that. Her mother knew that Hector Lewis was married, with kids. *She* had no reason to hope for a happy ending, because she had already chosen a story in which someone had to get hurt—herself or the other woman and her kids. Hector Lewis, overachiever, managed to hurt them all.

That first night with Billy, it was possible to believe in a world where no one ever got hurt. The pain was minimal, and he coaxed her through it, gentle and considerate, stopping as needed. He used his mouth on her. Later he would patiently instruct her on how to use her mouth on him, and that became his preference. He would do less and less for her. But that first night he took good care of her. It was natural to believe that she had found someone who might be able to take care of her in all sorts of ways. Was it so wrong to want that? No one had ever taken care of her. Not her father and not her mother, not really. Helen didn't doubt that her mother loved her, but where was the ferocious maternal love that should have prompted her to protect Helen against her father? So many stories in childhood center on this alleged fact, that a mother will do anything for her child. Having a mother who fell short of that standard made Helen wonder if there was something wrong with her, if she were at fault for not inspiring true maternal feelings. Billy was the first person who made her feel cared for.

"You're lucky he's asleep," her mother said when Helen came home at 1:00 A.M., hours after the restaurant would have closed.

"I'm allowed to hang out with friends on weekend nights, I guess."

"I hope you're using birth control," her mother said, sighing.

She was. Condoms that first night; then Billy took her to Planned Parenthood, had her ask for an IUD while he waited in the parking lot. "Shouldn't we keep using condoms, too?"

46

"You don't need those if you're faithful," Billy said. She thought that meant they were going to be faithful to each other, then later realized that Billy meant only that he was sure she would be faithful to him, that he was not at risk from anything she might do.

As it turned out, he was wrong about that.

Thursday, October 6

When Heloise began shopping for a house in Turner's Grove, she was amused by the standard feature known as "Mother's office," a small built-in desk, usually in a corridor between the kitchen and pantry, where a woman could keep a laptop and—the realtors always showed this with a grand flourish, as if it were truly something wondrous—the household papers, in a drawer already set up for legal-size hanging files.

"Isn't the whole house Mother's office?" her half sister, Meghan, once observed.

Besides, Heloise's files could never be kept in a drawer next to the kitchen, where a child in search of scratch paper might end up pulling out the applications used by would-be customers of the Women's Full Employment Network.

The issue of paper was central to Heloise's life long before various companies began begging its customers to go paperless and save the environment—along with their overhead. (Heloise has always been amused by the good causes that capitalism will embrace in order to save money. Paperless billing! No daily laundry in hotels! Adjusting thermostats! But ask them to reduce their actual dependence on fossil fuel? Impossible.)

Heloise, like the best madams, keeps an enormous amount of information in her head, but she still has to maintain some financial records, and paper is actually the least vulnerable medium. When she had the basement office of the Turner's Grove house renovated, she ended up designing her own file cabinets, then searched for the least curious contractor she could find. The winning bidder was a Polish immigrant who never smiled, although she thought she saw the wisp of one when he studied the drawings for her file cabinets. They look like old-fashioned barrister cabinets, not at all Heloise's usual taste, but she sacrificed her sleek aesthetics for this project. The banks of stacked cabinets alternate—hanging files in drawers with false bottoms are placed above drawers fitted with shredders. The top drawer has two locks. One is a real lock, the other releases the files through the trapdoor of the false bottom into the always-on shredders. Last year Scott had worked on a project for school about reducing the family home's energy usage, and he was appalled to find out how much power dormant appliances required. He dutifully followed the instructions, hooking up everything he could find to surge protectors, then turning them off in the evening. He was disappointed how little their energy bill dropped. Heloise couldn't bear to tell him it was because of her office, where Audrey mans the phones until midnight and the shredders are never turned off.

Heloise is aware that there could be a raid in which neither she nor Audrey would be able to get to the files first, or that the cabinets could be carted away and opened in a different location. Still, it was the best system she could figure out, and most of the paper is benign, although a good forensic accountant might be able to piece together how her business works. If she could, she would conduct all business by carrier pigeon, throw the papers into a fire, then roast and eat the pigeon for good measure. After all, isn't that what squab is? But such a system is impossible, so she saves what she must save—payroll, the necessary tax records, the expenditures she files with the state to prove that she's within the lobbying regs—in her hanging files and hopes she never makes the mistake of using the wrong key.

She has pulled out her files today to go over the quarterly filing, due next week. Her accountant, Leo, is a young man, at least chronologically. He carries himself with an older man's stooped, defeated posture. He has large, unblinking eyes behind thick glasses, and he always wears a suit, even for an afternoon meeting such as this. He has worked for her for five years, and Heloise isn't sure if he's ever figured out the gigantic ruse that is the Women's Full Employment Network and its rather baffling subsidiary, The Store Unlimited. Whatever he's managed to glean about her business, it's more important that he be absolutely nonjudgmental, which he appears to be. The Leos of the world, single men with no social skills, are some of her best customers. If he ever tells her that he's figured out what she does, she'll happily have one of her girls service him. In lieu of fees, of course. But so far Leo cares only about receipts and documentation, all of which Heloise maintains scrupulously. He comments on nothing.

Once he did ask about her inventory costs, but that's because there were tax implications. Where was she stocking the items—the jewelry, the Hermès scarves, the Vuitton luggage—she sold through her Web site?

"I have no inventory costs," she said, having anticipated the question. When Heloise can't sleep, which is often, she uses the time to try to think of any question she might be asked and how she might answer it. "I'm more of a personal shopper. People hire me to find exquisite things for them. I then charge a percentage of the full retail cost after procuring it at a discount, sort of like an interior decorator. The photographs are examples of what I might find, not actual items in stock."

Leo didn't blink. Of course. She wishes he would, every now and then, because that unwavering stare makes him hard to read. He doesn't even slide his eyes to the right or left. She assumes this is possible because he never lies. That makes one of them.

Heloise runs four businesses—two of them essentially legitimate, or would be if they weren't used primarily in the service of an illegal one and a bogus one. The legitimate ones earn the least, barely breaking even, but they save her money and reduce risk.

There is the main company, the Women's Full Employment Network, and she is a registered lobbyist with the state of Maryland, in case anyone checks. Much of her paperwork is generated by the reports she has to file with the state. She also has to make sure she shows enough expenditures to look legitimate. She takes care of that by sending all the state pols food baskets the day after *sine die,* when the legislature adjourns, and making lunch dates when the legislature is out of session.

She also maintains a very discreet online store, one that

cannot be found by any search engine. Cannot be entered, in fact, without an invitation and a password. There, customers who insist on using credit cards for WFEN's services can select various luxury items. These charges then appear on the monthly bills as "The Store Unlimited." Heloise resisted taking credit cards for as long as she could, but it was costing her business, so she now allows Visa and MasterCard. She still tries to dissuade her clients from using them, saying it's for their own good to deal in cash. But some of her customers are single, with no wives peering at their credit cards, and others insist—*insist*—that their wives never see the bills. These are the men who get caught. When they do, Heloise procures the item for which they have been billed and it arrives in the distinctive black-striped box designed by a local graphic artist. She doesn't bill them again, which allows them to show their wives that the gift was always meant for them, not a mistress or a girl-friend. They then pay her back in cash.

And she records it, every cent. Tax evasion is the big risk for her, not sex. Tax evasion is what took down Al Capone. It is very hard to prove that someone has been paid for sex, the difference between an hourly rate and cab fare on the dresser, an appreciative gift. One clever call girl spells it out on her Web site: *"I don't take money, but you are free to give me gifts."* She even has a registry of sorts. The other night Audrey was watching one of those god-awful reality shows about so-called housewives, and one of the women proudly proclaimed that she blew her husband for diamonds. A straight-up confession on national television about trading sex for items of value. If that's not prostitution, what is? But no one's going to arrest that woman, nor should anyone. Although someone might want to give her a few pointers about what class really is.

Heloise's other two businesses, the legitimate ones, were set up when she realized she required certain services and that she might save money—and protect herself from exposure—by providing them herself. There is a travel agency, which handles booking trips—relatively rare, but Heloise likes pocketing the percentage she gets back. And she also has a very small car service, with only two leased sedans and two drivers. The drivers, who are allowed to work as independent contractors when not being used by Heloise, provide an extra layer of security for her girls. Also, if the girls are going to drink or even do drugs with their clients—and all do the former and some do the latter, despite the fact that both are prohibited under WFEN's rules—it's better for them not to drive. A drunk girl crashing her car while on Heloise's payroll could end with her being sued.

Besides, Heloise also cares about the girls' personal safety. They all wear so-called slave bracelets, designed by her, with a GPS chip hidden inside. She hates the connotation of "slave," but that's the proper term for a bracelet that can be removed only with a key, which the girls never carry. Of course, the bracelets won't save them if they meet someone sick enough to remove a girl's left arm. That's another one of the worries that leads to Heloise's insomnia, the nights of staring at the ceiling trying to think of questions she might have to answer.

The girls think the bracelets are funny, call them HoJacks. And when they leave her employ—and they all do, after they've graduated from college or solved their money problems—they can have the chip removed and keep the bangle as a souvenir, a badge.

Heloise also gives the girls a safe word, which changes weekly: At the end of each date, the girl must text that word to Heloise and Audrey. The text also serves as a time stamp on the appointment, confirming that the client has not gone overtime. Customers are screened by a private investigator that Heloise keeps on retainer. The PI, a pragmatic young woman from the city, probably has an inkling that Heloise's business is not exactly on the up-and-up, but there is nothing illegal about what she does for Heloise. She once told Heloise that the same results could be achieved for less money just by subscribing to one of the various Internet-based services, such as Intelius. But then those names, those histories, would be on Heloise's hard drive somewhere, a de facto black book. Again Heloise is paying in part for the privilege of paper. She takes the reports and she shreds them once read. Her arrangement with the PI was set up by Heloise's lawyer, so their transactions are confidential. No one can get to her clients—or to Heloise—through the PI.

So yes, she has gone to great lengths to do everything she can to protect the men who pay her and the girls who work for her. Everything she can think of, but it turns out that no one can think of everything. She has failed one of her girls, which is one reason her accountant is here tonight.

"Sophie's prescriptions now cost seventeen hundred

dollars a month. Your health plan doesn't even have a pre-scription component, and you're paying that out of pocket. How long is she going to be on leave?"

"I'm not sure, but I said I would pay it, so I am."

"But why are you paying her cash, under the table? It's the same as income, doesn't matter if she uses the money for prescription drugs. Does she understand that? Is she report-ing it?"

"I think so." Heloise doubts it.

"Look, you can afford this kind of outlay—for now—but it can't go on this way indefinitely."

"Sophie's on a paid medical leave."

"For how long?"

"For as long as she needs to be." Forever. For fucking forever.

"So you're paying her base salary *and* you're buying her drugs. Fine, that's your choice. But as her medical bills start to rise, that will impact the group. You might see a big increase in premiums. If you don't expect her to return to work, it actually would be better to let her go, then use your money to cover her COBRA costs for eighteen months. Then she's guaranteed medical insurance through one of the big insurers and the group policy doesn't take the hit."

"And what will she live on? How will she pay for those prescriptions?"

"She can work," Leo says, but it's really more of a ques-tion. "I mean, I don't really know her, I don't know what her skills are or what kind of education she has, but she might be able to work again, right?"

"I promised to take care of her," Heloise insists.

"Okay, but you're putting the cost of the plan at risk. Except for you and Scott, because you're on your own family plan. Which, by the way, now costs seven hundred fifty a month."

"If that's what it costs, it's what it costs."

"You and Scott have to have more comprehensive coverage, because kids see doctors a lot oftener. But that's all the more reason for you to find another way to help Sophie out." Leo sighs. "All I can do is advise. I realize you feel sorry for the girl, but it's not your fault she has HIV."

Except it is.

Sophie, like most of Heloise's employees, was recruited through an ad in a college newspaper. She was premed at Johns Hopkins, very beautiful, very brainy—and very bored. Like Leo, she'd been born old, but a different kind of old, the preternatural weariness of being desired from a very early age. Boys chased her. Girls chased her. Professors chased her. She had a wealth of sexual experience, but it had provided her no genuine pleasure.

"I feel," she told Heloise at their first meeting, "as if I have this really valuable commodity—myself—and yet I'm not supposed to do anything with it."

"Absolutely," Heloise said. "Beauty is a commodity in our world."

They were at One World Café, directly across from the Hopkins campus, eating vegetarian fare. Sophie had explained that she was very particular about what she put into her body. No meat, no soda, no alcohol. She said this with a young woman's earnestness, as if no one else in the world had ever thought of such a thing.

"The way things work, I'm allowed to trade it to only one man, and then it's on his terms, you know? And it's totally a *transaction*. Like, if I find some rich guy, he might ask me to sign a prenup. At the very least, I'd have to live where he wants to live, have his kids. Whereas if I could sell it piecemeal, I'd make so much more. It's like a really big diamond—sometimes it's worth more if you make lots of little diamonds from it."

Heloise wasn't sure that was true, but Sophie probably knew more about diamonds than she did. Although Sophie's family wasn't rich, she had grown up in New York City, in proximity to people with great fortunes. Still, Heloise understood how Sophie felt. Her beauty, her sexual allure, was a commodity, yet she was prohibited to trade on it. To be sure, Sophie could "make" more by marrying a millionaire than she would working for Heloise for a few years, but she would be on call 24/7. Why not work eight to ten hours a week and earn thousands?

When Heloise hired Sophie, she gave her the talk she gave all the girls: No drugs, they're illegal. Bondage had to be preapproved; don't let just anyone tie you up. And it was better to use condoms, always, for everything. Yes, Heloise asked her clients to submit blood tests, but they could be up to six months old. (Most men who went to prostitutes didn't mind taking regular blood tests, she had found. She just wished she could get a piece of *that* action, own a lab. The fees they charged were ridiculous.) But there were men who would pay extra for not wearing a condom. Technically, Heloise forbade this, but it was ultimately between the girls and the clients, just like tipping. And, as with tipping, she couldn't prevent it or regulate it. She recommended reporting cash income, or at least some of it. She recommended using condoms and avoiding drugs. What the girls did, however, was between them and their consciences.

Some people would call what Heloise did turning a blind eye. But she wasn't blind. She knew. She *knew*. What she had given Sophie was a winking eye—go ahead, have unprotected sex for the extra bucks! What had it added up to, in the end? A pair of beautiful shoes, a dress, a sofa? Not enough for a modest car, even. And certainly not enough to buy Trizivir every month, at seventeen hundred bucks a month, for the rest of her life, which would probably be at once too short and too long.

Leo was right: There was nothing to keep Sophie from working some kind of job, technically. Except for her raging self-pity. She sat in the little apartment she rented in North Baltimore, in one of the older, shabby-chic buildings along University Parkway. It was the same building that housed the One World Café, not that Sophie cared about what she put into her body anymore. She ate the most astonishing array of junk, although she remained thin, too thin. She was still beautiful, but it was more ethereal now. The juicy promise that had attracted everyone to her was gone.

All of Sophie's regular clients were gone, too, expunged from Heloise's rolls. She had been straightforward, notifying each that he'd been with a girl infected with HIV. She urged all of them to get tested. Of the ten men who had been with Sophie in the three months before her diagnosis, seven railed at Heloise, said she was running a slipshod business and that they would take her for everything she was worth if they found out they were infected. Three accepted the news quietly.

Heloise was pretty sure that the man who had infected Sophie was one of the first group, although she could never decide which one it was. Deny, deny, deny. That's the way it goes. To be safe, she felt she had to let them all go, which she could ill afford. Ten regulars, gone from the rolls. After Sophie, new girls were told that failing to practice safe sex was grounds for firing. Barn door, meet the gone horse.

"I'll visit her soon," Heloise promises Leo. "See what she wants to do."

"I talked to her not long ago," he says.

"You did? I would prefer you not talk to the employees directly."

"She called me. Said it was a question about her W-2, but she also wanted to know if she qualified for workers' compensation. I told her that was only for injuries and liabilities that were part of a job, not for long-term illnesses, no matter how grave. I'm not sure even a hospital worker could get coverage for HIV—that is, unless the worker could prove some sort of negligence on the employer's part. But, of course, it has no bearing here."

Leo's face is bland, so bland. He doesn't blink. Then again, he never blinks. *This is trouble,* Heloise thinks. She's just not sure what brand of trouble it is.

1992

Early in her relationship with Billy, Helen worked out a way to "meet" him at the movies, a ruse that meant he didn't have to come to the house. Now seventeen, she was technically allowed to date by her father's ever-shifting rules, but Billy had become increasingly paranoid. He said he'd learned that he had violated statutory-rape laws with her. He said he was fearful her father would not approve of him, and it was better to go behind his back than to seek his permission, be denied, and then go against an out-and-out prohibition. He said—

"It's okay, Billy. I'll meet you there, like you want."

On this particular night, he arrived late, with only a few minutes to spare. He had forgotten his wallet. She bought their tickets and refreshments—popcorn and Sno-Caps and a large soda for Billy, a Diet Coke for herself. Billy often mentioned how beautiful his mother was before she gained weight. Her husband, Gus, clearly thought she was still a looker, but he didn't know how gorgeous she'd been when Billy was a little boy. Billy knew it was shallow, but he could never love a woman who wasn't thin. Helen, who had never been particularly concerned about her weight, had become very self-conscious about her body. But Billy did so much to care for her. Watching her weight seemed the least she could do for him.

The movie was about a woman with a perfect life. Which meant, of course, that it was all a lie. In Helen's experience, movies either began with perfection and shattered it or proceeded in the opposite direction, starting with someone poor and miserable and rewarding that person with a fairy-tale ending. At least those were the sorts of movies that came to the multiplex in Helen's hometown. In this movie the woman was beautiful, with one of those vague jobs that intrigued Helen. Her main responsibility seemed to be walking through an art gallery in beautiful clothes, making vague gestures at the paintings and sculptures. She and her handsome husband lived in an apartment filled with beautiful things, and they went to parties where everyone else was gorgeous, if not quite as gorgeous as they were. They were in negotiations to buy an even more beautiful house, something starkly modern overlooking water, so their beautiful daughter could play outside with their adorably ugly dog.

Then a friend from the gallery called the beautiful woman and said he had something urgent to discuss. "But not on the phone!" Helen hid her face in the crook of Billy's arm, knowing that the friend would soon be dead. The beautiful woman saw her husband in the Diamond District when he was supposed to be in Toronto. The beautiful husband turned out to have a different name, a whole different life from what he had claimed. He'd been stealing things from her gallery for years and replacing them with clever copies. He tried to kill her, but she tricked him, using her knowledge of trompe l'oeil—"It means 'fool the eye,'" Helen whispered to Billy, thinking he would be impressed by her knowledge—to lure him into an elevator shaft, where he fell to his death. Somehow the movie seemed to think this was a happy ending—he was dead, but it wasn't her fault, not exactly. The final frames showed the beautiful woman, beautiful daughter, and adorably ugly dog in a new apartment—smaller, more casual, but still expensive to Helen's eye, which wasn't easily fooled.

"I can't get over what a dope she was," Helen said. Billy shrugged.

"I can't get over what a dope I was."

It was six months later, and Helen was sitting on a sagging mattress in a cheap motel in Baltimore. Addicts are good liars, especially if you love them, and it had taken her a long time to sort out Billy's lies, to become aware of his giveaway tic, which was the laundry list of reasons he provided whenever he knew he was on thin ice. Billy's lies, like trends, came in threes.

Not that she was oblivious to his lies, but most of them were harmless, a habit born, he said—he lied—from his stepfather's terrifying strictness. Even that proved to be a lie; Billy's stepfather had not come along until he was almost twenty. But Helen, who lied to Hector all the time, was vulnerable to believing that lying could be essential to one's survival. Billy lied about the things that made him late, inventing traffic jams and accidents. He lied about his age. He was twenty-six, not twenty-three. He had thought twenty-six would scare her off. He lied about his role at the restaurant, although it's possible that he and his mother really did believe he was being groomed to run it. His step-father, however, had no such illusions.

About three months into Helen's relationship with Billy, Mr. Gus showed up one day about an hour before open-ing, when the waitresses were doing their prep. He said he wanted to meet with each of them one-on-one.

"The cash register is short on certain days," he said when Helen took a seat opposite him. "It's always when you're working."

She felt as if she'd been hit. The odd thing was that Mr. Gus's voice wasn't angry or accusatory, although his dour face gave every pronouncement a melancholy edge. He sat back, waiting for her response.

"I never—I wouldn't—this is a good job, Mr. Gus, and I value it. Plus, I don't even touch the cash register, except to cash out my charge tips, and then Rhonda or someone does it for me, per the rules—"

"Never by more than twenty or forty, but always short. If it were just people being bad at making change, the odds should favor me every now and then, don't you think?"

She tried to regain her composure but found she could not stop gasping. She had withstood beatings from her father more easily than this.

Mr. Gus continued. "And once or twice some inventory disappeared. Booze, the top-shelf stuff. Again you were working both nights."

Her instinct, ugly and swift, was to shift the blame to someone else. She realized that it wasn't an attractive impulse. "Am I the only one who worked all those shifts? No one else? Rhonda picks up most of the same shifts I do."

"It's not Rhonda," he said. "And you know what? I don't think it's you. But there is something else common to every shift you work, no?"

"Well, I work Friday and Saturday nights now, unless I switch with someone. And those are the busiest nights, with the most cash coming in, but—"

He held up a palm. His hands were huge, scarred from his early days as a line cook. He had come to the United States in the 1940s with his parents. He'd been a marine in the Korean War. Billy said gangsters had given him his start and that he was still friendly with what Billy called the "criminal element" of central Pennsylvania.

"I know the *malaka* comes to see you whenever you work."

"Sir?"

"My stepson, the idiot. I know you are with him."

She honestly thought they had hidden their relationship from everyone. The other waitresses assumed that she'd slept with Billy once or twice, because he stopped paying attention to her at work. After all, that's what had happened to all of them. Sex was okay, apparently, with Billy's mother. She drew the line only at relationships.

"Does his mother—"

"She doesn't see what she doesn't want to see when it comes to him. So no, she doesn't see that he likes a girl who is much too young for him. And too good for him, but there's not a girl on this earth who's not too good for him.

She doesn't see that he has nice clothes and a nice car, better than he could afford on the allowance that she gives him."

"Allowance?"

"Yeah, she calls it a salary, but it comes out of her pocket, so what would you call it? An allowance, like children get, only he is a man. And he's stealing from me. I want you to tell him to stop."

"But—why me?" She was thinking that no one could be more formidable than Mr. Gus. There was no doubt that Billy feared him. Whereas she seemed to have less and less control over him. A cynical person would say that was because she had given in to him, that he'd gotten what he wanted from her, but Helen believed it was more complicated than that. Her mother couldn't get Hector to do anything, whereas Barbara, his first wife, occasionally wangled money or gifts from him. It had something to do with those rats that Helen had learned about at school and the little lever they pushed for food. Her father always got the pellet from her mother. Not just sex but wholehearted approval, constant, cringing affection. Barbara blew hot and cold. She didn't *like* him, and Hector wanted to be liked.

But Helen couldn't hold anything back from Billy, didn't want to. It felt good to love someone.

"Why don't I talk to him? Because if I tell him, he will go to his mother and cry, and she will make my life a misery. But if you tell him that he must stop or you will lose your job, then he cannot cry to her. He will have to choose." He gave her what he seemed to think was a sympathetic look, although even Mr. Gus's sympathetic looks were a little scary. "If you're lucky, he will have you fired."

"I don't see how that would be lucky. I need this job. I'll have to get another one if I lose it, and there aren't many good restaurants in town."

"If it comes to that, I will help you. Gladly. You're a good girl—or were, before him. But you have to know he's no good. What kind of person steals like that, from family? I'll tell you—a drug addict."

"Oh, no, Billy doesn't use drugs."

Mr. Gus snorted. "Good luck," he said, showing her the door.

Billy said it was lies, all lies. That his stepfather was jealous of him and trying to get rid of him. That he once or twice made change from the cash register but had never taken so much as a dollar. He said Mr. Gus was sleeping with Rhonda and they had cooked up this plan to get rid of both of them. But he wasn't an addict. He was going to be the manager of Il Cielo—how could he stay away? But for her he would.

And he did, for almost a month, a month in which he became increasingly jumpy and paranoid. He knew things about his stepfather, he said. Things that could get him arrested. His stepfather knew he knew and was going to make Billy disappear, make it look like an accident. He needed to blow town, but he didn't have the funds. Besides, how could he leave her? He loved her. He had abandoned his own future for her.

"I have money, Billy," she told him. "Not a lot, but I've managed to save some."

66

"No, I couldn't do that to you."

His initial refusal made him seem trustworthy.

"I want you to. I want you to be safe."

"There's no life for me without you."

"Then I'll go with you."

"Okay, but only if we get married. You can do it fast, down in Baltimore, without a blood test. We could be married tomorrow."

Marriage. She had never thought about it. She had thought about going to college, getting a job. *Marriage.* Her father had refused to give that to her mother, so it must be a precious thing. Yes, she would marry him. That wouldn't keep her from doing anything else. She was already working and going to school at the same time. She could do that in Baltimore, too.

"Yes," she said.

"When you come to work on Saturday, bring your money—and a suitcase, with as many clothes as you can manage. Stash it behind the Dumpster, and I'll put it in the trunk of my car."

He showed up that Saturday in a suit, presiding as manager. He ignored Helen so thoroughly that she began to wonder if she had imagined his instructions. At closing he chewed her out, said one of her tables had complained about her attitude and that he was going to make her stay late and start inventory as punishment. Once everyone was gone, he showed her the night's cash receipts, waiting to be deposited. "Going to be deposited straight in our account, baby." They headed out of town in his car, not the sports car he had once driven but a plain, boxy old Datsun. "Gotta keep a low profile," he said. "He'll be coming after us."

They would get married the very next day, he promised. Well, not the next day, but Monday, at the courthouse. They were going to start over. Billy was going to open a real restaurant, a good one, where the desserts weren't made of Marshmallow Fluff.

She fell asleep in the car. The next thing she knew, they were in a motel room outside Baltimore, Maryland, which turned out not to be the place that one could get married right away. That was a different county, back in the direction they had driven. Here, in the city, there was a forty-eight-hour waiting period after taking out the license, a fact that threw Billy off. Plus, he was annoyed at the cost of the license. And he was out of drugs—not that she understood that yet—and he was getting irritable, and it turned out that maybe he had taken some things from his stepfather that weren't his to take—not just that night's receipts but all those other shortages, the booze, jewelry from his mother's bedroom—and maybe there were other people, less forgiving, who wanted money from him, too. See, Billy didn't use drugs, but he sold them, and there had been some bad luck, someone had stolen his stash, which he hadn't exactly paid for, but how could he pay for it if he didn't have the drugs to sell? They needed fast money, cash money, and the best place to make that, Billy had heard, was on the Block, where Helen would make great tips just for dancing. Just dancing! And what did it matter if men saw her naked? She was beautiful; men should see her and admire her. They wouldn't be allowed to touch her. Other men could look, but only Billy could touch.

Things didn't happen as fast as Billy thought they would. But they happened as he said they would. She got a job dancing. She made slightly more than she'd made on the good shifts at Il Cielo. She brought it all home, and Billy, instead of paying the debts he owed, put it up his nose.

She started bringing home a little less, hiding money as she had hidden it from her father. She started doing extras, to make a little more. Lap dances. As Billy had promised, no one touched her. Nothing touched her. He no longer touched her. She seldom seemed to catch him in the right phase of his chemical arc for sex, and she didn't want it much either.

So this is it, she thought. *I fell in love with the wrong guy, an addict, and this is the life I get.* Going home didn't seem to be an option. She had called once, to say she was in Maryland and planning to get married, and her father had called her a whore and slammed down the phone. Prophetic Hector. *How could I be such a dope?* She didn't think she could feel anything, ever again.

She was eighteen years old.

Friday, October 7

Heloise is having dinner with Scott when the home phone rings. She lets it go to voice mail. Calls to the landline are almost always telemarketers, although girls have started calling Scott, who does not have his own cell phone and is not allowed to chat on Facebook. And even if tonight's call is something uncharacteristically urgent, it can wait. Almost everything can wait. It's funny how few people figure this out, how they allow their phones and their BlackBerrys and their computers to enslave them. Heloise can't completely leave work behind on the nights she doesn't have appointments—there are almost always girls out on call, although Fridays tend to be slow—but she leaves it to Audrey to monitor the office, checking the GPS program from time to time, making sure everyone is where she's supposed to be. The ritual of the meal with Scott is important to her, even if she has never learned to enjoy food. She blames her father, the way she had to rush through dinner in order to escape him.

Food has never mattered that much to Heloise. Her mother was too exhausted to rise above the cheap conveniences she could afford—frozen vegetables and waffles, Hamburger Helper, casseroles made with Campbell's chicken soup. Heloise's experience behind the scenes at Il Cielo, her memories of being up to her elbows in Marshmallow Fluff, left her skeptical of all restaurants. Even when she dines in celebrated places, she finds it hard to have much of an appetite. During the years with Val, that cocaine-addled household had huge quantities of food, but it tended toward junk food and doggie bags from high-end chains, Styrofoam containers of unfinished sandwiches. Val didn't believe in wasting food. He was thrifty about everything. Even human beings. He squeezed every ounce out of them. Val was the person who could always get one more dab of toothpaste out of a spent tube, one more trick from an almost-done hooker.

Yet Scott, completely on his own, has become a little foodie. He bakes, he knows what an emulsion is. Heloise thinks his fascination with food must have started when he began watching cooking shows with Audrey or a previous baby-sitter. The cooking shows were probably an accident, sandwiched between the hideous reality shows that Audrey loves. Heloise cannot understand this. Audrey, whom she introduces as her au pair—her odd speaking voice makes her sound as if she's from some unplaceable foreign land, although she grew up in Wilkes-Barre, then moved to Aberdeen, Maryland—has had more reality in her relatively short life than most women could stand. Married at eighteen, she was abused by her husband for several years. One of the beatings resulted in a partial hearing loss, which is what makes her speech sound odd. Then, after catching *The Burning Bed* in a rerun, she decided that the old television film was meant to be instructional, that God wanted her to watch it and learn from it. Audrey doused her husband's bed with lighter fluid and set him on fire. The thing that troubled prosecutors was that it had been months since she'd been beaten. "But it was only a matter of time before he hit me again," Audrey told Heloise when they met. "And those were the worst times. The waiting. The best times were immediately after the beating, and not just because he was nicer. He wasn't, not always. He would apologize, but in that lame way where you say you're sorry but make it clear that the other person is at fault. Sort of like, 'I'm sorry that you behaved so badly I felt I had to hit you. I'll try to do better, but you have to try, too.' Although at least I wasn't wondering when he was going to hit me again."

Heloise understood. The prosecutor did not, nor did the police, and Audrey was convicted and imprisoned for manslaughter.

Five years later, pardoned by the governor, one of a group of women released for their violent crimes after the circumstances were shown to be connected to domestic violence, Audrey had somehow come across the Women's Full Employment Network and taken the firm at its word. She was a woman. She needed full employment, and no one would hire her.

Heloise was touched, but Audrey was not suitable for one of the six positions she kept on her roster, all of which were labeled "legislative liaison." It grieved Heloise to judge another woman this way, but Audrey was unattractive, with thick glasses and hair worn in the most unflattering braids, crowning her head. In a film one would take off the glasses, release the hair, and a beauty would be revealed. In real life, Audrey without her glasses had the sleepy, unfocused eyes of a newborn kitten, and her hair, when loose, was a Medusa-like mass. There would be no transformation.

Not that it mattered. Audrey disapproved of adultery. She had been faithful to a very bad husband. Certainly, more fortunate men and women should be able to maintain their vows. So when Heloise softened and decided to give her a job, it was simply as the "au pair," although Scott was in grade school and needed little supervision. The whole point of Heloise's job was to work a schedule that allowed her as much time with Scott as possible.

Audrey was sheltered. Audrey was a small-town girl. But she was not stupid. She sussed out Heloise's real job just as she sussed out everything else in life—by watching television. All it took was one Tori Spelling movie on Lifetime and Audrey had figured it out. A straight shooter, she came to Heloise the next day and said, "You're running an escort service, aren't you?"

"I am running a lobbying firm dedicated to women's issues, primarily pay equity."

"Do the girls who work for you—do they have sex for money?"

"That's illegal, Audrey. My girls meet with men who have the power to change things and use their best persuasive skills to convince them to introduce legislation that could help us toward our goal."

Audrey's eyes, behind her glasses, goggled. An old cartoon jingle flitted through Heloise's mind. *Barney Google with the goo-goo-googly eyes.* She flinched at the memory, then pinned down the reason: Hector Lewis used to sing it, tunelessly, when tending to some small chore. He did only small chores.

"Heloise, please don't lie to me," Audrey said. "I owe you everything. You gave me a job when no one else wanted to hire me. You trust me with your son. Trust me with this."

But Heloise couldn't, not right away. She told Audrey that WFEN was highly specialized, that it might seem to be similar to an escort service, but it was serious. Deadly serious. She said that Tori Spelling movies were not very realistic, in her experience. (She was right about that. Later she caught the film that had sparked Audrey's curiosity, and it had much more in common with the turn-of-the-century melodramas about virtuous young things who can't pay the rent and fall into bad company. She gave Audrey a copy of *Sister Carrie,* hoping to improve her mind.)

Still, Audrey had put her finger on something key: Heloise trusted her with the most precious person in her life. But that was part of the problem, too. Audrey had to be Scott's buffer. It was dangerous for anyone close to Scott to know everything about Heloise. Compartmentalize, compartmentalize, compartmentalize. Sometimes she felt that her entire life was about creating boxes and storing pieces of herself in each one. She never got the boxes mixed up, but it required ferocious concentration on her part, an eternal vigilance. How could she trust anyone else to keep it straight? No one else had as much to lose.

A few months after their conversation, Audrey was

74

driving Scott home from school in Heloise's car, a nice SUV but not particularly extravagant or in demand. They were waiting at a light, making idle conversation, when a man opened Audrey's door and told her to get out. Scott was probably too small to be seen in the backseat, but perhaps the would-be carjacker didn't care. He jabbed something pointed at Audrey through his Windbreaker pocket.

He hadn't counted on dealing with someone who was *done* being bullied.

"No," Audrey said. "Show me your gun. I don't believe you have one."

The would-be carjacker reached across her and unfastened her seat belt, even as Audrey pulled hair from his scalp. Screaming in pain, he threw her to the ground and took her place behind the wheel. But before he could close the door, Audrey was up and on the running board, clawing at him with one hand, straining for the panic button on the keys, trying to stomp the emergency brake, yet somehow maintaining a completely calm tone with Scott all the while.

"It's okay, buddy, it's all okay. Don't worry about a thing."

The man stopped the car, pushed Audrey out of the way, and took off on foot. He was arrested at the local ER several hours later, where he went for treatment for a scratched cornea. He also had scratches all over his face. But it was the bald patch that gave him away.

Such an incident would have attracted a lot of attention anywhere, but in a suburb such as Turner's Grove reporters slavered for the story. The world's bravest nanny! Television

75

news crews converged on Audrey from both directions, Baltimore and D.C. The local papers dispatched their best reporters. The *Today* show sent her a fruit basket. Heloise declined to speak to anyone, using the credible excuse that additional exposure could endanger her son. But she knew she could not keep Audrey from enjoying the attention, the prospect of which was heady.

Yet Audrey also told the press, through Heloise's lawyer, that she had no desire to be interviewed or photographed. She said no over and over, for about three days, and then a new shiny toy of a story came along to distract the media types. Heloise understood that Audrey had done this to protect Scott and, by extension, Heloise.

The cliché was inevitable: "How can I ever repay you, Audrey?"

The reply was unexpected: "By trusting me."

So she did. She let Audrey in. Into her confidences, her world, and, ultimately, her office. Audrey was the only person allowed to inhabit the two spheres of Heloise's life. After the years of strict compartmentalization, it was a relief to have someone who moved back and forth between the two worlds as Heloise did. A relief to have someone with whom she never had to be guarded. As Scott required less attention, Audrey asked for more responsibilities at WFEN. Over time she became Heloise's office manager. The euphemisms of Heloise's inventory list were helpful to Audrey, who still did not approve of what these men were doing, of what Heloise was facilitating. And her fierce maternal instincts were perfect for the task of ensuring the girls' safety.

So Heloise forgave and even indulged Audrey's terrible taste in television. Having Scott be a little foodie wasn't the worst thing in the world. Heloise even learned to cook, after a fashion. She was too impatient to be a truly good cook, and she had horrible knife skills, but she became good at simple sauces and began to glimpse why some people cared passionately about food, although she would never be one of them. Scott was the far better cook, if spectacularly messy and very hard on the cookware. Tonight, for example, he has made a shrimp stir-fry, and Heloise's heart sinks a little, looking at the splattered grease, the scorched pan, the odds and ends scattered along the counter, the dusting of corn-starch and five-spice powder across the floor. She will need an hour to restore the kitchen to order.

Then she looks at the cook, who is waiting expectantly for her verdict. Brown eyes. Red hair. Some would call his face foxy, but there is no guile there. Val—Val had the foxy look. But did he always? Was he born that way? Heloise knows very little about Val's past. She has seen no photos from his childhood. She knows nothing about Val's parents, Scott's grandparents. She lives in dread of the unknown genetic gifts passed down on that side of the family.

Not that her side is much better. She is, after all, Hector Lewis's daughter. She has done harm. Not intentionally, but by error and omission. A man died because of her. Maybe more than one. A woman has HIV because Heloise was willing to wink at her own rules. Another woman— She prefers not to think about that other woman.

"Mom?"

"It's delicious, Val."

"What?"

"I said *pal*. It's delicious, pal."

"You never called me that before."

"I know."

"You're *weird*, Mom."

"That I am, Scott. That I am."

She bolts her glass of wine.

1993

There were many things that Val Deluca didn't like to be called. Short. His full name. Most of all he hated to be called a pimp. He said he was a CEO, an entrepreneur, a self-made man. He told Helen that he was her savior—and maybe he was.

But he was, inarguably, short. Shorter than Helen, fine-boned, seemingly incapable of putting on weight although he tried just about everything to add mass to his frame. Protein shakes, heavy lifting. Not steroids, though, never steroids. He heard they gave you pimples on your back and shrank your testicles. A redhead, Val had found *freckles* difficult enough to surmount and had no inclination to see his testicles reduced.

He had bright red hair, the orangey kind, Bozo hair, the type of hair that people are teased about. Only no one teased Val, not in all the time that Helen knew him. Occasionally a new person moving in his circles made the mistake of underestimating him, but that didn't happen often. Most people were quick to figure out that a small man with that hair had not gotten where he was by being soft.

Yet he was soft, tender even, with Helen. *Of course,* people would say, if there had been people who actually spoke to Helen at that time in her life. The only people she knew

79

were Billy and the other dancers and employees at the club, and while they exchanged desultory conversation, they didn't really talk. But she knew the conventional wisdom. *That's what pimps do. They lure you in, they treat you nicely at first, make you dependent on them, and then lower the boom.*

In Helen's experience that was what *men* did. Her father had done it to her mother, or so she assumed. Billy had done it to her. Besides, she was already essentially tricking when she met Val. That's how she first encountered him, in a private room at the club. He liked her, something clicked. He came back to see her. When he came back a third time, Helen began to think that Val might be able to help her solve what she thought of as her Billy problem. Billy wasn't human to her anymore. He was just a huge hole, waiting for her back in the motel room every night. He swallowed up everything he could. She had no doubt that he would eventually swallow her.

Helen had to give Billy this much: He wasn't paranoid. People *were* out to get him at this point. His stepfather wanted to swear out a warrant on him, according to Billy's mother, whom he called—collect—every Friday, when he knew that his stepfather would be at one of his diners. His mother had kept Mr. Gus from making a formal criminal complaint, but Helen thought an arrest might be the best way to keep Billy safe. The other people who'd been ripped off by Billy weren't going to bother with warrants. They would find him, ask for the money they were owed, then kill him when he couldn't pay them back. And if Helen was there at the inopportune moment that the bill came due, they wouldn't hesitate to kill her as well. What was she? Some girl, a whore, a dancer on the Block. Collateral damage.

Helen was naïve enough to think that she could get Val to help her solve the Billy problem without being forever in his debt. When she realized he was drawn to her, that she had a brief window of being able to leverage him, she told him the details of her situation, how she feared for her life as long as she lived with Billy.

"Then don't live with him," Val said. "Live with me."

"It's not that easy," she said. "He's out of his mind. If I try to leave, he'll try to stop me. He relies on me for money—I pay the rent, buy what little food he eats. He doesn't care about me at this point, but he won't want to lose his meal ticket."

Val locked his eyes on her. He had brown eyes, unusual in such a fair, freckled redhead. There was a slight tilt to them, and she wondered if his mother, or perhaps grandmother, had been Asian. "Do you understand what you're asking me to do?"

"Oh, I'm not asking for anything," she said. This was true: She couldn't ask for anything, because she didn't know what she wanted. She had hoped Val might present her a laundry list of choices, see the solution in the way that outsiders sometimes can. She didn't want Billy to come to harm. But she couldn't prevent it, and she didn't want to be there when that moment arrived. Besides, Billy would make a scene if she left. He needed her. She brought in the only money they had.

81

She changed the subject. "If I did live with you, it would just be until I got on my feet."

Val stroked her arm. They were in a twenty-four-hour restaurant, of which there were surprisingly few in Baltimore, so the cops and the pimps and the whores and all the other night people ended up hanging out together at this one place, Burke's. It was an informal, neutral ground, a place where everyone coexisted in harmony as long as no one did anything stupid.

"You weren't meant to be on your feet. You're good, one of the best I've ever had. How many men have you been with?"

She blushed, which made him laugh.

"C'mon. You can tell me. You fuck like you started really early, before you even knew what it was. Someone help you out? You got a nasty daddy, a pervy uncle? Don't be ashamed. All the girls, it's the same story more or less."

"Billy was my first boyfriend. Since we came down here—well, you know what I do. It was a way to make cash on the side. I keep it mainly to lap dances. Except for you."

He laughed. "Bullshit."

"It's true." It wasn't. "I kept hoping I could put together a little bankroll, get away from him. But there's no place I can hide money that he doesn't find it. I've never seen anything like it."

"He's an addict. I think you could take a dope fiend and turn him upside down and run him along a beach and he'd find more dough than any metal detector." Val didn't use drugs, just a little weed. And although he liked to drink, his

82

tolerance wasn't very good, probably because of his size, and he didn't like being drunk-drunk. He smoked and drank to take the edge off, although Val's edge was never really off.

"I feel like I'm in quicksand. The more I struggle to get out, the deeper I get."

"You heard of these places called banks? You can put your money there."

She shook her head, thinking of the crumpled and soiled bills she would carry to a bank. No matter what she wore or how she handled herself, they would know that it was truly dirty money. Besides, she would need proof of address, and a by-the-week motel near the bus station probably didn't count as an address. She had no utility bill, and the girl on her driver's license was so distant from who she was now that it might as well be a seventeenth-century Flemish painting in a museum.

"Look, I want you to be with me, exclusively. I'll be honest—I'll never be exclusive to you. That's not how I am. And I'd expect you to keep your job. I guess I'm liberated that way." He smiled at his own joke.

"The dancing?"

"No." He laughed. "Good as you fuck, you are shit as a dancer. What I'm saying is, I've got a big nut, everyone contributes. But it's a nice life. Basically I'm offering you what you have, but with more money, a nicer place to stay. I've got a house out in the east part of the county. It's almost countrylike, out on one of those little inlets, with a dock and everything. You'll have your own room for when I don't want you in mine. You'll work shifts at these motels I use.

83

We screen the guys, bring them to you. It's very safe. No standing out in the cold, soliciting. Of course, that also means I know exactly how many tricks you work and how much you take in, so don't ever try to fool me."

Those words sank in. *Don't ever try to fool me.*

"And Billy?"

"He's a dope fiend. If I give him enough money, he'll leave you alone."

She never knew how much money Val had paid Billy for her. He said it was a lot. He said it was a hundred thousand dollars, but she didn't believe him. Over time the amount would change with each telling of the story, but the bottom line was that it was more than she could ever repay.

She moved into his house. It was as he had promised. Val didn't lie very often. People with power don't have to lie. She had her own room—the one closest to Val's, which established her as his favorite—and the property was large enough to allow her to wander in her hours off. She liked sitting on the dock at sunset, discovering the plantings left behind by the previous owners. Val seemed indifferent to it all, preferring to spend his time in the big den, watching a large-screen television and keeping an eye on the video feeds from the various security cameras posted around his property.

About three months into Helen's stay at Val's house, Billy showed up one day at the foot of the driveway, pressing the buzzer, his face appearing on the grainy video monitor. It was like a horror movie, seeing this once-beautiful man reduced to a shambling skeleton, spittle flying as he screamed into the speaker. Helen, who had been nipping a little bit too much into the various drugs around the house, despite Val's obvious displeasure, decided at that moment that she would stop cold turkey, and she did.

"I can't have this," Val said, watching the monitor, his arms crossed. "How did he find you? You been talking to him?"

She shook her head. "I would never, Val."

"You've been talking to someone, though."

Helen was pretty sure she hadn't. That was another thing about her life that hadn't changed. She didn't really have anyone to speak to. She was either here, drifting through the pretty house, or working. She didn't talk about herself with the clients. Come to think of it, she didn't talk much at all. Val had made it clear that he didn't have much interest in her outside his bed. The other girls were vapid and envious of her role as Val's favorite, but Helen didn't see that it was a big deal.

Val's security detail had arrived at the foot of the driveway now. When they parted the gates, Billy darted in, but they caught him by the arms. George I and George II, as Val called them, were as large and dark as Val was small and pale. Bald, they had extremely dark skin, skin so dark that it didn't seem to reflect any light at all. One was skinny and the other was fat, and both could move quickly when they had to. They seldom had to.

Billy had a junkie's wiry sidewinder moves, and he broke free, ran a few feet. He was out of the range of the camera now, and with no one pressing the button, there was nothing to hear.

That was the last Helen saw of Billy. Sometimes, when she was in town working and she came across a discarded newspaper, she would leaf through it, assuming there would be news of Billy's death. She never found anything. Maybe he wasn't dead. Or maybe George I and George II were very good at cleaning up after themselves.

She was not happy, but safe. She was Val's favorite, in his bed more often than not. He didn't let her keep the money she made, but if she wanted something, he saw that she got it. The refrigerator was stocked with food and beer and wine; Val had a horror of there being no food in the house. This was a clue to his childhood, although he never spoke of his early life. Deprivation was a big theme to Val. The other girls, while rivals of a sort, were respectful of her position. Helen was very, very good at what she did, and that pleased her work ethic, much as she had once delighted at being the best waitress at Il Cielo—not only a good earner but someone who looked for useful things to do during downtimes, even if it meant making that awful marshmallow topping.

The only serious argument she and Val had during those early months was when she asked if she could get a GED through a correspondence course. She had the time. But Val wouldn't hear of it. It turned into the first argument in which he hit her. It wasn't an angry or passionate hit, strange as that might sound. Val, as Helen would come to learn, hit girls the way some people hit dogs. He would actually announce it, very calmly. "I'm going to hit you now, so you don't do this again. Okay?" Which, of course,

86

made it all the more horrible, that split second of knowing she was going to be hit.

Later, icing her eye—Val said he hit her in the face on purpose, so it would be harder for her to work; that was part of the lesson—she asked George II, who was slightly more approachable, why Val had gotten so angry with her about her desire to complete high school.

"Because he can't read, girl."

"Of course he can read. I mean, I know he didn't finish school, but he made it through junior high. He has to be able to read."

"Nope. Watch him. He's got tricks, things he's learned to do. He can't read 'cat on the mat.'"

"But he's smart."

"That he is. Smarter than you or I." Helen secretly disagreed with this part, at least as far as she was concerned. "But he didn't learn to read, he learned to fake it. By the time the school figured it out, it was easier just to keep passing him from grade to grade until he could drop out legally."

"But what does that have to do with me?"

George II gave her a look as if he thought her stupid. Fair enough. She had just thought the same thing of him.

Helen gave up on the idea of a diploma, which meant giving up on the little fantasy beyond it, that she still might go to college. She was nineteen. Other girls her age, girls she had known in high school, were walking across campuses with heavy knapsacks filled with books, listening raptly to professors speak of amazing things. Did they know how lucky they were? Probably not. No one ever does, not really. Back in Pennsylvania, Helen had been lucky, and she couldn't see it. *Smarter to be lucky than it's lucky to be smart.* That was one of Hector Lewis's sayings, his way of explaining that it was lack of luck that held him down, not his own laziness. Well, she could still be smart. She would find a way to get educated somehow, without upsetting Val. She was a good liar when it came down to it. She had to be.

Sunday, October 9

Like a lot of parents of her generation, Heloise has no strong religious beliefs other than the belief that some kind of organized religion is good for kids. Pressed to define her actual convictions, she would probably use a lot of verbiage to avoid saying the word "atheist." She would love to have faith, but she also feels that all religions are self-interested, a con game with all the subtlety of those old Ronco commercials: *Wait—there's more! For only $19.95 in easy weekly installments, you can have eternal life just by following our contradictory laws and not asking why.* If forced to pick a label, Heloise will admit to being agnostic. But in her view an agnostic is an atheist who's covering her bets.

Yet around the time she and Scott moved to Turner's Grove, she decided to start attending a church, any church. After thinking about her own upbringing in the Lutheran Church, which she was allowed to abandon at age thirteen largely because neither parent cared to get up early on Sundays, she decided she wanted something open-minded and loose, with good music and an engaging pastor who didn't take too much of an interest in the parishioners' personal lives.

She has found all these in the Abbott Community Church, an extremely inclusive congregation led by a charismatic young minister, Frida Rosenweig, whose primary subject, week in and week out, is herself. The sermons are entertaining, more memoir than Scripture, but Heloise has to wonder if it's really godly to hold oneself in such high regard. Today, for example, Reverend Frida's sermon is ostensibly about Yom Kippur, which ended the day before, and what it means to atone. But it also is the story about how a young girl named Frida Rosenweig, growing up in an Orthodox household on the Upper West Side of New York City, decided to covert to Christianity when she realized that the Orthodox sect did not allow female rabbis.

"Why not simply embrace the Conservative sect of Judaism?" she asks from the pulpit, a lectern on a stage in a community center. The question is rhetorical, of course. Sometimes Heloise thinks all of Reverend Frida's questions—even "How are you?"—are rhetorical. At any rate, Reverend Frida inevitably ends up providing the answers to the questions she asks.

Heloise's thoughts drift. Her thoughts always drift here. She sees the mother of Scott's best friend, Lindsey, a few pews ahead of her. The Blake family joined here after Heloise did; she sometimes thinks Coranne has a nonsexual crush on her. As a stay-at-home mom, she probably romanticizes Heloise's life, which is orderly and organized compared to the ceaseless chaos in the Blake household. *Lord, does Coranne have a bald spot?* She's only a few years older than Heloise, no more than forty, yet she seems convinced that she is an "old" mother since giving birth last year to a particularly difficult baby girl, one who has suffered from reflux and colic and just about everything else that is stressful but not serious. Diaper rashes, eczema. "It could be worse," Coranne always says. "She could have leukemia, a hole in her heart. It could be worse!"

It's a strange way, Heloise thinks, to comfort oneself. Yes, things can always be worse, but they can also be better. One of her favorite sermons this year was Reverend Frida's take on the story of Job, in which she actually called God an asshole. More precisely, what she said was "In reading Job, is it not easy to wonder if God is simply an asshole at times?" The answer, according to the Reverend Frida, was nuanced—and, of course, circled back to her. Faith must be tested, as hers had been tested when . . . well, frankly, Heloise had lost the thread at that point. Still, it was a good sermon, right up there with her deconstruction of the story of Isaac. "Is it so much to ask, one little murder? Don't you love me above all others?" Reverend Frida had said, taking on an older woman's querulous tone, then switching to her own mellifluous voice. "Really, the argument can be made that God is the first Jewish mother." Which, she reminded her parishioners, she was allowed to say because she is Jewish, in terms of cultural identity if not faith. She scoffed at the verse "In sorrow thy shall bring forth children," saying that it probably meant only physical pain, nothing more, that children were a blessing. Not that she had any.

Reverend Frida also insists that Moses was the son of the pharaoh's daughter, that the whole bulrushes story was "bull"—long, dramatic pause—"malarkey." Pharaoh's daughter—"Why no name?"—got pregnant, hid the pregnancy from her father, then went through the charade of finding the baby. "Could a young woman in an ancient time have executed such a daring plan?" the Reverend Frida asked her congregation.

It was, of course, a rhetorical question, but Heloise is inclined to say yes.

Later, at the fellowship meeting—Heloise would love to skip it, but the promise of cookies and punch is the only thing that gets Scott through church—she watches him take off with Lindsey. Coranne seems to assume that this means she and Heloise should pair off—her husband almost never makes it to church, a fact for which Coranne apologizes endlessly. Coranne is the type of woman who apologizes for everything, beginning with her name. It was supposed to be Cora Anne, she told Heloise the first time they met, but it was entered incorrectly on her birth certificate, and her parents seemed to think the legal document trumped their own intentions. She also apologizes for Lindsey's name, saying she knows it has become more common for girls but that it was a boy's name at one point. Luckily, Lindsey is a self-possessed little tank of a kid, bulletproof when it comes to teasing.

"So," she begins, "school seems to be off to a good start. Except for Mr. Mathers."

Mr. Mathers is the social-studies teacher. He's also a jerk. Or, as the Reverend Frida might ask, is it possible to know the stories about Mr. Mathers and not think he's an asshole?

"I talked to the principal about him," Heloise says.

"You *didn't*." Coranne is almost breathless with admiration—and shock. The principal has made it clear that he does not want parents to complain about faculty members unless a teacher's misconduct reaches the level of felony, and Mr. Mathers is simply strict and unimaginative. The principal's implicit threat is that students will suffer more if their parents complain. Heloise doesn't buy it. But then, there are different rules for her, in her well-tailored clothes, than there are for Coranne, with patches of scalp showing through her hair, poor dear. That's not right, but it's the way things are, and for Heloise *not* to use her power doesn't gain Coranne anything. Besides, Lindsey is in Scott's class. If Mr. Mathers backs off on his pedantic style and ruthless discipline, all the kids will benefit.

"I did. The principal acted as if he wouldn't do anything, but there hasn't been one of those stupid pop quizzes followed by enforced 'quiet study' for two weeks."

"Well—that's great." Yet Coranne's tone implies more complicated, conflicted feelings, that Heloise's intercession with the principal is great and awful and rude and awesome. That it is another reminder that life is unfair, with different rules for different people.

The Reverend Frida joins them. She is very good about apportioning herself out equally to her congregants, and she does it with an attitude that suggests she considers this incredibly generous, because of course everyone wants her time and attention. Heloise can't help admiring the young woman's bountiful self-regard. It seems like a great way to be, even if the rest of the world considers you self-centered. But then, being as self-centered as she is, Frida has no clue that anyone experiences her as something less than wonderful.

"What did you think of the sermon today?"

"I loved it," Heloise says. Then some imp seizes her, and she adds, "I thought it was amazing how you managed to bring it around to yourself. It's so—brave. Most clergymen—clergywomen? Clergypeople? At any rate, they don't risk that level of *exposure*."

Frida beams at the compliment even as Coranne all but chokes on a cookie. "I do think it's important to break down that wall between the person standing at the pulpit and those in the congregation. We're not *anointed*, for goodness' sake."

"Not even with oil on occasion?"

Coranne coughs a piece of cookie into her napkin. But the Reverend Frida whoops with laughter, too. She punches Heloise in the arm, says, "You are *so* funny."

"But seriously, Reverend Frida?"

"Just Frida is fine."

"I know this is going to sound odd, but I would love it if you would one day do a sermon on the role of prostitutes in the Bible. I mean—they're all over the place. For example, I don't think most people know that the two women who come before Solomon in the dispute over the baby are prostitutes."

"Really?" Coranne says.

"See?" Heloise says.

The Reverend Frida furrows her brow, bringing her straight dark eyebrows together in a way that calls to mind her namesake, Frida Kahlo. "Well, prostitution is such a predictable feminist topic that I feel I'd have to do something surprising with it. There was the time I went to Barcelona—"

"I'm sure you'll find an unusual way to talk about it," Heloise says, her face all bland innocence. Coranne is dying now, coughing and spluttering. Heloise realizes she enjoys making her laugh.

But then the Reverend Frida moves away, and Coranne asks, "Are you free this afternoon? Lindsey wants to go ice-skating at the rink. If Scott wanted to go, you and I could repair to the little café across the street. I've never under-stood that use of 'repair,' actually—it's so strange. Anyway, if you don't have anything to do—"

"I'm terribly sorry," says Heloise, who's not the least bit sorry, "but I have to spend the day catching up on paperwork."

Heloise was telling Coranne the truth, not that she would have had any problem lying to her. She has set aside this rainy Sunday afternoon for clerical work, annoying but essential. Even though she eschews paperwork as much as possible, there's still no shortage of it.

It is not easy to become a new client of WFEN, even in this economy. Heloise prefers referrals from trusted sources—longtime customers who have a stake in the busi-ness, as it were. Men like Paul believe they will suffer might-ily if she is ever arrested—and that's a good thing. A little fear goes a long way, as her various mentors have taught her.

But her customers will never be as careful as she is. No one is as careful as she is. No one ever values another per-son's livelihood as much as that person does. Or another person's money or even another person's time, especially another person's time. *No one values her.* That was a painful lesson to learn at her father's knee—at the end of her father's arm, at the flat of his palm—but once she absorbed it, she flourished. It doesn't matter what others think she is worth. She sets the price.

Once a referral has been made, Heloise requests the kind of basic information that one might see on a credit-card application. Name, address, Social Security number. Almost all clients balk at providing their Social. Heloise expects them to do just that. She then agrees to waive the requirement, stressing that she never, ever does that for any client. Then she gets it anyway, through her private detective's sources, and presents it to the applicant, usually with a full credit report. This puts the men on notice. She's got their number, as the saying goes.

Despising impulse customers as she does—they carry too much risk—Heloise structures WFEN more like a country club. New customers are asked to pay an initiation fee of sorts, which is then applied to the first six dates. Once a man has enjoyed six visits, he has a habit. Once a man has a habit, she has a regular.

Sometimes, when business is particularly soft—regulars cutting back, the legislature not in session—she tells a certain kind of would-be customer that she has too many clients and he will have to wait for an opening. She based this tactic on a story she'd heard about a laundry in North Baltimore that doesn't accept new customers unless an old one dies or moves away. And sometimes not even then—customers are allowed to leave their spots to others in their wills. This makes people desperate to have their shirts laundered there. They beg, they plead, they offer to pay more. When Heloise senses that a man is very rich and very connected, she plays this game. It's usually good for several more clients. Because the new customer has to brag, of course, tell his friends about this exclusive deal he's getting, and they all want it, too.

It's not like she can use Groupon.

Heloise's customers are all men, although it's not uncommon to field requests from married couples looking for something novel. No judgment, no judgment at all, but Heloise avoids that type of trade. She never wants to be outnumbered. Besides, someone always gets jealous, the wife or the husband. Usually the husband, who had the fantasy to begin with. Heloise figures such couples are really looking for drama, even if they don't know it.

The bane of her existence is the rating services. Although she and her girls generally get top marks from the two best-known services, all it takes is one disgruntled customer to torpedo a girl's rating. Of course, everyone and everything gets rated online these days. Restaurants, professors, movies. Once Heloise spent an afternoon with a touring novelist—she takes on the occasional one-timer if he has strong references—and he became so exercised on this topic that he almost risked running out his hour without receiving any benefits. (His ex-wife had organized a group of her friends to sabotage his latest book with a bunch of one-star ratings at Amazon and Goodreads.) Strangely, some clients provide low ratings yet continue to use WFEN. When Heloise puts that together, she drops the customer. Then she contacts the service and asks to have the rating taken down, claiming that the reviewer has a grudge because he was dropped for bad behavior.

Today she is poring over a new applicant's file. The guy looks fine to her, but Audrey has flagged his folder. Heloise sends her a text, asking her to come down from the den, where she is watching television with Scott. Yes, he probably would have enjoyed ice-skating with Lindsey, but Heloise didn't want Coranne to think she was taking advantage, parking her son with a stay-at-home mom while she caught up on her work.

And she'd rather plunge a knife into her chest than spend the afternoon drinking spiked hot chocolate with Coranne.

"Why are you suggesting we reject"—she peers at the name in the file—"Mr. Callender?"

Audrey looks nervous yet defiant. "I didn't like his tone."

"His tone?"

"He sounded coarse."

Heloise flips through the papers. "Financials check out. He has no court record."

"He's single," Audrey says.

"We have lots of single customers, Audrey. You'd prefer it if I had nothing but single customers, I thought."

"He sounded as if he would be mean. You don't like the mean ones, because some of the girls can't handle them, so you don't have as much flexibility with scheduling. I just have a feeling."

Feelings, intuition. Heloise has little patience for such silliness. The whole point of the vetting process is not to rely on feelings. There are two primary risks she is trying to avoid: cops and kinksters.

Kinksters are guys who get off on being cruel to her girls, physically or mentally. They're actually pretty rare. Sociopaths who prey on prostitutes choose easier targets, street-level workers.

Cops—they're the enemy. Heloise's insomnia is rooted in her fear of cops. Her girls are all instructed to leave any situation that hints at a sting. That's one instance where she has no problem honoring someone's feelings. Although it's not really intuition. There are things to look for. One key is the insistence on talking about the money up front. The average customer is not anxious to have a prolonged conversation about the transaction at hand; he's still pretending, on some level, that he's not paying for it. Or else he's done it a lot, he knows how it works. A guy who asks over and over again if they're going to have sex for money—better to lose the gig than risk an arrest. Heloise's girls know what to say: *We're going to have some fun, I hope. Whatever happens, happens.* Some girls think they're safe as long as they have sex first and accept the money afterward, but that's not the case based on the legal precedents that Heloise has studied.

Folklore also has it that a girl who asks if a man is a police officer is protected; if he lies, the charge won't hold up. But it's folklore, and it wouldn't protect Heloise in any event. One arrest, even if it ends with charges being dropped, will destroy her life. Although if Mr. Callender is a cop, why has he gone through with the paperwork, and how did he fake the financials? It's not impossible to obtain a fake Social Security number, but getting a credit report to match up with it—that's pretty labor-intensive. Her business is too small, by design, to attract that kind of sting. Heloise has thrived by being not quite top-tier, more BCBG than Prada. State pols who are happy to stay state pols, the occasional cabinet secretary, but always one of the positions that people forget exist, like Interior or Commerce. True, there's always a crusading state's attorney here or there who would love to bust one of her pols, yet it's a funny thing about the crusaders—they almost always have a kink or two of their own.

To placate Audrey, however, who is hypersensitive about her standing, Heloise calls the customer who made the referral. It is bad form to call on a Sunday, but she wants to lock the office door behind her this afternoon with the sense of accomplishment that comes from finishing everything on her to-do list.

She punches in the reference's cell-phone number. Her number will show up on his caller ID—Heloise assumes everyone has caller ID—as WFEN. That's less suspicious than a blocked call.

"Hi, Ellis, I hate to bother you on the weekend—"

"Yes, what's up?" His voice is pitched high, tight. Someone is nearby.

"I'm calling for a reference on Mr. Callender. He said you recommended him to us."

"I don't think so." Less nervous, but still in a hurry to get off the phone. "I don't know a Mr. Callender. And I haven't suggested that anyone"—long pause, as if he can't think what to say next, although it's fairly obvious—"call you."

Good boy, Ellis.

"No one?"

"No one." Barked. "I've gotta go. We're at the movies. Family time, okay?"

He seems so relieved. He shouldn't, Heloise thinks. Mr. Callender knows that Ellis uses the services of WFEN and what they're for, but Ellis doesn't know Mr. Callender. Private detective, she thinks. Divorce action. It won't be the first time. How did he slip past *her* private detective? How did he fake being so rich?

She reads the file again, trying to find something concrete. She can't see it. Ellis probably lied reflexively, unnerved by the phone call. There is no concrete reason to reject this application, but she's going to let Audrey have her way on this one. People vastly overrate their own capacity for making good decisions. They remember only those times that their hunches have played out, not all the other times they were wrong in their funny feelings. Heloise has never once had any sense of what was truly going to cause trouble in her life. Or the trouble was so obvious that it didn't count—Val, for example.

Overall, being born seems to have been the only thing she needed to find trouble. This isn't self-pity or melodrama on her part, merely acknowledgment of the hand she was dealt. She used to think about it all the time, the forces that brought her parents together. Later, when she began to read on her own, her would-be mentor gave her a poem by Sharon Olds that captured what it's like to owe one's existence to two willfully mismatched people. You hate knowing what they are going to do to each other and to you, but there is no you unless those things happen. In the poem the parents meet while in college and the poet is more generous to them than Heloise could ever be to her parents, noting their youth and their ignorance. *College,* she thought with contempt. Her parents didn't meet outside an arch of ocher sandstone, with black iron gates. (Heloise had to look up the word "ocher.")

No, what she sees is: Wide-eyed Beth Harbison in her carhop outfit, the flared boots that showed her then-beautiful legs to such advantage. Hector Lewis, the car salesman across the street, making sure he always pulled into her slot—as it were, he would say with a snicker—taking her for "test drives" in the dealership's nicer vehicles when she finished her shift. Heloise realizes there was a moment, much like her first time with Billy, when her mother believed herself to be in love. But why didn't she walk out the first time he hit her? She had the job, she had the resources. She had more going for her than Heloise did when she found herself pregnant with Scott. Hector Lewis was a brute, but he wasn't the kind of man who would chase a woman down and kill her if she tried to leave him.

Scott, like Heloise, owes his existence to two people who should never have come together. But at least she got away from Scott's father—even if she still has to visit him every other week for as long as they both might live.

1994

Val's business, the part in which Helen was employed—
he called it a subsidiary—was an unusual combination of
whorehouse, escort service, and street-level prostitution. A
van took the live-in girls to a not-as-sleazy-as-you-might-
think hotel, one whose legitimate trade was foreign tourists
who thought the neighborhood was more central than it
was. The lucky girls, the ones in Val's favor, were assigned
regulars and callers, who arrived in three shifts—lunch,
after-work, and after-hours. The girls who were on the shit
list had to walk, which ranged from unpleasant to dangerous. Plus, there were quotas to meet.

Helen's goal was to stay off the street, which meant staying in Val's good graces, something at which she excelled.
The trick was persuading him that his happiness was the
only thing that mattered to her, that she alone cared about
him, but—and this was key—that she did not require his
reciprocal attention, she was fine when he ignored her. It
was that little core of coolness that kept her in good stead.
This self-containment was, she realized, the quality that
had driven her father mad. *You can hit me, but you can't
touch me.*

Remaining Val's favorite became trickier when she
decided that she was going to use her downtime at the hotel

to go to the nearby library and read. For one thing, the girls weren't supposed to leave their rooms unless they were going out to hustle. After all, if a call came in, they had to be available. Plus, if they left, they might try to generate business on their own, which was strictly prohibited. The two Georges were charged with watching them, making sure they were where they were supposed to be.

So Helen did the riskiest thing possible—she told George I the truth, that she wanted to go to the library and read. It was only two blocks away. She could be back at the hotel faster than any client if he beeped her. George II was the kinder of the two, but George I was a sneak, the sort of person who enjoyed having leverage over people just for the hell of it. It amused him to know that Helen was going behind Val's back to read books at the library. At first he extracted a few sexual favors from her to show he could. She was too skinny for him, he would tell her, smacking her rear quite hard as he rode her, mocking its size. But mainly he got off on knowing that he had something on her, so he · let it go. He also made it clear to her that when Val found out—and he was adamant that Val would find out—he would throw her to the dogs. He'd rather be dressed down for pretending that she had fooled him than let Val know he had betrayed him in even this small way.

Despite having George I's protection secured, Helen did not start going into the library, not right off. She was intimidated by its scale. It was a large, imposing place, almost as grand as the cathedral on the other side of the street. Once she managed to cross the threshold, she was entranced by the soaring ceilings, the beautiful paintings that ringed the main atrium. Her hometown library had been nice but modern, all glass and pale wood. Yet the two places smelled the same. Standing in the center of the atrium, inhaling the sweet odor of musty hardcovers, Helen remembered the girl she once was, the straight-A student with hopes of a scholarship. She was embarrassed to walk to the information desk in her work clothes, but it was her only chance. Luckily, the librarian was a man, and men were always nice to her. At first.

He was cute, too, in a nerdy way. He wore a big, lumpy sweater, and he had messy curls. And glasses, of course, which enhanced his large amber eyes and the thicket of dark lashes.

"I want . . . I want . . ." she began.

"As William Blake himself might say," he said, a finger holding his place in the book he was reading.

"What?"

"I'm sorry, a stupid joke. What do you want?"

"I want to read the Great Books."

"According to whom?"

That stumped her. "Well—me, I guess. I mean, it's my plan, not a school assignment or anything. It's just something I want to do. For fun."

"No, I mean, according to what source? There are a lot of conflicting ideas about what the canon is, or should be. Some people want to read the hundred best American novels, for example, while others want to follow a course of study more like the St. John's College curriculum, in which one reads chronologically through the great thinkers of our time—"

It was all she could do not to turn and run—well, totter, given the shoes. She never got used to the shoes Val made them wear.

The librarian took pity on her and came from behind the desk, grasping her elbow. "Let's go over to adult fiction, start there. I had a text in college, written by Robert Penn Warren and two other professors." He paused, clearly expecting her to know the name, and it was dimly familiar, something she might have studied back in Pennsylvania, but that part of her was so distant now. "Anyway, we'll start with what they considered the essential classics of American literature, into the mid-twentieth century. And yes, every one is written by a dead white male, although maybe we'll mix in some Willa Cather. Plus, you'll get to Jane Austen soon enough."

But it was not Cather or Austen to whom she responded most strongly. And it was not *The Scarlet Letter,* the first book on the list, through which she trudged as so many before her had trudged. The book that touched her was *Sister Carrie. Yes,* she wanted to shout—except she was in the library and couldn't—*this is life, this is how it works.* You get on a train, intending nothing more than a visit to your sister, and a man says nice things to you, and the world falls apart.

She had to read in the library on stolen bits of time because she lacked the forms of ID required for a card. Jules—for that was the librarian's name—was baffled. *No driver's license? Not a local one. A gas bill? No. Any utility bill?*

No. Besides, she lived in the county. At least she was pretty sure it was the county. That was okay, he said, there was a reciprocity agreement. But she needed something to prove her address. She didn't even know her address. No, she had no ID at all, except her expired Pennsylvania driver's license. Oh, and her Social Security card. She still had that, from back in her days at Il Cielo. But it didn't establish residence.

So she ended up having sex with Jules. It was what she did; it was the only currency at her disposal. And it turned out to be pretty fun, at least for a while. But then he had to put a word to it, claim it was love, and she had to explain to him that it couldn't be.

"Are you married?" he asked her one day. They were in the library, in a seldom-used women's bathroom on the third floor. He would sneak in and take the stall at the far end, and she would arrive five minutes later. It was funny, being the one who had to remind the librarian to keep his voice down. He was crazy for her, frenzied and incautious.

"In a way," she said, then covered his mouth with hers, to keep him from talking at all. Surfacing: "And you have a girlfriend. I saw her photo on your desk."

"I'll break up with her."

"Don't," she said, picking up the pace.

"Don't," he said. "I don't want to—" He did anyway.

"I'm trying to keep you safe," she told him, caressing the back of his neck.

"There's no safety in love," he said.

"This isn't love. It's just really good sex. And it's good because it's forbidden. If you break up with your girlfriend

107

and I leave my guy, it won't be the same. Trust me. I'm older than you. I know some things."

"I don't believe you're older than I am. I bet we're the same age," he said.

"We might have been born the same year, but it's been a long time since we were the same age."

She was actually younger than he was. She was only twenty. It broke her heart a little, knowing how easily she could pass for someone older now.

Still, it was a nice relationship. He gave her books, shabby ones that were going to be tossed or sold. She smuggled them back to Val's house in her purse and hid them on the property. There were books concealed everywhere, and although she didn't dare read them in front of anyone, it gave her a thrill to walk past one of the hiding places. She had a secret. She realized she hadn't had any secrets for a long time, and there was power in being able to keep something to herself, for herself. Her secrets were the only things she really owned.

She read and she read and she read, indiscriminately. The only thing she didn't really like was poetry. Jules gave her a poem about some woman's parents meeting at college, and the woman just seemed so sorry for herself it made Helen competitive in a weird way. Poets seemed conceited to her, full of themselves. One wrote that the old masters—Helen had to look that up before she understood that it wasn't about slavery—were never wrong about suffering. *Bullshit. How have you suffered?* she wanted to ask. *What do you know about it?* Helen liked facts. They were useful. A well-dropped fact could charm a man, and a man who was charmed might tip a girl.

Eventually Jules got crazy, melodramatic. He broke up with his girlfriend despite Helen's advice, and, alas, the sex got better, contrary to her sage wisdom, so now they had something of a problem. He lobbied for her to spend the night at his apartment, and she could not begin to explain to him how impossible that was, how dangerous, for both of them. He asked her where she lived. She refused to tell him. He tried to follow her, but he was inept. Still, she thought she was in control of things. And is there any greater folly in human history than thinking that one is in control of something?

The universe, forever random and cruel, threw them into the same Pulaski Highway diner at 2:00 A.M.—Helen, Jules, and Val. Jules wasn't stupid enough to say anything, but he was stupid enough to look at her long and hard. He looked at her with his puppy eyes, he licked his lips, he bumped the counter as he paid his bill and staggered out to the parking lot, where he sat in his car for a long time, trying to pretend he wasn't watching the couple illuminated in the window.

She was no longer a nothing face. Men looked at Helen all the time, but those were judging, appraising looks, the kind of looks in which Val trafficked. Jules's gaze was different, longing informed by knowledge.

"Tell me about college boy," Val said the next morning.

"Who?"

"The cocksucker in the sweater, drinking coffee and pretending to read a book while looking at you."

"Don't know him."

"Don't lie to me, Helen."

"Okay, I fucked him once to get a library card."

"Don't be clever."

"That's the truth." She was scared, cowed. She hadn't been beaten for a while, and she began to see a connection. Jules had fed some part of her, so she had been careful and compliant in the rest of her life, never risking Val's wrath. She had never been a better partner to Val than while she was having her fling with Jules.

Val worked his fingers into her hair as if to stroke her head, then pulled her to him so sharply that it brought tears to her eyes. "Why would you want a library card?"

"I get stir-crazy in that room. I have to get out. And then sometimes it's cold, so I need a place to sit."

"You don't need a card for that."

"I had to start checking out books to keep them from being onto me. They may be librarians, but they're not stupid. They know what I am, in those shoes, those clothes. As long as I check out a book and bring it back, they don't give me a hard time. But I don't have the ID necessary to have a card, so I had to throw that guy a freebie. He didn't understand it was a one-off, just, you know, business. He's inexperienced that way."

"I bet he is. Show me your card."

"What?"

"Show me your library card."

She went to get it out of her purse, not knowing whether it would be her salvation or damnation. Val studied it, and she pretended not to know that he couldn't decode anything but the bright colors on it.

"Hey, George II," he called out. "Look at this. Could it be a counterfeit?"

"Looks like the real thing to me, boss."

The card was a flimsy plastic, yet more durable than the old paper cards she had known in her girlhood. It couldn't be torn, not even by George II's large, capable hands. Val took out a knife and sliced it into slivers.

"Did you turn tricks on the side?"

"No," she said. It was strange how the truth could sound like a lie.

"I'm going to ask you again, Helen: Were you freelancing?"

"No, I swear—I just wanted a place to sit."

But it was too improbable, as the truth often is, and Val fell on her, kicking her until George II finally pulled him off. George I just smiled.

Helen saw Jules only one more time, when she was in a man's car on Park Avenue several weeks later. She had been busted down to street work for her disloyalty. Downtown emptied out pretty quickly after the workday ended, so it was safe to do some jobs in parked cars. She lifted her head from her customer's lap and saw Jules staring sorrowfully at her. He might have been crying, but he turned and walked away so quickly that she couldn't tell.

Hey, she wanted to call out to him from her stinging mouth, *you're alive, and that's no small thing. You have no idea how close you came to dying. I saved your life.*

Jules lived on, though, in the lists of books he'd made for

her. She hid these in the pages of the fashion magazines that Val never challenged and, of course, never read. Sometimes the other girls would come across Helen's lists, but they didn't recognize them as contraband. Helen couldn't go back to the library, so she shoplifted the books as she found them. There were more bookstores in downtown Baltimore then. When possible, she took the books back or left them in places where others might benefit from them—public restrooms, the old Greyhound station while it was still there, even Penn Station. She found fiction less and less interesting, reverting to her teenage passion for history and politics, which led her to reading more about economics. One of her regulars was getting what was known as a week-end M.B.A., which provided a nice cover for him to get out of the house to get laid once in a while. (He told his wife he was going to the library. Was that irony? Something close to it, Helen decided.) The program fascinated her, but she knew that if Val wouldn't let her get a GED, he definitely wouldn't approve of an M.B.A. Helen began to shrink, literally, losing too much weight, with bad consequences for her breasts and her face. She was trapped. When Val disappeared, which he did for as many as two weeks every month, on business he would never discuss or detail, she crawled under her covers with a book and a flashlight, but it seemed more and more futile. What was she reading for? What was the point?

Then Val brought Martin into the house.

Monday, October 10

"I liked January," Paul says. "A lot."

Heloise is having lunch with Paul at the Maryland Inn. Heloise never goes to committee hearings, is seldom seen in the State House hallways, yet everyone knows her as the redheaded lobbyist who has lunch with Paul Marriotti. That's all the credibility she needs, in both her real and her ersatz professions.

Paul was her first big customer, and many of her referrals in state legislative circles have come from him. She has even landed a few big Washington players through Paul. There was one Marylander, a cabinet member in a previous administration, who had waffled about leaving his longtime service in northern Virginia. "Buy Maryland," Heloise told him, appealing to his civic pride. Dead now, five years, a real gentleman.

"I'm glad she worked out," she says, spearing a stalk of out-of-season asparagus. When eating with a client, Heloise chooses her meals based on what can be eaten daintily. She is sensitive about her manners, despite the time she has put in trying to improve them, and lives in terror of doing something gauche in front of others. She's selling a classy image. Asparagus is one food she feels comfortable eating in public, although one has to watch for threads.

"She's a smart girl, very ambitious."

"Yes, she's a graduate student. Public health." Heloise thinks, *You'd never catch January allowing a client to go bareback.*

"I believe she's more ambitious than you realize. She tried to set up a private date with me."

This is serious, a firing offense. And stupid, which January never is.

"Tell me exactly what she said."

"She asked if I wanted to meet with her 'off the books.' I told her that I was loyal to you. And that I would report the conversation back to you."

Heloise twists this around in her mind while she tries to find manageable bites in her salad. She thought she was ordering a chopped salad, which is easier to eat neatly. But this salad has enormous leaves that require judicious cutting. She takes a long time slicing her lettuce leaves.

"She knew that. Before she said a thing to you, she knew where it was headed. She *wanted* you to report back to me."

Paul nods. "I thought so, too."

"Why would she do that?"

Paul lowers his head, forcing her to make eye contact with him instead of her salad. "Why do you think, Heloise?"

"Because she wants me to fire her? That makes no sense. It's not as if she could get unemployment benefits." Wait, she could. Heloise has always paid into the system.

"She wants to do what you do. She's a sophisticated girl, January. Who told me her real name, by the way, Anna Marie."

"My, you got downright chummy in just one session."

Now Paul averts his gaze, and Heloise realizes he is not telling her everything. He reported the improper overture and said he rejected it. But maybe Anna Marie threw him a freebie. Makes economic sense when trying to steal someone's loyal customer. Heloise will have to track the GPS records on the bracelet. The girls forget that the bracelets are never turned off, that Heloise can follow them even when they're not working.

"She believes that what you do should be legal. Feels it makes sense from a public-health position, but also in feminist terms. She admires you, Heloise. She could be a hell of a protégée if you would consider having a protégée."

"Well, I won't," Heloise says. "If I were to train anyone to take over, it would be my assistant, Audrey. She understands the ins and outs of the business, and I trust her. How can I trust January, knowing she's gone behind my back?"

"She didn't really. I admit she was clumsy, in how she did it. She's not as smooth at politics as you are. But then, you've known a lot more politicians, for a lot longer."

She thinks about the younger Paul, the one who came to her seven years ago. Darker hair and more of it. Desperate in his deprivation. He was, perhaps, one of the few men entitled to say, *My wife doesn't understand me.* She didn't. She was cold, perhaps clinically frigid. They had five kids, good Catholics that they were. Paul claimed they'd had sex exactly ten times since the birth of their youngest.

Yet it wasn't even the infrequency of their sex life that

had worn Paul down. His wife would not entertain the mildest variations in sex, which she treated as a workout, something she had to do. She didn't bother with excuses. She just didn't like it much. But she wanted to be married, at least as long as their children were at home. If Paul hadn't been a politician, he would have left her long ago.

But Paul is a politician, and an ambitious one. Not wildly ambitious—he doesn't want to be governor or a U.S. senator. His goal was to reach a powerful job where one could stay for years, and he has managed that trick. Paul seldom appears in the papers, nor is he a sound-bite guy. But he is a committee chair, well connected and well liked. He cannot afford a sex scandal. He also can't live without sex. This was what had brought him to Heloise for sex once a week, twice if he had a big floor vote coming up.

"How old are you, Heloise?"

Heloise resumes sawing her lettuce. She is suddenly very hungry and frustrated with her food. She's going to hit a drive-through on the way home, indulge in something greasy, gobbled behind the wheel while no one is watching.

"Don't be hurt. You look great. You'll probably look great for another ten years. But you're like a pro athlete, with a limited time to play your game. You need a five-year plan."

"It always amuses me," says Heloise, ever the history student, "that what started as Stalin's program to increase productivity among workers is now a cliché used by every job seeker."

"Call it what you like. And of course you could go into

management mode. Hey, for all I know, there are clients for postmenopausal women." Paul makes a face. He clearly won't be one of them. "But you might make more money if you get out sooner rather than later. Your business is strong now. It may not always be. I think Anna Marie could put together backers, or come up with a way to buy you out over time."

It's interesting how he uses her real name.

"And what would I do then? It's not like I invented Google. I'm not going to make so much money that I can retire forever."

Paul shrugs. "I don't know. Maybe you can finally do what you've always claimed to do."

"What?" Does he know she has failed to take care of one of her girls, which was supposed to be her point of pride, proof of the fact that she was a good person in a dirty business? Does Anna Marie know about Sophie?

"Be a lobbyist. You're registered, right? You have good relationships with several delegates and senators." Paul allows himself a rakish smile.

"Who would pay me to do that?"

"I'll ask around if you want me to."

"Would I make as much as I do now?"

"Probably not."

It all happens in the briefest of moments. She allows herself to believe, for no more than a second, that she could reinvent herself as a legitimate citizen. It's amazing how much it hurts to surrender the fantasy. But her life—Scott's life—requires a certain income.

She shakes her head, stabs her salad. "I'm not ready, Paul. And now I have to let January go."

"Aw, c'mon. Can't you see your way to giving her another chance? For me?"

"I don't do second chances, Paul. Not even for you."

1995

It was hard to remember later, when everything went bad, but Martin began as Val's protégé. He was tall, taller than Val. Almost all men were taller than Val, but Martin was so absurdly tall that Val didn't take offense. Like the Georges, Martin was allowed his size. It helped that he was thin, and not in the ropy, muscular way of Val. He was floppy and weak.

Plus, he was young, worshipful. In a different business environment, he would have been Val's intern, running meaningless errands in order to be close to the man he admired, happy to take his abuse. Helen was never quite sure what Martin did for Val, but then she also was never quite clear on the scope of Val's business. He continued to disappear for days at a time. He tried to put Martin in charge when he did, but the girls walked all over him, and Val had to use the Georges. Although increasingly it was George I, with George II disappearing with his boss. When Val was away, Martin drifted around the house, as melancholy as a dog who missed his master.

Helen didn't like Martin, not at first. She should have been glad for Val to have someone on whom to focus, especially if that person wasn't a straight-up rival. As much as she disliked her life with Val, she wouldn't tolerate any threat to it. When a new girl seemed to be gaining favor, she found a way to charm him again. She was extra sweet, accommodating, thinking about him, offering back rubs and making him breakfast, asking for nothing, letting the new girl shoot her triumphant glances as she headed to Val's bedroom, thinking Helen was over. She was never over. The girls usually did themselves in. They were greedy, they pushed. They mistook Val's besottedness for something that gave them real power. They were new toys, cheap ones, and they all broke soon enough.

But a guy shouldn't have mattered to Helen, especially a guy as clueless as Martin. Helen should have been thrilled at the way he distracted Val for a time, which freed her up to escape to her secret reading places on the property. (George II had caught her once, reading beneath the dock, but he didn't seem to understand how profoundly she was betraying Val. At any rate, he didn't bust her, and she didn't think he would as long as he believed them to be on the same side. And they were on the same side. Protecting, placating Val was a side, after all.)

Yet she resented Martin. She disliked his obvious worship of Val, the endless sucking up, the ready laughter at Val's mildest jokes, which were never that good. She hated how he took Val's abuse, too. She saw herself in Martin, in a way she had never seen herself in the other girls. And she could not bear being reminded of what a fool she'd been to think that she could manipulate Val into saving her and then someday be free of him.

"You're the boss!" Martin sang out several times a day,

cheerfully at first. He became less cheerful over time. What did he expect? Val was too vain, too paranoid, to groom a true protégé. He would require a successor only in the event of death or prison, and he had no intention of succumbing to either. None of us believe we're going to die, not really. It's an impossible concept, Helen decided. We can imagine ourselves not being before we were born—that's easy. We weren't there, once. We watch the home movies, if there are any, and tolerate the scenes of life before us—the older siblings and, if there are no older siblings, then our ridiculously childless parents, going through the motions of various celebrations as if anything could have been meaningful before we arrived. Helen had not grown up with home movies, but she had the first family of Hector Lewis to remind her there was a time when she did not exist.

But once we do exist—imagining that as not being true is impossible. It was especially true for Val, precisely because a bad outcome was so likely. Death or prison. There were no other options. He accepted that, never pretended that he was angling for retirement or a legitimate life. But acceptance is not true belief. The result was that Val was fearless. And therefore lethal.

Martin began to assert himself in small ways. He wasn't as quick to fill Val's hand with a drink. His laughter was less ready, less raucous. He began to win at cards. *Mistake*, Helen wanted to tell him. Eventually she did.

"Go back to letting him win," she said in the kitchen one day as Martin prepared Val's half-and-half. The trick to Val's half-and-half was that it was really two-thirds and one-third (lemonade to iced tea) or sometimes, if he had a hangover, one-quarter to three-quarters, and a person just had to know what was required or risk having it flung in his face. Martin also was expected to bring Val a broiled grapefruit sprinkled with brown sugar, and the sugar must be very even. Helen sometimes thought that landing a jet on a carrier had more margin for error than fixing Val's breakfast.

"I never let him win," Martin said, eyes darting around to see if anyone was listening.

"You mean you just always lost, always, and then you started winning? Well, I guess that's how it goes. In streaks. I'd say you're due for another unlucky streak. It would be healthier."

He shook his head as if she knew nothing of the man with whom she had been living for three years, and then he scuttled out of the kitchen with Val's breakfast tray. In a few minutes, there was the sound of glass breaking. Whatever the proportions of the half-and-half, they were wrong. Martin returned to the kitchen, face dripping, a small cut near his hairline, and started over.

Several weeks later she found him crying, a disastrous thing to do. He might as well have tried to have sex with one of the Georges. Val didn't like his *women* to cry.

"Why is he so mean?" he said, trying to cover up the evidence of his tears with ineffectual backhanded swipes, so like a little boy's.

"Well, he's short. So he has that complex."

"Yeah, Napoleon, whatever."

"He wasn't, though."

"What?"

"Napoleon wasn't that short." Helen was reading *Désirée* about then. "It's a myth. He was five-six, which was average for his time."

"But not for ours, and that's Val's height, give or take. Five-six."

Closer to five-four, Helen thought. Even in private, Martin was scared to say Val's true height out loud. But then, so was Helen.

"I don't think Val acts the way he does because of his height. I always thought it was his name."

"His name?"

It was Helen's turn to be conspiratorial, to look around before speaking. "Valentine. Valentine Day Deluca. I think his mother hated him a little. Don't ever say it. He doesn't even know I know it, but I saw it once, on his birth certificate. When he's giving you shit, though, you can think it. That's what I do, and somehow it makes it easier."

A gift, a coping tool, nothing more. She didn't have a lot of respect for Martin, but she didn't think he was stupid. Then again, he was apprenticing himself to a man who ran ugly, illegal enterprises, a man who didn't want an apprentice. So maybe Martin was stupid after all. Or simply very young. He might have grown out of it. If he had lived.

Instead, a few weeks later, he reached out his arms to gather up the chips in a particularly high-stakes game of poker, having ignored Helen's advice to rediscover his unluckiness in order to be luckier. "Sorry, Valentine Day."

"What?" Val's voice was matter-of-fact, flat. Too flat. His

eyes cut to Helen, but her face was prepared, which is to say it was blank. She had decided that if she looked surprised or aghast, Val would blame her for sharing the information. She should look puzzled, confused. No one knew Val's name, right?

"Nothing," Martin said guiltily, knowing he had gone too far. Did that make it better or worse? If he had brazened it through, acted as if he didn't realize the affront, would that have saved him? Probably not.

"I gotta take a leak."

Val left the room. It seemed as if everyone stopped breathing—Helen, the Georges, the other girls—but that couldn't be possible. How could everyone stop breathing for three, four minutes?

Val walked back in, placed a gun at the base of Martin's head, and pulled the trigger. Martin never saw it coming. That was the part that amazed Helen. Val didn't require Martin's fear or foreknowledge, any more than he would need to make eye contact with a cockroach before squashing it. Something had annoyed him. He eradicated it. End of story.

"Do what you have to do," he told the Georges.

That night, for the first time in several weeks, Val asked her to come to his room. Helen assumed that her patience had once again regained her the place as the house favorite, that her longevity was desirable in the wake of the evening's strong emotions, the complications engendered by having to dispose of a dead body. He wanted to be with someone he really trusted.

124

Val tore into her with a silent violence that made clear he knew she was Martin's confidante. No beating ever hurt as much as he made sex hurt that night. She was in pain for days, and these were days in which Val insisted she up her quota, work longer hours, more jobs. He put her on the street. At one point she began bleeding during a job, and the john recoiled in horror. Quick-thinking, she blamed him, said he was too big, and he ended up giving her extra money and a ride to the ER.

At home that night, she watched Shelley, the current favorite, laugh and giggle from what she believed to be her privileged position in Val's lap. He whispered in her ear, stroked her neck, but he had eyes only for Helen. Later he came to her and held her all night long. Again no words, but the apology was as evident as the punishment had been. Toward dawn he said, "You'll always be my favorite. Forever and ever. You know why? Because we're so much alike. We do whatever we have to do."

She wanted to disagree, but he wouldn't like that, he would hurt her again.

Besides, he had a point.

Tuesday, October 11

The official name for the prison in which Val has lived for more than a decade now is the Maryland Correctional Adjustment Center, an odd name to give to a facility that houses men in perpetual solitary, with no contact permitted among inmates. They are kept in their cells twenty-three hours a day, allowed only one hour out, except for the weekends, when they have to stay inside for twenty-four hours. They may receive only four visits a month. Heloise sees Val twice a month. As far as she knows, no one else ever visits him at all. She is unsure where his parents are, if they are even alive. Val has always been very good about not sharing information about himself.

As is she.

"Hi, Helen," he says, one of the last people in her life, along with Tom, to use that name. Although her mother would probably use it—if Heloise ever spoke to her.

"You look good."

"Don't bullshit . . ." He doesn't bother to finish the cliché.

"I'm not."

She isn't. Val has grown very pale in prison, but it suits him. His red hair has darkened. The freckles that bothered him when he was younger—his twenties? thirties? Val's actual age is also unclear to her—are gone. He has finally gained weight yet exercised intensely, so his frame remains wiry and muscular. Scott might look like this one day. Scott's short for his age, which bothers him. He often asks Heloise how tall his father was. "Normal," she lies. She's not sure why. But Scott could still get a growth spurt. Hector Lewis was very tall, and Heloise did contribute some genes to her son, even if they aren't overwhelmingly apparent. The only real resemblance between mother and son is their hair, and she dyes hers, in part so she will look more like him.

Val is angry today, distracted. It happens. Although he can be good company, he has never reconciled himself to the circumstances that brought him here. He blames his lawyer. He blames the witnesses. He blames the state's attorney. Sometimes he even blames Martin.

"I thought you would be in better spirits," Heloise says, then remembers: Paul has spoken to her in confidence. Val probably doesn't know about the compromised ballistics expert. Yet. The state, according to Paul, is trying to assess what the damage will be, how many cases might have to be retried.

"Why?"

"I don't know," she says, moving toward a lie with her usual smoothness. "You always seem a little less restless in the fall."

"Really? Because I've lost all sense of what the seasons are like. I'm aware of time passing. It's like a drip from a faucet. Drives me crazy, but if the drip ends, so do I. Yet I don't really notice the seasons. Does that make sense?"

"Sure. What are you reading?" After his conviction Val

owned up to his illiteracy and received intensive tutoring through a pilot program. He was the star pupil. Most adults who learn to read can't expect to develop much more than basic proficiency, but Val reads at a very high level, albeit slowly. "What's the rush?" he jokes. He gravitates toward history, military history in particular. It pains Heloise how similar they are in this regard, their love of history, their autodidact natures. It's hard not to imagine a parallel universe where the un-fucked-up versions of themselves meet and marry, carry out the normal lives denied them. Not that she yearns for such a thing, not even for Scott's sake. She fears Val too much to love him, and Val's feelings for her could best be described as high regard. He holds her in high regard. She is a singular person in his life. But they could have loved each other, in another world.

"Shelby Foote."

"Ah, more Civil War."

"I read the Bruce Catton. Might as well hear the other side of the story, although I don't get why people are drawn to the Confederacy. They lost. If they were fighting for something great, maybe, but to be pro-slavery *and* losers." He shrugs. Heloise knows that it's the losing part that bothers him. Being here, as Val sees it, is the only defeat he has experienced in his life.

"You ever go to those places?" he asks Heloise, a segue that makes sense to him but leaves her stranded. Val spends a lot of time in his own head, which makes him a tricky conversationalist.

"What places?"

"The nearby battlefields. Gettysburg. Antietam. I'd like to see Antietam, at the same time of year as the battle."

"It's never occurred to me," she says honestly.

"You should get out more, see things. If I ever got out of here—the things I would do, the places I would go. I can't believe how much time we spent cooped up inside that house."

If I ever got out of here. No. Tom said it was impossible.

"Yes." She doesn't mention that their agoraphobic life-style was at his behest, that he wouldn't go out and he didn't want anyone else to leave the property. That they couldn't leave the property because of the cameras everywhere. It had taken her a long time to figure out the spots not captured by his various surveillance cameras. It had taken even longer to start hiding money, digging holes with a toy shovel, of all things. She wondered if some of those little caches of bills were still out there. As it ended up, there wasn't enough time to go back and get them all. But she needed them to be placed haphazardly, messily, so it looked like a child's game. If she put all her money in one place, it would be obvious to Val that she wasn't reporting the tips she sometimes extricated from her customers, the cash she got by returning items she had shoplifted.

"What do you do when you're not working?"

The question surprises her. Val has never shown much curiosity about her life, only her business, which he helped her conceptualize when it became clear that he wouldn't be able to run any kind of enterprise. In return she still kicks money back to him every month. He has no use for money, not really, yet that was the deal they struck, and she abides by it. Locked up, Val has nothing but money with which to keep score. He records the amounts on legal pads, keeps the figures in his head, questions her closely when revenues go down. He thinks he's getting 50 percent of the net, but it's more like 35.

What *does* she do when not working? Almost all the answers lead to Scott.

"Read," she says. "Watch television. Shop on the Internet. That's my primary vice. Now, *that* should be illegal."

"Shopping?"

"These ads that stalk you, drawing on your own Internet history. That creeps me out. I'll be composing an e-mail, and bam, there's a pair of beautiful shoes dancing across the top of the page, almost as if someone's reading my mind, although it's just my own browsing history. Then again, if I could advertise, I wouldn't mind having ads for the business pop up on other people's screens. I don't deal with impulse buyers, but it wouldn't hurt to have an ad that allowed them to jump to the application page."

"E-mail? Who would you write an e-mail to?"

Who indeed? Scott's school. Scott's teacher. The mother who sometimes picked Scott up after band practice. And Coranne Blake, the mother of his best friend. Why do all roads seem to lead back to Scott today? Why has Val become so curious?

"I have that half sister down in Florida."

"I thought you hated her guts."

"I do, but keep your friends close—"

"Your enemies closer," Val finishes. "So she's an enemy?"

"She's a very angry woman who knows what I do for a living. I can't afford for her to nurse any grudges against me."

"Do you have to pay her off?"

"No. I have something on her, she has something on me. That's sufficient."

"Mutual assured destruction, huh? Be careful. You never know when the Berlin Wall is going to fall."

"What's that supposed to mean?"

"You become used to a current reality, then the reality changes. That's all. The way things are today may not be the way they are tomorrow. Just because you've got everything figured out, that doesn't mean you've got *everything* figured out. If you learn anything from my situation, that should be it. I thought I was so smart—"

"You were. You are." Placating him remains automatic.

"And they got me. I don't know how, but they did."

This conversation is unsettling. She's used to seeing him in funks, but Val's mood today is not quite like any she has encountered over the past ten years. She decides to turn it on herself, see if she can make him feel sorry for her.

"Lately people in my life, people who know what I do, have been suggesting I need an exit strategy."

"They're right."

This catches her off guard.

"I thought you of all people would want me to keep going as long as I can."

"You should move over into management. You had to

wear two hats when you started out, building the business. But there's no reason for you to continue to see clients."

"I would make less money that way."

"You also would be exposed to less risk."

"If I took a pay cut, would you take a smaller cut of what I make?"

"Do you think I ever let anyone pay me less?"

He is taunting her, baiting her. Why? Because he can. Because he's on the other side of a glass, in a world without people, and Val in his odd way had liked having people around him, as long as they were quiet. He was happiest when the house was full of slumbering bodies and he stood vigil. Sat vigil, actually, watching the enormous television in his den.

"You're very crabby today," she risks.

"My apologies."

"You're entitled."

"Why, thank you. Thank you for giving me permission to be in a bad mood because I've been locked up for over a decade for something I didn't even do."

She shoots him a look. Val has always maintained in official interviews that he didn't kill Martin. But has he forgotten that she was there? That she saw everything?

He smiles. "Gotta be consistent, my love. Remember that. Whatever you say, keep saying it." He taps the phone on which he speaks. "The walls have ears. There are very few secrets in the world when you get down to it."

Later, as she weaves through the city toward the interstate, she can't help thinking he was warning her. Stranger still, he was warning her about *him*. He knows something or suspects it. Where has she slipped up? When has she been inconsistent? Why did he want her to know that he suspected her?

She will take his advice, go to Antietam, bring Scott, then report back to Val. Perhaps that will soften his mood when she sees him next. He always liked playing the mentor. For a while. The trick was for the protégé to get out before Val tired of him. Or her.

1999

She got pregnant when she was twenty-five. She was old for the life she was in. The other girls made fun of her, called her Granny, asked her if she was having hot flashes. They were jealous and dismayed by her staying power, especially Mollie, a new girl. Helen looked good, all things considered. She had become adept at home-spa treatments, so her skin was soft and her nails immaculately groomed. She started practicing yoga for the mental benefits and found that the physical benefits were almost as impressive. She wore a hat in the sun. She didn't smoke, and she drank sparingly, largely because she felt she couldn't afford the looseness that came with a few drinks. Twenty-five. There were people, she realized, whose lives began at twenty-five, or even thirty, forty. If she had been able to go to college and graduate school, find a teaching job, she might be coming up for tenure now or moving on to a bigger, better school. It was a perfectly reasonable age at which to get pregnant—if one wasn't a whore.

There was no doubt that the baby was Val's. He liked to have sex without condoms, as long as he knew that the girl was clean—and he was obsessive about his girls' cleanliness. On the edge of the next millennium, a certain complacency had settled in about AIDS, with most men convinced that they couldn't get it from straight hetero sex. Still, Val sent the girls in for regular blood tests. If someone came back infected, he gave her money and sent her away. Val didn't want to see anyone die, not unless he was the one pulling a trigger. A slow, wasting death disturbed him more than anything. He understood, accepted, and even facilitated sudden death. Day-by-day dying was different. Helen always wondered if someone close to him had died this way, but Val revealed even less about his origins than she did. The others gabbed, including the Georges. They got melancholy or mellow and began to tell stories about themselves, looking to make some kind of connection. The tricks did it, too, sometimes, telling long, pointless stories that were meant to justify how they ended up cheating on their wives with paid sex. It was baffling to Helen, this belief that personal knowledge would lead to intimacy, something good, anything good. It was information. Information was power. Why would she give away any more power?

Yet it was on such a night—people sitting around talking, drinking, smoking, trapped in the house by a vicious blizzard—that her child was conceived. One of the girls, Bettina, told a long, hard-to-follow story about her father, and Helen must have rolled her eyes or shrugged at what was supposed to be the heartbreaking moment, because the girl came at her, went airborne across the debris-strewn coffee table and began pulling Helen's hair. Which made Helen laugh. What was this, *The Jerry Springer Show*? George I pulled Bettina off, also shaking with mirth. Val was laughing, too. Everyone laughed, except Bettina.

Later that night Val came to Helen's room. He almost caught her reading one of her stolen books, but she heard his footsteps and slid it beneath her bed, exchanging it for one of the fashion magazines she kept there. Val almost never came to the girls' rooms, instead summoning them to his, where he had everything as he liked it—the big bed, the television that was never off. Yet here he was, and his desire for her was touchingly straightforward. It felt almost like an encounter between a normal man and woman, although Helen's only experience with such things was with Billy, a decade ago.

Perhaps because her body was her business, she knew within a week that he had knocked her up. She shoplifted—or tried to shoplift—a home pregnancy test from the Rite Aid, only to have the cashier pull it out of her purse at the register. "Forget this?" he said. "Oh, yeah. I put it there because my hands were full," she said. The clerk was going to make a fuss, but a cop stepped in, said, "Let me handle it."

That was how she met Tom.

An undercover vice cop, he had been watching her for quite some time, it turned out. He took her in on the shoplifting charge, hoping to scare her into becoming an informant, but she was far more scared of Val than she was of the Baltimore Police Department. She gave him nothing. Then. And they couldn't hold her for shoplifting because she hadn't left the store with the kit.

Still, Tom thought he might be able to use Helen, and Helen began to wonder if she could use Tom.

A week later they met for coffee, and he tried to convince her to be his confidential informant.

"I don't know anything," she said.

"You work for someone who runs a lot of drugs, sort of like a wholesaler. Maybe firearms, too. By Baltimore standards he's organized crime. True, our standards are pretty low."

"I don't work for anyone." They were sitting in a diner, a really crummy one. "I don't even work."

"I've been watching you for a long time. I know what you do."

"You've been watching me?" She gave her voice a flirtatious lilt.

He squirmed. Good. The hook was in.

"It's my job."

"Do you like it? Watching me, I mean."

"It's my job."

"Nice work if you can get it."

"You think it's such a good gig, watching you?"

She smiled as she took a sip of the horrible coffee. Places such as this diner fascinated her. All mediocrity did. How did a diner with bad food and bad coffee survive? The service was the bare minimum, the location wasn't that great. But Helen knew: It survived because it took for granted that certain customers were beaten down enough to come back, that the world was full of people whose expectations were so low that they couldn't be disappointed. And she was on the verge of becoming one of them.

She assumed they were going to have sex, accepted it as

the freight she had to carry. But Tom had brought a pregnancy kit to replace the one she had tried to swipe. He waited for her to take it in the diner bathroom. Maybe he supposed that a positive would make her weaker, willing to do whatever he wanted, beholden to him, more in need of his protection.

Ten minutes is a long time to wait for a mark on a stick. She sat in the stall, crouching, really, as there was no lid and she wasn't going to sit on that seat a moment longer than necessary. She felt like someone in a legend, King Arthur perhaps, waiting for a sign. Her future was about to be foretold.

The woman who came out of that diner bathroom was a thousand times stronger than the one who went in. She had stared at the stick, the blurry mark, reread the instructions on the box, but she knew. She had known all along. She was going to have a child. How would that work? How could that be? She looked in the clouded mirror. *This child must never know its father.* She could not save her baby from Val's genes, but if she could keep the knowledge of Val from his child—then it must be done. How, where to begin? How would she support herself? How would she keep Val from knowing? Val would want his child, she had no doubt of that. The baby would be raised in the house with the same care and tenderness lavished on the various pets. Only the baby wouldn't be a pet. It would grow, it would have a mind of its own, it would challenge Val—and Val would turn on it.

138

Helen splashed water on her face, dried her hands on the old-fashioned towel, the kind that hung in a single loop. You pulled down and supposedly dried your hands on the fresh part, but when had it last been replaced? Her life was like this. She pulled and pulled but always ended up making a full circle, and each pass was dirtier than the last.

She took her seat across from Tom. "I can give you Val Deluca on a murder. I can give you the gun. You already have the body. But no one can ever know it was me who told, ever. I mean until the end of time, because Val will find a way to kill whoever is responsible for locking him up, even if it takes the rest of his life. Can you make that happen?"

"I think so."

"You have to be sure."

Wednesday, October 12

It is one of the oddities of life in Maryland that no single supermarket can serve a household's entire needs. The organic and semiorganic ones—Whole Foods, Roots—don't offer a full range of paper products and cleaners. (Heloise tries to be "green," for Scott's sake, but if it's a choice between greenliness and cleanliness, cleanliness wins.) The big chain stores often don't stock the exotic items required by Scott's newfound love of cooking—five-spice powder, tamarind seed, Manchego cheese, even arugula. Produce is best when bought from farmers' markets and the small seasonal stands that dot the back roads, even in Heloise's upscale neighborhood. And almost no grocery store is allowed to sell beer and wine, thanks in part to the efforts of one of Maryland's best lobbyists, a man whom Heloise can't help but admire: He's better at seducing senators and delegates than she is—and makes more money than she does.

But the main thing grocery stores have taught Heloise is that it's better to be a one-stop shop.

This afternoon she has chosen Tommy's Market, a local upscale grocery in Turner's Grove, for a last-minute shopping trip. She is coming from work and so is nicely dressed, which marks her as out of place at this time of day. Everyone else here is a stay-at-home mom, a nanny, or a teenager just released from the nearby high school. No one notices her. No one ever really notices anyone. Her father was right—she was born with a nothing face. But so is everyone.

Yet one man, as out of place at three in the afternoon as she is, seems to be tracking her. He has on khakis and an oxford-cloth shirt, blue striped. His hair is very blond, almost platinum, yet his eyes and brows are quite dark.

"Can you help me pick out a tomato?" he asks Heloise.

"You don't want to buy a tomato in October," she tells him, having learned this from Scott.

"But these are plum tomatoes, for a dish I make with shrimp and feta cheese. You can use canned, according to the recipe. Even the worst real tomato has to be better than canned, right? So I don't think it matters that much."

"If it doesn't matter, why are you asking me?"

He gives her a winning smile. "Because I needed an excuse to talk to you."

It's sweet, and Heloise is flattered, almost charmed. But not tempted, never tempted. Of all the things in the world she cannot have, "real" men top the list.

"Have a nice day," she says as kindly as possible, pushing her cart past him.

He follows her, pulls his cart alongside hers. "I'm sorry if I seemed overly bold. Are you married? I didn't see a ring—"

She holds up her left hand. There is a ring there, because Scott believes that his mother was married and his father died tragically and she can never love anyone else as she loved him. She wears the ring for Scott. And moments like this.

141

"I'm sorry," he repeats. "You must think I'm a louse, hitting on a married woman."

He looks humiliated, and Heloise does something she almost never does—she takes pity on a man.

"I'm a widow," she says.

"Wow, that's sad. How long?"

"Twelve years. He died when I was pregnant."

"Oh." He looks confused. "That's a long time."

"In some ways. Do you know the cliché about raising a child? The days are long, but the years are short."

"I don't have kids. And I don't have a wife, past or present." He holds up his naked left hand. He has exceptionally nice hands—clean and trimmed nails, long, delicate fingers—although there are calluses on the palms, as if he clutches something tightly on a regular basis. Weights, from the look of those shoulders.

"As if the absence of a wedding ring proves anything on a man."

She's teasing him. He was so horrified by her ring that she has to think he's a well-intentioned sort. But that's as far as she dares to take this light flirtation. "I have to go."

"Can I at least know your name?"

"Don't worry about the plum tomatoes. If the recipe says canned is okay, use canned. Why make extra work for yourself?"

"I'm making more than just one person can eat," he calls after her.

"Freeze it."

*

142

Later, in the parking lot, she catches him watching her as she loads her car. It's about as respectful as such a gaze can be. Wistful, not leering. She feels a little pang of regret as she drives away.

That night, at dinner, she allows herself an extra glass of wine and, once Scott is in bed, a little extra melancholy. She has had such encounters before, although usually even briefer. It's like receiving a postcard from a land where she will never travel. A nice man in an oxford-cloth shirt might as well be the Taj Mahal. Or one of the wonders of the world that no longer exists. She can't get there, and even if she could, the Hanging Gardens of Babylon aren't there waiting for her.

The man in the grocery store is not the only reason for her funk. There was a letter in the mail, one with the return address she wishes she didn't know, had never known. It's not the first time she has received such a letter, but it's been at least four, five years. She can't even bring herself to open it. Just the envelope, the familiar handwriting, feels like a burden. *I don't owe you anything,* she tells the letter. Heloise shuts it up in the lap drawer of the desk in Mother's office. Later she'll take it downstairs and shred it.

She continues to sit at the seldom-used desk, this cubbyhole where some developer, no doubt a man, imagined Mommy cheerfully doing accounts within earshot of her family. The desk is positioned so that she can see the family room, the large windows at the rear of the house. With her own house dark except for the glow of her laptop, she has a view of lighted windows, the shadows of families beyond them. She knows that the women are tired, probably much more tired than she is. They don't have enough time for themselves. They don't have *any* time for themselves. If they have jobs, they feel guilty. If they don't have jobs, they feel guilty. If they work part-time, they are convinced that they are deficient on both fronts, children and office. Some of them, too, probably are sitting with a glass of wine right now, staring out windows or at large plasma television screens, not registering the program flashing by.

As for the women who are going it alone, as she does—there are none here in Turner's Grove. But they are not far away, the divorcées and the widows, maybe a town or two over. What would they give for a nice-looking man—one who cooks yet!—making a pass at them in the grocery store? What will Heloise give for the same experience in a few years?

She fired January today. Business is slow, she can afford to be one woman, one month down. Anna Marie is a nice girl, one of her best, and it hurt to let her go, but Heloise has to be consistent. She reminded Anna Marie of the confidentiality clause she had signed when she came to work for WFEN. It's a funny thing about that contract: It's grossly tilted to Heloise's favor; no reputable lawyer would ever allow a client to sign it. But the girls she recruits never ask a lawyer to look at it, of course. The very fact that Heloise wants them to sign a legal document makes them feel better about their choice of employment. How illegal can a business be if it starts with such a proper contract?

Technically Sophie will be in violation of the contract if

she tries to file for workers' comp and reveals the nature of WFEN's clientele. But that technicality can't save Heloise. Sophie's too broke to fear a financial judgment. Sophie's too broke and too angry to fear anything, and that makes her extremely dangerous.

Anna Marie wasn't angry. She seemed chastened, apologetic. "I really thought you would be open to it. I just didn't know how to go about it. I guess I mishandled it."

"Yes, you did. Once someone has gone behind my back, whatever the motive, I can't trust that person. If you move to another service, I hope you'll do me the courtesy of not trying to poach clients."

She always says this, but she understands it's the first thing Anna Marie will try to do. Heloise might lose a client or two, but not Paul. Sure, he'll be tempted to cheat on her, but she'll ignore it, let him get it out of his system.

"I don't think I'm going to continue in this line of work. My college loan is almost paid off, the one from undergrad. And I've got a stipend for next semester."

"Really? A week ago you were plotting to buy my business, and now you're not sure you're even going to continue working in the industry?"

"It was Paul who first brought it up."

"Paul?"

"He liked my thoughts about public health, finding ways to decriminalize, if not completely legalize, the sex trade. He said he knew someone who might be interested, a money guy who could back me. He sort of encouraged me to follow my ideas to the logical conclusion."

Sure, that's what Paul liked. Her *ideas*. Still, it's interesting information, and Heloise files it away, just in case it's true.

She doesn't blame men for wanting younger women. It's evolution at work, hardwired into their brains. Once women can't have children and the children no longer require care, then what are women for? She read recently that women were supposed to die before or around the time of menopause, which explains why menopause is so awful: It's supposed to make you grateful to die. *The world is done with you. Get out.* Yet Heloise then stumbled on the writings of a scientist who said that menopause itself no longer serves a purpose. When childbirth was a serious health risk, it was better if middle-aged women, already loaded down with kids, didn't have to worry about an untimely death in pregnancy. Now women are taunting science, having children past the age of fifty. In her heart Heloise doesn't think that's right, but she can't help cheering for anything that levels the playing field. If men can have children up until death, it seems only fair that women can, too.

Like a pro athlete, Paul had told her. *And Val agreed.* That was more hurtful, Val's ready agreement that she should move exclusively to the management side. All her life the only thing men have wanted her for is sex. What else can she possibly provide, at her age, in this economy? What is she qualified to do?

She hears Scott give a little yelp in his sleep. She waits to see if he's going to wake up, need her, but it's just one of the noises that children make in the night. Scott has been

146

remarkably free from nightmares. His bad dreams usually come closer to sunrise and generally involve an enormous dog not unlike one that scared him badly when he was a toddler. She pours another glass of wine, finishing a bottle for the first time in years, yet feeling as if she's not drinking alone, far from it. She's one of a dozen, a hundred, a thousand, a million women, holding a glass and staring into space, asking herself the musical questions she used to hear on soupy, soapy WFEN radio: *What's it all about? Is that all there is? What are you doing the rest of your life?*

Heloise misses the randomness of that radio station, someone else calling the shots, picking the songs from some remote location in the country's heartland. Nowadays life is à la carte—watch your favorite television show when you want to watch it, create your own radio station on Pandora or your iPod, tick off the sexual acts you wish to enjoy on this handy order form. Not that she has an order form, but she could, come to think of it, a piece of paper like those handed out in sushi bars. Get what you want when you want it. Her business is steeped in this philosophy, thrives because of it.

Her life? Pretty much the opposite.

1999

Val was neither sentimental nor stupid. He had to know that keeping a gun used to kill someone was an exceedingly poor idea. But perhaps he thought it would be enough to conceal it well, while the two Georges tossed Martin's body into the bay. Martin's body had traveled a very long way before he was found, washing up one day in the trash nets of the Inner Harbor. It took longer still to identify him, and while his murder had remained an open case all these years, as all homicides do, no one had much hope of solving it. A naked man, a bullet in his head, a known associate of bad people—young Martin was not a priority.

Yet a week after Helen took her pregnancy test in the diner bathroom, four years after Martin's death, police arrived at Val's front gates with a warrant. It was not the first time that Val's home had been searched, and he did not pay much attention as the team of officers worked their way through the large house. He sat in the family room—his name for it, used without irony—watching television, surrounded by his people. His family. Helen, the two Georges, three other girls, including Mollie, his current favorite. She sat tight as a tick by his side, trying to distract him with little pats and kisses. Helen could see that her attentions merely annoyed Val, that he neither needed nor desired to be distracted.

Helen worried that the cops would do their job too quickly, revealing their inside knowledge, but Tom had prepped them well. Besides, they had full run of the house— why not take advantage of it? As one hour turned into two and the men continued riffling drawers, she began to worry that her message had been garbled through the chain of command. Or maybe she was wrong and the gun had been moved. Val had not even pretended to read the search warrant, and he assumed it was the usual nuisance visit. If he had known what was at stake, would he have been nervous? But maybe he did understand and wasn't worried because the gun was gone.

After two hours in the house, the cops fanned across the grounds. Was Val nervous now? He owned more than three acres, although much of it was heavily wooded, a buffer between him and the world. Helen wondered if the cops even knew anything about nature, if they would be able to find the ash tree among the oaks, if Tom had paid attention when she told him about the odd knot in the trunk. It was almost dark when the cops returned to the house with the dirt-covered gun and announced that Val was under arrest for the murder of Kristofer Martin.

"Who?" Val said, very convincingly. Maybe he didn't recognize the name, which had surprised Helen. Or maybe he no longer remembered the full name of the young man he'd shot four years ago, for the simple crime of using Val's full name.

They took Val away, held him without bail. The house felt odd without him there, even though he was normally gone at least ten days a month. The Georges drove the girls into town, brought them home again as if nothing had changed. It occurred to Helen that she wasn't sure where the bills went or who paid them. Val had once told her that he didn't keep anything in his name, but whose name did he use? She called his lawyer, asked for help, but the lawyer refused to tell her anything. She wasn't a wife or a relative, he said. He wasn't authorized to speak to her.

"Where do the bills go?" she asked the Georges. "How do we keep the lights on? Is there a mortgage?"

She didn't really care. But in asking, in pretending to care, worrying about her day-to-day expenses, she was setting up her reason for leaving.

"Don't worry," they said. "Val won't let his house slip away."

She was now four weeks along. She probably had six to eight more weeks before the changes in her body would become obvious. But Val knew her body so well. She went to visit him in county lockup. Martin's corpse might have washed up in the city, but the murder had happened in the county—and the county would go for the death penalty if it could, although there didn't appear to be grounds for a capital case. Flight risk, the judge had ruled, but Helen was the real flight risk.

"The charge isn't going to hold," Val said, confident as ever. "But I can't wait to get to discovery, find out who the CI was."

"The CI?"

"Confidential informant. Has to be one of the Georges, I'm thinking. Who else would know where that gun was?"

150

It would be in character for her to defend them, Helen decided, so she did.

"There were others, too," she said. "There was a girl that night—the one you let go because she developed such a bad cocaine habit. Bettina."

"Yeah," he said, remembering.

"And—" *Careful,* she warned herself. *Don't overplay it. The less said, the better.* They had watched a lot of cop shows together over the years, and that was what Val always said. *Most of these people hang themselves. They're too clever. They never shut up.*

"What?"

"Nothing," she said.

"No, go on, you were going to say something."

"Well, Mollie has a big mouth, too, if it comes to that. She wasn't with us then, but she might have heard some things."

He smiled. "Look at Helen being catty."

"No, I was just saying."

"Sure you were. I like it when you get territorial. Look, Mollie's not competition. Besides, like you said, she wasn't there then. So how would she know? It has to be Bettina. Or that other girl. What's her name? Brown hair? West Virginia? The one who liked to make out with other girls when she was drunk, remember?"

Helen wanted desperately to escape this topic. "Val, what do we do for money while you're here?"

"Do? You go to work. Whatever you make, you can use to pay your way. I've got the house and the utilities covered.

But when I come out—and I will be coming out, although there's no avoiding a trial—things go back to normal."

"It's just—my mom, she's really sick."

"Your mom? You have a mom?"

"Of course I do. Everyone does."

"You never spoke of her."

"And you never spoke of yours."

"Not about to start either."

She is curious about Val's origins, especially now. *Who were your people? Did they make you this way or were you born this way?* But those are questions she can never ask.

"My mom—they say she has three months, tops." Deliberately picking a small number, fewer months than she needed, believing it would be easier to claim urgency, then get home and relay the unexpected good news, that her mother had made it to six months, nine months.

"What's she got?"

"Colon cancer."

"That's a bad one."

"Yeah."

"Did she get that thing where they put that camera up your butt?"

"I doubt it. She's not even fifty."

"Are you close?"

She didn't understand the question at first, thought he was asking if she was close to getting the procedure, or even if she was close to fifty. It was a normal question under the circumstances. *Are you close to your mother?* Helen didn't have much experience with normal questions.

"In a way. Not in the keeping-in-touch way, because I couldn't see how to make that work. I send her cards at Christmas and stuff. But she was always good to me. I didn't leave home because of her."

She waited to see if he would ask, *Then why did you leave home?* But Val seldom asked such questions. None of the men in her life asked her questions about herself, except for George II, and those were rare, brought out by these very mellow moods he got when he smoked a lot of dope and became chatty.

"I want to go home. I know I won't be earning while I'm gone, but as you said, I would have been supporting myself, right? It's just up the road in Pennsylvania. She needs me."

"And if I said I needed you?"

A test. But Helen was good at tests.

"I would stay here. I would do whatever you needed me to do."

It was the right answer. He nodded. "I'd been counting on you holding things together kind of, but if this is how things are, if I don't have you to keep an eye on things . . . Tell the other girls to get out. Make sure they go. Make sure they take only what's theirs—clothes, makeup, that kind of shit. You and the Georges supervise them. Then, when they're gone, you can go to your mother. But keep me posted, okay? And keep coming to visit. It's not so far that you couldn't visit, right?"

"Three, four hours, one way," she lied, knowing that she would never make the trip.

"I won't be here long," he said.

153

"I know, Val. You always come out on top."

The weird thing was, she almost found herself rooting for it, if only because Val's ability to survive was one of the few tenets in her life. *Val always came out on top.*

She was riding in silence alongside George I before she remembered that Val had been arrested because she'd told Tom where cops could find the gun, then given them a full report on the death of Kristofer Martin.

But when Val's trial finally wended its way to discovery, he would be told that the informant was someone else. Someone who, with any luck, wouldn't even be alive, a reliable CI dying of cirrhosis—and happy to have the money that Helen funneled to him, through Tom, to pay for the funeral of his dreams.

Thursday, October 13

Heloise is cleaning up from dinner, letting Scott finish a report at the kitchen table. He's supposed to have his homework done before dinner, but soccer makes that impossible. Don't the teachers know about the sports? Don't the coaches understand how much homework kids get these days? They must. But they rationalize that it falls to the kids, which means it falls to the parents, to reconcile all these conflicts.

"Mom, do you know what mitochondria are?" Scott asks.

Such questions often give her a pang. She has tried hard, read much, but she was never strong in science and her mathematical skills stalled out at the arithmetic stage. She tells herself that other mothers, ones who had the luxury of all the education they craved, probably don't remember what mitochondria are, that if Scott is studying them (it?) now, she must have studied them (it?), too, in her own grade-school days. Something to do with a cell, right?

Luckily, Scott is just showing off his own knowledge. He recites the definition with confidence—so it *is* a plural—then goes back to his work. Chastened, Heloise settles down with a novel. Her new self-improvement list involves reading the work of Nobel Prize winners. It is slow going. Her "pleasure" read, the one by her bedside table, is a much livelier story about the origins of the current economic crisis, but it's like reading a horror story right before bed-time. At any rate, when Scott does his homework, she does her homework. She is finally beginning to adapt to the writer's old-fashioned rhythms when the doorbell rings.

"Who could that be?" Scott says, sounding for all the world like a fussy old lady, as if they are two spinsters living together. Heloise is reminded why she's determined for him to play soccer, how good it is for him to have some male attention, even if it's secondhand and second-rate. Personally, Heloise wouldn't mind if they were two fussy old spinsters growing old together, but she knows that's no life for a boy.

"Probably a neighbor. I'm sure I've violated the homeowners' rules again." Heloise tries to be scrupulous about staying within the law, as defined by Turner's Grove. Nothing gets meaner faster than a neighborhood dispute.

It's Leo, her accountant and he looks strange to Heloise. Drunk, she thinks at first, but there's not a whiff of alcohol on him and he's steady on his feet. Still, he's loose and giddy.

"I wasn't expecting you," she says. Rude, but—Heloise does not like anyone arriving at her home unannounced.

"Quarterly filings," he says. "I was in the neighborhood, thought I'd stop by and get your signature."

"Don't you usually messenger those over?"

"I do. And it costs seventy-five dollars, which I charge to your account. This visit is free!" His voice soars a little on the last word—he sounds like that squealing pig in the insurance commercial that Scott and Audrey love—and Leo giggles at the sound.

"Do you have a pen?" Again, rude. She should ask him in, offer coffee or a drink, even something to eat. After all, he knows about Scott. As her accountant, he had to know she has a dependent. She was tempted, when Scott was young, not to claim him, calculating that the tax benefit was not worth creating a paper trail for his existence. But another accountant, Leo's predecessor, had convinced her that it was in Scott's best interest. She was paying into Social Security, he was her only heir, if anything should happen to her, God forbid—so Leo belongs to the "legitimate" side of her life ledger, and she has tried her best to keep him there.

He pats his chest. "How about that? I don't."

There is nothing to do but open the door and let him in. He goes to the dining-room table where Scott is working. "I don't suppose I could have a soda," he asks Heloise.

"We don't have soda," Scott says. "It's very bad for your bones."

"Juice? Iced tea? Oh, what the hell, I'll have a glass of that." He indicates the quite nice pinot noir that Heloise is nursing. Disciplined as always, she has cut back, so it's her first glass of the night. But she resents sharing a twenty-five-dollar bottle of wine with Leo. She pours him a rather stingy serving, using a milk glass.

"Hell of a season," he says. "Seems like more and more of our clients are treating October fifteenth like April fifteenth."

"Not me," Heloise says.

"Not I," Scott corrects her matter-of-factly, and it's odd how shame and pride can simultaneously fill her heart,

157

although she knows it's a grammar lesson learned from the musical *Peter Pan,* which Scott loves. She reminds herself that educated people make such gaffes all the time, that she has brilliant clients who say "between you and I" and use "whom" even when "who" is correct.

"No, I wish all my clients were like you," Leo says. "So honest. So ethical. I've never seen anyone as careful as you."

A compliment. That is, it should be a compliment. But there is an odd tone under his words.

"You're really worried about being audited," Leo says.

"Isn't everyone?" she asks.

"Abstractly, yes. No one wants to be audited. But it's like a lot of things in life. As much as we don't want it to happen, as easy as it would be to set up a system to simplify our own lives—like filing stuff, you know? You buy things, you get all those warranties and instruction manuals, and you know you should have a system for filing them, but they're just in a big stack on your desk. Or passwords! Passwords. You say, 'I am going to write that down in a safe place, or at least put the hints down in a safe place,' and"—he threw his hands up in the air—"you never do. Well, you probably do. I never do. Most people don't. That's what I'm saying. You're so careful. Being audited must be a powerful disincentive for you in a way it's not for most of the people I work with. It's almost like you would *die* if you were audited."

She tops off his glass, then turns to her son. "Scott? Are you almost done? It's getting close to bedtime."

"Forty-five minutes," he says, correctly.

"Well, when you are done, you can watch television."

158

He slams the book shut. "I'm done!" He has probably skimped on some essential task. She really should check his work. But getting him away from Leo seems more important.

"Why don't you watch in my room?" she says. This is a treat. Although she has a television in her room, she seldom uses it, and Scott is not allowed to have any "screens" in his bedroom, not even the cell phone she reluctantly gave him this year after there was a mix-up and he was stranded at soccer practice. "Just put your pj's on first, so if you fall asleep, all I have to do is steer you to bed."

He runs upstairs, delighted by the novelty of it all, indifferent to Leo. Good.

"How did you know I would be home tonight?" she asks him. "It would have been a long way out of your way if I hadn't been here."

"Audrey has Thursdays off, right?"

"Not necessarily. It varies, according to my schedule."

"But Audrey usually has Thursdays off, which means you have to monitor the phones."

She glances at her BlackBerry. "I'm available to my employees, certainly."

"Like you were available to Sophie?"

"I'm not sure what you mean."

"I mean, you're sitting here in your five-hundred-seventy-five-thousand-dollar house—six hundred and fifty thousand before the bubble burst, but what do you care? your mortgage is only two hundred thousand—with your cute son, drinking wine, while girls are out there putting themselves at risk and you just sit on your ass and take forty percent off the top."

This is not the kind of detail that can be gleaned from her books.

"I own the firm. I am responsible for all the overhead costs, as you know. I have a silent partner who takes a big chunk of the profits in exchange for his original investment."

"Man, Sophie was right. You are a cool customer."

Heloise takes a healthy sip of her wine. This bottle might get finished tonight after all. A terrible thought crosses her mind. Ply Leo with liquor, send him on his way, hoping he wrecks his car on the famously curvy roads of Turner's Grove, roads that claim teenagers with such regularity that it's almost like human sacrifice. But no, she is not that person. She was once, but she decided she must not harm anyone again, if at all possible.

So where does Sophie fit within that vow?

"I'm terribly sorry about what happened to Sophie. You know that. You keep my books. You know that I've covered her prescription costs, that she receives the equivalent of a workers' comp payment."

"Yes, you're Lady Bountiful. Sophie's cool as long as you're cool. But if you decide to stop, she's fucked. With a legitimate workers' comp claim, she wouldn't have to worry. So why are you standing in her way? That's what I couldn't understand. Why would you pay out of pocket when a workers' comp claim would be a win-win for everyone?"

"Have you been talking to Sophie again? I asked you not to."

Leo gets up and walks over to the refrigerator, opens it, studies its contents. He begins yanking open drawers and helps himself to an unopened box of Mallomars. Heloise starts to protest that those are for Scott, a treat, but decides to stay still. A part of her mind registers the scene as comical—the bespectacled, never-blinking accountant establishing his dominance by helping himself to a box of Mallomars. She wants to tell him, *I've swum with the sharks, buddy, and come out alive. I've seen men do things that would make you piss yourself. Don't push me.*

"News flash, Heloise: It's a free country. You can't keep two people from talking to each other. Sophie needs help. She reached out to me. What kind of person would turn his back on her?"

Heloise assumes this is a rhetorical question.

"No honor among thieves, huh? And no honor among *whores,* I guess. You're supposed to take care of these girls. That's the promise you make them, right? That you've got all these systems, that no one who works for you has ever been hurt or arrested."

"That's true."

"So what do you call Sophie, in her situation?"

Foolish. "Unlucky. Very unlucky. But that's not my fault. And it's not your responsibility, Leo. Don't be taken in by her. She's using you to pressure me."

"A user? That's rich. I'm pretty sure that's what you are. You use these girls and cast them off, indifferent to what their lives are going to be like once they move on."

"That's not true," she says with some heat. More than

161

twenty girls have worked for her, and only one has had a bad outcome.

"I'm going to make sure you do right by Sophie," Leo says. "I'm your accountant. I know things."

"You signed a confidentiality agreement. As did Sophie. Trust me, you can't afford to talk to anyone."

"Hey, that agreement isn't binding if my silence means being an accessory to a crime."

"What crime? My accounts are in order. You said so yourself."

"Jesus, Heloise. You're a whore. Or a pimp. A madam, I guess. Whatever you call it. And that's illegal, and I prepared the tax returns that helped you cover it up."

"My tax returns are in order. I report all my income through my three businesses. I pay FICA, Medicare, unemployment—which Sophie can draw on if she wants to end her medical leave."

"So why can't she file for workers' comp?"

"Because she's not entitled to it, under the law. There is no evidence that her condition is related to her employment with me."

"She got sick while fucking your clients!"

"If Sophie had a consensual sexual relationship with one of our clients, that was her choice, but it was not a service provided by WFEN. We lobby for income parity for women—"

"Shut up!" He's pacing now, pulling at his hair. Her refusal to say what Leo wants to hear—that she's a whore, that she takes responsibility for Sophie—is only making

162

him more agitated, and she's beginning to wonder at her choice to stonewall him. But she will not hang herself with her own words, ever.

"Look, Leo, this is a horrible situation. You have to trust me. I'm going to continue to take care of Sophie. She was wrong to bring you into this. Clearly she figured out that you have a very tender heart." And a seldom-used cock. Leo is so innocent he probably doesn't require sex from Sophie—is probably terrified of it, given her HIV status. "She's appealing to your better nature, but she'll let you down. She lets everyone down eventually. She wouldn't be in this situation if she hadn't been greedy."

"Greedy! You're the greedy one."

"I assume one hundred percent of the risk and responsibilities of my business. I feel that entitles me to a percentage of what my employees earn. It's a pretty common business model."

He has stopped pacing, seems to be calming down.

"So it is, so it is. And I know the numbers. You make a good living, even in this economy."

"I'm not complaining."

"You must be very good at what you do."

She has been sitting this entire time. Leo now stands directly in front of her. "Do me."

"What?"

"Show me what those other men pay for. But use your mouth. For all I know, you're infected, too."

She speaks quietly but forcefully. "Are you out of your mind? My son is upstairs. This is my home."

"I'll be quiet. And you won't be able to talk at all." He is fumbling at his fly, his underwear, although it's clear that he's not quite ready for any kind of attention. He starts to rub himself. He's probably so used to pleasuring himself that it's instinctive to start this way.

"No, Leo."

"Yes. Or I will—"

She doesn't even wait to hear the threat, and she doesn't flinch at the mess she's about to make. She takes the wine bottle, unconcerned that it's not even half empty, and cracks it on the edge of her table. The wine splatters everywhere, and a dim part of her mind registers the warning that wine stains need to be removed as promptly as possible from granite and tile, or they will set. She'll get to them soon. She holds the jagged neck of the bottle at his crotch and says, "I will cut it off. I've seen men killed. I've had men killed." One man, her mind amends, and she didn't "have" it done, but she was responsible for it. "I'm going to write this off to the pressures you've been under during tax season. So why don't you leave? Go home and sleep on what you've done tonight, and we'll talk later about whether you're still my accountant."

It's a bluff, and if he calls it—if he attacks her, if he forces her—she can't imagine how it will end. Scott is probably snoozing upstairs by now, and she can't decide what would be worse: allowing herself to be raped as he sleeps or having him hear her screams, being forced to call 911.

But Leo is weak, inexperienced. He doesn't have the fortitude for this game. He skitters out, zipping up as he goes.

Heloise locks the door behind him and leans there for what seems like a long time, willing herself back to composure. Then she channels her namesake—gets out the granite cleaner and the tile cleaner, soaks her clothes in OxiClean, sweeps up the glass and puts it in the trash, figuring that the little pieces will be too dangerous in the recycling bin. Helen makes messes. Heloise cleans them up.

Upstairs, she finds that Scott has fallen asleep as the television plays a reality show about men with some horrible job. Do you know, Scott had asked her the other day, what the most dangerous job in the world is?

Mine, she thought, *mine.* Statistically that's not true, not even close. She's not at physical risk doing what she does. But her job threatens her life every day, in a sense.

She lets Scott spend the night in her bed, worrying that it's inappropriate, then smiles at her own fears. *Yes, Helen Lewis,* she says, which is how she addresses herself when she's rattled. *That's what Social Services is going to bust you for—letting your eleven-year-old son sleep in your bed.*

It had begun four or five years earlier, with a shovel, a child's toy, discarded under the dock, rusty and insubstantial. Yet, used with care and patience, it was capable of digging and then filling a small hole, something that wouldn't call attention to itself.

Not that anyone but Helen spent much time outdoors. After she had dug a hole or two with her shovel, she persuaded Val to let her take up gardening, a hobby that he allowed because he was house-proud in an odd way. He liked the subtle improvements to the grounds—and he liked not having to pay an outsider. He gave her better tools. She began hiding bills, the tips she cadged from her clients, in defiance of Val's rules. She wrapped them in napkins, then placed the little bundles in Ziplocs. The trick was remembering where she put them, how many there were, but she trained her memory as one would train a muscle, forcing it to take on more and more weight. She used all sorts of marking systems—stones and twigs, strange knots on trees. Her mother had liked to garden and Helen had worked by her side when she was a child, before Hector decided it was a waste of time and money and paved over much of the backyard. She planted bills with the fall bulbs, scooped out new hiding places while cutting back the liriope. That's how she came to find the gun. She was looking for a place to hide some money.

That would have been two years ago, give or take. Her little shovel, lacy with rust, yet still a sentimental favorite, almost broke when it hit whatever was hidden in the velvet Crown Royal bag. She rocked back on her heels, considering her discovery. Why had Val buried the gun on his property, with the bay right there, ready to carry away anything on its tides? True, Martin's body had been given to the bay, but it's not as if the two would wash up side by side. Val was cheap, the gun had value. Perhaps he hoped to recycle it one day.

Or maybe he just wanted a souvenir of the most reckless thing he'd ever done.

She put it back and found another place to hide her own money. But she never forgot where the gun was. She never forgot where her own money was either, and once Val was in jail and the household had been ordered to disperse, it was a simple afternoon's work to retrieve most of it. She didn't have even three thousand dollars to her name. It was enough. It would have to be.

Helen had told Val a semitruth: She did need to go home. But it was her father, not her mother, who was dying. She just figured a dying mother was more credible. Girls in her line of work don't tend to have close relationships with their fathers, and Val had inferred, over the years, that Helen's was the clichéd SOB. He even assumed that she'd been raped by her father, and Helen had let that assumption pass, much as she wanted to contradict it, to

167

say she wasn't like Bettina, with her pervy uncle, or Shelley, whose own brother had initiated her, then shared her with all his friends.

Hector Lewis was managing to die with as much inconsideration as he had lived. Ungrateful, belligerent, he disdained Beth's expert care yet also seemed in no hurry to arrive at his destination despite his oft-stated belief that he would be treated to something spectacular in the afterlife. Because he had never married Beth, he didn't have her health insurance. And Helen did not offer him any of her money, rationalizing that it would be like tossing a crumb to an insatiable ogre. Her savings would be wiped out in less than a month if she contributed them to Hector's care.

Instead she paid her mother for room and board, then helped her navigate the maze of Social Services. It quickly became obvious that they would have to bankrupt Hector and get him into a state Medicaid program. For once in his life, Hector—with his lack of bank accounts, no property in his name, all the ruses set up to keep the first Mrs. Lewis at bay—made something easy. It took less than a month to establish that he was indigent, with no money in his own name. He complained bitterly about the facility where he ended up, and in truth it was unpleasant. But it was still too good for him, as far as Helen was concerned. She visited him just often enough to deny him the pleasure of accusing her of abandonment.

To her dismay, her mother went to his room almost every evening, directly from work. She loved him, Lord help her. She was devastated by the idea of losing him. Her mother's devotion to Hector made Helen hard, harder. How could anyone love this man?

Yet even the first—technically only—Mrs. Lewis visited him on occasion. Helen saw her there one afternoon, looking disturbingly good—hair freshly dyed, nice clothes. She had finally granted Hector a divorce last year, just in time to avoid the messy complications of his final days.

"Helen," she said after a pause.

"Hello, Mrs. . . . " Her voice trailed off. How could she call another woman by what should be her mother's name, even if that woman held the title fair and square? "Barbara," she amended.

"Your mother didn't tell me you were married."

Helen started to disavow matrimony, then realized that the comment had been based on her now-bulging belly.

"I just started to show, and we were superstitious through the first trimester. You know how it goes. Besides—do you and my mother talk that much?"

"Meghan is married," the first Mrs. Lewis said, referring to her youngest, not quite six months younger than Helen, Hector's going-away gift to his first wife. He had doted on Meghan, but it was a Hector Lewis kind of doting—sporadic, fickle. Yet when it was time for Meghan to go to college, it turned out he had a little fund put aside for her, or so Helen had heard from her mother. It was perhaps the only time in Helen's memory that her mother had allowed herself to admit that she was angry with Hector.

"She met a very nice man at college, a real up-and-comer. She's pregnant with number three."

Helen realized that made her an aunt, or half aunt. She supposed she was expected to ask questions about the husband and his prospects, so Mrs. Lewis could continue to brag, but all she said was "That's nice."

"What does your husband do?"

"He's in pharmaceuticals. He travels a lot. That's why I came home."

"And to see your father, of course."

"Not really."

She had not bothered to lie to her parents about Val. She simply refused to tell them anything about the father of her unborn child. When she first began to show, her mother said, "Oh, dear." Her father said, "Once a whore, always a whore." He was right, but he didn't know it, so she took offense. As far as Helen's parents were concerned, she had been working as a secretary in Baltimore since things didn't work out with Billy. She said nothing, offered no information about herself. They were not entitled to it. Like her father, she had no health insurance. But, reunited with her Social Security number and an address that she could prove was hers, she qualified for welfare. She quickly became expert at ferreting out any additional help offered to pregnant women. There was a pilot program for prenatal care, and she was the star participant, doing everything right. At the monthly meetings, the other women eyed her skeptically, knowing she didn't really belong. Helen didn't care. She never belonged. She was never going to belong anywhere.

Back in Baltimore, Val's confidence was beginning to

erode. Martin turned out to have been a gabby type, who had told lots of people what he knew about Val's business and practices. Val was also bitter to learn, as the trial drew nearer, that the confidential informant who had told police where to find the gun was dead. A fiend, he apparently had done drugs with Bettina, exiled by Val long ago for her drug problems. She had told her drug buddy what it was like to see a man shot in front of her; he had sold the information to detectives. Because that's what it was, Val reminded Helen, a straight-up business transaction. He couldn't fault the CI, but Bettina was stupid, talking that way.

"If I ever find her—" he growled once on the phone.

"Be careful," Helen warned him, as if she cared whether the line was tapped. "Besides, she didn't mean to get you in trouble. It was only gossip. She didn't tell the cops. This guy did."

"Still, I wonder whatever happened to her."

"Lord knows. Nothing good."

Helen honestly didn't know what had happened to Bettina and doubted she was still alive. Bettina had a lot of bad habits. Besides, she had tried to fight Helen that one time.

"And now George I has flipped on me. Isn't that a kick in the ass? They pulled him in on a distribution charge, and he turned so fast that he left his shadow behind."

"I never liked George I," Helen said. This was true.

"That's interesting. He told me to watch out for you."

"See? That's what I mean. I've been nothing but loyal to you, and he tries to stir up shit. He's a troublemaker."

She had these conversations while lying in her parents' bed, evenings when Beth was at the hospital. She felt as if she was finally experiencing the teen years she had never known—hours on the phone talking to a boy, feeling him out, trying to be so entertaining that he would like her. Back in the day, Billy had never called her.

Of course, Val called collect. He had to, but Helen resented it a little, the way every conversation started with a demand that she "accept the charges." It was a loaded phrase between Val and her. At the same time, his calls to her mother's house strengthened her alibi. She was where she was supposed to be, if not doing what she said she would be doing. Sometimes she would claim to hear her mother shouting for her, beg off the call so she could tend to her.

"Maybe we should get married," Val said one day, out of the blue.

The odd thing was that part of her wanted to sing out, *Yes!* Her feelings for him were like a reflex. Hit it right and it would pop, just a little. *They could get married.* No one had wanted to marry her, not even Billy.

"Why?" she asked, nervous because it was out of character. "It's not as if I would testify against you anyway, for any reason."

"But it would make me look respectable, in front of the jury. You could wear a nice suit, sit in the courtroom every day. You look classy. When you try."

"That's not a good reason to get married, Val."

"Best one I can think of."

"Exactly. Marriage is not for you. You were always honest about that, and I never minded. Anyway, it's better if I stay here in Pennsylvania, look after my mother."

"You could testify *for* me. Character witness. You could say the opposite of whatever George I says."

"I'm not good at that." She didn't want to say *lying* because she understood that Val no longer realized it was a lie, that he had succumbed to his defense attorney's notion that all of this was a matter for debate, dueling theories, nothing more, like arguing over what really happened in a confusing movie.

"No, you're not," he agreed. Thank God he believed that she couldn't lie. His conviction in her inherent honesty was all she had going for her. She stroked her belly as she spoke to him. The boy inside her was a considerate child, who seldom kicked or caused her any discomfort. She swore he had figured out a way to position himself so she had less pressure on her bladder than the other women in her prenatal group had on theirs.

She was eight months pregnant now, but she tried to walk every day, even as the days grew colder, rawer. She waddled around the town with no destination in mind. One day she walked past the McDonald's, where she remembered seeing her father with Barbara Lewis. What if she hadn't seen them? Would he still have turned on her? Probably.

And one day she found herself walking past Il Cielo, reinvented as a Mexican restaurant and cheaply at that, with the name reconfigured to read "El Chappos." Helen was pretty sure that *chappos* was not a Spanish word, and the menu, posted in the front window, indicated that the owner's first language was neither English nor Spanish. Later her mother told her that El Chappos was run by a very nice Albanian family. Awful food but nice people. That put it one up on Il Cielo.

Standing outside the restaurant, seeing its past life—*her past life*—in the little bits of blue that peeked out at the corners and eaves, Helen remembered herself at seventeen, up to her elbows in Marshmallow Fluff. Now it was as if her whole life were stuck in Marshmallow Fluff. Once the baby arrived, she would be worse than stuck. She had no illusions about what it would mean to be a mother. Everything would be harder. The only possible reward would be the satisfaction of knowing she was a good mother, succeeding where her own had failed. No one would come before her child. Certainly no man.

But how to provide for her baby? What could she do? What kind of life could she give a child, with no degree, no education? The kindly social worker at the prenatal group wanted her to go to work as a motel maid or a cashier. "You'd be manager in no time," she said cheerfully. But Helen didn't want to stay here. She had to find a job where she could be her own boss, make her own hours. How did someone do that?

Luckily for her, Val was in the market for a new protégée, locked up as he was for killing the last one.

Friday, October 14

Heloise is taking a morning for herself, staying in Starbucks with her Venti latte and *Wall Street Journal* before heading out for a morning of treatments at a favorite spa—just the kind of expense, per Leo, that she should be able to deduct but never has. *Because she's so careful.* Her nerves ajangle all morning, she had hoped some extra caffeine would help, but it's only making her shakier.

A strange man dropping into the chair opposite her doesn't do anything to thwart that feeling. Especially when she can tell with a glance that he's a cop.

"Vice," he says. There are other words, too, but all she can hear is *vice.* Vice, vice, vice.

How would an average woman, a legitimate woman, feel about such a statement? She would think the man was crazy, dangerous. Or assume that she couldn't possibly have heard what she thought she'd heard. Heloise manufactures the horrified, frosty look that she believes one of the stay-at-home moms would give such a man.

"Excuse me?" she says, even as she pushes away from the table, prepares to leave. Why did she sit at a table anyway, which makes it easier for someone to join her like this? She should have taken one of the armchairs. But she was afraid that if she sank into an armchair, she would never get up again, not after the sleepless night she'd had.

"I said we share a vice." He points to the Venti in his hands, the markings in the little boxes, their coffee identities. They are the same, although the order is not a common one—Venti, half-caf/half-decaf, *minus* a shot, heavy on the milk, one Splenda.

Still, he's clearly a cop. A cop in a suit, a detective. It couldn't be more obvious to her that he's a cop if he were wearing a uniform and driving a marked car with the siren blaring. His suit's not quite sharp enough for a Baltimore city detective. He seems suburban to her. Damn. She has always assumed that the county police are stretched too thin to be worried about vice cases, especially as she's not stupid enough to do anything in her own home. But she can't stay out of Annapolis. It's 40 percent of her business. She takes a long draw of her coffee.

"You're Heloise Lewis, right? Your housekeeper said I might find you here. I was hoping we could talk."

"Why? What could you possibly want from me?" She's not about to relinquish her befuddled-citizen role, the woman keen to help authorities, but incredulous that she could.

"I'd like to talk to you about a homicide in Howard County, where I'm a detective."

On this particular score, she couldn't possibly feel less guilty. She is 100 percent sure that she has not killed anyone in Howard County. But now she trusts him even less.

"As a suspect?" A little too blunt for the persona she's channeling, but she's impatient.

He's not as surprised by her directness as she would like. "No, not at all. Just a talk. No big deal. We could probably do it here, right now, but the acoustics are god-awful."

He glances meaningfully around the coffeehouse. This time of day, it's mothers, the laptop crew, and that increasing army of people who seem to use Starbucks as their home office. Everyone eavesdrops here. Heloise knows because she eavesdrops here. She has picked up information about marriages going bad, problems at the local school, even stock tips, although she has never been tempted to take those because she is dubious about the business acumen of men who yell into their cell phones at Starbucks.

"I'd like to bring my lawyer, so let's schedule an appointment and I'll call him."

"No reason to do that," he says, his manner a little less friendly than it's been. "It's only a conversation."

"I have appointments all morning. Spa things. They charge you if you cancel with less than twenty-four hours' notice." She is thrilled to have this wonderfully legitimate excuse, almost hopes he'll challenge it. "Can we meet at your office at two?"

He nods, slides his card to her. Alan Jolson. Al Jolson!

She can't stop herself. "Why did your parents do that to you?"

"I think it's because they didn't want people to call me Al. And that was before the Paul Simon song. Everybody does, though. Calls me Al. Why did your folks stick you with Heloise?"

"Old family name." She lies for the sheer practice of it,

to test herself—and him. If he's been checking into her for any reason, the name change will kick up in the most basic LexisNexis search.

He sighs, brings his bulky frame up from the chair with some effort. "See you at two. Really, I wouldn't bring a lawyer."

"Do you have a son or a daughter?" she asks.

"I've got kids," he allows.

"If a police detective asked them to come in for a friendly conversation, would you allow them to go alone, without representation?"

"Yes I would. My kids know that we're on the right side."

She doubts it, but she lets it go. Heloise has always told Scott not to talk to the *principal* without her or Audrey in the room.

Several hours later, spa-pampered but not at all refreshed, Heloise arrives at police headquarters with her lawyer, Tyner Gray. An older man who has spent most of his adult life in a wheelchair, he has an electric energy that can feel like rudeness to those who don't know him. She likes it. He has never known the ins and outs of her business. She hopes he never will. But he has overseen all the confidentiality agreements she has used, and he is the one who put her in touch with the private detective who does her client background checks. He's probably figured it out, but they have been happy with their don't ask/don't tell relationship.

Perhaps to punish her for bringing a lawyer, Alan Jolson makes Heloise wait for forty-five minutes. That's okay.

Audrey's already on tap to pick up Scott from school. Still, the principle bugs Heloise. The point of an appointment is not to be left waiting. Civil servants.

"I'm thinking about adding a no-compete clause for my employees," she says to Tyner, making conversation. "I want to keep them from taking clients when they leave."

"Those are tricky in a business such as yours," he says.

"What do you mean?"

"It's all about relationships, right?" He could be speaking of her real business or a legitimate lobbying firm. "I can look into it. My hunch is that it will be a lot of billable hours and in the end I won't be able to craft a foolproof provision. I'd hate to do that to you."

The conversation peters out. He has no talent for small talk, and Heloise prefers to be paid for it. She notices the wedding ring on his hand, tries to imagine his wife. Was she with him before he was paralyzed? She envisions a patient, loving woman who has stood by him for forty years, someone as soft and yielding as he is hard and prickly. She bets he's a sweetheart with her—and no one else.

The silence between them is becoming more and more strained when Detective Jolson—Al Jolson, it still makes her smile—finally summons them in. He's angry, no mistake. He didn't want her to bring a lawyer. Yet he didn't make the usual threats, so she's clearly not a suspect. Cops just hate people who know their rights.

He pushes a photograph toward her—a woman appears to be sleeping on the steering wheel of her car, her face discolored.

"Recognize her?" he asks. Then, before she can answer: "Michelle Smith. Died earlier this month. They called her the Suburban Madam."

She cannot gauge if he's baiting her, if he knows what she does. It doesn't matter. She's not going to tell him anything about herself.

"I thought she committed suicide," Heloise says, even as Tyner shoots her a look. Right, they had agreed: Follow his lead, volunteer nothing, speak only with Tyner's nod of approval, direct and to the point.

"Yeah, funny about that. Everyone assumed that because it was asphyxiation, and we let it go. But it's a homicide. Official ruling's going to be released Monday."

She can't help herself. "Why Monday?"

"Because it's going to be a fucking big deal, and we'd all like to have a nice weekend free of media and Internet conspiracy theories."

Heloise sees a setting sun, feels the cool autumnal air, hears Tom's voice: *Be careful. Be careful.* This is what he was warning her about. Not his replacement in vice. A killer, someone who had murdered a woman not unlike her.

But she waits. No question has been asked of her.

"What do you think about that?" Jolson presses, not much better than the television reporters he hopes to evade for a weekend. *How does this make you feel?*

Tyner nods permission for her to speak, not caring that Jolson sees what he's doing, that he will understand the dynamic at work.

"It's horrible, of course. It's not what one expects, not in that neighborhood."

"Not for the everyday resident, but maybe not so surprising for a whore."

She flinches at the term. Still, no question has been asked. There is nothing for her to say.

"A whore," he repeats. "That's a nasty business. Nasty things happen."

"Was she killed by a client?" Tyner is allowed to speak as he wishes.

"You'd think so, right? I mean, that's how it works in the movies. Some guy's got a fetish, he goes around killing prostitutes. But let me tell you, those guys, they are not going to the high-end ladies." Heloise feels a bizarre flash of validation to hear her own theory supported. "And this lady wasn't supposed to be seeing customers, being under indictment and all."

"Right," Tyner says. "But she had a black book."

"You need to stop thinking that newspapers get stuff right," Jolson says, not unkindly. "There was no black book, not really. She had a coded list of customers. We broke it pretty easy. The most ordinary guys you could imagine. No senators, no bigwigs."

Bigwigs? Heloise has never heard someone use that term in earnest.

"I'm not saying these guys didn't care about being found out. They were shitting bricks, but it was all about their wives and bosses and neighbors, you know? The ones we talked to—they have alibis or it's just not plausible. I mean, you cannot imagine these guys carrying off something like this. Trust me, they would have confessed. They confessed to everything. I felt more like a priest than a detective."

Silence. What is there to say? Heloise feels as if she can pinpoint the exact location of her heart. It is like a pigeon caught in a chimney, flapping its wings, desperate to get out, blind in the darkness.

"What do you want from my client, Detective?"

"A show of emotion, at the very least. You know her, right?"

Tyner has to poke Heloise. She hasn't registered Jolson's comment as a question. "I don't think so."

Jolson pushes a photo across the desk. Now it's the living version of the woman as she appeared in her last court appearance. Thin, dark eyes—Heloise shakes her head, happily sincere. She has no idea what he's talking about.

"Does she look familiar to you in this photo?" The next one is a Polaroid of two women—the wraithlike, coked-up Bettina, eyes enormous, her arm around a juicier version of the dead woman, making out in a halfhearted way. But that's Shelley, not Michelle Smith. A brief favorite of Val's long ago. Lord, Heloise hasn't thought about her in, well, forever.

Heloise has been so sure of her absolute innocence in whatever matter was at hand that she hasn't asked Tyner what to do if asked about something she doesn't wish to discuss. She has to make a split-second decision. She goes to her default. She lies.

"No," she says.

"You sure?"

"Pretty sure." Michelle Smith. A different name, and she looks so different. She hasn't aged well at all. Funny, she got so thin and Bettina got so plump—

"You have something in common."

Heloise wonders if she is going to throw up, and if she can plead food poisoning if she does. "Really?"

"She's on the visitors list for a convicted killer named Valentine Day Deluca."

Don't say his full name, she wants to warn automatically. Instead she allows herself to furrow her brow as if she's trying to be a good Girl Scout, put together these connections.

"You are, too."

She is so well trained she won't even affirm this until Tyner makes eye contact and nods.

"Yes, I am."

"Why?"

"Because I visit him."

"I mean, why do you visit him?"

"I knew him."

"Were you one of his whores?"

"I was his girlfriend." It's hard not to say this without laughing. Still, they can't prove she was a prostitute. She was never arrested, not even once. The closest she came was the time she shoplifted the home pregnancy kit. And she knows Tom won't give her up, to anyone, not even to another cop. "His work life—I admit I turned a blind eye, tried to ignore what was right in front of me."

"He's a pretty bad guy. How did a nice lady like you ever become involved with him?"

"I was very young when I came to Baltimore. Also very broke and very desperate. I didn't have the best taste in companions. Val's arrest set me straight, made me see that I needed to get out and start over."

"Why do you still visit him?"

"I was under the impression he didn't have anyone. Now I know different." *Why was Shelley visiting him?*

"But you didn't know her?"

"I might have met her, but it was a very long time ago and I don't remember much about her."

"And the other woman in the photo?"

She shrugs as if she doesn't even understand the question.

"Did you know her?"

"I don't think so, no." She's still trying to process the fact that Shelley is *the* Suburban Madam. Shelley is on Val's visiting list. That's the only reason Heloise is here. This so-called detective doesn't have an inkling what she does. Yet.

And then her brain adds, *Shelley was murdered.*

"It's a weird thing about the photo," Jolson says. "It was on the seat beside her, in the car. Like it mattered. If it had been a suicide, it would be sentimental. But we never thought it was a suicide. And you know what? I don't think whoever did it wanted us to think it was a suicide. The person who killed her—this is either someone excessively stupid or someone who just doesn't give a shit that we know it's a murder. It was almost like he—or she—was offering us a little cover by putting her in the car, giving us some lead time. Very deliberate. So why would this person leave the photo there?"

184

Heloise maintains eye contact, unafraid to let Jolson see her disdain. Her complete lack of interest, which is not the same thing as disinterest. *Why the fuck would I know, asshole?*

"Michelle Smith is connected to Valentine Deluca," Jolson says. "So are you. I'm not sure anyone expected us to figure that out. But maybe they did and you're supposed to be able to tell us who the other woman is. What do you think, Heloise?"

"I don't know," she says. "I'm not very good at things like this. That's why I'm not a detective."

"But as a concerned citizen—"

"I'm not," she says.

"You're not?"

Well, that had come out wrong.

"I'm very sorry someone has been murdered," she says. "I wish I could help. But I know nothing about Michelle Smith."

"Didn't even know she was visiting the man you visited?"

"I had no clue." She's being honest there.

"There's nothing you want to tell me?"

She has stood to go, figuring it's the one thing she can do that Tyner can't.

"No, no. Come to think of it, there is one more thing." Tyner has grabbed her elbow, his grip almost painful, but she won't stop talking. "I would hope that this woman's professional life wouldn't blind you to the fact that there could be other people who wanted to kill her, for other reasons. I'm afraid all you see is a dead prostitute."

"And what do you see?"

"A dead woman."

But also: a woman sitting on Val's lap the night he shot Martin, whispering in his ear, consoling him. Shelley. Yet it was meaningless. He never cared about Shelley.

So why was she on his visitors list? Why did someone leave a photograph of Shelley with Bettina?

"A dead woman," she repeats. "It's tragic, and I hope you figure out what happened, but I really don't see how I can be of any help. I'm afraid this is nothing more than a coincidence."

Someone's daughter, someone's sister, someone's mother. That's what she'd said to the snooty woman in the Starbucks, the one who wanted Heloise to disavow the Suburban Madam when she was a stranger to her.

And now she has done exactly that.

"You got fat," Val said.

"A little."

"I never would have let you run yourself down that way."

"Anxiety eating. I was so worried—"

"And now you're fat and I'm in prison for life, so all the eating in the world didn't solve a thing, did it?"

"No." She hung her head as if ashamed, but she was relieved that Val believed her puffy body was the result of bad eating habits.

Scott had been born only seven weeks ago, on the final day of the year. "Oh, look," the nurse said. "He showed up in time to give you a tax deduction. How considerate."

It had been a long, hard labor, almost thirty-six hours, complicated by the fact that Hector decided to die in the middle of it, almost as if he were giving up his place in line to his grandson. Beth, forced to choose between life and death in a way almost no one ever is, not really, decided she'd rather be at Hector's bedside. Helen understood. Sort of. She even believed that it was probably the best choice, a dying man's final hours over a baby's seeming infinite number to come.

Besides, Beth might as well get used to not seeing Scott, because Heloise didn't intend for her mother to spend any time with him at all, once she was cleared by the doctors to head back to Baltimore.

Considerate, the nurse had said, and Scott was that. Ten pounds at birth, he began sleeping through the night before he was a month old. But the delivery hurt. Lord, it hurt. Heloise had believed there was no new pain or indignity that could be visited on her body at this point in her life. Men had pretty much punished every inch of it over the years, but here were completely new sensations. Perhaps there were always new pains, fresh injuries that one couldn't imagine.

But this was the only pain that brought joy. Pure, uncomplicated, terrifying joy. She would show her mother how it was done, what a woman was supposed to be to her child. And the first step of that was to cut her mother completely out of her life.

Val's case went to the jury about a week after Heloise brought Scott home. They deliberated for three days, which his lawyer thought a good sign. But the jurors returned a guilty verdict, and he was given the death penalty. The news jolted her. She realized she didn't want Val to die. She just wanted him to stay inside forever and ever.

The news jolted Val, too. He was furious, but his anger had nowhere to go. George I was in prison, somewhere on the Eastern Shore. That didn't mean he was safe from Val's wrath, or so Val said, but there would be no face-to-face retribution. The confidential informant had died in the autumn, as Tom had promised. Bettina, the fake informant to the fake informant, was long gone, almost certainly dead from her own bad habits. Still, Val focused angrily on her. How could she have known where he had hidden the gun? She was an idiot. Had Helen ever noticed her looking for anything in the garden?

She almost started to say, *But it wasn't in the garden—it was in a copse of trees at the edge of the property.* She could no longer remember if that information had been shared, discussed. Would she know that? Should she know that?

"Stupid people make discoveries all the time," she offered instead. "They just don't see the bigger picture. That's what makes them stupid."

He liked this answer. It fit with Val's sense of himself—a smart person who saw the big picture and the tiny details. No one had outwitted him. He had just been unlucky.

"So what are you going to do?" he asked Helen.

"Figure out a way to make a living." She remembered that Val thought she'd been doing that all along. "I'm not cut out for the street life, Val. I'm just not. I stayed independent, thinking you would be free, but now—" She shrugged. She noticed a dampness in her bra and prayed that she wouldn't spurt breast milk in front of Val. She had fed Scott before she left her mother's house, pumped in a truck-stop restroom. She hunched over, as if ashamed of her body.

Val gave her an appraising look. "You doing as well as you used to?"

"No." That was honest at least.

"You ought to consider moving into the management side of things."

"You mean—" They had never used the word "pimp." Val found it undignified. Not to mention incomplete. He had a lot of operations going. His hospitality business—his term—was only one facet. Again, his term.

"You mean do what you did?"

"No, that's the wrong model for you. How are you going to offer protection? Or intimidate anyone? If you tried to run a straightforward business like mine, the girls would end up ripping you off because there would be no downside to it."

"I'm not soft."

"No, you're not. But you don't scare people either. Anyway, I've been thinking. I have a lot of time to think. You know this Amazon.com?"

She was surprised he did. Why would Val know about a bookstore, much less an online enterprise? He knew almost nothing about computers.

"A guy in here, he told me about it. The business model was really simple. They started with books because they're portable, easy to ship, never spoil. But now they're moving into all sorts of things. They got an auction site, they're selling CDs now. They're going to sell everything one day."

She couldn't follow his train of thought.

"It's the future," he said. "And it's perfect for escort services. I'll show you how to do it—in exchange for a share." A beat. "A big share. A forever share."

"Why do you need money?"

"Because I'm not going to be in here forever." Val had high hopes for his appeal, too high in almost everyone's opinion. Only Helen would be unsurprised when he got his death penalty knocked down to life. Unsurprised and strangely relieved.

At the time Helen didn't even own a computer. She couldn't begin to understand how she would set up a Web site, generate traffic to a site without risk. She and Val agreed that she should apprentice herself to someone who was beginning to make use of these tools—then steal every idea and customer she could.

Her unwitting mentor called herself Madame Dundee. She worked out of a Catonsville storefront that did psychic readings. That was clever, Helen had to give her that. Madame Dundee's Web site asked all sorts of questions about "love": *Have you met your true love? What will she look like? How will you know her?* The use of the feminine pronouns should have been a tip-off; men do not go to psychics asking questions about love. Men who contacted the service were asked to come in for a reading. Madame Dundee had a special tarot deck, featuring photographs of her girls. She laid out the cards in the traditional format, and the gentleman indicated which card was to his liking. He picked a girl and a service.

"Aw, the Queen of Cups," she might say, "and the Hanged Man. Yes, I see a big love in your future."

The man, if he was a return customer, would then be ushered into a lounge behind the parlor, meet his girl, and go upstairs. It was an all-cash business, which made it easier for the girls to earn extra behind Madame Dundee's back. Helen was not one of the more popular ones, not at first, which was new and humbling for her. Val encouraged her not to brood on the problem but to address it as she would a bad evaluation from a boss. What could she do better?

She lost her pregnancy weight and used her earnings to improve herself as she could. Her teeth had never been properly cared for. She got them whitened but decided against veneers. The idea of taking one's real teeth down to stubs to make them look healthy—the paradox gave her chills. She began getting regular facials, expensive treatments for her skin. Her skin was her business, her business was her skin. If she had been motivated by sheer vanity alone, she never would have taken the time, much less the money, to do these things. But one had to reinvest capital. Helen put her money into herself and waited, knowing that her time would come.

Madame Dundee was busted, eventually. She made the mistake of not reporting the bulk of her income, thinking her all-cash enterprise would protect her. Helen, meanwhile, was dutifully filing quarterly taxes, claiming she was employed as a freelance masseuse. She didn't report all her income, but she reported most of it.

"Proving someone is having money for sex is hard," Val counseled her. "But mail fraud, income-tax evasion—those things are easier to prove and carry real time. Don't be stupid. Don't be greedy."

With Madame Dundee busted, it was time for Helen to make her move. She was ready now. Val agreed. But she didn't want to do it as Madame Dundee had, maintaining a physical space. It was too much of a risk. It was also too much overhead. But she also would never conduct business in her home, not with Scott there. She needed to use hotels, or have clients who could afford them.

"This is what you do," Val told her. He had ideas about everything. She leaned her head toward the glass, eager to absorb what he knew. Unconsciously he mirrored her posture, and their foreheads inclined toward each other, only the glass between them. Val was not in prison, Helen told herself, because he was stupid about business. He was here because had lost his temper over something silly and inconsequential. Men and their stupid pride. If Helen had picked up a gun every time her pride had been wounded, she would have killed half a dozen or so people by now. *Bam-bam*, Daddy. *Bam-bam*, Barbara Lewis, and here's a volley of shots for your horrible sons, who yell at me in the street. (She would spare the youngest, Meghan, who was too polite or too scared to taunt her.) *Bam*, Billy, and maybe Billy's mother, too. *Bam*, Bettina, for trying to beat her up that time, and *Bam* for every girl who thought she could displace Helen as Val's favorite.

Bam, Val.

But she had as good as killed him when she put him here. Did that make it hypocritical to take his advice, to let him instruct her in how to set up her own illegal enterprise?

Probably. But if there were no hypocrisy in the world, there wouldn't be any prostitutes.

Monday, October 17

The restaurant on Thirty-ninth Street has had many lives, but Heloise still remembers it as Jeannier's. Val took her there once, as a treat. It was an odd thing for him to do. He didn't like to go out, he didn't care about food, and he wasn't particularly interested in making her happy. But he had been away for almost a month, and he seemed unusually solicitous upon his return. So he took her to Jeannier's, where he solved the problem of not being able to read the menu by telling the waiter to bring whatever he thought best, the specialties of the house. These included sweetbreads, which neither Val nor Heloise had ever had. They liked them, and Heloise, still Helen, decided to risk appearing ignorant and ask if the "bread" was the crispy coating. Once the dish was explained to her, she felt queasy. Val teased her. "You liked it going down," he said. "Why does knowing what it is change that?"

A good question, in all things.

But now Jeannier's is Italian, less grand to her eye, although perhaps that's a reflection on her, the restaurants she has seen, the meals she has eaten since that night almost thirteen years ago. She wonders why Sophie has chosen this particular place. She thought she would prefer the most expensive spot possible, soak Heloise for the cost of a pricey meal with wine. Heloise hadn't wanted a meal at all, only a meeting, and had asked if they could do it at lunch. Sophie insisted on dinner. She is dictating all the terms—the place, the time.

Sophie arrives twenty minutes late. Her apartment is around the corner; she could have crawled here in that amount of time. She orders a martini. Heloise, a forty-minute drive home looming at the end of the meal, is allowing herself one glass of wine, no more.

"You look well," she tells Sophie.

"Not really. I just don't look as sick as you think I should," Sophie says.

She really does look fine. If one didn't know of Sophie's former glory, she might even seem reasonably attractive. But the lusciousness is gone. She's like a piece of fruit on its way to being overripe. There's no visible decay, but you wouldn't want to bite into her for fear that the sensation would be mushy and mealy.

"Leo tells me you want workers' comp." Heloise has decided, for now, not to mention what else transpired during Leo's visit.

"I'm entitled, under the law. It was a direct consequence of my work for you."

"Not necessarily. You know that none of your clients came back positive, right?"

"Did everyone get tested?"

Sophie has her there, not that Heloise will ever admit it. "The bottom line is, it's incumbent on you to prove that this is work-related, and you can't do that. It's like if someone threw out his back at home, he can't get compensation from his employer just because he works on a loading dock."

"I didn't have any contact that wasn't through the firm," Sophie says. "Firm" is the nomenclature on which Heloise has always insisted. It's a good sign, she thinks, that Sophie is still using it.

"Did you share needles?"

"I don't use needles. You know I'm not a junkie."

Heloise did know. Like Val, she won't tolerate drug use among her employees. Still, a few girls have slipped through from time to time.

"I've gone over this with Leo," Sophie continues. "Workers' comp is my best bet. It's for life. No one can ever take it away from me."

"It's for life if you can prove a permanent disability," says Heloise, who has studied the law in preparation for this discussion. She quotes from the state Web site: "'Both arms, both eyes, both feet, both hands, both legs; or a combination of any two of the following: an arm, eye, foot, hand or leg.' I don't think vagina counts."

"Well, it would be interesting to find out, don't you think? Besides, it's my only option. Unless"—she gives Heloise her best look, the one that once melted every man and almost every woman in her life—"you want to give me a large enough cash settlement so I won't have to do that."

"You're blackmailing me."

"I don't see it that way. I am entitled to workers' comp. I got sick on the job. You're lucky I don't go to one of the big asbestos lawyers, start a class-action suit."

"I'm not Beth Steel, Sophie. If you go to the state, I'll be shut down, and then there's no money for anyone."

"Then I guess you'd better come up with a solution."

Sophie has ordered an enormous amount of food—two appetizers, a salad, and an entrée—and she seems to take great pleasure, as the meal proceeds, in wasting it all, taking a bite here and there, mucking her fork through things so they can't even be carried away in doggie bags. She's already establishing her right to use Heloise's money as she sees fit. Few things make Heloise angrier than someone presuming to waste anything of hers—money, time, energy.

"And what if the business just goes away?"

Sophie looks scornful. "What else would you do? You didn't even graduate high school."

Heloise had been parrying, trying to find a foothold in the argument. Val persuaded her a long time ago that no one can afford to be blackmailed, that you have to find a way to end the threat before it gets too far. But what leverage does she have over Sophie?

"Do your parents know you're ill?"

"I don't talk to them anymore."

This is sadly typical, a commonality among almost every girl who has worked for her. They're not close to their parents. To anyone. It's true of Heloise, too.

"Sophie, I understand that you're scared. You think money will make you less fearful, but I simply don't have it. The firm isn't as profitable as you think."

"Leo says you live pretty well."

Ah, here it is. She is dealing with two punks, not one. "What else does Leo say?"

Sophie leans across the table. "He says he loves me. He says he'll do whatever he can to help me. He says it even when I'm *not* blowing him."

"Isn't he scared of being infected?"

"We practice safe sex."

"If only you had done the same when you were working."

"Don't be so prim, Heloise. You all but told me it was a way to sweeten what I earned, to make up for the obscene cut you take."

"It's not obscene. I provide a lot for what I take. The clients, security. All the overhead is on me."

"Yes, you keep the girls in the dark as much as possible. We don't know one another, can never compare notes. Divide and conquer, right? But Leo knows everything."

"Leo knows what's on the ledger. That's all. He's seen the books for a lobbying firm and a personal shopping service."

"It's enough."

"I don't think so."

"Well, I guess we'll find out, won't we? I want a half million, Heloise—and for you to continue paying for my meds, whatever happens. My meds, then a monthly stipend. I know you don't have that much cash on hand, but Leo thinks the house will get that much, and you don't have a huge mortgage."

"Where will I live?"

"Not my problem," Sophie said. "Figure out a way to

meet my demands by Thanksgiving or I file a claim with workers' comp. Look, I'm not stupid. I know I won't get anything from the state. But I will get famous. The story will go everywhere—the sex worker with HIV, demanding equal treatment under the law. You could argue that I should go straight to Plan B, not ever bother messing with you, that's it more lucrative for me in the long run."

"How so?"

"A book deal, a movie deal, who knows? The sky's the limit."

She orders dessert, tiramisu, and takes exactly one bite from one ladyfinger.

Heloise calls Leo on the drive home. She says his services will no longer be required. Attempted rape might have been overlooked if he'd apologized convincingly, but telling someone about her personal finances is unforgivable. Tomorrow she will have Tyner follow up, send Leo a scary-proper letter reminding him of the confidentiality agreement he signed when she hired him. She doesn't vent or say anything about the meeting with Sophie. She doesn't tell him he's an idiot, that she now realizes Sophie will use him up and throw him away like the condoms she should have used for her work.

At home, Scott wants to show her things he has found on YouTube, including a lot of programs he loved when he was younger. One of the hardest things about raising Scott was having no real base on which to build, no role model. That had been one of the rare advantages of having her half sister

Meghan living nearby. Meghan was a wretched person but a good mother, a combination that Heloise had not realized was possible. She wondered if that meant it was possible to be a good person and a wretched mother. Possibly, although she doubts it.

As a self-taught mother, she was a reborn child. She and Scott had watched things and read things that seemed odd to others, such as the Mary Martin version of *Peter Pan*. Now someone had transferred it to YouTube, complete if fuzzy in picture and sound, and Scott was delighted with this bit of piracy about pirates, so delighted that Heloise didn't want to lecture him about property rights. He showed her their favorite part of all, Captain Hook's tarantella. She had forgotten his little dip of melancholia in the middle, his realization that he could be victorious but still not be beloved. "That's where the canker g-naws."

"G-naws," Scott repeats, knowing it is one of her favorite lines, and she tries to smile, focus on him, but her mind keeps drifting back to Sophie. The dig about her education is what really hurt. For almost a decade, she has helped girls fund and finish the education she was denied. True, she never got a real M.B.A., but she had taken courses online and worked her way through list after list of so-called Great Books. She read the newspaper carefully. She was better informed on current events than almost anyone she knew. To have Sophie laugh at her, to throw her lack of formal education in her face—

That's where the canker gnaws.

She wanders over to the Mom cubbyhole. The envelope

from Pennsylvania, the one she is sure she shoved into a drawer, is on top. It hasn't been opened, best she can tell. Was Scott snooping? Audrey? It didn't seem like something either one would do. She plays with the glue on the seal. It opens with suspicious ease, but—it's a cheap envelope. Of course her mother would buy a cheap envelope. Heloise looks at the handwriting, so neat and orderly, a relic of days when penmanship was an entry on one's report card. The words suck her in; she reads in spite of herself.

Shit.

"Mom—that's a five-dollar fine," Scott says, pointing to the curse jar instituted by Audrey. Heloise wasn't even aware that she had spoken out loud.

"Bath time," she says.

"Five-dollar curse word," Scott replies, making her laugh. Audrey doesn't think it's funny at all when Scott does that—"It's just like saying the curse, if you ask me"—but Heloise can't help admiring the way he has figured out the loophole in Audrey's plan. It's not as if profanity is a problem in this household.

Once she hears the water running, she picks up the phone and calls Audrey, who is enjoying her girl's night out—one girl, singular, an evening that usually revolves around Chick-fil-A and a movie—and asks her to juggle the schedule for the day after next, subbing out Heloise's two appointments, picking up Scott from soccer, although chances are she will return in time. Lord, she hopes it doesn't take more than a few hours.

"Where are you going?" Audrey asks, probably stunned

that Heloise would allow any of her girls to take on these two appointments, regulars of whom she's quite fond.

Where indeed? She doesn't even want to say the town's name, much less refer to it as home. "I have to settle an old account," she says at last.

Motherhood was a revelation to Helen. Scott was a dream baby. He had a sweet, logical nature and seldom seemed to want things he couldn't have. He was mellow during diaper changes, loved bath time, went to sleep with a gurgle of pleasure, then awakened the same way twelve hours later.

It was the hardest fucking thing she had ever done in her life.

Being alone was what made it hard, although Helen doubted that things would be much better with a husband, unless she had one of those touchy-feely ones, and she had a feeling she would never end up with one of the touchy-feely ones. Even Tom, who still came around to check on her and had started throwing her longing looks, wouldn't be a hands-on dad. From what she heard—really, overheard, because she could not afford to make close friends—from the mothers who crossed her path, the hands-on father might be a bit of a unicorn. Everyone wanted to believe in it, but no one had actually seen one.

Still, it would be nice to have someone other than paid baby-sitters to spell her. To sleep in on Mother's Day, to have someone hold the baby while she took a shower or even a pee. Now that Scott was more than a year old, she sometimes found herself holding him on her lap while she went to the bathroom, which made her think of the wildly dysfunctional things mothers did in novels where their little boys grew up to be serial killers. She could prevent Scott from knowing what Mommy did for a living, but she couldn't shield him from the fact that she also was in thrall to certain bodily functions.

She read books. She had always read books. But in this circumstance the books let her down. She needed more from them. She also needed less. More practical advice, less generic hysteria. What she required was a very particular volume, written just for her: *What to Expect from Your Toddler When You Are Trying to Put Together Your Own Escort Service.*

First there was the matter of the baby-sitter. She wanted someone trustworthy yet capable of not noticing anything about Helen's life. It frightened her, bringing a stranger into her home. But it was an unavoidable risk. She interviewed several girls from the local community college and UMBC, hiring the incurious one who never stopped talking about herself. Helen didn't like her much, but at least she could be certain that this girl would never notice anything.

Helen and Scott were living in Catonsville now, not that far from where Madame Dundee had plied her trade and her tarot cards. It was a pretty suburb, very grand in places. Helen rented a small house on one of the more modest blocks. She chose the house for the neighbors— none on one side, an elderly couple behind her, an elderly woman on the other side. She thought long and hard about what kind of relationship she should have with them. Her neighbors didn't venture out much, especially the one who lived alone. They had lawn services, so there were no conversations along the back or the side fence. They did not bring Helen gifts when she moved in, or make a call to introduce themselves, or offer assistance. Helen supposed most people would have found that daunting, but it was exactly the kind of coolness she required.

And yet—she felt she should be on good terms with them. She introduced herself and explained that she had a toddler but hoped he wouldn't be a nuisance. (As if sweet Scott could ever be a nuisance.) She carried their newspapers to the doorstep on inclement days. She offered to run errands. The couple declined all her offers, politely. They were a self-contained unit, together almost sixty years, not even particularly perturbed by the infrequency with which they saw their grown children. They were like two trees that had grown together, and they would probably topple together.

But the woman living alone, Mrs. Sampson, brightened at any attention from Helen. And if Scott was with Helen, Mrs. Sampson lowered herself to the floor, all seventy-five creaking years, and tried to engage him. Scott was cool to strangers, but he was kind to Mrs. Sampson. He scooted around the rug in her living room, offering her found treasures from among her own things—a magazine, a piece of lint, the back of an earring that had probably lived in the rug for decades.

"His father is—" Mrs. Sampson probed with delicacy.

"A redhead, too," Helen said.

"I mean—where is he?"

"Dead," Helen said, flinching at how cold her voice sounded. She would have to pretend greater affection for this mythical creature once Scott was old enough to ask and wonder.

"Oh, I'm so sorry. How long has it been?"

"Before Scott was born."

"That must have been horrible."

"Yes." Right, yes. It would be especially horrible to lose a beloved husband in the early weeks of a pregnancy. Helen had so little cause to speak of her circumstances that she had not thought of the emotional authenticity she must bring to the story.

"What happened?"

"An accident."

That was good enough for Mrs. Sampson. But others might not be so easily satisfied. Helen needed a story at once more precise and generic.

"I can't imagine."

"Neither could I—until it happened to me."

They both watched Scott, scooting across the floor with impressive speed. He found many dangerous things in Mrs. Sampson's house, but Helen knew it was her responsibility to protect him there. Mrs. Sampson had no reason to baby-proof her house.

"I hope he had life insurance," Mrs. Sampson said.

"No, I'm afraid he didn't. That's why I have to work."

She saw the question hurtling toward her, realized she had seconds to come up with an answer. It didn't have to be the forever-and-ever answer, but she would need one eventually. She would never be nostalgic for her time in Val's house, but it was easier when someone else was the boss.

"What do you do?"

"I'm a librarian," she said, thinking of the sweet boy she had known at the Enoch Pratt Library. "But I'm going back to school to get my M.B.A."

The latter was not quite true. Helen had started taking classes online but had to settle for an unaccredited program, one that didn't require a transcript.

"How marvelous," Mrs. Sampson said. "You young girls today—so much ambition. I was a teacher. What will you do with your M.B.A.?"

What would she do? She realized at that moment that she had a tiny fantasy, so deep inside that she hadn't admitted it to herself. She had thought she might go out into the world and look for a real job, that the online degree, phony as it was, could be her passport to a straight life. But it would mean working for someone, and while there were advantages to not being the boss, Helen was finding she *liked* being the boss. She had three girls working for her. Like her baby-sitter, they had been recruited from the local colleges, only with a very different ad. A subtle blurb in the classifieds, because she was looking for subtle girls. The ad had promised "freedom" and "flexible hours" for "just the right girl," someone "outgoing." A "people person." Of those who had applied, a few assumed it was some sort of sales job. They weren't right for her. Others knew exactly what they were signing up for but were simply not attractive enough. Finally Helen found three beauties who got it, who wanted to work much less and make much more.

In each case the girls she ended up hiring put the cards on the table first. "This is an escort service, right?"

"What makes you think so?" Helen asked. She met them in a downtown hotel, over coffee. She wore a suit, one tailored to emphasize her figure, and put her hair up. The concierge in the hotel was one of her contacts, and the waitstaff knew exactly how much attention to lavish on her. The smart girls took this all in, but they weren't particularly awed. They were pretty. They had grown blasé when it came to special treatment.

No matter how well the conversations went, Helen didn't commit herself, not during that first interview. She culled the best ones, then set up dinner appointments where specifics were discussed. The final "interview" was a date with one of her regulars, Dwayne. A carryover from her Madame Dundee days, he was comfortable with Helen watching the date on a closed-circuit television. Four girls made it to that part, but she had to drop one, who was unnerved by the knowledge that she was being watched. If she was that prissy with gentle Dwayne, she wasn't tough enough.

Eventually the girls asked her advice about how to explain their flush incomes and short hours. What should they tell their friends, their parents, about their part-time jobs? Helen had been wrestling with this for several weeks, counseling them simply to not talk, but she knew that did not come naturally to beautiful young women. And now here was Mrs. Sampson asking the same thing. Helen needed a better answer.

The question continued to plague her, even as she took on new clients. While most escort services rely heavily on impulse buys, men reaching for the phone in an hour of need, Helen was determined to reduce risk by working with as many regulars as possible, cultivating men who were committed to paid sex the way some men are committed to golf. One of her new clients was Paul. She asked to meet him in public before committing to a date; she wanted to test his temperament, see if he was the nervous type. There were, in Helen's assessment, three types of public figures to avoid: The super famous, who are always under scrutiny. Really not a risk for her, although the hotel concierges sometimes made inquiries for big-name actors. Hypocrites, whose public images are based on being do-gooders. They're juicy targets, too. Finally Helen was determined to avoid the kind of nervous Nellies who would be too quick to flip, cooperate with an investigation to save themselves. She wanted to see how Paul would behave with her in public, if he could lie as smoothly and well as she could.

"Everyone's going to think you're a lobbyist," he joked when they walked into the Maryland Inn. She knew the term in the vague way that most Americans knew the term—something unsavory yet legal, people in the employ of special interests. In some ways the lobbying profession was held in even lower esteem than hers, which she found intriguing. But the trick was to create a professional identity about which people had no questions. If she said, *I'm a lobbyist,* people would say, *For what causes?*

She needed to encourage people's lack of interest in her, to create the professional equivalent of what her father had called her *nothing face.* What was it that bored people? Other people, in her experience.

One day, heading for an appointment in an Annapolis hotel, a Paul referral, she saw a short, stocky woman in a red suit having coffee with two delegates in the lobby. The men could not have been more obviously bored—glancing at their watches, using their BlackBerrys. The woman suffered their rudeness in good humor, waiting her turn to speak as they spoke on their cell phones or interrupted her to glad-hand others passing through the hotel. The woman reminded Helen of an exceptionally well-trained dog, one who sat and waited for his treat despite having a mercurial master who might not remember the treat at all. She was the kind of dog one saw lashed to street signs outside coffee-houses and bars, left alone for hours, hopeful and forlorn.

An hour later, her appointment done, Helen waited in the same valet line as the woman in the red suit. Helen, who never spoke to anyone, found herself wanting to talk to this woman, to ask about what she did.

"I saw you meeting with Rheems and Jones," she said with a sympathetic smile, as if she knew how difficult they were. Rheems was, actually, forever disputing the time. She asked her girls to take kitchen timers to their meetings with him.

The woman smiled and sighed simultaneously. "They're

not bad guys. It's my job to make them care about what I care about. That's what I get paid for. But women's issues—they never seem to be in vogue down here. When the economy is good, all these guys want to do is make sure they get their pork, and when it's bad, they say there's no political will to change things. They like to think that everything got solved back in 1968 and there's nothing left to talk about."

"You lobby for women?"

"Officially, no. I represent tech-industry people who want to address the lack of women in their field. Women are still overwhelmingly employed in so-called pink-collar jobs—"

Helen wondered if her job counted as a pink-collar job. Certainly the field was dominated by women. She always thought part of the reason prostitution was illegal was that so few men could make a living at it. Criminalized, it created jobs for men like Val, but legalized— She realized that even she was tuning out this nice, well-meaning woman.

"Well," she said lamely, "keep up the good work."

"You, too," the woman said. "You, too."

Had she really mistaken Helen for one of her own? Helen looked down at her own red suit, the white silk blouse buttoned to the throat, the heels high enough to flatter her calves but not so high that anyone would call them fuck-me pumps. If a lobbyist thought Helen was a lobbyist, why couldn't she be one?

By the time the valet pulled Helen's car around, she had named her new business, the Women's Full Employment Network. It took its initials from the radio station to which she had listened so many years ago, WFEN, the home of those soupy, soppy ballads meant to cheer women as they prepared dinner and cleaned the kitchen. It worked just as Helen hoped. All she had to say was "income parity" and everyone was ready to change the conversation.

Wednesday, October 19

It is easy to date Heloise's last journey home: It was for Scott's birth and Hector's death, at the dawn of the new millennium. She is not officially estranged from her mother. Beth has her address—well, the P.O. box where Heloise receives her mail, hating the use of communal mailboxes in Turner's Grove. She sends Christmas cards and birthday cards, presumably. "Presumably" because they go straight into the shredder. It's not just easier for Heloise to allow Scott to believe that his grandmother is dead. It's safer. If Scott met his grandmother, he would want to know about his grandfather, and Heloise could never stomach the lies that Beth would tell, the endless rationalizations about how misunderstood he was.

But now, as she heads north on a brilliant autumn day, Heloise finds herself worrying about how isolated Scott is. One parent, no siblings, no grandparents. He was thrilled, during the years that her half sister lived nearby, to discover his four first cousins. He still visits them, down in Florida. Heloise isn't crazy about that arrangement, but it means the world to Scott. Besides, Meghan has her own secrets, and they have an understanding: Heloise won't disturb the neat fictions of Meghan's life, and Meghan won't poke at the web of lies holding Heloise's together.

The two women don't like each other. Fact is, they despise each other. But they respect each other, Hector Lewis's two daughters, not even six months apart. And if anything should happen to Heloise, Meghan will be Scott's guardian. At least that's Heloise's plan. For all her discipline and organization, Heloise has never named a guardian for Scott nor drawn up a will, although she has spoken to Tyner about her general desires. She has life insurance, a good sum, purchased when she was in her early thirties, and Scott is the beneficiary. Still, like everyone, she has a hard time planning for her own death. Even now, knowing that Shelley was murdered, she doesn't feel vulnerable. *She* wasn't in the photo.

Her town is little changed. It's a small town, by anyone's standards, not even twenty-five thousand people, a number that has stayed static since the middle of the twentieth century. Nothing really changes here, although the neighborhood where she grew up looks improved, spruced up—except for her mother's house.

She rings the bell and does not know what to do with the woman who answers the door. Hug her? No. Shake her hand? No. They stand, arms by their sides. Despite her mother's stooped shoulders and gray-brown hair, Heloise sees similarities between them that she never noticed when she was young. Nothing Face, meet Nothing Face.

"Thank you for coming, Helen," her mother says. Her meekness is irritating. Heloise enters the room, glancing at the clock with the mirror that still hangs in the stairwell landing. Her mother stays loyal to *everything*.

"Would you like lunch? I've put out a spread."

Heloise wants to say no, to hurry through this meeting, but she finds herself unexpectedly hungry for her mother's food—the German potato salad, the bowl of Utz potato chips, the hearty sandwiches, local pickles. She sits at the kitchen table and can almost remember the relatively nice days, before the bad times began.

Almost.

"Soda?" Her mother proffers generic cans from the Giant. "I've got one lemon-lime, one black cherry. You gave me so little notice I didn't have time to get to the store."

"Sure. I'll take whichever one you don't want." Heloise ends up with the black cherry, although she suspects it's what her mother prefers, that she can't help giving her daughter what she thinks is the better of the two choices. Lord, the endlessly twisted passivity of women, the inability to say, *I want this.* She tells her mother to take the soda she wants. Her mother thinks she's lying and gives her the soda she actually wants, assuming that's what anyone would want. And Heloise really preferred the lemon-lime. It's exhausting, this relationship.

"So what's the problem? Why do you have to sell the house? Are you being evicted?" The house should have been paid off long ago, but Beth is the kind of financial naïf who would have borrowed against a house in the boom times, then ended upside down in it.

"No, I'm fine, moneywise. For now."

"Then why are you moving? Why did you summon me here?"

Her mother stares into space as if she can no longer remember. She seems far away, lost in some private reverie. She sighs, shakes her head, brings herself back.

"I have ALS. Lou Gehrig's disease. In a typical diagnosis, that means I have three to five years."

"Three to five years to what?"

"Three to five years to live."

The news jolts Heloise. She's not sure she can burn through all her hate for her mother in that period of time.

"Typical—what determines if a case is typical?"

"That's not predictable." Her mother's voice takes on her professional tone, her nurse voice, soothing a patient's family, although she is the patient and Heloise is all the family she has. "Twenty percent live more than five years. Ten percent live up to ten years. And five percent live more than twenty years. But I think we both know I've never been one out of five, or even one out of twenty. I have to prepare for when I can't take care of myself."

"What does that mean?"

"Well, I'm selling the house and moving into an apartment. Something on one floor. The money from the house, along with what I get from Social Security disability, will mean I can afford assisted living."

"I can help," Heloise says, wondering if it's even true. She still hasn't figured out what to do with Sophie.

"That's not why I asked you to come see me."

"Why, then?"

"I want you to help me kill myself, when the time comes."

Her mother's manner is calm, resigned, as if she's asking

216

for nothing more than a commitment to a potluck dinner. She actually seems happy.

"Are you absolutely sure of the diagnosis? I mean, no offense to the local hospital, but—"

"I went to Hopkins for a second opinion."

She thinks of her mother at the Baltimore hospital, not even a mile from where Val is in prison. Depending on the day, they might have passed on the street, the highway.

"Why can't you be one of the five percent? Isn't there some drug for ALS?"

"Only one. It's a thousand dollars a month."

"You have insurance, right? And again, I can help—"

Her mother shakes her head. "No. That's not what I want. I want to die, Helen."

"That's a terrible thing to say."

"Is it? My husband died more than a decade ago. My only daughter doesn't speak to me, and my grandson thinks I'm dead. He does, doesn't he? That's why he never writes, never acknowledges the birthday cards. I mean, I know it's not much, the five- and ten-dollar bills I send, but I know you, Helen. You're proper. You care about appearances. You've raised him to write thank-you notes, I bet."

She has, actually. And now she feels guilty about the money, insignificant as it was, that has passed through her shredder because she never opened the envelopes.

"Well, now you'll get to make your story true. Frankly, I thought you'd enjoy it."

Why does she feel guilty? Her mother is the one who should be squirming, the one who should be held to account. Her mother sat by while her father pushed her down the road that would destroy her—into Il Cielo, into Billy's arms, which led to Val. Passive for most of her life, Beth wants credit for being active now, for choosing her death?

"It was easier," she says. "Not seeing you. For a lot of reasons. You can't blame me for feeling that way."

"I don't. But you know what, Helen? There's going to come a time when you won't blame me anymore. I did the best I could. I really did."

"You stayed with an abusive man who started abusing me. You let him undercut my education, make me take that stupid job—"

"All true, all true. But you know, I worked my way through nursing school when I had a baby. A part-time job wasn't the end of the world."

"Billy was."

"Who chose him, Helen? Who sneaked out to see him? That's one area of your life where listening to your father wouldn't have been the worst idea in the world. If Hector knew anything, it was that a man could ruin a girl's life."

It's hard to remain at the table. She wants to flee her mother's house, escape this conversation. She's not at fault. It couldn't possibly be her fault.

"Mother, do you know what I do for a living?"

"No. I Googled you one time, but I didn't find anything."

Heloise has designed her life for just that answer, but now it feels like the saddest accomplishment in the world, a statement of nonexistence. Invisible to Google.

218

"I own my own business. I'm quite successful."

"That's great. I'm not surprised. I see how you dress, the car you drove up in. But I don't want your money, I want you to—"

Heloise holds her hand up. "Please don't keep saying that. Can't we agree that you'll at least try the drug or find a clinical trial? You have to have hope."

"Why?"

Such a simple question, yet as impossible to answer as most simple questions. Why does there have to be hope? Because the old myth, the one about Pandora's box, told us hope was in there? Because without hope how does one get out of bed in the morning? But what if hope is an illusion, a pretty story we tell ourselves? Why does there have to be hope? Heloise can't begin to answer the why of hope, but she discovers, in this moment, that she does believe in it.

"Because I say so." And she smiles at her own joke, a daughter using a mother's line back to her.

Beth doesn't smile.

"That's fine for you," her mother says. "But I'm determined to do this my way. If you help, I can risk going a little longer. If not, I have to be prepared to take measures into my own hands while I still control my hands But there's something else you could do for me."

"Okay." Wary, not committing. One doesn't have to be a cynic to suspect that the first request was meant to shock her into agreeing to what her mother is going to ask now, that Beth was never serious about the assisted suicide.

"I want to see my grandson before I get really sick."

Anticipating what Heloise might offer, she quickly adds, "Not at a distance, on some playground, and not as some mythical old friend. And not just one time. I want him to know me as his grandmother."

"How would I ever explain that?"

Her mother appraises her coolly. "I don't know, but my hunch is that you're good at thinking of things. If I'm dead to my grandson, Helen, you can resurrect me. It's the least you can do."

"I have to think about this," Heloise says, rising to go. When her mother wrote that she was selling the house and it was imperative that Helen come see her before that happened, she had thought they would be tagging things for storage, packing. Now it looks as if she could have kept one of her afternoon appointments and met Scott at soccer practice.

"Helen—I know you hate me. And it's not without justification. I loved your father. I loved you. I couldn't choose."

"But you did. You chose him."

"He stayed, you left."

She can't believe that this is her mother's argument. Children leave. They are supposed to leave.

So she does. Again.

Traffic is bad, and it's almost five when Heloise finds herself at the exit to Turner's Grove. Famished—she walked out of her mother's house after only a few bites—she stops at a wine bar to get something to eat. It is happy hour, and she is surrounded by people who seem pretty happy. She long ago surrendered the notion that she would ever be one of these people. But it was what she wanted for her son. Perhaps wanting a better life for one's child is not selfless. Perhaps it's just another type of selfishness. Heloise wants to be able to provide Scott with a childhood free from all wants, material and emotional. She wants him to wake up every day knowing he is loved and safe. Heloise can't remember the last time she felt those two things. Probably when she was not much older than Scott is now. Even then she was aware that things were precarious in her household, that they didn't have what others had, that there was some nasty whiff of a rumor clinging to her parents. Okay, she's selfish. She wants her son to grow up to be one of the self-assured young people in this bar, people who can afford a ten-dollar glass of wine on a Wednesday afternoon. She wants his life to be better than hers, and according to the news that's not likely.

Funny thing, incomewise, Heloise is in that fabled 1 percent, that sector of the economy that is being blamed for everything. It takes a lot less money than people think to be in the 1 percent. She thought that money would protect her, save her, and, by extension, protect and save Scott. Now she sits eating food that might as well be dust in her mouth, overwhelmed by the way things have mounted up. Sophie's blackmail, her mother's illness. Shelley's murder—which, to be honest, bothers her primarily because it brought her to the attention of a cop.

And all because Shelley was on Val's visiting list. What was that about? She'll find a way to ask him at next week's visit, super casual, so it won't be apparent it bothers her as much as it does.

She is paying her bill when a man comes in, tries to catch her eye. She shrugs on her coat, shrugs him off at the same time. But he blocks her path.

"Are you following me?" he asks with a smile.

It's the man from the grocery store.

"I'm kidding," he says. "I guess it's just one of those things."

She manages, "Are *you* following me?"

He laughs. "I would if I knew who you are. But you wouldn't tell me, remember?"

"I'm sorry. A pickup in the grocery store, it just seemed, oh, tacky."

"A bar is so much better."

"Are you trying to pick me up now?" Teasing, challenging.

"No, you're much too classy. I think a man has to have better game than that if he wants to get to know you."

There's something about his open admiration that soothes her nerves. He's so fresh-looking. Wholesome. *Why not a man?* she thinks. Why not marriage to some-one, someone who could care for her and Scott? Close the business, disappear, run away from all this. Not necessar-ily this man, although he might make for good practice. She'll probably have to settle for someone older, a widower or a divorcé, one of those men who can't live alone. Men have always been the root of her problems, but perhaps they—one, the right one—could be the solution, too? Not in a happily-ever-after fairy-tale way, but in the spirit of pragmatism that has governed her relations with men for the last decade.

"I am, at heart, an old-fashioned girl," she says.

"Too old-fashioned to use e-mail? That's simple enough, right? A little back-and-forth in the safety of our laptops. And maybe a drink, right now, just to get us started."

She is more tempted than she thought she would be. "I really have to get home, but . . ." She takes out a business card, writes down her private e-mail, the one that the PTA gets. "We can correspond."

"I'll be proper." He hands her a card. Terrence Acheson, security consultant.

"You'd better be. I have an aggressive spam filter. Don't shock my computer. Or me."

He kisses her hand. He's the kind of man who can carry that off, kissing a hand. He's the kind of man who takes care of women, she can tell. Could she really allow a man—not just this man but *any* man—to take care of her at this point in her life?

"You'll hear from me," he says.

She knows she will. More than knows. Hopes.

By the time Scott started preschool, Helen felt that she was in control of her life. Business was good. She had a reliable baby-sitter, an older woman with absolutely no imagination. None. Lonnie—a nickname derived from Lenore—was the most literal-minded person that Helen had ever met. If Scott banged a spoon on an upended piece of Tupperware and declared, "I play drums!" Lonnie seemed to feel obligated to say, "That's actually a piece of Tupperware."

Perhaps this made Lonnie less than an ideal baby-sitter, but Helen rationalized that Scott's Montessori school nurtured his imagination. And Lonnie was ideal in every other aspect. Prompt, never sick, never thrown into tizzies as college girls could be. She also loved Scott, but who wouldn't? The dream baby was now a dream boy, unusually sweet and kind, with real empathy for people, animals, even objects. He was into everything, as boys often are, transforming the most unlikely things into vehicles and weapons, although Helen had shielded him from guns and violent cartoons. The other mothers at his nursery school spoke of the same dilemma, how boys seemed to have this innate interest in weapons. (These lamentations were overheard, of course. Helen didn't feel she could risk anything more than the most superficial greetings, coming and going.)

Still, she worried about what his father's genes might have contributed to the mix. Not to mention her own. She tried to encourage Scott's sensitive side, giving him soft, silky things to pat and stroke. At night she took him into her lap and made a ritual out of brushing his hair, which was coppery red. She dyed her hair to match, but she could never forget that Scott had Val's hair and Val's eyes, too. She remembered a saying she'd heard around West Baltimore: "There's no denying that child." If she ever crossed paths with anyone from her old life, that person would recognize Scott as Val's son.

But she never did. How could she? Val was in prison, George I was in prison. George II had disappeared, along with the other girls. She was grateful now for the small, tightly circumscribed world that Val had created, claustrophobic as it felt at the time. She never had to worry about bumping into her old life. Tom was the only remnant, and as far as she was concerned, their relationship was a pragmatic one. He was a captain in vice now. He heard things, he knew things. He told her if there was any threat to her, or if a certain hotel was under scrutiny. Not for money or even sex. They were friends. She had risked a lot helping him hand Val over to county homicide. She deserved Tom's eternal protection.

Yes, Helen had everything figured out. Perhaps she was daring to think that exact self-congratulatory thought as she waited in line at the Giant on Route 40 one night. *I have everything figured out*. She might even have allowed herself a smug, happy sigh. She made some kind of sound, because why else would the woman two people ahead of her in line glance her way, turn around, then swivel her head back, frankly studying her.

"Helen."

She widened her eyes, pretending confusion.

"Helen."

She couldn't decide whether to deny her name or merely the acquaintance. "I'm so sorry, I have a horrible memory," she lied.

"It's Bettina. From . . . back in the day."

Bettina. Not dead and no longer a fiend, judging by her plump, rosy features. She had gotten healthy, only to let herself go. Was she a mom? At the very least, a wife, someone not actively looking for a man.

"Hi, Bettina."

"Do you live around here? How funny. I mean, life is just funny. I always say that, and it's true."

Helen apologized to the women standing between them. "Sorry to talk over you this way."

Bettina turned to complete her transaction and left the store. Helen thought she had escaped, but Bettina was outside the hissing doors, lying in wait.

"Life is funny," she repeated. "I always wondered what happened to you."

Helen couldn't muster the dishonesty to say that she ever thought about Bettina. She should, she knew she should, but some lies came hard to her.

"That was the best thing that ever happened to me, Val throwing me out." When Helen didn't follow up, Bettina prompted her. "Aren't you going to ask?"

"Bettina, I have a lot of frozen food—"

"And it's barely forty degrees out here. I think you're okay for now. Especially in that coat."

The coat was cashmere, nothing showy. Showy didn't pay. Showy was for what was worn under the coat, the dress, but never on the outside. The coat was expensive, though, and if one had any eye for clothes, that was apparent. Who knew that Bettina, in her enormous rainbow-striped down coat, had such an eye?

"Anyway, I kept working after I left, but I got busted and I couldn't make bail. Stayed in city lockup so long I detoxed by the time I got to trial, and then the case was thrown out. The public defender took an interest in me. Got me to go back to school. I got a degree—A.A., over to Dundalk, worked in a flower shop, ended up being manager. Did a lot of weddings. I was working with this young girl, only twenty, and one day her daddy walked in, and he turned out to be no more than forty-five, cute as a bug. And widowed. Well, you can believe I closed that deal."

"That's great, Bettina."

"So you're not the only one."

"The only one?"

"Who got out. You did get out, didn't you?" She swept her eyes up and down Helen, taking in the coat, the boots, the earrings. Helen remembered how Val once said a dope fiend could find loose change anywhere. Bettina still had that quality, an ability to assess the value of objects, people. She had been a good whore before she fell in love with drugs, excellent at cadging extras from the men she serviced. Not as good as Helen, but few were.

"I've done okay."

"Married?"

If you have to stop to consider the lie, the opportunity has passed. Some instinct told Helen it would be better to say that she was, that she could then create a phantom husband who was responsible for the fine things she wore. Would that make Bettina more or less jealous? But now it was too late to tell anything except the truth.

"No."

"Never?"

"Briefly. Widowed."

"Kids?"

She hesitates, then nods. A kid bolsters her story.

"I'm trying. Lord knows I'm trying."

Helen couldn't help being shocked that Bettina's weight gain wasn't a postpregnancy phenomenon. She must feel very secure in her relationship with the forty-five-year-old.

"I can *get* pregnant, but I can't seem to hold on to a pregnancy. Breaks my heart. I got a grandkid. Well, step-grandkid. But I want my own kids. And Nestor is a man—Mexican, too—he's not going to be open to adoption. So the only thing available to us is IVF, but health insurance doesn't cover it. Life's unfair. Isn't life unfair?"

"It is." Helen had no problem being sincere in her agreement on this point.

"And it's not like I have family or that Nestor can afford it. I mean, I thought he was pretty well fixed, the way he was throwing money around on that wedding, but it turned out that the maternal grandmother had put money aside for the little princess."

A saga, an entire miniseries opened up with that sentence. Bettina, setting her cap for a man she believed to be rich, winning him, only to find out that the deep pockets belonged to his former mother-in-law. Oh, and she clearly hated her stepdaughter, who probably wasn't too thrilled with Bettina.

"I'm sorry," Helen said, unsure of what Bettina wanted to hear.

Bettina leaned over her cart. She looked like a jealous dog, someone who would slap you if you so much as dared to touch one of the frozen pizzas or cans of Pringles.

"I need a loan, Hel." How Helen hated that abbreviation of her name. Only Val used it, and that was because she couldn't tell Val what to do.

"Have you tried the banks? Or a second line of credit on your home? Equity loans are pretty easy to get now, and the terms—"

"What's it worth to you for me not to let people in your life know what you used to be?"

"I have no people in my life," she said, quite truthfully.

"C'mon, I know you're married. I'm not buying the widow crap. Look at you. You didn't put those clothes on your own back."

She wanted to argue that she had, but it didn't seem the best idea.

"I really am widowed, Bettina."

"So he left you a good life-insurance policy?"

Helen said nothing.

"He left you *something*. What did you do, pick out some geezer and ride him in bed until he had a heart attack?"

"No, Bettina, I think that was your plan."

Oh, whatever pleasure she took in that little barb was quickly taken from her when she realized that she had harmed her own cause.

"I want money, Hel. When you leave here tonight, I'm going to follow you. And maybe you'll give me the slip, but not before I get your license plate. You know how easy it is to get someone's address if you have the license plate? I'll come to your neighborhood, I'll go door-to-door saying Helen Lewis—that was your name, right, Lewis?—used to be a whore."

Used to be. If only you knew.

"How much?" she asked.

Again that calculating look. "Twenty—no, twenty-five thousand. Sell the earrings if you have to."

"This really isn't about IVF, is it?"

Bettina was already rolling her cart away. "You let me worry about how I spend my money."

She put her groceries into a Subaru Outback, then waited, emergency lights blinking even as people circled, eager for her parking spot. Helen was parked only one aisle over, and she couldn't wait Bettina out. For one thing, she was already fifteen minutes late relieving Lonnie. She drove off. Bettina did in fact follow her home, flashing her brights from time to time, reminding Helen that she was there. As if she could forget.

It was hard getting through the next few hours without letting Scott see that something was weighing on her. She put the groceries away with shaking hands, fixed his dinner, read him a bedtime story, acquiesced to his requests for one more, one more, one more. It was almost 9:00 P.M. before she could take the time to think about her situation.

She knew, instinctively, that Bettina was like a stray cat: Feed her once and she would never go away. Helen could afford twenty-five thousand dollars, if it came to that. What she couldn't afford was for Bettina to keep coming back to her. She already had to pay Val a monthly fee. She couldn't afford someone else on her payroll.

Val would know what to do, she realized. If only to protect his own share, Val would tell her how to get rid of Bettina.

Val would get rid of Bettina.

Tuesday, October 25

As Heloise dresses for her usual visit with Val, she finds herself thinking about the questions on the eHarmony compatibility match. These questions are not easily found if one doesn't wish to register for the service, which Heloise has no intent of doing. But she figured someone, somewhere, had to have posted the questions to an open forum, and she has finally located those on a blog.

How important is chemistry to you?

Now, if she were to actually take this test—and she might end up doing that, if she really begins to panic about the Sophie situation, but she is holding on to the hope that she will find another solution, just as she did with Bettina all those years ago—how would she answer that? Clearly chemistry is not important to someone who has slept with—let's not put a number to it—a large sampling of men not actually of her choosing. But she hasn't decided to live with any of these men. Besides, would she want to be with someone who said chemistry wasn't important? Everyone wants chemistry. Someone who doesn't care would be suspect.

Describe your parents' relationship.

Pass.

Which of the following quirks would bother you most in a

partner? Uses poor grammar, tends to cling to you in social situ-
ations, superstitious, is not familiar with current events.

How about all of the above and the fact that he has to rely on a matchmaking site to find me?

Heloise has always paid close attention to the marketing of matchmaking services. She has even allowed herself a few minutes with the horrible reality show about a matchmaker, a woman who seems to think she knows what men want. (She's right about the long hair, though. Men do want that.) But it's the heavily advertised services that fascinate her—eHarmony, Match.com, Great Expectations, JDate, the one with the ad in which the woman imagines getting thrown around the room by a gorgeous man and decides she'd rather just go to a movie. The fact that Heloise can't remember the name of that one would indicate that its marketing is a fail. WFEN is *supposed* to be forgettable, but a good matchmaking service should have a name that's instantly memorable.

Yet they're in the same business, in a way. She knows that few would agree with her, but the way Heloise sees it, she and the matchmakers both traffic in lonely people. Same market, different solutions. She bets a lot of guys who end up searching matchmaking sites would just like to get laid.

And the men who hire Heloise and her employees are lonely, achingly so. Some of the regulars swear it's not so, that it's "just" sex, which is like a man dying from thirst, finding an oasis, and trying to claim, manfully, it's "just" water. They have been denied a basic human need. They should feel entitled to go to any lengths to satisfy it, as long

233

as everyone involved—the men, the workers, the wives and the girlfriends—are granted basic dignity. Heloise believes there's more dignity in her business than in the matchmaking sites, where people can be rejected. Once someone has passed her screening, he is assured that no one's going to say no.

Her forays into the virtual matchmaking world have paralleled her correspondence with Terrence—Terry, as it turns out—which has proceeded at the perfect pace as far as Heloise is concerned. His e-mails have been flirtatious, but not overly so, and he has shown just the right amount of interest in her—lots of questions about her likes and dislikes, what she was like as a little girl, not so much about her family. Her instinct was not to tell him about Scott, but she realizes that this is important information she shouldn't hold back. She will tell him over lunch tomorrow, make a clean breast of things.

The phrase strikes her, as phrases sometimes do, and she can't help herself: She goes to her laptop, which is never far away these days, as it might chime at any moment with another message from Terry. She quickly types "clean breast of things origin" into Google, conjecturing that it will go back to poultry, the literal cleaning of. But no, it derives from a reference to the chest cavity, which holds the heart. To make a clean breast is to bare one's heart.

What if she began to feel something for Terry? Would she tell him everything? Make a clean breast of it all? She can't imagine that. Terry is a private treat she is allowing herself during a time when it's better not to be too active at work. With Shelley's homicide pulling her into the sight line of that homicide cop, it's downright convenient having a real man around, going out like a normal person. A little fake normalcy is just the ticket right now. Solve the Sophie problem. Wait out the Shelley investigation. Ignore her mother's requests, both of which seem equally impossible to Heloise. She'll figure everything out. She always does.

She likes the fact that Terry has set a lunch for their first date. It means sex is unlikely, although not impossible, obviously. She's pretty sure she won't have sex with him; she doesn't plan on doing that until their third date. (She has been researching the so-called Rules, too, and is amazed by how some of them mesh with her own advice: *Be honest but mysterious. Be a creature like no other.*)

First, however, she has to get through her visit with Val. She has waited until their regular Tuesday to ask the questions that have been nagging at her since Jolson brought her in: *Why was Shelley on your visiting list? Do you know anything about her death? Did you even know she was dead?* Instinct—no, not instinct or intuition, but her hard-earned knowledge of Val—tells her that she can't come at the topic too directly, reveal how desperately she wants the answers. She's not even sure she should tell Val that a Howard County homicide cop has questioned her, much less mention the photograph of Shelley and Bettina. And she's definitely not going to let Jolson see how interested she is in this topic. Only Val can tell her why he was in touch with Shelley— and why he never mentioned it.

*

"I made a connection the other day that I can't believe I didn't notice before," she says about fifteen minutes into her conversation with Val, after providing a detailed account of the trip she and Scott had made to Antietam, which she found unexpectedly moving. Now she and Scott are watching the Ken Burns series together. Of course, there is no Scott in her account, which is a shame, as that's what made the trip particularly effective. Scott was entranced by the vista, had no problem imagining the thousands of men crossing the open fields, whereas warfare is always a little hazy to Heloise.

"Hmmmm." Val has never been very good at following up on conversational cues. He never had to be.

"That woman, the so-called Suburban Madam? The one they found dead and now say was a homicide?"

"Yeah?"

"It was Shelley. Shelley Smith, but going by a different name now." He stares impassively through the glass. "She worked for you. Briefly. Back around"—no, better not to reference Martin's murder—"mid- to late nineties."

"Christ, I barely remember her. Brown hair? West Virginia?"

There it is, the lie. She can call him on it or pretend that she doesn't know what she knows. Why would he lie? But clearly, if he wanted her to know about Shelley, he would have shared the information earlier. Val was always squirrelly that way, controlling people by not letting anyone know the whole story.

"Dirty blond when we knew her, and I think it was

Burns documentary on the Civil War? You really
me."

sh they would rerun that," he says, his eyes lighting
se familiar eyes, the ones she looks into every day.
BS on that rinky-dink TV they let me have, but I
's just one big Lawrence Welk pledge drive."

talk about Little Round Top for the rest of the visit.

Virginia. The thing is—police questioned me about her death."

"Really?"

Val's not quite as good a liar as she is, having had to do it less often. That's the ultimate perk of power, not having to lie, because there are no consequences for telling the truth.

Or maybe he just doesn't care that she can see through him.

"Yes. We were connected in a way I didn't realize."

A quizzical look.

"She's on your visitors list."

"Oh." As if this had slipped his mind. "You know, I don't think she ever did, though. Visit me. Not regular, like you. I think that goes way back to when I was first locked up. No reason to take her off, though."

Why is Heloise scared to confront a man on the other side of a glass, a man who is locked up for life? "But she was gone by then. She disappeared a few months after"—she's going to say it this time—"after Martin was killed. I always thought she was a little freaked out."

"Yeah, we stayed in touch for a while. Back then."

"Val, did you set her up? Did you give her the idea for *her* business?"

He grins. "You jealous, Hel? Did you think you were my one and only?"

Yes.

"It just would have been nice to have a heads-up. Can you imagine what ran through my mind when a cop said he wanted to talk to me about her death?"

Virginia. The thing is—police questioned me about her death."

"Really?"

Val's not quite as good a liar as she is, having had to do it less often. That's the ultimate perk of power, not having to lie, because there are no consequences for telling the truth.

Or maybe he just doesn't care that she can see through him.

"Yes. We were connected in a way I didn't realize."

A quizzical look.

"She's on your visitors list."

"Oh." As if this had slipped his mind. "You know, I don't think she ever did, though. Visit me. Not regular, like you. I think that goes way back to when I was first locked up. No reason to take her off, though."

Why is Heloise scared to confront a man on the other side of a glass, a man who is locked up for life? "But she was gone by then. She disappeared a few months after"—she's going to say it this time—"after Martin was killed. I always thought she was a little freaked out."

"Yeah, we stayed in touch for a while. Back then."

"Val, did you set her up? Did you give her the idea for *her* business?"

He grins. "You jealous, Hel? Did you think you were my one and only?"

Yes.

"It just would have been nice to have a heads-up. Can you imagine what ran through my mind when a cop said he wanted to talk to me about her death?"

237

"But I bet you were convincing. I mean, you didn't know that you had any connection with her, and you hadn't seen her for years, so you were probably really persuasive when you told him you don't know anything about her being murdered."

"Yes, but it means a suburban cop could figure out I was in the life, once upon a time, although I denied it. I don't want to be on any cop's radar."

"A homicide cop in Howard County doesn't care about a prostitute who works out of Arundel County. Cops are funny that way. Hierarchical. And homicide cops are always full of themselves, think what they do is so much more important than all the other squads. You've got nothing for him, legitimately. He'll leave you alone."

"Jesus, Val, aren't you the least bit upset? Or curious? This is someone you knew. Someone you must have liked on some level, if you did business with her. And she was murdered, possibly because of what she did."

"You know, Shelley always was a scaredy-cat," he says. "You're right about the timing. Martin got killed"—even now, after all these years, he never spoke of this event except in the passive voice—"and she couldn't hack it. She asked me if she could leave, which I don't usually let people do, as you know. She had a lot of earning left in her. We worked out an arrangement, sort of the beta plan for what you ended up doing. So you're really riding her coattails, benefiting from what I learned being in business with her, although you're more suited to it. She never got the high-end trade that you have, didn't have the discipline to run it like a real business."

He's trying to compliment her, but what Heloise is hearing is something very different. She's been a dupe, a sap. She is, in short, as unwitting as her own mother, the second Mrs. Hector Lewis. No, even more so. Her mother never suffered from the delusion that she was Hector's one and only. Stupid to feel cheated on, when it was a business deal, but Heloise always believed Val when he said she was the only person like him, the only one who understood him.

"Anyway, I truly thought Shelley offed herself, though. I mean, you could see why she might have. No income coming in. Jail looming. But now they say homicide? Maybe she began to look around her life, see what she had to bargain with."

"What are you telling me, Val?"

"Just making an observation. I think she pissed someone off, threatened to name names, and it came back to haunt her. Nobody likes a snitch, Helen."

Val never calls her Heloise, but he almost never calls her Helen either. He usually falls back on the shared first syllable, Hel. Hell.

She thinks about the photograph discovered with Shelley's body, the Polaroid of Shelley kissing Bettina. Does Val know about the photograph? If he knew that the cop would talk to her, did he also know that the cop would share this photo, ask her about the other woman in the photo? She thought Val had put the Bettina thing behind him a long time ago, assumed she was dead. Did he have Shelley killed? Is he trying to find Bettina, have her killed?

"Did I tell you," Heloise says, "that I'm finally watching

the Ken Burns documentary on the Civil War? You really inspired me."

"I wish they would rerun that," he says, his eyes lighting up. Those familiar eyes, the ones she looks into every day. "I get PBS on that rinky-dink TV they let me have, but I swear it's just one big Lawrence Welk pledge drive."

They talk about Little Round Top for the rest of the visit.

Val was proud of Helen. There it was, she had said it, and—
she was going to admit this to herself, too—she felt something warm and powerful in his pride. She knew enough
about the rudiments of psychology, as almost everyone
does in our modern age, to realize that this was bound up
with her feelings about her father, who had seldom compli-
mented her on anything, and then it was never meaningful,
a grunt of thanks for bringing him a beer or finding the
remote control when he had left it somewhere unfathom-
able. (The glove compartment of his car, for example.)

Val at least admired the things for which she wanted to
be admired: her mind and her appearance. She tried not to
put too much stock in her looks, realizing that placing all
her self-esteem behind that asset was like putting all one's
money into a beautiful boat with a small but unfixable hole.
One day that asset would be lost to her. All the more reason
to make it pay now.

In prison Val cared even more about her beauty. Where
once it had generated income for him, perhaps inspired
envy in other men—poor Jules—now, when she visited
him at Supermax, her beauty redounded to Val in a way she
had not anticipated. The pretty redhead was the subject of
much speculation, a legend. No other inmates saw her, but

many described her, based on the guards' gossip. Val never said anything about her at all, fueling the interest.

"The latest rumor," he said when she settled in for her bimonthly visit, "is that you're a former model. One guard swears you were Playmate of the Year fifteen years ago."

"Fifteen years ago? Fifteen years ago I was sixteen. I like to think I look good for my age."

"Oh, don't be sensitive. He's black."

Helen looked at Val, even more confused.

"Black people, they're not fooled by white people's ages. It's the damnedest thing. It's like they've been looking at our skin in a way we don't. They see the most subtle signs, even in a very well-kept woman such as yourself."

Helen filed this away, as she filed away every interesting insight about human nature, even when unsure if it was true. Could this be? She knew that the obverse was true, that African Americans aged better. "Black don't crack." Of course, that wasn't the obverse exactly, but a corollary, she supposed—

"You seem like you're somewhere else," Val said, annoyed. Her visits were supposed to be focused on him.

"I ran into—" At the last minute, she declined to say Bettina's name. She knew that Val wanted Bettina dead. And heading here today, Helen had every intention to set things in motion, to see if Val would take care of Bettina for her. Besides, it would be helpful for her to know if Val could do such a thing. If he couldn't . . . well, then she would be safe, too. A win-win.

So why did she say, "Mollie. I ran into Mollie"?

"That cunt."

"She's fat now."

"I saw that coming."

"Really? How?"

"She was greedy. Nothing could fill her up. She was big as a bucket, inside and out. She still working?"

"No. She hooked some poor sap who met her while she was working as a florist. Older man. She thought he was rich. He's not."

Val laughed, pleased by Mollie's fate. "More than she deserves. You know, I sometimes wondered if she ratted me out."

This was territory they had covered before. Helen decided to push past it.

"I ran into her at the grocery store. She says if I don't pay her ten thousand dollars, she'll tell all my neighbors what I used to do."

"She used to do it, too."

"But she doesn't anymore."

"Does her husband—the jerk she lassoed, does he know?"

"Probably not."

"Well, there you go. That's dynamic tension, baby. You've got as much on her as she's got on you."

"But if she poked around, she might figure out I'm still in the business. I have more to lose." She could not mention Scott, her primary concern, so Val didn't have any idea just how much she had to lose. If he did—maybe she should have introduced the idea of a child earlier, claimed to have gotten knocked up a year later than she did? No, Val had

243

seen her almost every month since Scott was seven weeks old. Even if she had tried to fake a pregnancy, he would have figured it out immediately, put together her absence during his trial, known that the child was his.

"Look, she could make things hot for you, but you could ruin her life. You can move, mix things up. All she has is the meal ticket. You know what? You should fuck him. The husband."

"Why?"

"I don't know. I just think that would be funny."

"It would only make Mollie angrier."

"Yeah, you've got a point. Maybe have one of your girls do him?"

"I don't want to do that. I think he's a genuinely nice guy who's in love with Mollie."

"Those two things can't be true. If he's a genuinely nice guy, he's in love with an idea of Mollie, a fake person that she created to land him."

Helen had to marvel at Val's intuition about people. Even with some key details fudged—Mollie instead of Bettina—he was on top of the situation. "She was a horrible person, out for herself," Val continued. "I bet she gave you some great bullshit line about why she needs money."

Helen felt naïve, a feeling no one enjoys, ever, despite the fact that we often pretend it's a virtue. Naïveté is just a euphemism for ignorance. "She says she needs money for fertility treatments."

"Like she would ever be a mom, wipe someone else's ass. She probably does want a kid, though, to anchor the guy.

She's feeling insecure about him, take my word. Make it clear that you'll take the husband away, and she'll get lost. Scare her, Hel. You don't have to *do* anything if a person is genuinely scared of you. TCB, like Elvis and his gang used to say."

"TCB?"

"Taking care of business, that's all it is. Taking care of business."

A silence fell. Helen thought about Martin and wondered if Val was thinking about him, too. Of all the people in his life, Val had failed to make this most unlikely young man scared of him, or at least scared enough so it would last through the buzz of cognac and a winning streak. Helen doubted that Martin was the only person Val had killed in his life, but part of his success was that he used violence sparingly. He was a bad daddy, and a bad daddy kept everyone in line by erupting only now and then.

She pressed her fingertips against the glass and thanked him for his insight.

Supermax was near downtown Baltimore, right off the Jones Falls Expressway. As she headed out that afternoon, she checked her watch, calculated if she had the time to take a literal trip down memory lane. She drove east, to the house on the water that had been her world with Val. It had been sold. She was unclear if the state had seized it as one of Val's assets or if it was owned by someone who'd sold it for him and funneled the proceeds to him, to the offshore accounts maintained by Val's lawyer, the same accounts to which she made deposits every month. Legitimate people lived there now. It was a beautiful house—why shouldn't a more traditional family want it?

Did they know? she wondered. Did they know about the weird family that had lived here, the murder, the way it had ended? Had they found all the hidden places—the safe in the wall, the tunnel to the dock? Val had believed that if the police came for him, he would have enough notice to walk out through the tunnel, get on his boat, and head for the bay, take it all the way down the eastern seaboard to Jamaica or the Bahamas. The boat was kept ready, shipshape. The only flaw in the plan was that Val never learned how to pilot it himself.

That was one of Martin's jobs. Besides, the day the police came, Val didn't take it seriously, didn't think he had anything for them to find.

She was home in time for Scott's supper, bath, and bedtime, as usual. She tried to take no more than two evening gigs a week. They paid the best, being longer, but there were plenty of lunchtime engagements, and besides—she got a cut of everything. Because she hired smart girls, there was inevitably a moment when they asked themselves what she was really providing. Couldn't they leave and take their clients with them? She didn't argue with them. She let them go, and yes, some of them managed to take her clients.

They promptly got busted, too, after she tipped off Tom. Word spread. It happened less and less.

Maybe she knew more about TCB than she realized. She called Tom, asked if he wanted to come by. Poor guy, he always did. She wished he didn't love her. She told him that all the time, was very up-front about the fact that she didn't love him and never would.

"I want you to pay a visit to someone for me."

"A competitor?"

"Not exactly."

Tom went to Bettina's house, which wasn't even two miles from Helen's. He showed her his badge, asked for a cup of coffee, said he needed to talk about the old days. He said some things were best forgotten by everyone. He told her to go on with her life and let others get on with theirs. He stayed until her husband came home, then said he was a Baltimore County detective and he was worried about some break-ins in the neighborhood, was asking stay-at-home types like Bettina to keep their eyes and ears open. "You're a lucky man," he said. "And while I guess it's not politically correct, I think it's nice that you have a wife who stays at home, even without kids. I like an old-fashioned girl."

He never mentioned Helen's name. He didn't have to. The message was clear: *If you come near anyone in my life, your life will be exposed, too.* Bettina could have the satisfaction of destroying Helen's life, but she'd have to take her own with it. Val was right. Bettina had something to lose, too. It was a game of chicken, and Helen kept her foot on the accelerator while Bettina swerved.

That Sunday, Helen began studying the real-estate section. She also began researching how to change her name. She was stuck with Lewis, because it was the name on all Scott's legal documents, and he was already too inquisitive a child to accept a new surname without multiple questions.

She couldn't really start over, but she could paper over what she had, make it look shiny and new. She thought of her mother, doing the Jumble in the afternoon paper, devouring the advice columns, never noticing that her daughter, more than anyone, needed some sound advice. Ann Lewis? Too plain. Abby Lewis—ugh.

Heloise Lewis. That worked.

Wednesday, October 26

She is exactly, precisely on time for her lunch date with Terry, which is probably a mistake, but her internal clock is finely calibrated. It was a good technique to learn when she was starting out, something that allowed her to end her tricks at exactly the right time without stealing glances at clocks or phones. The tendency for most new girls, the ones who work by the hour and not the act, is to short their customers—an hour is actually quite a bit of time when it's just (just) sex. Meanwhile, some customers are always trying to steal a little extra. One man actually suggested a punch card—one free date for every paid ten. He owned a chain of sandwich shops that made such an offer, and he argued that almost no one actually collected on it, so it was a good way to appear customer-oriented without having to outlay that much.

But Terry is late, and Heloise feels self-conscious, although she is often alone in public and doesn't think twice about it. But then, she's never in the position of doubting that the other person will show up. She doesn't have a book or anything to occupy her, although there's always her phone. She checks e-mail, looks at her schedule. The weekend is thin in terms of work, top-heavy with things for Scott—

"I'm sorry," Terry says, and he looks truly distressed at his lateness. "There's a terrible accident on Route 50, but I don't have your number, just your e-mail—"

She slides her phone into her purse. Corresponding with Terry has been too much fun. She doesn't want to start talking to a disembodied voice, not yet. She wants him to continue to write, explain himself to her.

So far he has told her that he grew up in Northern California, the only child of two professors. His household sounds like Heloise's fantasy—full of books and art, attending theater and even opera when he was younger than Scott is now. Scott is not a reader, much to her regret, and she can't imagine what he would do if she tried to take him to an opera. Still, it sounds appealing, Terry's family.

He also has volunteered that he's twice divorced, which is daunting yet also endearing. Certainly no one would lie about that.

He had described the two relationships as two starter marriages.

"How does one have two starter marriages?" she wrote back.

"By learning nothing from the first one," he replied.

She was, by habit, less free with information about herself. She mentioned that she was widowed but did not bring up Scott. She said she had grown up in a small town but managed not to add the state and the fact that her mother was a nurse. She did not say her mother was dead, as she usually does. She didn't say she was alive either, just left it alone. When her half sister, Meghan, was living in the same neighborhood, Meghan thought it was hilarious that

Heloise had "killed" Beth, said she was going to start killing all sorts of useless people in her life. It had seemed funny. Then.

"So," he says. They are in that odd state of knowing so much yet knowing so little about each other. They have agreed, by Heloise's initiative, to avoid the "What do you do?" discussion as long as possible. *"I'm not what I do,"* she wrote him. *"Besides, it's really boring."*

"So," she says. "There's something I should tell you, I guess. There just never seemed to be a right moment. But I know it matters."

"Maybe not to me."

"Maybe. I have a son."

"Actually, you did tell me. The first time we met, in the grocery store."

"I did?" How strange. She has no memory of this. But then, she immediately put him on that side of the ledger, the one with teachers and neighbors.

"In passing. How old is he?"

"Eleven. Twelve in a few months. On New Year's Eve, actually, poor guy. It takes a lot for him not to get lost in the shuffle of holidays."

"That's a great age, eleven. Where's his dad?"

"Out of the picture. Gone before he was born." Great, now she's having trouble killing Val.

"Gone as in—"

"Dead. Car accident. He didn't even know I was pregnant."

"Wow. So whatever you do—that thing you are *not,* as

251

we agreed—you must be doing well. Nice car, a house out here—"

"I never told you where I live."

"I just assumed it was somewhere nearby, since you had a kid. I bet you wouldn't want to go too far on what is technically our first date. And I guess this means I have to lure you back to my place." He laughs, for which she is thankful, but suddenly she does want to go back to his place.

Instead she orders lunch and picks a dish redolent with garlic, something she seldom has when out with a man. Terry is as easy to talk to in person as he is in e-mail, and he tells her more stories of his magical childhood. It's easier for her to imagine Harry Potter's life than it is to believe in Terry's stories, where everyone is sweet and charming and loving.

She doesn't have similar stories to share, so she talks about Scott. She finds herself sharing an anecdote about his only truly bad act, shoplifting a candy bar when he was seven, how she made him take it back and apologize to the man at the pharmacy.

"You're an honorable person," Terry says. "I think that's what I like best about you. I can tell, even with our limited knowledge of each other, that you try to do the right thing."

She loses her appetite for the lamb stew, delicious as it is.

"When can I see you again?" He has waited until the parking lot to ask. "This weekend?"

"Weekends are for my son. I work so much."

"Okay, then Monday."

Monday is good, Monday is slow. So many of her regulars start the week pretending that this is the week they won't call.

He gives her a polite kiss on the cheek but strokes her arm in a way that's undeniably sexy. Promising. This is a man who will take care of her, if she lets him.

"Monday," she repeats. Thinking, *By Monday I could be as honorable as you think I am. I might not be able to make a clean breast, but I can do the right thing. I can do it right now.*

Luckily, Bettina still lives in the same house. Heloise wouldn't know how to find her otherwise. It seems as if a thousand years have passed since their encounter in the Giant, but it's really only six. Heloise knocks, but no one answers. So she waits in her car, hoping Bettina will return soon. Before she loses her nerve.

A ditty runs through her head. *One of these things is not like the others.*

Bettina's not in the life, hasn't been for a long time.

Two of these things are kind of the same.

Shelley and Heloise were in the same business. She was probably kicking back money to Val, too. Lord, for a man with no real expenses, he required a lot of tribute.

But the photo was of Shelley and Bettina, arms wrapped around each other. Who was the photo for? Why had it been left there?

One of these things is not like the others.

Shelley is dead.

Two of these things are kind of the same.

253

Shelley was threatening to tell police something about Val. Why did he care? He can't do *more* than life. Did he think he had a shot of being released, did he worry that Shelley would complicate that for him? All the disallowed evidence in the world won't mean a thing if there are eyewitnesses willing to testify against him. Yet Val believes that Bettina is the person who put him in prison. And that's Heloise's fault. She never meant to hurt anyone else, only to save herself, protect her child.

She has to warn Bettina. She has to do the right thing.

A Ford Explorer pulls up, Bettina at the wheel. When she gets out, she looks much older than the woman Heloise saw six years ago, perhaps because she is thinner, which hasn't been good for her face. But she looks happy, content.

That—and maybe the thinness, come to think of it—can be explained by the blond toddler she lifts from a car seat. Children can wear a woman to a nub like nothing else.

Heloise rushes up the walk, "Bettina, it's—" Even as she pauses, making the mental adjustment necessary to use her real name, Bettina is backing away from her wide-eyed, anxious, fumbling with her keys.

"Leave me alone," she says. "I haven't caused you any trouble. You have no right to cause me any."

"I'm not." She thinks guiltily of Tom's visit, made with her approval. "That's not why I'm here. Bettina, something has happened. Something for grown-up ears."

The boy is large; she can't judge his age. He looks up at the word "ears," pulls his own, laughs.

"Bettina, it's important. To you."

254

"Jesus, you make it sound life-or-death."

"It very well could be."

The house is a museum devoted to two works—photographs of the little boy and a much older girl, presumably the one whose wedding landed Bettina her husband. She steers the boy to the television, then invites Heloise into the dining area.

"You have a lot of nerve, coming to me for anything."

"A woman was murdered a couple of weeks ago. The madam, out in Howard County?"

"Yeah. I heard something about that."

"It was Shelley. From back in the day. She was using the name Michelle, but it was really Shelley."

"You know, I thought that might be her, but she really changed, didn't she? She got old. I mean, I know what I look like, but she really looked like hell." A bitter glance at Heloise. "You've managed to keep it together pretty well. Money *can* buy some things, can't it?"

"There was a photograph left with the body. A Polaroid picture of her—and you."

Bettina looks dubious. "I didn't hear anything about that, and no one's tried to talk to me. How do you know?"

"The police showed it to me, thinking I might help them."

"Why?"

Heloise is still leery of Bettina—the woman, after all, tried to blackmail her once. "They found out I had a connection to Shelley, thought I could tell them something. I couldn't. And I didn't tell them I knew the other woman in the photograph. I figured it didn't matter."

"Oh, but now it does. Look, we are not well fixed—"

"I'm not here for money." *I'm not you.* "I think Val had Shelley killed. And I think he might come after you next."

"Why would he care about me? He threw me out. Best thing that ever happened to me, although it didn't seem like it at the time."

Here it is. Heloise has to confess what she did. "Right, he threw you out. Everyone assumed you'd live on the street until you died. You were pretty messed up, Bettina. I forgot, I guess, that people can get lucky, that anyone's life ever changes for the better."

"Yours did."

Heloise decides to try to appeal to her through their strongest mutual bond. "I got pregnant, Bettina, and I decided to tell a police detective what I knew about Martin's death, where the murder weapon was hidden. But I was terrified of even being a confidential informant. I didn't think Val would let me live if it came to light—and, like I said, I was having a kid. A cop friend of mine had a CI who was dying of cirrhosis, had nothing to lose. He agreed to be the cover, to say he heard about the shooting and where the gun was hidden from a girl who was there that night. No one ever said your name, *ever.*"

Ah, but that's a lie. *She* said it. Heloise rushes on, as though she can outrun her mistakes if she just talks quickly enough.

"There were three of us there that night. Plus the Georges. But Val always thought it was you, for some reason."

It takes Bettina a beat to absorb this. She never was the

brightest girl, and even being drug-free can't make her sharp. But she sorts things through and says, "You bitch."

"I'm really sorry, Bettina. You should go to the police, say you were a friend of Shelley's, that she once saw a murder. They'll show you the photograph, maybe, and you can identify yourself, tell them what I suspect about Val—I'm sure they'll give you protection—"

"Yeah? Why don't you go tell them all this?"

"I can't, I just can't."

"Because you're still a whore, aren't you? Oh, yeah, I added that up, especially after that vice cop came over to talk to me. And now you want me to put everything in my life at risk so you don't have to risk yours."

"You're a respectable citizen. Married to a nice man, beyond suspicion. The police will protect you. Val won't be able to get to you once they know. He doesn't know where you are, isn't even sure you're alive. He can find me."

"You're amazing." She draws out the syllables as a teenager might. A-MAY-zing. "You come over here like you're doing me a favor, but you're still trying to pin this on me. Here's my suggestion: *You* go to the police, *you* cop to what you did, and *you* deal with the fallout. Leave me out of it."

"I can't. I would if I could, but I can't unring this bell. Please, Bettina, go see Detective Alan Jolson in Howard County. I'm sure he'll be discreet."

"But not so discreet that you're willing to trust your life story with him, right?" Bettina has been keeping one eye on the boy, entranced by the television, visible through the door to the small den. Now she closes it and comes back and stands over Heloise. She remembers their fight, all those years ago, how comical everyone found it when Bettina lunged at her, almost as provocative as the kissing sessions with Shelley. And certainly more sincere. She flinches, ready to absorb a blow.

"Look, you always were a snooty bitch, thought you were better than everyone. Because of your looks, because Val liked you best, because you were sneaking around with those books. But what were you? You were just another whore. Like Shelley, like me. Only I got out. I have a legitimate life, with a legitimate kid. And you want to wreck that? I don't think so. Yeah, I'll go see your detective, and I will tell him everything. Everything, Helen. Who you are, what you do."

"I really wish you wouldn't."

"Or maybe I'll write Val a letter, explain it all. How about that? Man, you painted a target on me and then just went about your life, thinking—hoping—that I was dead and it wouldn't matter. And even when you knew where I was, you didn't have the guts to tell me what you did. For, what?—six years you've just left me hanging. I'm surprised you didn't tell Val where I lived, back when I tried to get a loan from you. That would have solved everything."

"But I didn't," Heloise said, relieved to have this one tiny parcel of high ground. "Precisely because I didn't want anything to happen to you, despite the fact that you were trying to put the screws to me."

Bettina shakes her head. "Get out. Just get out. Val obviously doesn't know where I am. Everyone in my life knows me as Betty Martinez. I don't even look like my old self. First time I ever felt good about that. I'm just another neighborhood lady. You want to make amends, you need to be talking to someone else. A cop, a priest."

What can Heloise say? Bettina has the ultimate advantage of being right. Heloise has been a coward. Bettina got out, Heloise stayed in. She didn't think Bettina's life was much to envy when their paths crossed six years ago—older husband, problematic stepdaughter, not a lot of money—but now it looks pretty damn sweet.

"I'm sorry," she says. "I'm really sorry."

"Go fuck yourself."

2005–October 28, 2011

It was not the best time to shop for a house, although Heloise would later comfort herself with the notion that it could have been worse, that she didn't buy at the top. Besides, in 2005 seemingly everyone believed that prices would rise forever, that a house simply could not lose value. Heloise, preapproved for a ridiculous amount of money, a sum she would never lend herself, was advised to offer above the asking price or waive an inspection to get what she wanted. The advice made her feel like a sap. She wasn't used to being at the whim of an irrational market. The commodity she provided did not experience wild price fluctuations. Demand went up slightly in overheated times such as these and slumped in recessions, but there were no giddy bubbles. Heloise envied the funeral-home business, wondered how it responded to an economy where everything was measured by percentage increases in profits. Did funeral homes have stockholders? If so, how did they appease them? Presumably with suggestive selling, suckering the bereaved with extras they didn't need, items with ridiculous markups.

Heloise didn't have such items in her inventory. A blow job was a blow job was a blow job. You couldn't paint it gold and add two thousand dollars, you couldn't—

"And this is Mother's office," the realtor told her, pointing out the little cubbyhole off the kitchen, the one that had been pointed out in every house she had seen in the suburbs she'd selected between Baltimore and D.C. The agent opened the file drawer with a flourish.

Whose mother's? Heloise wanted to ask.

Besides, it was a different office that intrigued Heloise in this particular house, the basement lair of a psychiatrist who had worked at home. Soundproof, with a steel door, ugly as sin. Yes, this was the place for her.

"The house is nice," she told the realtor. "But I hate what they've done down here. I wanted to find a house with a playroom in the basement, or at least a space that could be easily converted."

"Well, there's always the family room off the kitchen—"

"Not the same," she said. "A shame. The rest of the house is at least inoffensive in its decor."

"Inoffensive? It has all the latest top-line fixtures."

"If you say so," Heloise said with pained politeness.

The realtor, used to needy supplicants, became invested in winning Heloise over, extolling the house's virtues, falling back on the usual glossary—"marble" and "granite" and "high-end"—as if these were incantations that would cast a spell. Heloise played it cooler and cooler. She made the realtor doubt the house's desirability. It wasn't enough that others might want it. Why didn't this well-dressed, preapproved woman want it? Before the week was through, the seller accepted the original asking price for the house in Turner's Grove, which was considered a huge coup at the time. *Buying a house for the asking price.*

261

Really, Heloise thought, something was askew.

Turner's Grove came by its prosaic name honestly. Ezekiel Turner had owned acres and acres of fruit trees in what was now the center of a sprawling subdivision in Anne Arundel County, where Helen—reinvented as Heloise—decided to buy. Location, location, location. It was thirty-five minutes from downtown Baltimore, forty from D.C., and not even fifteen from Annapolis. The houses, while expensive, were not quite as pricey as one might expect, because only a small stretch of Turner's Grove had water access. Water, the bay and its rivers, was what drew most well-to-do people to this particular county. Heloise considered the lack of water a plus. Didn't people know that drowning was a greater risk to children, that a pool in the backyard was more dangerous than a gun in the home? Hadn't anyone else read this new book *Freakonomics*? She rejected several houses in the neighborhood she wanted because they all had pools.

But the best thing about Turner's Grove was the size of the lots, at least a half acre, which the original housing covenants decreed must never be subdivided. It was the most private place she found in her search, which wasn't saying much. She could still see the silhouettes of three different neighbor families at night.

She hadn't even reached moving day—the daily rental truck disgorging a pitiful amount of furniture, not enough to fill even a third of the house—before those neighbors, and others farther afield, started to speculate about this single mother with the big house.

The initial gossip about Heloise was spread by the realtor,

a top-heavy woman with a penchant for grudges. Not that she had much gossip to spread, but when had that ever stopped anyone? A single woman, she told her friends, who told their friends. Widowed, apparently, although given her profession—lobbyist, and one had to be a lawyer to be a lobbyist, no? (no)—maybe she was that rare woman who had done very well by her divorce. Hamilton Point, the neighborhood Heloise had chosen, was the best in Turner's Grove, no spec houses here, all custom-built creations.

Why does a woman with one child need so much space? the realtor asked everyone she met. And so cool, almost snobbish. The realtor was less forthcoming with the information that Heloise had gotten a relative deal on the property.

Stranger still—the gossip moved on to a second generation, based on what the neighbors had observed about this oddly private creature—she managed to do things that even stay-at-home mothers struggled with. There she was, in the drop-off lane every morning and in the pickup lane more afternoons than not. She drove Scott to T-ball, never missed field day or a school concert. If baked goods were required, she offered store-bought ones from gourmet bakeries. What kind of job was that, which allowed one to be present *and* garbed in Prada? She was more like a man than a mother, and it was true she tended to gravitate to the part of the field where the fathers gathered, still in their work clothes. She looked less out of place among them. Her dead husband must have had quite a life-insurance policy. The women eyed their still-living husbands with something akin to resentment, wondering how their lives might change for the better if their men would suddenly disappear and be replaced by an enormous chunk of cash. How had he died? A car crash? With a semitrailer? There must have been some deep pockets involved, a corporate entity held responsible for the errant driver.

The talk swirled around and around, feasting on itself, with no help from Heloise. It was like birds pecking at one another long after the last crumb was gone. Still Heloise refused to make friends, despite knowing that her reserve was fueling the gossip. Too dangerous. Every person added to her life was a liability. She drove Scott to and from play-dates, let him have friends to the house, but she never volunteered to do anything with other parents and limited sleepovers to a few times a year. On the sidelines at soccer practice, she never said, *Oh, I'll take the kids to Pizza Hut,* and she seemed nervous when Scott wanted to go off with a group. She kept to herself. What could be more suspicious than a woman who didn't desire their company?

Over the years Heloise changed a few things. When Lonnie became problematic as a baby-sitter—the poor thing had fallen asleep with a pan blazing on the stove, and who knows what might have happened if Scott hadn't wandered into the kitchen for a glass of water?—Heloise let her go and hired Audrey, whom she introduced as her au pair. (Audrey's odd speech made it plausible that English was her second language.) Au pairs were not a luxury the way full-time nannies were, so no one envied her Audrey. Besides, the women gossiped, they wouldn't want someone with such poor language skills to care for *their* children.

The thing that finally normalized Heloise in the other women's eyes was her half sister Meghan, who moved into a nearby subdivision a year later, a coincidence that Heloise bemoaned yet managed to survive. Meghan's family didn't stay long; she found herself genuinely widowed, and she cashed in her chips—her term—and moved to Florida, where the money went further now that the bust was on. But the mere existence of a bona fide relative somehow persuaded the other families that Heloise was authentic, hiding nothing. Funny, because Meghan was quite the most disreputable asset that Heloise could have summoned, given that they had the same father and were only six months apart. But no one did the math. No one ever does the math, in Heloise's experience. In reality, people probably gossiped less about her than she imagined.

No, Turner's Grove was altogether satisfactory. Life went on, which is the one thing it can be counted on to do. Scott entered kindergarten, Scott went to grade school, Scott went to middle school. He was happy and productive, a good student, the kind of boy whose manners drew compliments from teachers and strangers, yet other boys didn't find him prissy. Heloise assumed that the shoe of adolescence would drop eventually, that he would become querulous and difficult. But with his twelfth birthday looming, he remained her dream child.

Or so she thinks until the Friday afternoon she returns from a midday appointment and finds her office door

265

unlocked, which it never, ever is. Audrey is so paranoid about Heloise's rules on this that she locks herself inside the office when she's working there alone.

Unlocked, but undisturbed. The filing cabinets are locked, the desk is as clean as ever. Still, she can't help remembering that open letter upstairs, the one from her mother. Is Scott becoming a sneak?

She boots up the computer and has typed nothing more than *"P"* when the obliging Google box offers her list upon list of pornographic sites. Party girls. Poontang. On and on and on. She clicks through to one site. It makes her sad, as most pornography does, because of the low production values, its tendency to make sex look ugly.

Eleven and looking at porn on a computer. Was he precocious? Should she be proud? Scott has known where babies come from since he was seven. He also has known the alleged story of where he came from, the lovely redheaded father killed in a car accident before his son appeared in the world. But he has never asked her about sex in any other context but procreation. If he had, she would have talked to him about it. She would have told him it felt good but that it was complicated. She had planned to tell him that sex is a promise you make with your body, that it must involve mutual respect, that it is powerful, more powerful than most people want to recognize. That people (men usually) have died for it, that women use it to get what they want. Sex is like a gun. If you know what you're doing, you'll be safe, but if you don't take precautions—oh, yes, there is so much information about sex in her head, but her son (tellingly?) has never asked his mother for any facts beyond the basics.

Later that afternoon she picks him up at school and announces that they are going for a treat, which is not out of the ordinary on a Friday. They drive to an ice-cream stand next to a farm with a pen of tame ponies. Scott had once delighted in this place, but he seems jaded now. How you going to keep him down on the farm? Who wants ponies once he's discovered poontang?

"Scott," she begins, sipping her strawberry shake, "were you in my office today?"

"I'm not supposed to go in your office," he says, licking the edge of his cone.

"Yes." He's slicing the onion pretty thin. "But *did* you?"

He meets her eye and says with sincerity, "No! If you tell me not to do something, I don't do it."

The no—emphatic, almost shocked—might have won the discussion for him. But he's gone slightly too far. Heloise looks into her son's foxy brown eyes and is reminded of—not Val but herself. Because she's the liar. She's been lying so long, about so many things, that the lies don't register anymore. And somehow Scott realizes this, even if he doesn't know he realizes it. Everything she has done has been for him, but how does she explain that? How does she explain that she lied to protect herself, then lied to protect him? Bettina was right: She is a coward.

Her mother's voice chimes in: *And if you're lucky, you'll never have to ask your child for forgiveness.*

"Scott, I know you were. I also know you looked at a letter that was in my upstairs desk."

"I needed paper clips. I'm allowed to go into your upstairs desk."

She almost wants to stop to school him a little in effective lying. *Admit nothing.*

"And you saw the letter?"

"I saw a letter addressed to Helen Lewis. I don't know who that is."

"That was my name, once. I changed it legally."

"Why?"

It feels awful to lie when she's trying to teach her son the value of honesty. She manages a semitruth. "It sounded grander. I wanted an impressive name, a memorable one, for my business."

"And who's B. Lewis? That's what was in the return address."

"Did you open the letter?"

"No."

This has the ring of truth.

"A relative. Someone I'm not close to, back in Pennsylvania."

"An aunt, like Aunt Meghan?"

"Something like that." A grandmother is something like an aunt, no? "Scott, are there . . . things you need to ask me?"

He looks down at his cone. "Why aren't there any photos of my dad?"

A lie is at the ready. *When I moved after your father's death,*

268

a lot of things got lost. A lie has always been at the ready for Heloise, even when she was Helen.

"Your father wasn't much for photos," she says. That's true. She suddenly thinks about the Polaroid, the one of Shelley and Bettina, making out for the men's amusement, a silly thing she refused to do and that Val never forced on her. She always thought he respected her for having some dignity. Polaroids were almost campy by the nineties, but Val had never been an early adopter, except when it came to his television, which was always the biggest, the newest, with bells and whistles that he learned to master through trial and error, being incapable then of reading an instruction booklet. On a boring night, he would bring out the camera, ask girls to pose for him, make the guys do stupid shit, too.

They were doing that the night Martin died, before the card game. Could that photo be from that very night? But the only person who could expect her to be questioned in Shelley's death would have to be someone who knew what they had in common. And who knew that besides Val?

"I hate not having a dad," Scott says. There's no self-pity in his voice, but it's such a stark, terrible truth that Heloise again feels that odd sensation she experienced in the police station. Her heart lunges against her rib cage, avid for escape.

To make a clean breast indeed.

But it's the one thing she can never do with her son. Her own mother, whatever her failings, let Heloise see her mistakes. All Scott knows is that he lives in a house of secrets.

"I hate it, too," she says. For almost thirteen years, from the moment she took that pregnancy test in the diner bathroom, all she has wanted is to give her son everything. But she can't give him a father. A stepfather, maybe, but never a father.

A single word forms in her head: *Out.*

She has to get out.

Not because Shelley was murdered.

Not because Sophie is blackmailing her.

She's going to get out so she doesn't have to lie to her son about what she does.

"Scott, how would you feel about leaving Turner's Grove?"

"It depends. Could we go to Florida, where all my cousins are?"

"Well, maybe not Orlando, but somewhere nearby."

"Do they have soccer?"

"Probably, yes."

"Could we wait a year, until high school? Because I have to change schools then anyway."

"Maybe. I'm not sure. I'll do my best."

"And will Audrey come with us?"

"I hope so."

Why did anyone need to hope? her mother had asked, or words to that effect. Heloise feels supremely hopeful as she and Scott pat their faces with napkins and then pat the ponies for old times' sake. "I loved doing this when I was little," Scott remarks, another sucker punch to her heart, but a sweet one. She conceals a smile at his perspective on himself, the idea that he is surveying his childhood from some great distance, and says only, "I love doing it now." It may be the single truest thing she has ever said. In the fast-falling twilight of an October afternoon, she feels a peace she has never known. She loves her son. She's going to put her past behind her and find a new future, for him.

She agrees to let Scott cook dinner, knowing that it will mean a disaster of a kitchen for her to clean and careful supervision of his knife work, now that he insists on using the Wüsthof chef's knife that Audrey gave him. They pick up the groceries he needs to make meatballs—ground beef, pork, *and* veal—and drive home in companionable silence, Scott playing with his iPod in the backseat while she toggles among her news stations—NPR, WTOP, WBAL, soothed as always by the world's events washing over her, a wall of sound and activity that persuades her that things always could be worse, always.

A word, a name, jumps out at her: "Martinez." She has to wait for the news to cycle around again on WBAL before she hears the full report.

"A Baltimore County woman was murdered in her Catonsville home today in what police say appeared to be a burglary gone wrong. Betty Martinez was stabbed to death in her kitchen while her husband was out with their young son—"

"Mom, why are you pulling off here?"

"Gas. I need gas. Can't risk running out even if we have such a short distance to go."

She doesn't; she has more than half a tank. But sitting in the full-service lane allows her the time she needs to control her wildly beating heart, which now seems to have broken free from her chest and risen to her throat, where it's on the verge of choking her.

Monday, November 7

Heloise surveys herself in the mirror. It's odd, worrying that she needs to look her best for Paul, who has seen her in so many lights over the years. Mainly hotel-room light and the light at the Maryland Inn, but metaphorical lights, too.

Now, though, she has to strike his eye as someone new, as someone who is changing, or at least capable of changing. So she is wearing a new suit, a St. John knit, the purchase of which was hard to rationalize, but the creamy beige color is insanely flattering. She has paired the suit with kelly green pumps and a very good fake Birkin. (The years of pretending to shop for luxury goods has made her appreciative of them, if not appreciative enough to pay the full price.) On her wrist is a heavy gold charm bracelet with only one charm, the locket from the necklace that her father gave her when she was fifteen. The chain was cheap—big surprise, Hector Lewis buying something cheap—but the locket is eighteen-karat gold, and she has carried Scott's photo in it since she found the locket in a jumble of costume jewelry, amazed that she still had it, that it somehow survived Billy's most manic pawning phase, when everything went out the door. The heart, with its precious photo and own wily talent for survival, is a talisman, something she needs: a little extra luck.

The radio keeps her company on the drive to the District, although the steady backdrop of news is no longer calming. It has been ten days since the death of the woman that reporters keep calling Betty Martinez, and the story has been featured in almost every local newscast, although it is starting to lose steam for lack of new developments. A burglary gone wrong is the working theory, a theory buttressed by two other break-ins in the neighborhood that same morning. But those houses were empty, whereas Betty had the misfortune to be at home. Caught off guard, the burglar panicked and attacked Betty with a kitchen knife. Everyone seems satisfied with this version of events, and Heloise is still struggling with whether she should contact Detective Jolson. Anonymously, of course. *This is the woman in the photograph with Shelley.* But what if he hasn't shared that photograph with anyone else? He'll know that the note is from her. A tip line has been set up, offering a reward, not that Heloise wants one, but it might be easier to call and inform the operator about the connection between Shelley and Bettina. Jolson will still know it's her. How does she do the right thing without hurting herself?

Has she ever done the right thing? The thought shoots through her, hot and painful. Bettina is dead, and it's almost certainly her fault. Not that she'll ask Val about it when she sees him tomorrow. For now her only desire is to get through each meeting with Val in a state of cheerful, fake normalcy. By year's end, if everything goes according to plan, she figures she'll never have to see him again.

The sad irony is that Heloise feels safer than she has in

years. The shoe has finally dropped; Val has his revenge against his presumed Judas and must be satisfied. Yet a little boy has lost his mother, and that's Heloise's fault. She is not inclined to romanticize Bettina, who was a pretty awful person in her own way, but she apparently was sincere in her yearning for a child, and she was tender with her little boy in the few minutes that Heloise observed. Heloise tries to remind herself that she had no way of knowing what would happen when she dropped Bettina's name to Val all those years ago. She'd assumed that the woman was dead, or as good as; she couldn't prophesy that there would be a husband and a child, a genuine second chance for the junkie-prostitute who had once lunged at her and attempted to pull her hair out at the roots. She was just trying to keep Scott safe, and that required staying alive.

There have been fleeting moments in the past two weeks when she thinks she should find a way to befriend Bettina's widower, marry him, raise their children together. It would be a fitting penance, giving herself to a loveless relationship in order to care for the child she has robbed.

Then the sun finally comes up, and such 3:00 A.M. thoughts are banished, as they should be.

She and Paul have agreed to meet at the Mandarin Oriental, a Washington hotel. She told him she had business in the District and asked if he would meet her there, but that was a lie. *He's* the business. Or will be, she hopes. Although they have sometimes met in D.C. before, it's usually at hotels closer to the K Street corridor. The Mandarin Oriental feels off the beaten path, although it's not that far from downtown. She wonders, as she hands her keys to the valet, at the provisory use of the word "Oriental," why it's still allowed for hotels and rugs and art.

She is early, by design, and she sips green tea, unaccountably nervous. Why is she so nervous? She's merely following up on the very things that Paul has suggested.

He arrives, his eyes sweeping the room out of habit, but he knows no one here and no one knows him. Is it just her imagination, or does Paul look smaller outside Annapolis, in a room other than the low-ceilinged bar at the Maryland Inn?

"I thought we could do the tasting menu," Heloise says. "My treat."

"Really?" Paul is surprised by both her generosity and her hunger. But then, Heloise has never been able to do her job on a too-full stomach.

"I take you to a few meals here and there, so I have something to file."

"Yes, but it's usually a wedge salad and crab cakes, with dessert if I'm lucky. Okay, I'm in. But no alcohol. Can't afford a DWI on the drive back."

"None at all?" Paul almost always has a drink with lunch.

"Well—one vodka martini. Is it *just* lunch today?"

"Just lunch," she says demurely. "I don't have the kind of relationship that would let me take a room here without drawing attention to us. But it is a business lunch. Paul—do you think your . . . uh, associate might still be interested in buying my business? The potential backer that Anna Marie referenced to me when I fired her?"

The question clearly surprises him. Good. That's always an advantage. She's been thinking about this for a while; he probably abandoned the idea after she fired Anna Marie.

"I think the interested party could be cajoled into a negotiation. By business—what do you mean, exactly? What are you selling?"

"The client list, essentially. The current employees, except me. They're under contract. The software I've had developed for billing and bookkeeping, all relevant files— everything but the actual name. I'm keeping that."

"Why?"

The waiter arrives, and they go through the little dance that the tasting menu requires—no, no known allergies; no, no dislikes. (Paul actually points to Heloise and says, "She'll put anything in her mouth." It's not the first time he's made a slightly crude joke at her expense, but it's the first time it has annoyed her. She's not on the clock today.) It occurs to Heloise, belatedly, that one is not supposed to eat fish on Monday, at least according to Scott, her little foodie. She's not sure where he's lapped up that particular piece of wisdom. Still, she has to believe that a place such as the Mandarin is invested enough in its reputation to make sure its diners are safe.

Like you *did?* asks the mocking voice that seems to accompany her everywhere she goes these days. It's Val's voice, even though he doesn't know about her specific problems with Sophie.

"That's part two of what I wanted to talk to you about," she says, returning to their interrupted conversation. "I thought I would take your advice and become a real lobbyist."

Paul's just-arrived vodka martini is brimming, and he drinks off a bit—more than necessary to keep the glass from overflowing. "That's a pretty tough transition, Heloise."

"You were the one who suggested it."

"I was *joking*."

She's hurt. But this is business. She can't afford the luxury of taking things personally. "Really? I mean, I understood you were teasing, of course, but I thought there was a germ of a good idea."

"There is. You have the skills. You have the contacts. There's a real overlap. Theoretically, it makes sense."

"What's the problem in reality?"

"Unless you have a lot of money put away, it will take you years to get the kind of paying gigs that will replace your income."

She hasn't considered this. "I could sign on with one of the big firms, take a salary."

"They won't want you. The big boys, Heloise. The hardcore ones, the cutthroats who make a million a year—"

"Yes, I know who they are."

"And they know who *you* are."

"I've never dealt with any of them professionally. I've been careful about that." She has in fact eliminated a few lobbyists through her screening process, inferring that they were trying to get their feet in the door to find out if they could offer her services much as they gave away sports tickets and cases of liquor. Why use a middleman when she had already tapped the source?

"Do you honestly think they don't know about you? Dirt is currency for these guys."

"I'm not dirt," she says.

"Of course you're not. It's only—these guys make it a point to know everything. And to use everything they know."

"Okay, so they've heard about me. Why couldn't one of them hire me, put me on salary while I develop a boutique sideline within the firm, doing the kind of social-justice issues that don't appeal to them anyway? Make the lie of income parity true once and for all."

Paul sips his miso. "That almost could work. Except— Look, I'm just going to tell you the truth, Heloise. The best guys have rivals, and the rivals would expose you in a heartbeat, if they thought it would work to their advantage."

The waiter arrives with an extra course, an *amuse bouche*. Heloise doesn't think any part of her can be amused just now.

"Besides, most of these guys would expect you to do for free what you've been charging for. Not out-and-out sex. But you would be hired for your, um, decorative quality, your manners. You'd be like a geisha. Yeah, they'd let you lobby for this little issue or that one, for appearances' sake, but you wouldn't have any effect. They'd want you for the list of men you'd slept with. You'd be sort of an implicit threat of blackmail. 'Look who works for me, wink, wink, nudge, nudge.' Is that what you want?"

It occurs to Heloise that Paul can't help but be self-interested on this score. He's particularly vulnerable to the very scenario he's sketched.

"I still want to keep the name," she says. "Do you really have a buyer, or was that another *joke*?"

"I do," Paul says. "But he has to stay anonymous."

"That means he wants to pay cash, I assume?"

"Of course. And if he pays cash, you can't report it, Heloise. I know you've always been careful about money, staying legit with the IRS, but this can't be one of those times."

"I figured as much." She had, but the idea still makes her stomach flip. She may not fear Val anymore, but she still fears the IRS.

"And by the way"—Paul clears his throat, takes another hearty swig of his drink, coughs when it goes down wrong— "I'd expect a finder's fee. From your end."

She's pretty sure that Paul is getting it from both ends, but she merely nods in agreement.

"Even without putting anything in writing, it would be good for you to have a lawyer, maybe an accountant, who can review this for you."

"That I have," she says, smooth as the tofu that she is fishing out of her miso. She will consult Tyner if needed.

"May I ask why you changed your mind?"

She shrugs. "Time for something new."

"Is there heat?" Worriedly, his self-interest rising to the surface again. But who is Heloise to criticize someone for being self-interested?

"No, not on the business." She considers, for a moment,

280

telling him about Shelley and Bettina, about Val. Maybe even Scott, the real reason for the change. The truth is, she's about as close to Paul as she is to any other adult—except for Val. Audrey knows more about her, but she's still an employee, and a little too worshipful of Heloise to be a true confidante. Heloise and Paul are kindred spirits, bound by their pragmatism, she supposes, a willingness to pretend to play by rules they don't endorse. They not only accept the need for appearances, they excel at them.

No, even now she will not tell him about Scott.

"Do you like your wife?" she asks. Blurts, really.

Paul almost chokes on the lovely tuna tartare that is the first course. The dish has become omnipresent in Heloise's considerable restaurant-going experience, but when it's done right, even her mediocre palate can appreciate it. "Where did that come from?"

"I mean—I understand your problems, why you stay. But you loved her, right? The day you got married? You were in love?"

"I was twenty-three the day I got married," he says. "That young man felt and believed a lot of things that this guy can barely remember."

"Of course. Yet—you go home to her. Eventually." She knows that Paul stays in Annapolis whenever he can make the excuse of work and not just because he needs a cover for a meeting with Heloise or one of her girls. Sometimes he simply can't bear to go home, where Heloise knows he is lonelier than he is in a room at the Maryland Inn, watching CNN in his shorts.

"I admire her, as a mother and a person," he says. "She's been a good partner to me, supportive of what I wanted professionally. As for her—limitations. Well, for better or worse, right? Besides, divorce is expensive. You end up with two households, two sets of bills. I have better uses for my discretionary income."

He leers, another bit of innuendo at her expense. She won't miss these jokes. Heloise wants Paul to tell her something new about his marriage, something she hasn't heard before. "As I said, I understand the practical reasons you stay married. It's only that I would like to believe that there's some comfort there for you, some understanding, that when you do go home, you can sit in silence and be happy."

"That," Paul says, finishing off the martini he had been trying to pace through the six-course meal, "depends on the silence. Some are companionable. Some are meaningless. Some feel like I'm in a damn Indiana Jones movie, surrounded by snakes and booby traps, where the slightest movement could be lethal."

"All my silences are the same," Heloise says. "That's the thing about one-person silences."

"Do you live alone, Heloise?"

Here is the curiosity she thought she wanted, even if she always discouraged it. Turns out she doesn't like it. She sips her tea, envying him the drink, but she would never have a drink at midday.

"Sorry," Paul says. "Did I break a rule there, asking you a personal question?"

"I was trying to do the same thing with you. Break you out of the compartments we've inhabited all these years. A natural thing to do, I guess, as a relationship ends."

"Are we saying good-bye?"

"Soon. If not today, very soon."

They clink glasses.

"Of course, if you were a lobbyist, I'd still see you."

She can't help feeling a flare of hope. "You said it would never work."

"No, not the way you want it to, no. Best-case scenario? You'd be a joke, Heloise. People would laugh about the beautiful ex-hooker pretending to be a lobbyist."

"No one laughs now." She keeps the question mark out of her tone, but it's in her head.

"No, no one laughs now. I guess that's—irony? Human nature? The people who know you and know what you do—they respect you. Your skills and your discretion have earned you far more respect than any lobbyist enjoys. But if you tried to go legit, people would make fun of you."

"Hardly seems fair."

"It's not. But you'll have a nice chunk of change when you complete the sale, I think. You could go to law school or underwrite a new business. You'll have lots of options."

Paul's wrong about that. Options are the one thing that Heloise has never had.

They end up taking a room. Why not? As Heloise noted, it's good-bye for them, or soon to be. The Mandarin Oriental is a sophisticated place in all aspects; it's probably not the first time that an attractive couple has inquired about room availability after a leisurely lunch. Still, Heloise is not so nostalgic that she throws Paul a freebie. So even with valet parking and the expensive lunch, she comes out ahead for the day.

Leaving a discreet twenty-five minutes after Paul, Heloise glances at the concierge desk, where a woman very much like her—late thirties, a polished appearance that is more about impeccable styling than overt sexuality—is trying to soothe an agitated man with a florid face and an air of self-importance. Her manner is solicitous, her attitude unimpeachable, yet Heloise knows, or believes she knows, the inner dialogue, the mockery at a remove, as she calms this noisy baby of a man.

In the valet line, she remembers the moment when the inspiration for WFEN hit her and wonders, wistfully, if lightning might strike twice. But all she gets is her car. She drives north, listening to the news cycle around and around, listening to Betty Martinez's gradual disappearance from the public imagination. Will she disappear from her young son's mind in the same way? Is it better that he's too young to remember much about her, or does that set him up for a life of chronic sadness, a hole that can never be filled?

And for the first time, Heloise wonders how Scott's fictional dad figures in *his* thoughts. It's always been a story for her, a pretty fiction and pretty hollow, no different from all the other pretty myths that parents tell children. Santa Claus, the Tooth Fairy, your father. But for Scott the story about the handsome, loving, heroic redheaded father is true.

Heloise thinks back to Reverend Frida's attempt last month to soften the ugly Old Testament verse: *in sorrow thou shalt bring forth children.* She had said it was probably pain, not sorrow, that God was not cursing women to be sad about the act of motherhood, although the verse also conveys the understanding that all parents, fathers and mothers alike, are seldom at peace once a child is in the world.

Reverend Frida wasn't burdened by the actual knowledge of what it was to be a parent, but that didn't keep her from filtering every experience through her own. She did that awful thing that the childless sometimes do, equating her cats to progeny. Even Coranne was outraged.

Heloise remembers something she hasn't thought of for years, Scott's second day of life—the red-all-overness of him, from his feet to his hair, his squinched-up face. A nurse had come into her room to conduct a test to determine if the fluid had disappeared from his ears. Usually not a problem with vaginal births, she said cheerfully, but the test failed to deliver a satisfactory score. She tried it once, twice, three times and said she would not be allowed to release him if he didn't have a passing score in both ears. Then it turned out the testing equipment itself was malfunctioning and required only a reboot. Scott was fine.

Heloise never was again.

Tuesday, November 8

And still she has to visit Val. Visit him, cajole him, entertain him, never alluding to what she believes she knows about the death of Bettina. Even when she sells the business, she will probably have to continue to visit him. That's an argument in favor of moving, not that she can make it to Scott: *Let's go somewhere else so I never have to see your father again.*

Val's in good spirits today, which only confirms Heloise's belief that he had Bettina killed.

She risks, "You look like the cat who swallowed the canary."

"Nope. Just the usual feed." Still, his closed-mouth smile looks as if it might burst.

"Seriously, what's up, Val? It's clear you're gleeful about something."

He leans toward the glass, and she inclines her head toward his, an instinctive gesture after all these years. "I don't know if you've heard about this, but there's a ballistics guy, testified in my trial, and it turns out he lied about his credentials."

Tell me something I don't know. Tell me something that hasn't been keeping me awake for weeks.

All she says is "I think I heard something about that."

"Well, last night he attempted suicide."

286

"I didn't hear *that* on the news." And Lord knows she has been listening to the news.

"Maybe they're keeping it quiet. Privacy or whatever. It was kind of a bullshit attempt the way I heard it. Halfhearted. A real man would kill himself."

Even from Val, this sounds extreme. "Really?"

"Yeah. He's a liar. He hurt people. He shouldn't be able to live with himself."

She has to wonder if Val's words ever circle back to him. Heloise decides to risk disagreement, something Val allows as long as it's strictly intellectual, done in sport.

"I heard—I read, I mean—that he may have faked his credentials but his testimony will stand. Other ballistics experts will affirm what he said. It's pretty cut-and-dried stuff. Which is why it's weird that he felt it necessary to exaggerate his background."

"I'm sure that's what the prosecutors are putting out. We'll see. We'll see. My lawyer's readying the motion, going to put it in when the time is right."

"What's the advantage in waiting?"

"I don't second-guess his strategy."

That rings false, too. Val has always questioned everyone else's strategies, always believed himself the smartest person in the room. He wasn't wrong either, most of the time, but then—he chose who was in the room. Why would Val want his lawyer to wait? What could possibly change? Is he hoping that the ballistics expert will make another attempt on his life and succeed?

Or is he waiting for someone else to die?

Shelley. Bettina. Heloise. What do these three women have in common?

"What have you been reading?" Heloise asks, and uses his answer, which she knows will be detailed enough—he's still working his way through everything he can find on the Civil War—to allow her to follow her own thoughts.

Shelley dead.

Bettina dead.

Heloise alive.

Two were prostitutes. Two were suburban mothers. There was only one thing that united the three of them in the present day.

They had all seen Val kill Martin. He already believed that Bettina had ratted him out once. What was to stop Bettina from providing testimony if there was a retrial? Propriety, a desperate desire to keep that part of her life secret. But would Val understand that? She was at large in the world, and she had betrayed him. That would have been reason enough to kill her.

As for Shelley—hadn't Val suggested that her arrest had made her nervous, unreliable, that she was looking for things to trade? Heloise had thought that his only concern was that she would reveal he was still capable of running criminal enterprises while jailed. But maybe that was the least of Val's worries. If Shelley had been willing to testify against Val in the event of a retrial, she probably could have made a deal for herself.

Shelley had died before the information about the ballistics expert had become public. But people had known

288

already. Paul had shared it as idle gossip that had been in the pipeline for a while. Tom knew, too. Maybe Val's lawyer was more plugged in than anyone realized.

Now Val's going on about the Wilderness and Cold Harbor. As much as Heloise has read, as much as she loves history, she has no affinity for war. The only thing she can remember about these two battles is that they were in Virginia. And awful, but aren't they all? War strikes her as illogical beyond belief. To put on a uniform, to sign up for a job where the implicit directive is kill or be killed.

Kill or be killed. There are those who would argue that she has lived her life that way. She remembers Billy, gibbering into Val's surveillance camera. She didn't wish him dead, but if that's what it took to keep her alive . . . She sees herself in Jolson's office, denying any knowledge of Shelley. She thinks about Bettina, her second chance destroyed by Heloise's wayward lie.

And she sees Val, on the other side of the Plexiglas, his skin so beautifully fair now, glowing from the lack of light, a stunning contrast to his eyes and hair. If the state had wanted to kill him for Martin's murder, she wouldn't have regretted her decision to implicate Val. Meanwhile, add Martin to *her* scorecard. Wasn't she the one who'd supplied an immature young man with the information that ended up killing him? Who has killed more people, Val or Heloise?

"Heloise?"

"Yes, Grant. I know how much you admire him."

"I was talking about Meade," Val says, impatient with her for not keeping up.

"What?"

"Meade, that poor motherfucker. Couldn't catch a break. It's impossible not to admire Grant as a military man, but he *wasn't* perfect. I mean, seven thousand casualties in the space of an hour. Al-Qaeda needed four planes and two improperly built skyscrapers to achieve less than half as much."

"Fascinating," Heloise says.

He's appeased. For now.

Thursday, November 10

The offer from Paul's mystery buyer is low, even lower than Heloise feared.

She counters, via Paul, and it comes up slightly, but she's going to end up buying less time than she hoped. She's very clear that's the ultimate nature of the transaction. Every dollar buys her a minute, maybe literally. No, not even. A dollar a minute—she does the math—comes to $1,440, more than a half million annually. Once she's paid Val his share, then paid off Sophie, she'll be lucky to have six months of savings on which to live. Six months in which to figure out what to do next, even as she's spending the money she'll inevitably need as capital for a new start.

Selling the house and moving to Florida might be the way to go after all. But first she's going to have to lowball Sophie the way Paul's buyer has lowballed her. Not a seller's market, Paul-the-proxy has explained, yet he still wants a finder's fee of 5 percent. She wonders if Anna Marie is tied to the deal, if the girl was telling the truth when she said Paul recruited *her*. She wouldn't mind. Anna Marie would try to keep the group health-care plan intact, continue to use the HoJacks and the car service, whatever it takes to keep the girls safe. Heloise is keeping the travel agency and the shopping service, empty shells that they are once severed from the main business.

"It says here that a lawn service is a good business to start in a down economy," Audrey says. She is at Heloise's office desk, studying the Kiplinger site, where Heloise has been taking a series of tests to gauge if she's knowledgeable enough to start her own business. Surprise, surprise—she is. On the other hand, she's apparently doing a terrible job of saving for her retirement. It's because she's too risk-averse for her age, but if only Kiplinger knew: She's a ninety-year-old woman trapped in the body of a thirty-seven-year-old.

"That makes no sense to me," Heloise says, still resentful that she missed this particular question on the self-administered quiz. "When people have to cut their budgets, they start with things they can do themselves. Laundry, if they've been sending it out. Restaurant meals. Besides, I can see lots of women happily getting rid of the lawn service on the theory that their husbands could benefit from the exercise. And you know it's usually women who make out the household budgets."

"I'm just reading what it says here," Audrey counters. "Don't argue with me, argue with Mr. Kiplinger."

"At any rate, a lawn service isn't something I could do. I like gardening as a hobby."

"I've always thought," Audrey says, "that you could do better by your own landscaping here given that you use a service. It's a little bland. No real color or anything."

"I *like* it bland." This is not exactly true. But Heloise believes it's better to have a yard of no distinction, to live in a place that is not easily identified. Ordinary colors, even on the door, no distinguishing characteristics. Blend,

blend, blend. Luckily, this makes the house easier to sell, too, although Scott has decided that he'd prefer not to move until the end of the school year, if possible. Maybe, Heloise has said. Maybe.

However, to appease Sophie, who believes that the house is Heloise's primary asset, she has listed it on a for-sale-by-owner Web site, pricing it too high, which she has learned is the most common rookie mistake. As the house languishes online, it buys her time with Sophie. Heloise has been trying to figure out if she can put WFEN into a fake bankruptcy at the same time, calculating that a defunct business can't be sued for workers' compensation. However, that would involve outright fraud. WFEN is still solvent, thank God, earning a tidy profit, which is what makes it attractive to a buyer, who Heloise suspects is linked to one of the coming casinos. It is a nice synergy, a casino and an escort service, although the work is slightly different. A casino needs girls to prop the guys up, keep them gambling between small bouts of sex and comfort. She'll tell Sophie the house won't sell and offer her a third of what she demanded.

She hears her own voice in her head, from all those years ago, the last time she was blackmailed: *She'll come back, just like any alley cat you feed.* Bettina.

Audrey leaves the computer to Heloise and goes back to searching the files for any paperwork that can be discarded. They are shredding what they can, boxing up only the financial documents that would be needed in case of an audit, then putting aside a few things for the new owners, although most of the info on the clients remains in Heloise's head, still to be transcribed and shared. They also are shredding anything relating to Sophie, but that's more of an emotional journey. Thanks to Heloise's compliance, the state and federal government both have W-2s establishing Sophie's employment with WFEN. Heloise can't unring that bell.

"I don't see any medical records," Audrey says.

"We wouldn't have those. Privacy law and all. Those go to her directly."

"But you were paying for the drugs—"

"I was, but I just gave her cash, because our health insurance didn't include a provision for prescriptions."

Audrey looks at Heloise, puzzled. "Then how do you know she has AIDS?"

"Technically, she has HIV, but— Oh, *fuck* me."

"Heloise!" Audrey reprimands. "That's a five-dollar word."

"Fuck me," she repeats. "And I'll put in ten bucks when I get upstairs. Maybe I should put in twenty, because I don't think I'm through."

How does Heloise know that Sophie has HIV? *Because Sophie told her so.* And because Sophie looks different, but maybe she looks different to Heloise simply because Heloise believes she has HIV. Yet why would Sophie lie about something like that?

Because she got almost as much money to sit on her ass as she did to work. Heloise had given her cash for the drugs because there was no prescription plan, covered her rent, kicked in for the odd expense here and there.

Heloise's mind roots around for the truth, on its scent at last.

294

"I never liked her," Audrey says. "She was snooty, acted like she was better than everyone."

Yes, she was, Heloise thinks. Snooty and clever. Heloise doesn't like being outwitted by someone—who does?—and it's particularly shameful that this lazy young woman might have done just that. Whatever Heloise's mistakes and flaws, laziness isn't among them. She thinks about Sophie's abandoned degree—again something Heloise accepted as a consequence of Sophie's illness. And the severed relationship with her parents, which Heloise chalked up to shame, but there is no shame if there is no diagnosis. Why else would she be on the outs with her parents?

Because she's an addict.

Bingo. That would explain much—the need for money, the lack of support from parents and friends, assuming Sophie ever had friends. But, Jesus, how could Heloise miss that? How could her clients miss it? She thinks about the customers lost, the ones who declined the HIV test and the ones who took it. Obviously it's better for her if Sophie is lying. Then she truly has no leverage. Heloise won't have to pay her a cent. And she wouldn't wish HIV on anyone, not even an enemy. Which Sophie will avowedly be if she's lied all this time, undoing Heloise's relationship with Leo—and to what end? Really, she almost wishes that Audrey's instincts, always suspect in Heloise's experience, are wrong yet again.

There's only one way to find out. She picks up the phone. Sophie doesn't answer. She never does. Heloise imagines her on the sofa in a messy apartment, watching afternoon television, screening her calls. A chance at a degree from Hopkins, and she just throws it away, all the while mocking Heloise's own lack of education. Heloise leaves a curt message, saying things have come together more quickly than she hoped. They should meet sooner rather than later.

That afternoon, at Scott's soccer game, Tom drifts onto the field, hands in his pockets. It has been such a strange fall—warm well into October, a freak dusting of snow the day before Halloween, then a week of viciously cold temperatures, followed by this spate of balmy days. End-of-the-world weather, Heloise thinks. The boys are in high spirits, the game a little wild and undisciplined. Scott's ready for the season to be over, Heloise can tell. He likes the other boys, but he doesn't truly like soccer. He's better than average, but that's not enough for him. He likes to be good at things, preferably the best at things. She's pretty sure that's her gift to him, whether by nature or nurture.

And now she will be the best . . . at what? She still doesn't have an inkling. Yet it's the first thing she says to Tom when he comes up to her.

"I'm getting out."

"That's good," he says a little absently, scanning the field, finding the one redhead.

"Did you hear me?"

"You said you were getting out more. That's nice. You've always deserved more fun."

"No, I'm getting *out*. I'm going to"—she decides not to mention selling the business. Even Tom, soon-to-be-retired

296

cop that he is, might find that too juicy a target once she's detached, will figure the new owner isn't buying Heloise's protection from him. That wouldn't be fair to the new buyer, much less all her regulars. She's not going to screw Paul over now, even though she suspects he's screwing her a little. Finder's fee, her ass.

"I'm going to close down the business, come up with something legit to do."

"In this economy? That's going to be tough."

"I have enough savings to go for a while. And aren't you doing the same thing, leaving a safe job to try something new?"

"I've got a pension and a job waiting for me. What are you going to do, though? Do you have any ideas?"

His skepticism is hurtful. Tom, of all people, should believe in her.

"There are some interesting franchise opportunities." She doesn't know where this lie comes from; it flies out of her mouth, a tangential idea from her computer searches, where she has seen promises of burgeoning franchises. Frozen yogurt, tea shops. But that's not what really interests her. She wants to create another business from the ground up. Whatever Tom thinks about WFEN, it is a successful small business and almost wholly her creation. She has accomplished something that many people never do. She should be the kind of woman who's feted at banquets, celebrated for her achievements, the *Daily Record*'s Woman of the Year.

"Well, that's great," Tom says, but there's not much

oomph behind the words. He glances around, gauges their distance from everyone else. "So about this other business, the reason you asked me to drop by?"

"Yes?"

"I don't think I can go to Jolson and try to bullshit him that I knew Shelley and Bettina back in the day, like it just came to me."

"But you were investigating Val back then and you did meet Bettina once."

"Yeah, years later, and how do I explain that, Heloise? 'You see, six years ago Bettina tried to extort money from some other prostitute that I know, so I paid her a visit, persuaded her to change her mind.'"

Some other prostitute. That seems unnecessarily harsh.

"What should I do, Tom?"

"I don't know. Maybe accept that it worked out as you wanted. Val's in prison, and he has no idea that you're the person who put him there."

"But Bettina—"

"I know. But I'm in a different jurisdiction. I don't know the guys working her murder, don't know how to share information with them without being asked a lot of questions. Besides, if you're right, Heloise, the guy's probably a pro, did it right, learned from his mistakes on the first homicide. If you're wrong, it's bad info and it sends them in the wrong direction."

"I'm not wrong," she says. But she wavers because she wants to be wrong.

"Why do you care so much?"

"Because . . . because it's my fault. Don't you feel that way? *We* did this."

"I never put her name in play, Heloise. I provided a confidential informant who did what he had to do, then had the courtesy to die from cirrhosis, just as we planned. You're the one who had to embroider it, tell Val how the guy learned it from some other prostitute."

Some other prostitute—there are those words again, hurtful and cruel. Has she been wrong about Tom all these years? Does he feel only contempt for her?

"But if you think Val is the one who had her killed—"

"I could go either way on that, frankly. And either way you'll be fine. If he managed to put out a hit on her, he thinks he's done and you're safe. If he didn't do it, then it's random and you're still safe."

"Unless he gets a new trial and gets released. Then nothing can keep me safe."

"Jesus, how many times do we have to go over that? First of all, while the ballistics expert may have lied about his credentials, his information is still solid. Val's gun, hidden on Val's property, killed Kristofer Martin. He's not going to get a new trial, much less be acquitted."

"But what if he thought he was?"

"What if?"

"With Val the only thing that matters is what he believes. His reality is the only reality. Even if he thinks that Bettina is the one who ratted him out, he might fear me as a potential witness against him."

"Well, even in Val's reality, cockeyed as it is, he knows

you can't testify against him because you'd have to tell the courtroom what you did, who you are. And you'd never do that because—"

His eyes go to the field, searching out the boy that Heloise knows he wishes were his. They watch the game in silence, and she is reminded of what Paul told her, about all the different kinds of silence that a couple can inhabit. This is neither companionable nor cold, merely distant, the fraught quiet between a man who wanted more and a woman who wanted less. Tom loved her once, she's sure of that, but she realizes now that he hasn't loved her for a long time.

"Val doesn't know about Scott. Remember? He doesn't know how much I have to lose. And he doesn't know I'm getting out. When I tell him that, he might become fearful that I'll turn against him."

"So don't tell him." Tom doesn't know how often she sees Val, how intertwined he is in her life. Or does he? Maybe Tom knows more than she realizes. She thinks back to the last time they stood here, how they spoke of Shelley's death, then thought to be a suicide, and he told her to be careful. Has he known all along about her murder? Did he know that Shelley was one of Val's girls and not tell Heloise?

The outstanding player on Scott's team, a gorgeous Ethiopian boy adopted just two years ago, intercepts a flying ball with his head, knocks it to the ground, and snares it under his foot, then begins flying toward the goal, now in control. Heloise knows how the ball feels—under someone's foot, moving forward swiftly, but with no control over what's going to happen to her.

Tuesday, November 15

This time Sophie comes to her. Heloise sets up the meeting in the new Four Seasons Hotel, in the so-called Harbor East neighborhood. She has often done business in this neighborhood, because it is, to quote another poem that her librarian friend taught her years ago, a place where executives would never tamper. They like to play here in the evenings, try out the restaurants, but during the day the area is far removed from their part of Baltimore, in style if not actual miles. Their colleagues sit at the Center Club, whose name once made sense. Light and Pratt Streets were the city's nexus for many years. But now the view from that lofty private club, while still beautiful, is a little emptier. Harborplace, which kick-started the city's renaissance, is losing tenants; even the stalwart Phillips has moved east along the water. USF&G is gone, as is the big brokerage firm that once sat above The Gallery. The action has moved, too, as evidenced by the Four Seasons. If Heloise intended to keep going in the business, she would try to cultivate some contacts here. She likes the name of the restaurant, Wit & Wisdom, which is depicted as a fox and an owl. She hopes to corner the market on both commodities in this meeting.

Sophie tries not to look impressed by her surroundings when she arrives to find Heloise waiting for her. It's not always a sign of weakness to be the one who waits, especially if one is on the phone and halfway through a lovely appetizer. Not that Heloise requires a midafternoon snack of bison tartare, but it's all about appearances. She is dressed in the same suit she wore to meet with Paul. It flatters her.

Sophie, on the other hand, has a small stain on her blouse and looks a little rumpled. She also has a runny nose and a twitch. How had Heloise missed the telltale signs? Val never would have, she has to admit. He was onto Bettina the moment she started to go down that road. Sophie has probably been a full-fledged addict for at least two years.

"Traffic was horrible," Sophie says, and perhaps she's sincere. She thinks her payoff is coming; she's motivated.

"It gets worse and worse," Heloise says, loving the banality of their chatter, in no hurry at all to get down to brass tacks, whereas Sophie is impatient, crazed to know what she's going to get. "Would you like tea? A glass of wine? Something to eat?"

"A glass of wine would be great. Red, to warm the bones. It's not that it's cold out, but it's so damp."

Heloise places the order for Sophie, then says, "Can you drink while on Trizivir?" She knows the answer. She knows the answer to most of the questions she plans to ask today.

"What?" Sophie says.

"I mean, I assume so, but I wasn't sure. Are you allowed to drink, or does it interfere with your medication?"

"Oh. One drink is okay. It won't kill me." She rallies, skilled liar that she is. "I'd be lucky if alcohol was all I had to worry about."

"I suppose that's true." Heloise looks grave, concerned. "Do you have your paperwork together?"

"What paperwork? You didn't say anything about paperwork."

No, she hadn't. "I didn't? I've been so scattered, what with all I have to do. I thought I told you to bring your medical records."

"Why would I bring you my medical records?"

"Just to be complete. I want to know exactly where you are, in terms of your diagnosis, before I finalize your severance package."

"Severance package?" Sophie smiles, getting it, *thinking* she's getting it. "Yeah, that's what it is, isn't it? My golden parachute."

"People live a long time now with HIV, Sophie. No matter what I do, I don't think I can leave you fixed for life."

"Still, it would be nice to have something."

"Yes, yes, it would. But, as you know, I've always run WFEN like the business it is. There will be an official separation package. You will sign documents absolving me of liability going forward, agreeing not to ask me for money again."

Sophie grins, so sure of the upper hand. She probably thinks that Heloise has already forgotten about the medical records.

"Sure, have it your way." Thinking, no doubt, as all blackmailers think, that there will always be more money, that she can come back to the well as soon as she's dry. Not that Sophie's playing a truly long con. Drug addicts don't

303

have the attention span to do that. If it comes down to it, Sophie probably doesn't have the work ethic necessary to file the paperwork for workers' comp, even if she did have the required documentation. She's lazy. How did she get past Heloise for all these months? Everyone makes mistakes, and this is Heloise's only disastrous hire, but it still galls. She was blinded by her own envy of the girl, this polished New Yorker who had everything that Heloise wanted—and valued none of it. Unlike the other girls, she didn't even have a pressing financial need for the job. She just wanted to know her worth, her value.

"I'm serious, Sophie. This is a onetime offer. Once we reach our terms, that's it. You can't come back. For one thing, there won't be a WFEN anymore. I'm disbanding it."

"To do what?"

Ah, that vexing question again. "I have some irons in the fire. But the thing is, the business will be gone, its assets—of which there are almost none—dissipated."

"Okay, whatever. You know, I didn't say I would entertain counteroffers. I was pretty specific about what I wanted."

"Yes, you were. But I'm a businesswoman. I can't help myself—I have to counter."

She takes out a piece of a paper and writes carefully. Sophie seems to get more excited with each pen stroke. After all, the more pen strokes, the higher the offer, right? Heloise passes the paper across the table, neatly folded, and sips her tea happily while Sophie reads it.

"What is this bullshit?"

The note says:

Zero.

"I don't think you have HIV," Heloise says. "You lied. You just didn't want to work anymore. Probably because you have a drug problem and that's time-consuming. I know. I used to live with an addict. It's a demanding life that forces you to quit working, even though it's only through working that you can afford the drugs. It's very paradoxical. I once heard a man say that being a drug addict was the hardest job in America, and you're not really cut out for hard work."

"I do too have AIDS. HIV. You can't prove that I don't."

"I don't have to. You have to prove that you *do*. Look, I've done the research—you'd have trouble suing me even if you were HIV-positive. Infected workers in the porn industry haven't been able to sue successfully for workers' compensation." Heloise doesn't actually know if this is true, only that she couldn't find any examples. "If you're not . . . well, I guess that's good news, right? A classic case of good news and bad news. Good news: You're disease-free. Bad news: There's no payoff for that. If anything, I should sue you. For the cost of drugs you never bought, for the clients I lost."

"I am too," Sophie says. She sounds like a little kid, but then—she always sounded like a little kid. Petulant, caring only for her needs.

"If that's true, I am sincerely sorry. But I need to see your medical records."

"You say that like it's easy." The girl's mind is racing, she's probably trying to figure out a way to fake her diagnosis. Steal someone else's paper, get a friend to fake being her doctor and confide in Heloise, privacy laws be damned.

"My hunch is that it will be impossible," Heloise says, all seriousness now. "Really, Sophie—why?"

"What do you mean?"

"Why did you do this?"

"I didn't do anything. I'm the one who's sick from working for you." Still grasping, committed to her bit.

"If you needed money, if you had come to me—"

"Right." Sophie's tone is bitter, and it shames Heloise. She's correct—Heloise would have been loath to help out anyone financially, and she never would have given her anything if Sophie had been honest. A ride to rehab is all she would have offered.

She tries, "You have a problem."

"You have a problem." Sophie says this in a very childlike, you-are-rubber-I-am-glue way. But she has a followup. "I can still tell. I can still make things bad for you."

"Very soon there will be nothing to tell."

"Doesn't change what you've been."

"No, but it hurts others. Lots of others. Why do that to them, just to get at me?"

"Because I want money. How dim can you be, you stupid cunt?"

The word carries. People look up from their drinks. Heloise tries to keep her face impassive.

"There's not going to be any money. I'm sorry. When I thought you had HIV, I felt I had an obligation to help you.

And I did. But I don't think you have the virus, and I'm not going to help you anymore unless you prove me wrong."

"I'll tell your son."

Now it's Heloise's turn to say, "What?"

"Leo told me. You have a kid."

Accountants just know too fucking much about a person. How she wishes now that she had never claimed Scott as a dependent.

"Don't go there," Heloise says, knowing that the phrase is tired and threadbare, but it's also precise, literally and figuratively. She will kill Sophie if she tries to come to her house. "Don't talk about him."

"I'll talk about whatever the fuck I want to talk about, you hypocrite of a whore. You have a son. Give me money or I'll find him and tell him who his mommy is and what she does."

Heloise fights down a rage so virulent that it feels like the legacy of Hector Lewis. She wants to slap this girl or shake her. But she doesn't. She wills the anger to stop clouding her brain and says, "No you won't. You're too lazy."

"What?"

"You're too lazy except when it comes to getting whatever your drug of choice is. I'm going to guess coke, but it could be meth. I don't care. I do know that you don't have the initiative to get off your ass and do something that complicated. You could barely be bothered to get here on time today, and you thought you were going to get a nice little payoff."

"Leo will do it for me."

307

"Not after he finds out that you conned him, too, played on his sympathies. By the way, he'll probably want to have sex with you now, if he hasn't already."

"Oh, fuck you."

"You can't afford it, Sophie. I get more per hour than my employees do."

Sophie bolts her wine.

"That's the last thing I'll ever buy you."

"We'll see," Sophie says, standing. "You don't get to call all the shots. You always thought you did. You thought you were so grand, so above us. You're nothing but a pimp in better clothes, luring girls in with your ads and your promises and your I'm-so-enlightened bullshit. And the health insurance, which wasn't worth shit. We didn't even have a prescription plan. I got root canal, and the painkillers were like seventy-five dollars. What if I had gotten really sick, needed a hard-core chronic prescription?"

Ah, so that was the source of her brainstorm—and maybe the beginning of her problem.

"I can help you find a rehab," Heloise says. "I do think I owe you that. Some girls—they start to use to get through, although it doesn't really enhance their performance, which is probably why you started booking less. I will help you get clean, get back into school."

"I don't need to go to rehab."

"Okay," Heloise says. "Okay."

"You're gonna pay me. You're gonna pay me or wish you had. I'll find you."

Heloise sips her tea complacently. Sophie doesn't even

308

know her full name. The checks are signed by Audrey, who is WFEN's comptroller. Yes, Leo knows her address, but she's pretty sure that Leo will want nothing to do with Sophie after Heloise talks to him.

She pulls out three twenties, starts to leave them on the table, thinks better of it, and signals the waiter over. No fiend worth her salt would pass up cash.

"I'm going to find you," Sophie repeats, quietly this time.

"I've really got to go, Sophie. Let me know if you change your mind and you want help. That I will provide. But I'm not giving you any more cash. I feel bad that I didn't figure this out sooner, because I think I could have helped you if I'd understood everything."

"Help me? You destroyed me."

The words lodge like fishhooks. Heloise still feels them thirty-five minutes later as she turns in to her street. Could she? Did she? It was never her intention to ruin anyone. She was only offering girls the same life she had fashioned for herself.

Her mother, she realizes, could make the same rationalization. Not that her mother is given to much rationalization. She hasn't called or written since Heloise visited her. She pleaded her case and let it go. She has a lot more dignity than Sophie.

Heloise had thought, heading out today, that she would return home triumphant. Instead she feels like a boxer who has won on a technicality. She's got the belt, she's got the money, but she's bruised and battered and can barely see. She almost trips over the package on her doorstep, a white-paper ghost tented over a beautiful pot of narcissus.

The flowers are from Terry, who has been calling her for days. She can't see him, though, not now. She has tried to explain that to him, but her sudden decision to cut him off makes no sense to him. How can it? It baffles her, too. All she can do is hope that he will still be interested in a few months when her reinvention is complete. But she's pretty sure that's too much to ask.

Friday, November 18

Heloise is driving home from an appointment, listening to another profanity-laced message from Sophie, the girl's voice slurring and staggering over itself, broadcast into the car via the Bluetooth. Sophie has called every day to curse her, threaten her, but the messages are losing steam. Still, she will have to be careful not to answer the phone when Scott is in the car. Leo, who when sober seems equally terrified of both Heloise and Sophie, swore he didn't give Sophie the home number or address, and as the home phone has been blissfully quiet so far, it appears he's telling her the truth.

Nevertheless, she's unnerved to see a car parked at the corner, although she knows instantly that it's not Sophie's. It's too nice, too clean. She slows as she passes but doesn't make eye contact with the driver. Yet after changing to more comfortable clothes—leggings, a loose cashmere top, flat boots—she walks down to the end of the street and taps on his window.

"I'm sorry," Terry says. Sheepish, embarrassed.

"This is creepy, Terry. You're freaking me out. We never even—"

"I know, I know," he says. "I just never had someone drop me so quickly. Especially someone who seemed to like me."

She looks around. She can't decide what is best—speaking to him here or letting him enter the house. She still has an hour until Scott comes home.

"Do you want to come in? To talk, I mean. Leave your car here, though, and wait five minutes. I'll open the garage door and you can come in through the kitchen."

She's not even sure why she takes that precaution. The neighborhood has the empty, ghostly feel it always has during school hours. Regardless, she doesn't want anyone to see her walking down her street with a man. Old habits die hard.

Terry follows her instructions, seemingly eager to show how obedient he can be. Her stove is so powerful that the tea water is already warm. She fixes him a mug, although he hasn't asked for one.

"I don't know how to do this," he says.

"Me either," she replies, although she's not sure they're talking about the same "this." She doesn't know how she can have a relationship with a civilian when she's not sure how she's going to escape her old life. Even now, with the sale of her business set for the week after Thanksgiving and Sophie neutralized, Heloise can't decide what will be safest for her, and therefore best for Scott. Should they move? Will Scott reconsider his request to stay through the school year? Will it be harder or easier to find a job in a new place?

And what the hell is she going to do? That's the question she should have been asking all along. She put money away for retirement (although not in the right investments, according to Kiplinger, and with no employer to match her contributions). She had been prudent with her spending, living well within her means. She opened a 529 when Scott was two and is on pace to have enough to pay his college tuition—but only if she keeps earning at the same rate, and that isn't going to be possible. How has she failed to see this? She isn't someone in an industry that has been transformed by technology, although she supposes that day could come, that even sex could be digitized. How has she ignored the fact that she would have to change careers eventually or risk her son's knowledge of what she does? Even Val saw it coming, although he thought she should simply segue into management.

"I'm not wrong," Terry says. "You liked me."

"I like you. But I have a son, and we're thinking about making some changes. I might sell my business, try something new. We might move. It didn't seem fair to you to start something."

"Maybe you should let me decide what's fair to me."

She wants to bury her face in his neck, if only to smell him. She bets he smells great, of soap and shaving cream and some kind of old-fashioned, citrusy aftershave.

"I just have a lot going on right now. Maybe later." She wants to tell him that she's a caterpillar and he should wait for the butterfly version but fears she will sound insane.

He stands up, takes his mug to the sink, rinses it out, and puts it in the upper rack of the dishwasher. It's a bit ostentatious, almost as if he's going overboard to demonstrate his perfection. But then he walks over to Mother's office, as the realtors would have it, and turns his back to her for a second, facing the wall where the family calendar hangs, with Scott's myriad activities highlighted in purple marker. His shoulders are heaving. He doesn't want her to see that he's crying, or about to cry. It is equal parts freaky and flattering.

"I'm going to take you at your word," he says in a voice that doesn't quite quaver. "I'm going to let you be. You know how to get in touch with me. I could be good for you, Heloise, I really could. But I respect that you're not in a place right now where that works for you. Let me know if your situation changes."

He makes a very dignified exit through the kitchen door to the garage, only to have to return because the garage door is down. Heloise walks back to the kitchen door with him, punches in the code. In the split second before the door raises to the top, exposing them to the empty street, he pulls her to him and kisses her. It manages to be at once a passionate and respectful kiss, quick as it is. He walks away as soon as the door is up, and she watches him go.

Ten minutes later, when Audrey returns from running errands, Heloise is still standing there.

Audrey gives her a weird look but says only, "You're getting Scott today, right? It's Friday."

"Right."

"Heloise, are you okay?"

"Perfectly fine."

Sitting outside Scott's school, she feels— She's not quite sure what she feels. Not perfectly fine, that's for sure. She watches her son come toward her. Every day he's more guarded, closer to being a teenager, too cool to show that he's happy to see her. If she does her job right, he will grow up, go to college, thrive in a career he loves, marry a nice girl, have children of his own. He will be subsumed into his wife's family, as husbands usually are. And she will be— what? Lonely? Alone? Both? Will she consider it a good bargain, then? Will she regret the choices she has made? In living her life for her child, has she neglected herself as surely as her own mother neglected her? Her mother favored her husband over her child. Heloise has favored her child over herself. The first one is wrong, the second one is right—right?

"How was school today?"

"Okay."

"Should we have our usual Friday treat?"

"Of course! But don't forget, next Friday I have a sleepover at Lindsey's. You remember, right?"

The sleepover, a very big deal as Scott is allowed only a few, is the day after Thanksgiving. Heloise has agreed to it because she knows that some of her regulars will be wild to escape the house that weekend, will try to squeeze in appointments while their wives and families descend on the local malls. She's been booking cash dates, risking a little under-the-table income, keen to capture every dollar she can in these final days.

"I won't forget, buddy. But first we have Thanksgiving, right? And you're going to make the gravy this year."

"The gravy and the mashed potatoes. Plus, you promised

I could use all the real knives this time. Under supervision, you said."

"I did."

She has never been the kind of mother who calls her son "my little man" or "my best guy." And Scott was not the kind of child who ever announced he wanted to marry his mother. That's a good thing for a boy with no father. But he often tells her that she is pretty, the prettiest of all the mothers that he knows. He loves her. He's enough. Right? He has to be enough.

Sunday, November 20

"Does Paul really tell us that God forbids homosexuality in his Epistle to the Romans, perhaps his masterwork?

The Reverend Frida arches an eyebrow, aware that she has captured everyone's attention with that single word "homosexuality." Even its third syllable alone would have done the trick. Is it just Heloise's imagination, or does the Reverend Frida also touch her shaved nape, encouraging people to notice her short, short hair, daring her congregation to speculate, as she must know they have frequently speculated, on the nature of *her* sexuality? It's the one part of her life that the reverend has not shared. Yet.

"Let's look at the relevant passages even as most of you are thinking, 'Well, this is a heck of a way to kick off the Thanksgiving sermon.' I bet you were hoping for something about gratitude. But the flip side of gratitude is ingratitude, and Romans happens to touch on that subject, too."

And she's off. One has to decide early in a Frida sermon whether to follow or zone out. That's her genius. Or presumption, if one prefers. Her sermons zig and zag; it's impossible to predict where she will end up. Having gotten everyone's interest by declaring that she's stalking a somewhat bold and interesting topic, Frida is now reminding people of the context of the epistles, jumping to Paul's biography. Heloise wants to listen, she really does, but her mind is such a stew these days. She tries to settle in, only to think— *Do we have to have turkey for Thanksgiving? Even a small one means leftovers for days. Maybe I can talk Scott into quail, if I make it sound fancy enough.* Or: *Is frozen piecrust really so awful?* Being the mother of a foodie has its trials. She'll make it in the Cuisinart, which Scott also considers cheating, but of a lesser degree.

The Reverend Frida is talking about the road to Damascus now, the alternative theories about what happened to Paul, if there might be a scientific or medical explanation as to what struck him. Perhaps if Heloise can still her mind, she will be rewarded with her own epiphany; the answers to all her problems will become clear. But even as she longs for this, she doubts that it ever works that way. Brainstorms are always unbidden. She felt as if she was close to one the other day, leaving the Mandarin Oriental, or maybe it was the Wit & Wisdom. Something about a hotel, the parking valet. A bed-and-breakfast? God, no.

The Reverend Frida zags back to the passages in Romans concerning sex, the confusion over what women were doing with one another, if anything, the references to shrine prostitution, which may be better understood as false idolatry. Is it just Heloise's imagination, or does Coranne turn back and smile at her? What's that about? This is why Heloise has always been nervous about Scott's having close friends. He might unwittingly transmit information that is laden in ways he can't comprehend. *My mom gets to go out to the best restaurants in Washington and Baltimore. Who does she go with? Oh, different guys. She calls them clients.* All quite factual, all legitimate when explained in the context of her life as a lobbyist, but lies have a way of outing themselves when found in a more innocent mouth.

Then she remembers: Coranne was there when Heloise spoke to the Reverend Frida about prostitution in the Bible. She probably means the glance as tribute.

Besides, Coranne is as distracted as Heloise, her neck swiveling as her gaze bounces around the half-filled room. She's probably trying to still her own thoughts. She looks exhausted, her hair dribbling out of a lackadaisical chignon, her knit suit tight and rumpled. Would Heloise change places with her if she could? Would she be forty-something Coranne, who seems perpetually overextended yet cheerful? No, not cheerful exactly, but determined to be cheerful. There's a difference. Coranne has sold herself to one man, Heloise to many. Who came out ahead in that equation?

"What did you think of the sermon?" Coranne asks Heloise at the fellowship. "Was that the direction you thought she would take it, when you suggested the prostitutes of the Bible?"

Heloise realizes she has brought this upon herself. See where even a moment of pretend friendliness leads one.

"I thought it was almost *too* personal. I understand why the Reverend Frida is interested in the Scriptures' ideas about homosexuality—or think I do. For someone who talks so much about herself, she's pretty coy. And I usually like the way she wanders around a topic. But today it felt like a stretch, the whole ingratitude-to-gratitude peg. I would have liked to hear a straight-up sermon on gratitude, counting our blessings."

"Really?"

"Yes." *Yes.* Heloise finds herself interested in the conversation almost in spite of herself. "It seems to me that people very quickly get used to both the worst and the best life has to offer. We can be incredibly stoic and spoiled at the same time."

"Oh, I'm just spoiled," Coranne says. "My husband would be the first to tell you that."

"I don't see that at all."

"I complain constantly. I'm a stay-at-home mom, which is what I wanted. Rick would have been happy to have a second income. He works in a precarious industry, but he's hung in there and ended up making more money than ever. We don't want for anything, my kids are healthy—well, relatively, the baby always seems to have a cold or a stomach-ache—yet all I do is dwell on the negative."

Heloise is unnerved by how personal the conversation has become, wants to derail it. "Oh, you're too hard on yourself," she begins, but Coranne will not be deterred.

"I never have time for myself. That's why I look like such a wreck. And don't say I don't, because I know I do. And I don't feel like I can ask for help, because that's my job, right? Staying home with my kids? Only who else has a job where they're on call 24/7? I mean, yes, two of them are in school, but Jillian's home with me. She's fourteen months, she takes one nap a day. If I'm lucky. That's what I get to myself.

That and my own night's sleep—but, well, listen to me. I'm preaching out of self-interest, too. It's hard to avoid, I guess."

Heloise feels almost violated by this torrential confession. If a man had unleashed this kind of energy, she would expect to be paid. Her mind leapfrogs: *Maybe I could be a shrink.* No, too much school, more than a decade. Clinical social worker, psychologist? Whatever path she takes, she can't get around the fact that all she has is a GED and some business courses from an unaccredited online school. And it strikes her as unfair that she would make so much less, having her ears filled, than she has— She interrupts her own flow of thought, feeling she must say something to Coranne, find a way to answer the imploring look in her eyes.

"Look, if the sleepover this Friday is too much, we can cancel. I don't want to add to your burden."

"Oh, no, Scott is a dream guest. Do you know he strips the bed? I've had adult guests who haven't thought to do that."

Heloise smiles, thinking, *I taught him well.*

"His manners are simply wonderful. You'll have to tell me sometimes how you did that. Regular beatings? Just kidding." Her voice does the motherly deprecation trill, high and desperate. "Seriously, he's nice, Heloise. I mean, he's smart, too, and other things, but he's so considerate. It knocks me out."

"Me, too," Heloise admits. Then, "I can't take credit, really. He was sweet from day one. Just born that way."

"They do show up with their own temperaments. For better or worse."

The Reverend Frida is making the rounds. Trolling for praise—from Heloise's point of view, a little unseemly in a minister. Heloise never solicits praise from her clientele and doesn't worry if it's not articulated. If the men come back, that's all she needs to know. And some of the ones who don't come back have a fetish for novelty, so she doesn't worry about them, either. She almost wishes she could share this advice with the Reverend Frida, tell her just to note who keeps coming back week after week.

"How are you ladies doing today?"

"Great," Heloise says.

"Fine," Coranne says, but the waver in her voice makes it less than convincing.

"Coranne's having a tough week," Heloise says.

"Oh, it's not so bad," Coranne says.

"The holidays," the Reverend Frida says, nodding sympathetically. Hell, Heloise thinks, why provide the answer? Why not fucking *ask*? The rhetorical devices employed in sermons have made the Reverend Frida forget that it's allowed to ask people questions without knowing the answers.

"I know, right?" Coranne says, grateful for being spared having to answer. It's as if she'd rather agree to any banal assessment of her situation than admit what's really going on. Then again, how did Heloise reward Coranne's candor? She tells herself that she's not the reverend, that this isn't her gig. But out of guilt she decides to throw herself on the grenade that is Frida.

"Great sermon today," she says.

The Reverend Frida brightens. "You think so? I know it

322

was a little unusual, not what people expect. I was originally planning a sermon about what led me to my calling when I started out in investment banking—" And she was off to the races, blah, blah, blah. Heloise decides to zone out, having heard much of the story before. She tries to locate the tickle of an idea that she had when she was thinking about social work, but it's gone. That's what she gets for being nice and listening to Coranne. That's why she's not really suited to social work. Whatever she does, Heloise needs a job that allows her mind to slip away at times. The current one has been great for that.

And then, lo and behold, a miracle: The Reverend Frida says something helpful.

"What I learned is that sometimes you just have to leap even if you don't know where you're going to land," says this earnest young woman who has always had the safety net of a family's money—and unconditional love. That fact has come up in the sermons again and again. "I thought I could continue to work and go to seminary. A straddle. But I had to commit to leaving my job before I could see what I really wanted to do with my life. The moment I quit, I had utter clarity."

Well, that's what Heloise is doing in spite of herself, so why hasn't she achieved clarity, utter or otherwise? Will it happen when she has the cash in hand, when her days are suddenly empty?

No, she realizes. It will happen when she tells Val that she's quitting. Then it will be real, urgent. Once she tells Val, it will be true.

Tuesday, November 22

The familiar drive to the prison feels new, as if she's seeing it for the first time. It's an odd kind of nostalgia, nostalgia for nostalgia's sake, the preternatural desire to be done with a place so she can long for it. She sees Baltimore as so many people have seen it throughout the years from this highway, marveling at its ugly, hardworking façade, as embodied by the mountains of coal, the grain elevators, the huge cranes. This part of Baltimore looks as it did when she and Billy arrived twenty years ago.

But when she heads west, into the city, the landscape has changed. There are more and more signs in Spanish, businesses catering to an immigrant population that wasn't yet here in the early nineties. The high-rise housing project, Flag House, hasn't cast its shadow over the city in years. The area around Hopkins Hospital has been depopulated.

She enters the visiting area, her cheeks flushed, her smile barely compressed. How often is one lucky enough to recognize a seminal moment? So much in her life has happened *to* her. That's about to change.

Val picks up on her mood. "Well, if it isn't Miss Mary Fucking Sunshine."

"The weather's nice for this time of year."

"Sky looked overcast to me. The little of it that I can see."

Ugh, it's self-pitying Val today. She almost second-guesses herself. But no, she has promised herself this moment. Part of changing her life means fulfilling the promises she makes to herself.

"I've been thinking—"

"Aren't you always?"

The question seems a little freighted, but she pushes on. "I've had an offer for the business. It's a good one, and I'm going to take it."

"How much?"

She halves the number, halving Val's take as she does so. The way she sees it, Sophie's demands would have lightened his take anyway. And Val uses money only to keep score. She could hand him Monopoly dollars for all the good it will do him.

"Then what?"

"I'm not sure. Something new, something different." She shies away from saying *legitimate*. Val not only won't respect that choice, he'll see it as a criticism.

"And what about me?"

"You're getting half the money."

"Yeah, in a onetime payment. I mean, your buyer's not going to keep putting money in my accounts, right? Probably doesn't even know I exist."

More self-pity, yet a different flavor. It's been more than a decade since Val's arrest. Does anyone on the outside remember that he exists?

"I couldn't. You're a silent partner, remember. While you

helped me set up the business, you haven't been active. For obvious reasons."

"Yeah, we're like Steve Jobs and Steve Wozniak, only I'm Wozniak. Which means—"

"That I'm Steve Jobs? Why, thank you."

"It means I'm getting screwed out of the credit I deserve, but you'll die young and I'll be rich."

He's joking. She hopes. "You yourself said I couldn't do this forever."

"I expected you to keep managing the enterprise. I mean, Christ, Hel, what else can you do?"

How many more men are going to ask her that?

"I don't know. That's why I need to make a definitive split. I want to choose a life for once, not just fall into something. I feel like I've never had the luxury of choosing what I wanted to do."

"That makes two of us."

She's not going to argue with him. She must not argue with him. "I'm tired, Val."

"You're thirty-seven. Get over it. You'll be working until the day you die. Everybody does now. The thing is, you can't make this kind of money doing anything else. What, you think there's some job out there with health care and a pension, paid vacations? Not for you. Not for anyone, hardly."

His argument strikes her as prepared, as if he has seen this day coming and readied his talking points. How can that be? How could Val have anticipated this conversation? But Val, like Heloise, anticipates a lot.

"I want a change."

"Too bad."

She is not entirely surprised by his resistance. But she's also not cowed. "Jesus, Val, you don't even *need* the money. It's just something for you to keep score with."

"That's not for you to say. Besides, my appeal won't be free."

They sit staring at each other, at an impasse but far from impassive. Heloise realizes that she has never allowed Val to see her angry with him, has always pretended deference. No more.

"Val, I'm selling, and you can't do anything about it."

He smiles. "I can't prevent the sale, no."

"Are you saying I'll be harmed? That you'll do to me what you had done to Shelley and Bettina?"

He looks side to side, although she is the only visitor just now, then hunches forward, his eyes searching her face, locking on hers. She still can't get over his physical resemblance to Scott.

"You been talking to the cops, Hel?"

"No."

"Tell the truth."

"I am. You know they asked me about Shelley's death, but that's not my fault, is it? I certainly didn't know she was on your visitors list."

"Shelley's a good example, though."

"Of what?"

"Of what happens when someone gets in a bad situation, starts to wonder how to get out of it, what she has of value.

327

I'd hate to think you were here today trying to get me to admit to things I never did because you have some legal problems."

"I don't have legal problems."

"Then why now?"

Impossible to answer without mentioning Scott.

"I just feel it's time."

"I feel like it's not. And I have fifty-one percent of the voting stock."

"Really? When did we establish that?"

"That's just how I've always thought of it in my head. You still work for me. You owe me, Heloise. You can never get out from under me. I saved you. All those years ago. Remember?"

"It was a curious kind of saving."

"It was a better situation than you had. That stupid druggie was going to drag you down with him, and you knew it. You said as much. When my luck ran out, I didn't take you with me, did I? You owe me. You'd be dead without me."

That's the second time in this conversation he has pronounced her dead.

"You had Bettina killed," she says.

"I don't know what you're talking about."

"Shelley, Bettina. You think you have a shot of getting out if there are no living witnesses. But the ballistics testimony against you is going to stand, Val. It's not in contention. The expert was flawed, but not his expertise. Besides, there's always George."

"Haven't you heard? He took a bad fall in the shower

over at ECI last week. Hit his head so hard he broke his neck. Poor fucker is still alive, but he's not expected to make it."

"I haven't seen that in the news."

Val grins. "Who says it was in the news? It's not like some poor little Baltimore County housewife, killed by an intruder. But I expect it will make the paper when he finally dies. And he's going to die, Hel."

She sits back, taking it all in. So she's right. Everyone has to die before Val files his appeal. But she gets to live because she makes money for him. Only she doesn't want to make money for him anymore.

"I'm out, Val. I'm sorry, but I'm out."

"Then you're no good to me."

"I never was any good to you, nor you to me. We brought out the worst in each other."

"We're exactly like each other."

"No. No, I don't agree with that. I can't agree with that. I don't harm people. I haven't hurt anyone the way you have."

"What about your boyfriend, all those years ago? You think he didn't get hurt?"

"He was alive the last time I saw him."

"Honey, he had a bounty on his head. The two Georges drove him back to Pennsylvania in the trunk of a car, got a nice payoff. I think we bought lobsters or steak. Whatever it was, you ate it, you enjoyed it."

"I didn't ask you to do that."

"You didn't not ask. You knew what was happening, Hel. Always. And I did, too."

She supposes this is the kind of down-and-dirty fight that only a long-married couple can have, another thing she's been spared. The layers, the viciousness, the resentments—it's all new to her.

She sits quietly. For how long? Five seconds, ten? A minute? She knows only that she wants to change the mood, to make sure that he understands she's not speaking from anger or hurt.

"I put you here."

"What?"

"I'm the one. I was always the one. I was the one who knew where the gun was."

"No, there was a CI—"

"Yeah, a CI who was dying of cirrhosis. He was a straw man, willing to carry the tale for money. I told the cop, the cop told him what to say. I thought Bettina was dead, or on her way there, so I didn't see the harm in letting you think she was the one." A beat. "I see it now."

"You are in legal trouble, aren't you? You'll say anything right now to get me to say what they want you to get out of me."

"No, I'm not under anyone's thumb. For once. I'm telling you the truth. I'm—" The phrase comes back to her. "I'm making a clean breast of things."

"Why?"

Why indeed? Because she wants him to know that in the long chess game that has been their relationship, she finally has him in check. Fifty-fucking-one percent. She'll tell Tom, she'll get protection. She'll move Scott at midterm, change her name again. She has been scared every day of Scott's life, scared of so many things. Scared something will happen to Scott. Scared she'll be arrested. Scared that Val will hurt her.

She's still scared, and yet she's not.

She sits, waiting for him to lash out with words, assuming there will be threats. But Val doesn't rise to the occasion. He just stares at her, his face unreadable. Meanwhile, Heloise feels an odd sense of relief. Not exhilaration or anything that giddy. But she has faced down something she has dreaded for years, and like most people in that situation she has found that it was just as terrible as she feared. But it's done.

As she rises to leave, Val asks, "Will you still visit?"

"I don't think so." Yet she can't help holding out a bit of hope, pretending that they can go on. "Certainly not as often."

"I'll miss you," he says.

She realizes she will miss him, too. She came here out of duty and fear, but she enjoyed their conversations in spite of herself. She and Val are not, as he insists, exactly alike. But they've been together for almost twenty years. Released by circumstance from the daily burdens that weigh down most married couples, they have been free to speak about ideas and books and the news. Yet he doesn't know her as well as he thinks he does, can't see that she has managed to stay human despite all her mistakes.

"I'll miss parts of you, Val. You're smart. I like talking to you."

"And back in the day—the other thing. Did you enjoy that, too?"

His euphemism, if that's what it is, surprises her, catches her off guard. "Sometimes. You could be rough, though."

"Had to be, sometimes."

She nods. "A little fear goes a long way, as you often told me."

"But it only goes so far. You don't fear me anymore. Even with what you think you know about me—and let me be clear, I didn't have anything to do with those things—you're not scared of me, are you?"

She has to think about that. "No, I guess I'm not. Or maybe— I don't know. Maybe I just don't fear anything anymore."

"What, you got nothing to lose?"

"Something like that." She has everything to lose.

"I need that money coming in every month, Hel." His voice is low and wheedling, a tone he hasn't used since their early days together. "I *need* it. Everything else can be forgiven if you keep up your end of the bargain."

"I don't know what to tell you, Val. Pretty soon there won't be any more money. But you will get a nice lump sum. I can sweeten it a little, but that's the best I can do."

He nods, and she realizes she's safe for now. Until Val gets his share of the sale, he won't try to have her killed.

After that, all bets are off.

Wednesday, November 23

Scott has a half day the day before Thanksgiving, so Heloise clears her own calendar. By December she won't be taking any more appointments anyway. By December—oh, Lord, it's only a week away—she'll be long gone from here. The other regulars, the ones who aren't Paul, don't yet know. Having the conversation during an appointment seems wrong somehow, a reminder that the relationship has been pure commerce. She also doesn't want to be asked about her plans, given that she has none. All she wants is a long weekend free of worry, time with Scott apart from his sleepover with Lindsey, their intimate dinner, just the two of them. Her shopping is done, the house is clean, the compromise piecrust waiting for Scott to fill later today. Heloise has never understood people who groove on the adrenaline of doing things at the last minute.

She, for example, is already making arrangements to leave the country the moment she sells the business. She's going to take Scott out of school and head for Costa Rica or Belize, two countries that came up most often in her Internet searches for best places to retire. (She has to think that the article recommending Greece is out of date.) She figures she can buy two years abroad, maybe more if she chooses wisely.

And once she's abroad, she'll write Jolson—anonymously, of course—and tell him what she thinks she knows about the deaths of Michelle Smith and Betty Martinez.

A phone rings, the house phone. "Let it go," she tells Scott. This week Sophie has started calling the house phone, although she usually rings late at night. Damn Leo. Is there anything he didn't tell her? "But it's Lindsey's last name on the caller ID," Scott says. He's still young enough to like talking on the phone, whereas Heloise is one of those people who don't even like to listen to voice-mail messages.

"Hello? . . . Oh. Okay." He brings the phone to his mother. "It's for you. Lindsey's mom."

Heloise barely has time to say hello before Coranne, her voice thick with held-back sobs, starts stammering. "I—I didn't know who else to call. I took the baby in for her second part of the flu shot this morning, and she's had a reaction and we're in the emergency room—" Her voice fades in volume; she's talking to someone where she is. "Yes, I know I'm not supposed to use my cell phone here, but what would you have me do, go in the parking lot with my sick baby?—and there's all this stuff that has to get done for Thanksgiving. Rick's family is coming, and his mother is so judgey."

Mothers-in-law. Another thing Heloise has been spared.

Coranne has barely paused for a breath. "I thought I was so smart, I had a lot of things done ahead, but my order's over at Tommy's, the whole Thanksgiving dinner essentially, and they close at seven, and the linens are at the dry cleaners, and would you believe my furnace died, and I managed

334

to get a service call, but the window is four to eight, and I'm not sure when I'll get out of the ER, and while I'm okay with Lindsey being home alone, but not with letting some strange service guy in—I mean, that's like a scenario out of a Lifetime movie, he'll be a pedophile, and I'll be the mom who—"

"It's okay, Coranne," Heloise says. "It will all be okay." Meaning, *Leave me out of this.*

"I didn't know who else to call. I tried three other moms. Everyone is as frantic as I am, and I know you work, but I thought—"

"What do you need me to do?" But that's a mistake. She meant to say, *What do you expect me to do?*—a very different question.

"If you could go to the market and the dry cleaners, then stay at my house until I get there? Scott knows the garage code, and the kitchen door is open, of course." Her voice slows, calmed by the possibility that Heloise might really help her. "I know it's a lot to ask. I'm embarrassed to ask so much from someone who's never even asked me for a ride. I just didn't know who else to call."

Heloise's mind divides; it's almost like a cartoon, with the devil on one shoulder and an angel on the other. But in her case the two personas are Heloise, always in control and with a plan, and Helen, the poor sap to whom life just happens. If only she could have sent Audrey, but she let her leave early today for her own Thanksgiving break with some distant cousins in Greenbelt.

"Okay, give me the details again. Slowly."

The weather is clear, thank goodness for that. She and Scott take off in her Lexus, Bluetooth disconnected in case Sophie tries the cell number, hitting the dry cleaners first, then descending into the hell that is Tommy's Market on the day before Thanksgiving. At least Coranne was truthful: Her order is completely assembled. Heloise and Scott carry it into her house, which is basically a messier version of Heloise's.

She puts the groceries away and hangs up the linens in the hall closet, while Scott avails himself of some video game that she won't let him have. It is only three, and the repairman isn't due for an hour at the earliest. Bored out of her mind, she decides to start straightening, then out-and-out cleaning. Given that she has a housekeeping service, it's a bit of a novelty, almost fun. She checks in with the furnace people, who initially insist that the window is the window and they're slammed. But after working her way up to the office manager and telling the story about the sick baby, she earns some sympathy, and the woman agrees to juggle the appointments so the repairman will arrive at four. It turns out to be a problem with the thermostat, and, miracle of miracles, he has the right model in his truck. She and Scott could leave, but Heloise has noticed Coranne's daunting to-do list on the refrigerator and realizes that the turkey from Tommy's must be brined, which requires twelve hours of immersion. Assuming Coranne wants to put it in tomorrow morning, first thing, there's not much time to waste. With Scott's happy help, Heloise assembles the brine and they slide the turkey into the large plastic bag. "Their turkey is so big," Scott says in wonder, and Heloise feels guilty about their two-person tradition.

Coranne arrives while they're loading the dishwasher—and promptly bursts into tears, which embarrasses Heloise no end.

"How's the baby?" she asks, crouching down to inspect the sleeping Jillian in her car seat, which Coranne has carried in rather than risk waking her.

"Fine, fine. I probably overreacted, but it is a holiday weekend, and—well, you know. I didn't want to risk having it get worse."

"I know. Look, put your feet up, have a glass of wine." Heloise has seen a half-full bottle of chardonnay in the fridge. "Everything's been done. The furnace works, the turkey's in the brine, the dry cleaning's in the laundry room."

"You're a saint, Heloise. I mean it. I wish I could hire you."

Heloise laughs.

"My husband has an assistant who does all the little things for him. Remembers birthdays, runs personal errands. I always say, 'Where's my assistant?' But, you know, as a stay-at-home mom, I'm not supposed to require any help."

Heloise pours herself a glass of wine, although it had been her intention to bolt the second Coranne got home. Scott has disappeared with Lindsey, probably to the basement rec room that seems like such a novelty to him. She has that nagging tug of an idea again—the valet line, the Mandarin Oriental, the Four Seasons.

No, not the valet. The *concierge*. The woman who looked

337

like her, trying to assist that petulant man. Lord, the last thing she wants to do is wait on petulant men for less money than she makes now. But what if—

"Would you pay someone to help you?"

"I can't afford a full-time assistant."

"But what if you could hire someone hourly, à la carte, to do the things you need done? What if there had been a service you could call today? Is that something you would pay for?"

"Would I? And every mother I know at Hamilton Point would probably do the same. There's just so much fuck-ing—sorry—driving, and if you have more than one kid, there are so many conflicts. Rick is like, 'But you have all the time the kids are in school,' except I don't. We have a baby. She sleeps maybe two hours a day."

"Interesting," Heloise says, and Coranne shoots her a look. It *is* an odd thing to say. She lets the conversation switch to the more acceptable banalities, refuses Coranne's offer to open another bottle of wine, and announces she must take Scott home. He has a pie to make, many apples to peel and slice.

"We look forward to having you over Friday night," Coranne says to Scott, and Heloise is reminded that one thing she likes about the woman is the way she treats her son. He's an individual to Coranne, not merely Lindsey's friend.

The way home takes them back past Tommy's Market, now in even more chaos, and Heloise is stuck for a long time waiting for her left turn. But when her moment comes, she almost misses it, and Scott has to prod her.

338

"There's a gap, Mom, you can make it."

"What?" She is thinking again about the concierge. When they come back from Belize or Costa Rica—*if* they come back from Belize or Costa Rica. Doesn't it just figure that she gets an idea for a business when she's no longer trying to find one? The Reverend Frida was right. You have to leap. But what's the point of figuring it all out if it ends up that you have no place to land? It's about as useful as seeing every vivid detail in the landscape—right before you slam into it because you have no parachute.

That night, Scott in bed, his pie cooling on the counter, the wrecked kitchen reclaimed—Lord, she feels as if she's been cleaning all day—Heloise checks out various Web sites that offer expedited passports. Another service an à la carte concierge could offer a busy woman, she thinks. The house phone rings, startling her. Sophie.

"Yes?" she asks, not bothering to hide the sigh in her voice.

"Heloise, you can't just cut me off." Sophie's voice is slurry with some kind of alcohol or medication. She's given up hiding her bad habits from Heloise.

"I'm sorry, Sophie." She almost is. She tries on the empathy she found for Coranne this morning. But she can't feel anything for this girl.

"It's not like I can go home, you know? I've got no one, nothing, and now I don't even have any money. Look, I'm sorry I tried to shake you down, but if you could just keep paying for my meds—"

339

"I was happy to pay for your meds when I thought they were meds. But not this, Sophie. I can't give you money. If you want to go to rehab—" It's a safe offer to imply. Sophie's not going to rehab.

"You owe me. You ruined me. It's not like I can get married now or have a normal life. Once a whore, always a whore. You're living proof of that."

No I'm not, Heloise thinks, feeling a thrill of joy she has never known outside her relationship to Scott. *I'm not, I'm not.* What she told Terry is true: She's not defined by what she does.

"Sophie, I can't help you."

"You better. You better. I know where you live, you bitch."

She probably does. Goddamn Leo.

"Sophie, let's talk after the holiday, okay?"

"You better—" Her voice is trailing off. She doesn't even have the energy to keep up her own threats.

"After the holiday weekend, Sophie. I know it's a tough time to be alone. But we'll talk Monday."

Buying more time. After years of selling it, she can't get over how expensive time is, how much each increment is costing her. Placating Sophie. Placating Val. But as of Monday it's only three days until the sale goes through. On December 2, Val's share of the money will be deposited in the offshore account maintained by his lawyer—and she and Scott will be en route to Miami, where they will leave for a Caribbean cruise that Heloise booked just an hour ago. They simply won't return. Audrey has agreed to stay behind and take care of everything else—selling the house, selling everything in it. That's another thing she has to add to her to-do list—consulting Tyner, making sure that Audrey has limited power of attorney.

On the bright side—she now has a very good reason not to honor her mother's wish to have a relationship with Scott. *Sorry, I'll be murdered if I stay around. Toodle-oo.*

She can't help thinking that if she has to keep getting these distraught, needful calls, it would be better if they were from Terry. She could be kind to Terry. Just her luck, he's the one person in her life who's true to his word. He promised to leave her alone and did. Terry and her mom have that in common. Go figure.

Friday, November 25

Black Friday has traditionally been a good day for WFEN. Heloise is not one to indulge in stereotypes, but the women go shop and the men—well, "catch up on a few things at the office" is the usual excuse. Or golf, if the weather is mild, as it is today. Heloise has several customers who use golfing as a cover on a regular basis. "This is cheaper in the long run," one observed. "And I have a few hours left over to myself."

She meets with one man, not a true regular but getting there. She remembers his first time; he was so nervous that she almost walked out on him, suspecting that something wasn't right. He was just a guy white-knuckling his way through a terrible marriage for reasons not even he can articulate. "I've never failed at anything," he said one time in passing. Heloise knows that some people might judge his patronage of WFEN as a failure, but she admires his stoicism, his determination to do what he thinks is right for his kids. Perhaps that's why she finds herself telling him that the business is changing hands. That's the term she decides on at the last minute. It sounds more genteel.

"Will you stay on?"

"No, why would I do that?"

"It's not uncommon. Lot of people with successful start-ups remain as consultants."

"No, I think a clean break is best." She digs back in her memory for something Tom said, about the new captain in vice. "The new boss should be able to make the business his own. Her own." She waffles on the gender, still unclear who is buying her out. She wonders if the girls will continue to wear the GPS devices she designed, if the new owner will use the car service. It's harder to let go than she thought.

She has dropped Scott at Coranne's en route to her appointment, a rare bit of multitasking made necessary by Audrey's absence, and she dallies on the way home, reluctant to return to an empty house. No Scott, not even Audrey, who isn't due back until Saturday. Heloise is so desperate for something to do that she stops by a mall. By late afternoon the mania has abated somewhat. One of Heloise's short-timers, an economics expert who was spending three months at a D.C. think tank, once told her that Black Friday isn't necessarily the busiest shopping day of the year. It's an artificial construct that the media feeds, a myth that might as well be reality. A factoid. She was sorry the economist was just passing through. She always thought she might end up getting some good ideas from him. But his only legacy is her devotion to the Planet Money podcast from National Public Radio.

There's a party on her cul-de-sac, and the usually quiet street is jammed with cars. Heloise was invited, but declined to go. As, she is sure, was expected. It still stings, though, how readily people accept her aloofness. Will she make friends in her new country? That seems more intimidating than learning a new language.

She enters the house through the garage, her eyes struggling to adjust. It's dark. The days have shortened so quickly that she forgets to leave a light on, bullied as she is by Scott and his campaign against wasting energy. She reaches for the hall light, only to trip over what feels like a bunched-up rug. Even alone, Heloise finds it humiliating to stumble, and she scrambles to her feet with the outrage of a child whose dignity has been affronted.

The bunched-up rug is the hem of a big down coat, too warm for the day, but maybe it's the only coat that Sophie owned. For it is Sophie lying in her hallway. Sophie with a bullet hole in her forehead and a vaguely pissed expression to Heloise's eye, as if she cannot believe that it ends this way. Heloise can't either.

She's moving quickly, thinking quickly, her instincts on fire, but she's not fast enough. A man has blocked the door to the garage.

"Terry," she says.

"She was creating a disturbance," he says, pointing to Sophie. "You wouldn't want that, I know. Someone banging on your door, yelling and screaming, saying that you'd better let her in. So I did, Hel. Is it okay if I call you Hel? I know that's what your true friends call you. Not Heloise. Not Helen. Hel."

For one brief moment, Heloise allows herself to hope that Terry is simply so around the bend in his devotion to her—the near breakdown in the kitchen, the way he faced the wall to hide his tears from her—that he has overreacted in a sincere attempt to protect her.

344

The tears, facing the wall: He studied the calendar hanging by her desk, saw Scott's sleepover, Audrey's absence. The embrace by the garage door. He watched her enter the code.

So, no. No. This man is going to kill her. Probably killed Bettina and Shelley, too. Sophie is collateral damage, another body at her feet, literally this time.

"I thought I'd have more time," she says.

"Don't we all? Let's go down to your office. We have some paperwork to do before we can finish up here."

She thinks about making a run for the front door, but it's locked, that strange suburban notion of security. Double-lock the front door but leave the kitchen door open, assuming that a code will be enough to protect you and your loved ones. One, in Heloise's case.

She opens the basement door and descends into the room that she once valued for being a soundproof fortress. She has no doubt that she's going to be tortured. Bettina and Shelley were lucky after all.

Yet Terry wasn't being droll when he referenced paperwork. He sits Heloise at her desk, then puts a sheaf of papers in front of her. A will. *Her* will. She skims it. Her entire estate is to be left to Scott, but the trustee will be Ofelia Ocampo of Rochester, New York.

"Who is this?" she asks.

"Val's wife. Common-law, but they have three kids together. Where do you think he went when he went out of town back in the day?"

"Business," she says. "I thought it was business."

"That's what he wanted you to think. But this is where the money goes, every month. As long as you were providing income to Val, he let you live. When the money goes, you do, too. Oldest kid is a junior in high school. He's thinking about college. Sign at the Post-its." He gestures with the gun at the neat flaps sticking out, marked "Sign here."

"No."

"Look at it this way: If you sign, there's a will. No nasty questions. You'll be killed in a home invasion. I'm changing up again. I never wanted anyone to connect Shelley and Bettina—except you, of course. I'm not sure how the thing with the girl upstairs will play out—she worked for you, right?—but I can't risk moving her body. Maybe I'll put out some wineglasses, a bottle, make it look as if you were preparing for a friend's visit."

"Who are you?"

"Val's brother. Also his lawyer."

"I know Val's lawyer."

"You know his criminal lawyer. I take care of everything else."

"You look nothing like him."

"Foster brother. I'd tell you the story, only—I know Val never did, and I respect that. Suffice it to say we didn't have a very nice life when we were young. But Val took care of me, and now I take care of him."

"Why did you—take up with me?"

"After Shelley threatened to parlay her participation in Val's business into a Get Out of Jail Free card, Val didn't trust

346

anyone. Not even you, love. That's why he had me leave that photo, put you in play. He also asked me to befriend you and keep an eye on you. Learning about Scott was a bonus. And, of course, the moment I told him about Scott, he knew you were the one who did him all those years ago. Broke his fucking heart, Hel. It killed him, too, that I never got to meet the kid. He was dying to hear everything about him."

So he had known all along. Her big confession was all for naught. Except—it had felt powerful to her, changed her, put her on the road to becoming someone new. Or so she thought.

"Val doesn't think he's getting a new trial, does he?"

"He'll have his criminal attorney make the motions, sure. But he understands that the ballistics evidence is pretty overwhelming. Even if all the witnesses are dead."

"So why kill them?"

"Why not? Each one betrayed him."

"Not Bettina."

"Oh, her. Well, that was for you, darling. We thought it would keep you in the pocket, make it clear that Val could get to people—and that he plays a very long game. The thing is, you are a good earner. You've provided for Val's family all these years. Shelley did, too, but never at your level, and not at all for the past year."

"Didn't Val have any money on hand when he was arrested? He didn't live that large."

"When the cops hit him, it was a bad time. He had used most of his cash for a big score, and then George II took off with the product. Now, *that* was a smart fucker."

347

Heloise remembers how George II once implied he was smarter than she was, how she had doubted it. Now she has to agree with Terry. He was a smart fucker.

"So he set you up, improving on the model he developed for Shelley. It was great. Only Shelley gets popped. And then you decide you want to go legit. That's the one thing he didn't see coming. He was willing to forgive you as long as Ofelia was provided for. She's the love of his life."

"Nice to know."

"Sweet. Lives to serve her man. They were teenage sweethearts. She writes him every day. Every goddamn day, Hel. By hand. In this day and age. Can you imagine?"

"Why isn't she on the visitors list?"

"Because she thinks Val is overseas and can't return to the United States or he'll be picked up on a bogus murder charge. Far as Ofelia and the kids know, Val is a legitimate businessman caught up in a conspiracy. Being Filipina, she doesn't find that so incredible."

"So where does she send his letters?"

"She gives them to me."

"But how do you—?"

"Ofelia's not like you. She doesn't ask so many fucking questions."

Heloise stares at the document in front of her. The horrible thing is that Terry is making sense. The will means that Scott will be protected, to a certain extent. He'll get her money, he'll never know about his mother's other life. Of course, Scott's not going to like having to live in Rochester, New York, with three half siblings about whom he knows nothing, but . . . he'll have a family. And Ofelia does sound nice, if dim. The oldest kid is going to college. She must be doing something right. Heck, she's had three kids with Val and he treats her like a goddess. She may be smarter than Heloise as well.

Think, she wills herself. *You can outthink anyone, given time.*

"How did you find Bettina?"

"That day I met you for lunch, when I was late? I put a tracking device on your car. I couldn't be sure that you knew where Bettina lived. But if you did know, I had a hunch you'd go to her eventually, which is why I left that photo at the crime scene. Only decent thing you really did, trying to warn her—and it got her killed. That's ironic, isn't it?"

"It is," she agrees, thinking of another irony, one that can work for her. "There's a problem with this plan. I have another will, the kind you download from the Internet. Never got around to doing it proper, with a lawyer, but it's legally binding. They'll find it when they go through my files, and that will screw up everything. The estate will end up in probate, and Scott will be sent to my mom or my sister, because I didn't earmark a guardian."

"Val said your mom was dead."

"I lied."

Terry laughs. "Yeah, you're not much of one for family ties, are you? You know, Val was always a little scared of you. He said, in the end, that you were meaner than he was, that you had no loyalty to anyone."

"The will is in the top drawer. The locks are tricky—let me do it."

He lets her stand but presses close behind her, the gun in her back. She reaches in. "Shit—I must have put it between two folders, not in a hanging folder, and it's slipped through. I can't— Your arms are longer, can you reach?"

He comes around, keeping his eyes on her, believing her to be the real threat to him. He twists his body so he's facing her, the gun in his left hand, his right hand reaching behind him, his gaze never leaving her face.

"It's really down there," Heloise says. "Sweep your hands along the bottom."

"Why does it—" he begins, but Heloise has lunged forward and turned the dummy key, hip-checking him so he falls deeper into the drawer. She can't believe that her office, soundproof as it's supposed to be, can contain the scream Terry makes as the industrial paper shredder engages his fingertips. Only his fingertips, alas—she had hoped it would swallow him whole, or at least take him up to the elbow joint—but he manages to wrest his hand back in some adrenaline-charged bit of bravado. Instinctively, however, he cradles the wounded hand, so the gun is no longer pointing at her. That's her opportunity, and she takes it, bolting for the door. If she could, it would be better to force him out and lock herself in, but the wound has made him monstrous. She doesn't want any contact with his maimed hand, which is geysering blood everywhere.

Terry comes after her, shockingly fast, fueled on pain, in so much pain he's beyond it. He is screaming even as he shouts terrible threats about what he will do when he gets her. She has no doubt. She takes the steps two at a time, only to stumble once again over Sophie. Terry, in turn, trips as well and tries to grab Heloise's ankle as she crawls and kicks, but he has the gun in his left hand and his right hand can't maintain a grip. She heaves herself back up and heads for the unlocked kitchen door, but she has to stop to hit the code at the garage, and that wastes much of her advantage. He catches up to her again, hits her across the face with the gun, but using his left hand makes the blow less effective than it might otherwise have been. Still, Terry has the advantage of having killed before. He knows what's required and knows that he's up to it. Heloise is only beginning to discover how ready she is to kill someone, and she's not sure what it's going to take in terms of time and determination.

They are wrestling now, rolling over and over on the smooth concrete floor, and Heloise wishes for the first time that she were less orderly, that her garage was a messy hodgepodge of things she might grab and use—a leaf blower, a baseball bat, anything. But tools and toys are put away in their places, mocking her from their labeled boxes and cubbyholes. Although she tries to focus on the gun, Terry's mangled hand keeps distracting her. She struggles to knock the gun from his grip with her elbow even as he reaches for her throat with his bloody hand and attempts to throttle her. But he can't control that hand, which seems to be doing its own macabre dance. She wriggles away, starts to crawl to the door, but it's no use if she can't stand up to hit the code. He overtakes her, throwing his body on her as if she's on fire and he's trying to smother the flames. She rolls beneath him, terrified of being shot from behind, determined to make him look at her. But now he has her waist in a powerful scissors hold with his legs and he's forcing his right elbow into her neck. He's steadying her, she realizes, determined to make sure he needs only one shot. She bucks and rolls, trying to throw him off.

He has the upper part of his right arm across her windpipe now, suffocating her. She's finding it harder to move, but she knows that when she stops moving, she'll be dead. It's not her life that passes before her eyes, only her son's face. Maybe she should have signed the fucking will. She's going to die. She doesn't want to, but she accepts it as her fate. Shelley, Bettina, Billy. Sophie. Martin. Why shouldn't she join the pile? Why does she get to escape Val? She'd go peacefully if only she could be assured that Scott would be okay—

Terry slumps forward, and she feels a gush of warm liquid. Has she wet herself? Has he wet himself? No, it just keeps coming, blood and more blood, in a thicker, steadier stream than the blood from his hand. His body falls to the side—is thrown to the side.

Audrey is standing behind Terry, her chest heaving with her breath, one of Scott's coveted Wüsthofs in her fist.

"My cousin wanted to go to the outlets over on the shore, so I went with her and had her drop me off on the way home. I didn't think you would like being alone this weekend." She actually looks a little nervous, as if Heloise were going to reprimand her for arriving unannounced. "When I saw Sophie in the hall—"

"Let me guess," Heloise says, on her hands and knees, panting, keen to retch yet unable to. "You just had a feeling. Like the one about the client you didn't want me to take."

Audrey bends down. She probably expects Terry to get back up, like some character in a horror film. Then, to Heloise's shock, she moves her face closer to his, so close that she could kiss him. "Heloise—this *is* the client I told you not to take. I recognize him from the photo. He shaved his beard and dyed his hair, but it's absolutely the same guy."

Heloise nods. That makes sense. If anyone would know how to game her system, it would be Val, the man who loved listening to every detail about the business. She always thought he was simply proud of her. Maybe he was.

Tuesday, February 21, 2012

Heloise is nervous. She unfolds her paper, smooths it, looks up, takes a sip of water. Paul gives her a nod, which helps. She begins, "I am here today to testify in favor of Senate Bill 1212, which would decriminalize prostitution in the state of Maryland."

Paul nods again. After all, he helped to write her statement. The bill has no chance, he has told Heloise. He himself will not vote to support it. But he will treat it respectfully during this hearing and bring it to a committee vote, which will guarantee a small bump of media, even as it's voted down. The bill has a strong advocate on the committee, an almost freakishly lefty woman from Heloise's own county. But the bill will get attention because Heloise is briefly famous as the woman who fought off an attacker in her home on Thanksgiving weekend.

For some reason those two words, "Thanksgiving weekend," are always attached to what happened to Heloise. *The Thanksgiving-weekend incident, the Thanksgiving-weekend attack.* The implication seems to be that it's bad enough to be brutalized and almost murdered in one's home by a man who has killed another woman right in front of you, but it's particularly blasphemous on a day that's supposed to be put aside for Christmas shopping.

Black Friday. Yes, it was a very Black Friday indeed.

Heloise and Audrey did not call police immediately. Heloise went back to her office and shredded everything in the drawer that had caught Terry—throwing in the will that was still on her desk. She will admit this to police later. Not the part about the will, but that she then shredded everything in a fit of hysteria. That she was so overwhelmed by events that she returned to her office for reasons she can no longer remember. Of course, it's all Terry's blood, but who knows what experts will notice, in terms of splatters and partial footprints. The key thing, Heloise knew, was not to lie. She knew this because she called Tom before she dialed 911. Dialed him on Audrey's cell, which was then soaked in water and disappeared a few days later at the electronics recycling center in Halethorpe. Heloise is nothing if not cool in a crisis.

The story was that a man she had dated (true) and broken up with (true) had burst into her home (true), shot her employee (true) who was waiting there to meet with her (sort of true), and then tried to kill Heloise in her office, where she tricked him into reaching into her shredder, saying she had something special for him. Again true. If Terry's connection to Val was discovered—well, she could have claimed with great credibility that their relationship was unknown to her, just as she never knew of his connection to Shelley/Michelle. That is, it was unknown to Heloise as of 6:15 P.M. on Black Friday. Whatever Heloise and Terry discussed between that time and Audrey's intercession—that wasn't really germane, was it? Heloise was a beautiful woman who had broken up with a man. These things happen. Even to lobbyists and lawyers. Why complicate matters by mentioning wills and common-law wives in Rochester, New York? Heloise reset her mental clock to 6:15, the Friday after Thanksgiving. She learned nothing after that moment. Didn't know of Terry's connection to Val. Didn't know why he had targeted her. Didn't know that Terry had killed Shelley and Bettina.

And now no one else will know either. Their killer is dead, and that's a kind of justice, but what's the use of justice if the victims' loved ones have no idea it's been done?

The last part bugs her, will probably always bug her. She is never going to forget that image, glimpsed in the moment she thought she was going to die. All those bodies. Billy, Martin, Bettina. Sophie, too. Not Shelley, although that name had come to her. The fact that Heloise had planned to write Jolson an anonymous letter once she was out of the country—it didn't matter. None of her good intentions mattered. The dead were dead, a child was motherless. Sophie's parents had lost a daughter, and their estrangement from her probably only made it worse, Heloise was sure. It was a toss-up, who had caused more damage in the world, she or Val.

She has not spoken to Val since the night Terry visited her. She will never speak to Val again. She tells herself she is not the least bit perturbed by the revelations about Ofelia Ocampo, the three kids, the shocking similarities between her story and her mother's. She doesn't doubt that she, Heloise, was the love of Val's life, that he cared for her more than anyone, that he valued her mind, her acumen.

So she's Barbara Lewis in this scenario, the first "wife," the one he can never quite leave. Ofelia's just an *idea* of a wife, far away, raising three children on her own, writing every day of her loyalty and devotion. Easy to be loyal to a phantom who sends you money, takes nothing. Val demanded loyalty and devotion, but he didn't reward it, much less return it.

"Senate Bill 1212 will not make prostitution legal. But it will place it within a legal framework where it can be treated as the victimless crime it is," Heloise concludes.

The oldest senator on the committee is the first one who wants to question her. Paul has prepared her for this. Like the Reverend Frida, the old senator takes a long time to get to the point, and it's all about him, but he finally finds his way to an actual question: "Why would an attractive young mother such as yourself care about such women? What is your interest in this sordid business?"

She answers as Paul coached her. "For years I have worked here in Annapolis on issues central to income parity for women. But where does parity begin? It begins in opportunity. We live in a culture where women sell their bodies. That's simply a fact. Women have sold their bodies throughout history and will continue to do so. There's no point in creating euphemisms for this, but there's also no point in judging the women who do it. It is, however, humane to protect all members of our society. A drug dealer murdered by a rival does not forgo the right to have his murderer arrested and convicted. If we decriminalize prostitution, sex workers will enjoy more safety.

"I was the victim of a violent crime, an aberration, in my home. Sex workers—and that's what I prefer to call them—are at risk all the time. Are we going to say, as a society, that they are beyond our concern because of what they do? Their crime is not a violent one. It is not inherently harmful. It does not destroy marriages. It probably keeps some together."

Paul shoots her a look. She has gone off script with that last line.

"At any rate, as some people know, I left Annapolis and lobbying after my experience. It may be trite, but I looked death in the face and decided I would change my life if I were lucky enough to have one. Cut back on my work hours, spend more time in my community, do more volunteer work. It's easy to support popular issues. I wanted to throw my experience behind an unpopular one."

The rest of the questioning is, as Paul warned her, hostile. Patronizing, too, more questions in the vein of "What does a pretty lady like you know about such things?" Maryland, liberal as it is, is not ready for this. It won't be ready for it in her lifetime, but Heloise doesn't care. With a polite, composed face, she endures the lectures disguised as questions, thanks the committee for its time, and tries not to check her watch. She wants to pick up Scott by three.

She makes it, barely. He's at Coranne's, playing contentedly with Lindsey but happy to abandon the Wii for the adventure that Heloise has promised him.

Coranne says, "I have a plumber scheduled for next

Thursday, when Jillian has a pediatrician's appointment. Can you cover for me?"

Heloise takes out a bulging Filofax. She still prefers paper and finds she likes writing things down, now that she has no reason to fear leaving a record. Her new accountant marvels at her precision, her meticulous records. "Yes, I'm free in the afternoon. In the morning I'm meeting an exterminator at the Rileys'."

"An exterminator?"

"The twins' class had a lice infestation, and she's overreacting. Not for me to judge as long as she pays my rate, right?" Plus, Heloise is already developing relationships with certain local servicemen, who pay her for any business she swings their way. Some might call that a kickback, but she prefers Paul's term: finder's fee.

"How's business going?"

"Picking up, every day." WFEN, the Women's Full Employment Network, is now Wives for Everyone's Needs. "It sounds kinda dirty," Coranne had said when Heloise told her about the brainstorm inspired by Coranne's catastrophic day.

All Heloise had said was "It does, doesn't it?"

She and Scott head north, stopping at their favorite ice-cream place. Scott says again, "Remember when I used to love the ponies?"

"Don't you love them still?" Heloise asks.

Scott thinks about this. "I suppose I do." It appears to be a revelation to him, the idea that he can still love the ponies now that he's twelve, that one can outgrow something yet keep it in his heart. Heloise hopes he will hold that lesson close for the rest of his life.

In the aftermath of the Thanksgiving-weekend incident—as she shredded the will and briefed Audrey on what they would tell police—Heloise's only concern, as always, was Scott. Would Terry's attempt to murder her break down the divide that had governed her life when she was mere days away from escaping it? Would her past come out? But the wall between her lives proved sturdy. Certainly her customers weren't going to come forward, and neither was Val.

And everyone else who knew the whole story was dead.

More unexpectedly, the story seemed to make people squeamish. The paper shredder, the expert way Audrey had slit Terry's throat, which brought up the old stories about how Audrey had murdered her husband as he slept. Audrey, with her odd voice and appearance, was not what public-relations people call camera-ready, not that she agreed to any interviews. And it was a brainstorm of sorts for Heloise to say she dated Terry. It placed the incident into the niche of domestic violence, just another love story gone wrong. That was something people could understand, or thought they could. Nothing to see here, move along. The sale of Heloise's business went through. She didn't give Val his share of the profits. She actually felt a pang for Ofelia Ocampo and her family, wondered how that devoted woman would provide for her children, how Val would communicate with her now that Terry was dead. Who would carry back the tales of his heroism in remote and evil places.

But it was for Betty Martinez's family that Heloise really grieved. She made an anonymous donation for the boy, giving him much of the money that would have gone to Val. It wasn't enough. All the money in the world wouldn't be enough. But it was what she had.

As they approach their destination, Scott takes in the landmarks with little comment, asking only, "Don't they make Utz potato chips near here?"

"Yes," Heloise says, "but that's another town. This town doesn't really make anything."

They walk up a familiar walk; a familiar door is opened; Heloise reflexively checks her image in the old clock with the mirror, which still hangs at the foot of the stairs. She notices a pink Post-it on it. That means her mother wants to take it with her to the new apartment. Not the one in town, but one outside Annapolis, near Turner's Grove.

That's where the rest of Val's money went and some of Heloise's, too. Her mother has an apartment in one of those residences where she can stay the rest of her life, moving into the nursing center when her disease progresses to that point where she can no longer care for herself. There was a waiting list, but Heloise "knew" one of the executives of the company that runs the facility. She "knows" someone at Hopkins, too, a vice president who's going to make sure her mother gets cutting-edge care. It turns out that Heloise knows a lot of people. Most of her new clients are the wives of the men she once served, and if they interpreted her networking inquiries as blackmail, that's on them. Heloise is never going to out her former customers. "Happy wife, happy life," she tells them. No coercion, no threats. By the end of the year, if billings continue to pick up, she will be in the black. It's a more modest life, but she can manage the mortgage and keep Scott in Turner's Grove.

"Hello, Scott," Beth says solemnly. She is like a mail-order bride meeting her husband-to-be. Nervous, unsure, but hopeful for the best possible outcome.

"Hello— What should I call you?"

"I don't know. What would you like to call me?"

"Grandma, I guess."

"Okay, I'll be Grandma."

She brings out photo albums. Heloise is not even sure she knew that these albums existed, but there she is—as a baby, a toddler, at Scott's age. In her uniform from Il Cielo. There are photos of Hector, too. Those still hurt, but she sees something now that she couldn't see before. He was young. True, Beth was younger still, but he was a young man in a small town with two wives, five children, and no prospects.

Still, she can't find anything in her heart for him. She just can't.

"Why didn't I know about you?" Scott asks.

"Your mother and I lost touch. It happens sometimes." Heloise doesn't miss the fact that her mother doesn't assign blame for this.

"But you're not the grandmother for my cousins?" Scott asks.

"No. Your grandfather had another wife before me. It's complicated."

362

Boy, was it.

Heloise sits gingerly on the edge of the old sofa. Only it's not the old sofa, of course, the one where Hector once reigned. Not even her mother could live with the same sofa for thirty-seven years. Still, Heloise is nervous. She feels as if the house itself is a trap, that it could pull her back and she'll have to live her life all over again, make all the same mistakes. And she's still angry about so much. There's no use pretending she's not.

But as much as the house sets Heloise's teeth on edge, it's a palace of wonders to Scott. It's his first glimpse into his prehistory, his first chance to contemplate the world that made him. What else does Heloise have to show him? Her high school. A house in Baltimore County, although they probably couldn't get past the front gate? A copse of trees where a gun was hidden, those forsaken holes of dirty cash? A downtown hotel, the Central Library? Perhaps she should be grateful for this tacky little house.

The visit is constrained—intimacy can't be jump-started—but her mother is charmed by her only grandson, and Scott clearly likes the *idea* of a grandmother. Maybe they will have time to forge a real relationship, especially once she's closer to them. Maybe not. At any rate, Heloise will have done her best.

"Why did you change your mind?" her mother asks while Scott investigates such basement wonders as a dusty carpet sweeper and a waist-high deep freeze.

"One day I might need Scott to forgive me for some things," she says. "So I thought I would try to forgive you."

363

"For what?" her mother says. It's unclear which part she needs clarified. Can she really not know? Or does she see things differently?

"It's a long story." True on both counts.

"But you know it doesn't work that way, right? That forgiveness is not— What's the word?"

"It doesn't have transitive properties."

"What?"

"Just because I forgive you, it doesn't mean Scott will forgive me if that day will come."

"Aren't you fancy?"

Heloise believes she detects a note of pride in her mother's voice.

Back in Turner's Grove, sitting at the little shelf that really is Mother's office now—the basement office has been emptied and locked, never to be entered again as long as they live here—Heloise goes over her schedule for the next day, sips a glass of wine.

Audrey comes in to review which appointments she has to cover tomorrow, who's going to pick up Scott at school. Strangely, since Heloise started helping other women with their lives, her once-smooth-sailing routine seems slightly more chaotic, harder to control. Her male clientele was orderly, predictable. For the women she serves, the emergencies and conflicts never stop coming, and that backs up on her. She needs employees, but she can't afford their salaries, not yet.

So Audrey's still working for Heloise, although Heloise

can't offer her anything more than room and board. Instead Heloise has given her a partnership stake in the new business. Why not? It has to turn out better than the collaboration with Val.

"How was the visit?" Audrey asks.

"It was okay."

"Only okay?"

"Only okay."

Audrey takes Heloise's terse answers as her cue to leave. She's a true silent partner. Unlike Val. *He plays a very long game,* Terry had told Heloise. Okay, so she's not safe. That's the irony. She never was. She never will be. But then—no one is safe in this world. The best you can hope to do is create an illusion of safety for your children for as long as possible. Scott has nightmares now, real ones, even though he never saw what happened in the house. (Bless Coranne, who kept him all that terrible weekend and somehow kept him away from the news.) But he knows, of course. Heloise will sell if she can find something smaller in the same school district, get a good price for this now-infamous house. For the time being, they are stuck here, and for all the cleaning that has been done, she still finds errant spots of blood lurking on the moldings, hiding in the garage.

She works by the light of her laptop, enjoying the darkness, the view through the rear windows, her own still-impressive reflection rebounding back to her, although the dim light obscures the inch of roots in her hair. She sees the lights on in other homes, imagines other women still up, poring over schedules, trying to figure out how to get through life one day, one appointment, one obligation at a time. She's one of them now.

Maybe she always was.

Author's Note

This is a work of fiction. While I read quite a bit about prostitution—I'd like to single out Jeanette Angle (*Call Girl*) and Christine Wiltz (*The Last Madam*)—I once again took comfort in the wisdom of Donald Westlake: "I became a novelist so I could make things up." Heloise Lewis's business model is of my own design, and if she is mistaken in her beliefs about what will keep her safe from prosecution—well, that's sort of the point of the novel, isn't it? We are all, at some point or another in our lives, mistaken about the amount of control we have, how shrewd we might be. It has always been my contention that Heloise Lewis is an American everywoman—a single mother trying to maintain a civil relationship with her son's father, a small-business woman nervous about her future.

I also feel compelled to point out that Heloise first entered my imagination in 2001—before the real housewives of anywhere, before *Weeds,* before *Washingtonienne*. And also before the unrelated suicides of two different madams, one in D.C. and one in the Baltimore–D.C. suburbs. In the post-9/11 world in which I pitched stories about Heloise, I think I sounded a little daft. In 2006, however, Harlan Coben asked me to write a story for an anthology in which the theme was love. I asked: "What about a mother's love for her son? And what if that woman was a prostitute?" He had no problem with it. So thanks to Harlan for the chance to bring Heloise to life, finally. This book might not exist if it weren't for the invitation.

Two years later, a book of previously published short stories was heading to publication and my editor, Carrie Feron, asked if I could write at least one new piece for the collection. In two weeks, I wrote "Scratch a Woman," a novella about Heloise's twisted relationship with her half sister, Meghan. Still, I always knew I wanted to come back to this complicated woman and explore how she became who she was. How she got in and how she got out.

There are some small discrepancies between Heloise's historical record, if you will, and this novel. See above: "Donald Westlake . . . make things up." One character decided he deserved a different name. Scott's soccer skills eroded slightly as he aged, but that happens. Turner's Grove is completely fictional, as is Heloise's church and Tommy's Market. And, of course, every single politician referenced here is a fictional creation. Politicians with prostitutes! Some people probably think I've entered the fantasy genre with this book.

As always, I had help. As always, I'm the only one responsible for any errors. Thanks to William F. Zorzi Jr., who indulged my fictional flights about a bogus lobbyist and how she might operate; thanks to Bill Salganik, who provided me lots of information and sources about health care, which I ended up not using.

Then there is the Mouseketeer roll call of regulars: David

Simon; Alison Chaplin; Maureen Sugden; Vicky Bijur; Carrie Feron; and pretty much everyone at HarperCollins/ William Morrow, including, but not limited to, Michael Morrison, Liate Stehlik, Lynn Grady, Sharyn Rosenblum, Tessa Woodward, and Stephanie Kim. A shout-out to Beth Tindall, who deserves an island of her own. Finally, thanks again to Sara Kiehne for taking such good care of Georgia Rae Simon. Also, thanks to all the people on Facebook who tolerate my word counts and bursts of enthusiasm for kale and shoes.

The book is dedicated to three good friends, but also to all women. The fact is, I am eternally grateful that I didn't get to write Heloise's story for a decade. Like her, I had a long journey to make. And while I don't have a "Mother's office" in a McMansion, I've been known to have a glass of wine in the dark at the end of a long, exhausting day. Sometimes two.

Laura Lippman
April 2012